THE
CIRCLE

SARA B. ELFGREN
MATS STRANDBERG

THE
CIRCLE

THE ENGELSFORS TRILOGY
BOOK I

TRANSLATED FROM THE SWEDISH BY PER CARLSSON

THE OVERLOOK PRESS
NEW YORK, NY

This edition first published in hardcover in the United States in 2013 by

The Overlook Press, Peter Mayer Publishers, Inc.
141 Wooster Street
New York, NY 10012
www.overlookpress.com

For bulk and special sales, please contact sales@overlookny.com,
or write us at the above address.

First published in Great Britain in 2011 by Arrow Books
in association with Hammer

Cataloging-in-Publication Data is available from the Library of Congress

Manufactured in the United States of America
ISBN 978-1-4683-0658-3
2 4 6 8 10 9 7 5 3 1

This book is dedicated to our teenage selves.

A NOTE ON THE SWEDISH SCHOOL SYSTEM

In Sweden, grades 1-9 comprise primary school, and secondary school (high school) lasts for three years, the equivalent of US grades 10-12. The main characters in *The Circle* are therefore beginning tenth grade, their first year of high school.

Part I

CHAPTER 1

She's waiting for an answer but Elias doesn't know what to say. No answer would satisfy her. Instead he stares at his hands. They are so pale that he can see every vein in the harsh fluorescent lighting.

'Elias?'

How can she stand working in this pathetic little room with her binders, potted plants and that view over the school parking lot? How can she stand herself?

'Can you explain to me what's going on in your head?' she repeats.

Elias raises his head and looks at the principal. Of course she can stand herself. People like her have no problem fitting into this world. They always behave in a normal, predictable way. Above all, they're convinced that they have the solution to all problems. Solution number one: fit in and follow the rules. As principal, Adriana Lopez is queen of a world founded on that philosophy.

'I'm very concerned about this situation,' she says, but Elias notices that she's actually angry. That he can't just get a grip on himself. 'We're barely three weeks into the semester, and you've already missed fifty percent of your classes. I'm bringing this up with you now because I don't want you to fall behind completely.'

Elias thinks about Linnéa. It usually helps, but now all he remembers is how they shouted at each other last night. It hurts him to think of her tears. He couldn't comfort her, since he had caused them. Maybe she hates him now.

Linnéa is the one who keeps the darkness away. The one who stops him choosing other escape routes, the razor that gives him brief control of his anguish, the smoking that helps him forget it. But yesterday he couldn't cope, and Linnéa noticed, of course. And now maybe she hates him.

'Things are different in tenth grade,' the queen continues. 'You have more freedom, but with that freedom comes responsibility. No one is going to hold your hand. It's up to you what you do with the rest of your life. This is where it's all decided. Your entire future. Do you really want to throw it away?'

Elias almost bursts out laughing. Does she really believe that crap? He's not a person to her, just another student who's 'gone a little astray'. It's impossible that he could have problems that can't be explained away by 'puberty' or 'hormones' and resolved with 'firm rules' and 'clear boundaries'.

'There's the SAT, isn't there?' It just slipped out.

The principal's mouth becomes a thin line. 'Even the SAT requires good study habits.'

Elias sighs. This meeting had already gone on too long. 'I know,' he says without meeting her gaze. 'I really don't want to mess this up. I had intended tenth grade to be a new start for me, but it was more difficult than I thought . . . and I'm already so far behind the others. But I'll get through it.'

The principal looks surprised. Then a smile spreads across her face, the first natural smile of the whole meeting. Elias has said exactly what she wanted to hear.

'Good,' she says. 'You'll see that, once you decide to apply yourself, things will go smoothly.'

She leans forward, plucks a strand of hair from Elias's black shirt and twiddles it between her fingers. It glints in the sun, which is shining through the windows, a little lighter at the root, where his natural hair color has grown out by an inch. Adriana Lopez stares at it in fascination and Elias gets the crazy feeling that she's going to put it into her mouth and chew it.

She notices how he's looking at her and drops the hair into the wastebasket. 'Excuse me, I'm a bit nitpicky,' she says.

Elias smiles noncommittally – he's not really sure how to respond.

'Well, I think we've finished for today,' the principal says.

Elias stands up and leaves. The door doesn't quite shut behind him. He turns to close it and glimpses the principal in her office.

She's bent over the wastebasket, fishing something out with her long, thin fingers. She drops it into a little envelope and seals it.

Elias remains standing there, uncertain of what he just saw. After the last few days he can no longer trust his senses.

If it hadn't seemed so odd, he might have thought it was the strand of hair she'd just removed from his shirt.

The principal looks up. Her expression hardens. Before she manages a forced smile.

'Was there something else?' she asks.

'No,' Elias mumbles and shoves the door shut.

When it clicks securely behind him, he feels a disproportionate level of relief, as if he had just escaped with his life.

The school is empty and desolate. Only half an hour ago, when he went to the principal's office, it was bustling with students. It feels unnatural.

Elias dials Linnéa's number as his boots pound down the spiral staircase. She answers as he reaches the foot of the stairs and throws open the door to the ground-floor hallway.

'Linnéa.'

'It's me,' he says. He's aching with anxiety.

'Yes, it is,' she answers at last, as she always does.

Elias relaxes slightly. 'I feel so fucking bad about yesterday,' he says quickly. 'I'm sorry.'

He'd wanted to say it this morning as soon as he saw her, but he'd never had a chance. Linnéa had kept out of sight all day. And she had disappeared before last period.

'I see,' is her only response.

Her voice doesn't sound angry. Not even sad. It's empty and resigned – as if she'd *given up* – and that frightens Elias more than anything else. 'It's not . . . I haven't gone back to it. I'm not going to start again. It was just one joint.'

'You said that yesterday.'

'You didn't seem to believe me.'

Elias walks along the rows of lockers, past the deserted group of hard wooden benches screwed to the floor, past the bulletin board, and still Linnéa hasn't said anything. Suddenly he becomes aware of another sound. Footsteps that aren't his.

He turns around. There's nobody there.

'You promised you'd quit,' Linnéa's voice says.

'I know. I'm sorry. I let you down—'

'No,' Linnéa interrupts. 'You're fucking letting yourself down! You can't be doing this for *my* sake. Then you'd never—'

'I know, I know,' he says. 'I know all that.' Elias reaches his locker and opens it, stuffs a few books into his black cloth bag and slams the thin metal door. He hears the other footsteps again before they go silent. He turns. Nothing there. Nobody at all. And yet he feels watched.

'Why did you do it?'

She'd asked the same question yesterday, repeated it several times. But he hadn't told her the truth. It was too scary. Too crazy. Even for a head case like him.

'I told you. I was freaking out,' he says, trying to keep his voice free of irritation, so as not to provoke her again.

'I know there's something else.'

Elias hesitates. 'Okay,' he says softly. 'I'll tell you. Can I see you tonight?'

'Okay.'

'I'll sneak out as soon as my mom and dad have gone to sleep. Linnéa?'

'Yes?'

'Do you hate me?'

'I hate the fact that you're asking such a stupid question,' she hisses.

Finally. That's the Linnéa he knows. Elias hangs up. He smiles as he stands there in the hallway. There's hope. As long as she doesn't hate him there's hope. He has to tell Linnéa. She's his sister in all but blood. He doesn't have to go through this alone.

And at that moment the lights go out. Elias stiffens. A dim light filters its way through the windows at one end of the hallway. Somewhere close by a door shuts. Then silence settles in.

There's nothing to be afraid of, he tries to assure himself.

He starts walking toward the exit. Forces himself to keep to a slow, steady pace. Not to give in to the panic rising inside him. He rounds the row of lockers on the corner.

Someone is standing there.

The janitor. Elias has only seen him a few times, but he's impossible to forget. It's those big ice-blue eyes. Eyes that stare at Elias as if they could see all his secrets.

Elias stares at the floor as he walks past. And still he can feel those eyes burning into the back of his neck. He quickens his pace, nausea rising in his throat. It's as if his heart is throbbing so hard that it's triggering his gag reflex.

Everything's been getting better over the last six months.

He's felt that things are happening inside him, that he's changing. The new psychologist at the CAP center isn't an idiot like the last one, and it seems she actually understands him a little. Above all, he has Linnéa. She makes him feel alive, makes him want to leave the suffocating yet familiar darkness.

That's why it's so hard to understand why this is happening *now* – now when he can finally sleep at night, now that he can even feel happy.

Three days ago he had seen his face change in the mirror. He had seen it stretch and contort beyond recognition. And he had realized he was going crazy. Hearing voices and seeing hallucinations. It had scared the shit out of him.

For three days he had held out against the razor blades and Jonte's merchandise. He had avoided mirrors. But yesterday he had caught sight of himself in a store window, had seen his face quiver and pour away as if it were made of water.

That was when he called Jonte.

You're losing it.

A strange whisper in his head. Elias looks around and discovers he's climbed the spiral staircase again and is back in the hallway outside the principal's office. He doesn't know why. The lights flicker and go out.

The door to the stairwell slowly swings shut behind him. Just before it closes he hears it. The sound of a soft shoe sole on the stairs.

Hide.

Elias runs along the dark hallway. After each row of

lockers he expects someone *or something* to suddenly appear. Just as he's rounded a corner he hears the door to the stairwell open far behind him. The footsteps draw closer, slowly but surely.

He reaches the big stone steps that form the school's backbone.

Run up the stairs.

Elias's legs obey, clearing two at a time. Once he's reached the top floor, he continues running toward the little hallway where a locked door leads to the school's attic. It's a dead end, one of the school's forgotten places. There's a bathroom here that no one else uses. He and Linnéa usually meet here.

The footsteps draw closer.

Hide.

Elias opens the door to the bathroom and slips inside. He closes the door carefully behind him and tries to breathe as quietly as possible. Listens. The only sound he can hear is a motorcycle revving in the distance.

Elias puts his ear to the door.

He can't hear anything. But he knows. Someone's standing there. On the other side.

Elias.

The whispering is louder now, but Elias is sure that it's only in his head.

It's finally happened: I've lost my mind, he thinks, and at once the voice responds: *Yes. You have.*

He looks out of the window toward the pale blue sky. The white tiles glisten. It's cold in here. He's filled with an immense loneliness.

Part One

Turn around.

Elias doesn't want to, but he turns just the same. It's as if he's no longer in control of his body. The voice is controlling it, as if he were a puppet of flesh and blood.

He's standing in front of the row of three sinks with mirrors mounted above them. When he catches sight of his pale face he wants to shut his eyes, but he can't.

Smash the mirror.

Elias's body obeys. His grip tightens around the strap of his book bag and he swings it through the air.

The sound echoes off the tiled walls when the mirror shatters. Big shards break off and crash into the sink where they splinter into smaller pieces with a tinkling noise.

Someone must have heard, Elias thinks. Please, let someone have heard.

But no one comes. He's alone with the voice.

Elias's body goes up to the sink and picks up the largest shard. He understands what's going to happen. He feels dizzy with fear.

You're broken. Impossible to fix.

Slowly he backs into one of the open stalls.

It'll soon be over. Soon you'll never have to be afraid again.

The voice sounds almost comforting now.

Elias locks the door and sinks onto the toilet seat. He struggles to open his mouth, tries desperately to cry out. His grip on the glass shard tightens and the sharp edges cut into his palm.

No pain.

And he feels no pain. He sees the blood trickle from his hand and drip onto the gray-tiled floor but feels nothing. His body has gone numb. Only his thoughts remain. And the voice.

Life won't get better. Might as well end it now. Spare yourself the pain. Spare yourself the betrayals. It never gets any better anyway, Elias. Life is just a humiliating struggle. The dead are the lucky ones.

Elias doesn't try to resist as the glass shard cuts through the long sleeve of his shirt exposing the scarred skin beneath.

Mom, Dad, he thinks. They'll get through this. They have their faith. They believe we'll see each other again in Heaven.

I love you, he thinks, as the sharp edge starts to slice through his skin.

He hopes that Linnéa will understand that he didn't choose this. Everyone else is going to think he killed himself, and that doesn't matter. As long as she doesn't.

He cuts into his flesh differently from how he ever has before. Deeply and purposefully.

It'll soon be over, Elias. Just a little more. Then it'll be over. It'll be better like this. You've suffered so much.

The blood pumps from his arm. He sees it happening but feels nothing and now black spots dance before his eyes. They dance and grow until the whole world is pitch black. The last sound he hears is the footsteps out in the hall. Whoever's out there isn't bothering to move quietly any more. There's no reason to now.

He tries to keep thinking about Linnéa. Like when he was

little, and thought he could escape his nightmares if he could just hold on to one bright thought as he drifted off to sleep.

Forgive me.

He doesn't know whether those words came from him or the voice.

And that's when he feels the pain.

CHAPTER 2

When she regains consciousness, she's lying huddled in the corner where they had left her.

It's pitch dark in the cell. Her whole body aches.

She sits up, pulls her legs under her dress and wraps her arms around her knees. She still can't hear anything from her right ear and there is a throbbing ache behind her eye, which is sealed shut with pus and coagulated blood.

Footsteps echo outside and the heavy door opens. Torchlight fills the room and she looks away when she sees her scarred feet bound together with a thick chain. Two guards wrench her up from the floor and tie her hands behind her back while the torchbearer looks on. The rope cuts into her wrists, but she refuses to let them see how much it hurts.

The man with the torch saunters forward with an arrogant smirk. He has no teeth and his breath smells of rotten flesh. The heat from the torch sears her face as he brings it closer.

'Today you're going to die, harlot,' he says, and strokes her face with his free hand, letting it continue down toward her breasts.

Seething hatred fills her, makes her strong and hard.

'I curse you,' she hisses. 'Your prick shall fester and fall off! My lord Satan will come for you on your deathbed, and demons will torment you for all eternity.'

The man pulls away his hand as if burned.

'God spare us,' mumbles one of the guards.

It gives her a little consolation to see them so frightened.

Someone pulls a sack over her head, and she is dragged through the labyrinthine passageways.

A gate opens on creaking hinges.

Outside. There is the fresh smell of dew. She braces herself for the hateful baying of the mob, but all she hears is birdsong. The red light of dawn filters through the weave of the sackcloth over her head. A cuckoo caws to the south. It is a death knell. A deep, animal instinct takes over. She has to flee. Now.

Driven by panic, she rushes forward blindly. The iron shackles knock against her ankles as she runs. No one tries to stop her. They know there's no need. She doesn't get far before she falls headlong on to the damp ground. The guards laugh and call out behind her.

'Looks like she's in a hurry to get to her lord Satan,' she hears the toothless one shout.

Powerful hands lift her underneath her arms and someone else grabs hold of her feet. They toss her roughly through the air. She soars for a moment before slamming on something hard and getting the breath knocked out of her. A horse snorts and the world sways back and forth. She's lying in a cart, that much she can work out.

'Is anyone there?' she whispers.

Nobody answers.

Just as well, she thinks. We are all alone in death.

Minoo is woken by her shivering. She's freezing, as if she had slept with the window open all night. She's having trouble breathing – it feels as if something big and heavy is sitting on her chest.

She pulls the covers up to her chin and curls into a ball. She's had many nightmares, but never one that had such a physical effect on her. Never has she felt so relieved to see the familiar yellow and white striped wallpaper of her room.

After a while she starts to breathe more easily and the warmth slowly returns.

She checks her cell phone. Almost seven o'clock. Time to get up.

She climbs out of bed and opens the wardrobe. She wishes she had some kind of distinct style instead of the same lame jeans, tops and cardigans every day. She pulls down a navy blue long-sleeved shirt from a hanger and is disgusted with herself. She's so awfully . . . harmless. She hasn't even changed her hairstyle. Ever. But what would people say if she suddenly came to school in something different? The alternative crowd at school, those whose style she secretly admires, would think her a wannabe.

Plus she hates buying clothes. She feels like an illiterate in a bookstore. On other people clothes look ugly or attractive; she can see whether or not they suit the person wearing them. But when she's flipping through a catalog or standing in a store, she only ever makes safe choices. Black. Dark blue. Long sweaters. Jeans that aren't too tight. Nothing too low-cut. No patterns. Clothes are a language she understands, but can't speak herself.

She takes her outfit with her as she steps out into the hall. The door to her parents' bedroom is shut and in the bathroom, her father's razor is lying in a pool of water next to the sink. Minoo guesses he's already at work. Her mother's towel is damp so she must be up, too, even though it's her day off.

Minoo lays her clothes on a stool, climbs into the bathtub and pulls the shower curtain closed. Suddenly she catches a whiff of smoke. She holds a wisp of her long black hair up to her nose and sniffs it.

She has to shampoo her hair twice to get that inexplicable smell out. Afterward she wraps it up in a towel turban and brushes her teeth. Her eyes wander to the old framed map of Engelsfors that hangs beside the mirror. Last year she actually thought that her parents would let her go and stay with Aunt Bahar in Stockholm and go to high school there. She hates to see that map every morning and be reminded that she's still stuck here. In Engelsfors. Pretty name, shitty town. Out in the middle of nowhere, surrounded by deep forests where people often lose their way and disappear. Thirteen thousand inhabitants and high unemployment. The steel works closed down twenty-five years ago. The stores in the town center stand empty. Only the pizzerias survive.

The interstate and the railroad form a partition through

the town. To the east lie Dammsjön Lake, gas stations, workshops, the shuttered factory and a few depressing high-rise blocks of apartments. To the west lie the town center, the church and parsonage, streets of town houses, then the long-abandoned manor house and the fancy upscale houses by the idyllic canal.

It is here that the Falk Karimi family lives in a light-gray functionalist two-story house. The walls are covered with expensive wallpaper, and most of the furniture has been shipped in from designer boutiques in Stockholm.

Minoo's mother is sitting at the kitchen table when she comes down the stairs. The newspapers her father pores over in the morning are lying in a neat pile on the table. Her mother is immersed in a medical journal, with her usual breakfast – a cup of black coffee – next to her.

Minoo pours herself a bowl of strawberry yogurt and sits down across the table from her mother.

'Is that all you're going to eat?' her mother asks.

'You're one to talk,' Minoo retorts, and gets a smile in response.

'Yogurt, oatmeal, sandwich, yogurt, oatmeal, sandwich. It gets pretty tedious after a while.'

'But coffee doesn't?'

'One day you'll understand.' Her mother smiles. Then she suddenly gets that look in her eyes, the one that bores straight to the core. 'Did you sleep badly?'

'I had a nightmare,' Minoo says. She tells her about the dream and how she had felt when she woke up. Her mother feels her forehead.

Minoo recoils. 'I'm not sick. It wasn't that kind of shivering.'

Minoo recognizes her mother's switch into 'doctor mode'. Her voice becomes serious and professional, her body language more formal. The change had been evident even when Minoo was small. Her father had nursed her as a parent would when she was sick, spoiling her with candy and comics, but her mother had been like a doctor on a home visit.

Once, that had made Minoo sad. Now she suspects it's a defense mechanism. Perhaps without it her parental concern, combined with professional understanding of human ailments, would be impossible to handle.

'Was your pulse rapid?'

'Yes . . . But it passed.'

'Difficulty breathing?'

Minoo nods.

'It might have been a panic attack.'

'I don't get panic attacks.'

'It's not unlikely that you would, Minoo. You've just started tenth grade. It's a big adjustment.'

'It wasn't a panic attack, Mom. It was connected to my dream.'

It sounds strange when she says it, but that was exactly how it felt.

'It's unhealthy to bottle up your feelings,' her mother says. 'They're going to come out one way or another. The more you try to control them, the more uncontrolled their eventual release.'

'Have you switched from being a surgeon to a psychologist now?' Minoo teases.

'I once considered becoming a psychiatrist,' her mother answers a little pointedly. Then something shifts in her eyes. 'I know I haven't been a very good role model.'

'Stop it, Mother.'

'No. I'm a typical overachiever. I don't want to pass that on to you.'

'You haven't,' Minoo mumbles.

'Tell me if it happens again. Promise?'

Minoo nods. Even if her mother can be a little too intense at times, it's good to know that she cares. And for the most part, she understands Minoo.

God, how sad, Minoo thinks, swallowing the last spoonful of yogurt. My mother is my best friend.

Vanessa is woken up by the smell of smoke.

She throws off her comforter, runs to the door and yanks it open.

But the living room is still and quiet. No flames licking at the curtains. No noxious black clouds billowing from the kitchen. The coffee table is still strewn with pizza boxes and beer cans from yesterday. Their German Shepherd, Frasse, is asleep, basking in a pool of sunlight on the floor. Her mother, her stepfather Nicke, and her little brother Melvin are already in the kitchen having breakfast. A perfectly ordinary morning at Törnrosvägen 17A, fifth floor, first door to the right of the elevator.

Vanessa shakes her head, and that's when she realizes that

the smell is coming from her. Her hair stinks like it had when she was little, after she had stood staring at the stupid May Day bonfire on Olsson's Hill.

She crosses the living room, walks through the kitchen, where Melvin is playing with two spoons, tapping them on the table. Sometimes he's just so cute. It's unbelievable that he got half his genes from Nicke.

She tosses her nightshirt on the bathroom floor and turns on the shower. The pipes cough and a stream of ice-cold water spurts out. The shower has been a nuisance ever since Nicke had insisted on replacing some of the pipes himself and putting in a new faucet. Her mother had objected, but she always gives in to Nicke in the end.

Vanessa steps into the shower stall and is almost scalded before she manages to find the right temperature. She washes her hair with her mother's coconut shampoo. The mysterious smoke smell is still there. She pours out another thick blob and lathers her hair a second time.

When she gets back to her room, wrapped in her bathrobe, she switches on the radio. The commercials make everything sound a little more normal. She angles up the blinds and at once her mood improves. T-shirt weather! She wants to get out into the sun as quickly as possible.

'Turn that down!' Nicke hollers, from the kitchen, in his best cop voice.

Vanessa ignores him. It's not my problem if you're hung-over, she thinks, as she rolls deodorant under her arms.

Once dressed, she grabs her makeup bag and goes to the full-length mirror propped against the wall.

She's not there.

Vanessa stares into the empty mirror. She raises her hand and holds it in front of her. There it is, clear as day. She looks in the mirror again. Nothing.

It's a while before she realizes she's still asleep.

Vanessa smiles. But if she's aware that this is a dream, she should be able to control it.

She puts down her makeup bag and goes into the kitchen. 'Hi,' she says.

No one reacts. She really is invisible. Nicke is sitting there, half asleep with his head in his hands. He reeks of stale beer. Her mother, who looks just as tired, is listlessly chewing on a ham sandwich while flipping through a catalog from a place called the Crystal Cave. Only Melvin turns his head as if he's heard something, but it's obvious he can't see her.

Vanessa stands next to Nicke. 'Hungover today?' she whispers in his ear. No reaction. Vanessa giggles. She feels oddly exhilarated.

'Do you know how much I hate you?' she says to Nicke. 'You're such a fucking loser that you don't even know what a fucking loser you are. That's probably the worst thing about you, that you *think* you're so incredibly perfect.'

Suddenly she feels something wet and rough against her hand. She looks down. Frasse is standing there, licking her hand.

'Wha' Fasse doing?' Melvin asks, in his perky voice.

Her mother looks at the dog, who is licking thin air. 'You

never know what Frasse is doing,' she answers. 'He's probably chasing flies or something.'

'Don't make me come in there and smash that fucking radio,' Nicke shouts, at Vanessa's room.

Vanessa giggles and lets her gaze wander across the kitchen. Nicke's favorite mug is standing on the counter, a big blue one emblazoned with 'NYPD' in white lettering and the police logo. He probably thinks that being a policeman in Engelsfors is somehow similar to patrolling the streets of New York.

Vanessa knocks the mug on to the floor with a sweeping motion. It splits in two with a satisfying crack. Melvin jumps and starts crying. Immediately she feels a little guilty.

'What the hell?' shouts Nicke, and gets up so forcefully that his chair tips over.

'Shame you can't blame it on me,' Vanessa says triumphantly.

Nicke stares straight at her. Their eyes meet. The shock sends little jolts of electricity down her spine. He can see her.

'Who the hell else would I blame it on?' he hisses.

Melvin is bawling and Nicke lifts him up, stroking his tousled chocolate-brown hair. 'There there, buddy, it's all right,' he says comfortingly, while glaring at Vanessa.

'Vanessa, what are you doing?' her mother says, in her weariest voice.

Vanessa can't answer her. Is she still dreaming? If not, what's going on? 'Could you see me the whole time?' she asks.

All of a sudden her mother looks wide awake.

'Have you *taken* something?'

'You guys are such dicks!' Vanessa shouts, and rushes out into the hall.

She's scared now, scared to death, but she's not going to show it. Instead she steps into her sneakers and grabs her bag.

'You're not going anywhere!' her mother shouts.

'So I should miss school?' Vanessa slams the front door behind her with a bang that echoes up the stairwell.

She hurtles down the stairs, out through the front door and across the street to the number-five stop where she just makes it on to the bus.

Thank God she doesn't know anybody on board. She sits at the very back.

There are only two possible explanations for this insane morning. One is that she's lost her mind. The second is that she's been sleepwalking again. When she was younger it happened quite often. Her mother loves to embarrass Vanessa by telling people that she once squatted on the hall carpet and peed. Vanessa still remembers how it felt to be in that state between sleep and waking. But deep down she knows this was something completely different.

I must have been sleepwalking, she decides. The other explanation is terrifying.

Vanessa looks out of the window, and when the bus heads into a tunnel, she catches sight of her reflection in the glass. Two unmade-up eyes stare back at her.

'Oh, God.' She rummages in her bag.

All she finds is an old tube of lip gloss. Her makeup bag is still lying on the floor at home. Vanessa hasn't gone to school without makeup since she was ten and has no desire to start now. One trauma is enough for this morning.

The bus continues through deserted industrial areas. Her mother often goes on about how the old steel works was the pride of the town when she was a child, that then you could feel proud to come from Engelsfors. Vanessa doesn't understand what there was to be so proud of. The town must have been just as ugly and boring then as it is now.

The bus drives across the railroad tracks and enters the western part of the town. Outside the window, the area her mother mockingly refers to as the 'Beverly Hills of Bergslagen' rolls into view: large houses in bright colors set among well-tended gardens. It's as if the sun shines a little more brightly on this side of town. This is where the people with money live. Doctors. The few successful retailers. The descendants of the mill proprietors. There's still a way to go to her school, which is oddly distant from the town center.

Like a prison, isolated from the rest of civilization.

CHAPTER 3

Anna-Karin is longing for the autumn.

She's standing by the gates looking out across the playground, where summer-clad students are milling around. Tanned arms, legs and cleavages everywhere. All she wants is to crawl into her scruffy old duffle coat, pull on a woolen hat and Grandpa's knitted mittens.

Today she's wearing a baggy jacket, an extra-large T-shirt and jeans. It's already over seventy degrees, but she'd rather be hot than displaying skin. She doesn't want to get *too* hot, though. Now she's standing with her arms held a little out from her sides so she doesn't get sweat patches under her arms. In seventh grade somebody shoved her so she spilled water all over her shirt. Erik Forslund, who was standing next to her, immediately shouted that she had sweaty boobs. 'The B.O. Ho' was such a popular nickname that it had stuck until ninth grade. She has no intention of giving anyone the opportunity to use it now, too.

The playground is emptying. Anna-Karin joins the flow, head bowed, arms folded protectively across her breasts. She's started wearing a bra that's supposed to make them look smaller, but in the mirror you can't see any difference.

When she enters the building, she catches sight of Rebecka Mohlin, who's in her class, and Rebecka's boyfriend, Gustaf Åhlander. They're standing by the stairs with their arms around each other. Anna-Karin looks away with a rush of pitch-black self-pity. No boy is ever going to look at her in the way Gustaf is looking at Rebecka.

'Hi,' Rebecka says to her, as she walks past.

'Hi,' Gustaf echoes.

Anna-Karin doesn't answer.

Only once she's in the classroom, at her desk in the front row closest to the wall, can she relax a little. She sticks her hand into her jacket pocket and feels Pepper's warm body and sharp little claws. His fur is silky soft. When she strokes his tiny head, he starts to purr so that her pocket vibrates. Self-pity melts away, replaced with love.

Anna-Karin knows she shouldn't bring the kitten to school, but she doesn't feel strong enough to go alone. Not yet. Maybe next week.

So far things have been quite good. She's already gotten through two weeks of school, and the third has just begun. No one has laughed at her or thrown her bag out of the window. No one has tried to push her down the stairs. No one has pinched her breasts until she cries from the pain. Erik Forslund and Ida Holmström have passed her in the hallway several times without even looking at her.

She's dreamed of this moment for nine years and now it's happened.

She's finally become invisible.

Minoo hates being a teenager, mostly because it means being herded together with other teenagers. Coming to school is like being deported to an alien planet – every day. She has nothing to say to the inhabitants. She can't even pretend to be one of them because she doesn't know how.

Everything was supposed to be different in high school. That was her source of comfort all the way through middle school. The others were supposed to have caught up with her – at least, those who had also taken natural sciences classes.

Now, at the start of the third week, she's starting to realize that that was wishful thinking.

Even the building reminds her of the past few years: a four-story red-brick edifice with a flat roof. A lone pair of netless goalposts provide the only entertainment in the asphalt playground. At some point an attempt was made to spruce up the lifeless surface with trees. Most are dead now. Their twigs and branches have turned gray.

The doors are propped open to let in fresh air, yet it smells familiar, of dust and old linoleum, when she enters. The smell of school. The first person Minoo sees as she steps through the doors is Vanessa Dahl, who's standing next to Jari Mäkinen, one of the older boys. He's talking eagerly to her, but she looks annoyed.

Vanessa is Minoo's polar opposite: pretty, loud, bleached-blonde hair, voted sexiest girl in the school in tenth grade. She's wearing white short-shorts and matching sneakers. The lace edge of her push-up bra is sticking out over the neckline of her top.

Evelina, one of Vanessa's friends, runs up and jumps onto Jari's back, throwing her arms around his neck. She holds out her phone and takes a photo of them. When Jari tries to shake her off she clings to him even more tightly, so that her breasts press against his neck. She shrieks with laughter and everyone in the hallway turns to see what's going on.

Haven't they had enough after so many years in the spotlight? Minoo hurries past.

First period is Swedish. Vanessa walks into the classroom with Evelina. Michelle has laid claim to a few seats at the back and is powdering her nose.

'God, I'm, like, totally exhausted,' Evelina says, and sinks down on the chair next to Michelle.

'Me, too.' Michelle yawns and examines her face in the mirror of her glittery compact. 'I look like I'm fucking thirty today.'

Vanessa sighs. Michelle looks the same as she always does. She just has to hear how great that is a gazillion times a day. Now she adjusts her glistening dark hair and pouts at her reflection.

'You've got, like, a three-inch-thick layer of powder on your face now. I think that's enough,' Vanessa snipes.

Slowly Michelle lowers her compact and stares at her.

'What's your problem?' asks Evelina.

'I was only joking.'

'It didn't sound like it,' Michelle tells her airily.

29

'Do you have PMS or something?' asks Evelina. 'Did you and Wille have a fight?'

'Yeah,' answers Vanessa. 'We did.'

It was easier this way. How could she explain what had happened to her this morning? 'I was invisible for a while this morning – or maybe I just lost my mind.' Boy trouble, on the other hand, is a language Michelle and Evelina understand. They look relieved. Everything's back to normal.

'Oh, sweetheart,' Evelina says, and puts an arm around her.

Michelle nods in commiseration. Vanessa smiles gratefully and asks if she can borrow her makeup.

A group of boys are sitting at the very back of the classroom listening to hip-hop on a phone. Kevin Månsson is singing along in broken English. Minoo gives an inward smile of contempt.

She nods at Anna-Karin Nieminen in the front row, but gets no response. As usual, Anna-Karin is hunched over her desk with her tangled dark hair hanging like a veil over her face.

There's something heart-wrenchingly hopeless about Anna-Karin. Minoo tried to speak to her a few times last year, but Anna-Karin just pressed herself mutely against the wall as if she wanted it to swallow her up. Her passivity seemed to demand provocation. Minoo feels an almost shameful sense of relief that at least she isn't *that* far down the social pecking order.

She fishes out her math book. So far she's understood everything they've covered in class, but she's still nervous. She's always been the best in the class without much effort, but despite that – or perhaps because of it – her greatest fear is that one day she'll be exposed as a fraud.

The bell rings for the start of class and she looks up.

Max is standing in the doorway, holding a cup of coffee. He's twenty-four and moved to Engelsfors at the beginning of the summer. Though she can't understand why anyone would come here voluntarily.

Max locks the door. Seconds later someone is pounding on it.

'If you're late, you're *too* late,' Max says, and sets his cup down on the desk.

'Oh, come on! What if you've got a good reason?' shouts Kevin, with the new voice he acquired over the summer.

Minoo can't believe she has to put up with Kevin for another three years. Why did he choose natural science classes? In eighth grade he'd asked if a zebra was a cross between a horse and a tiger.

Max glances at Minoo as he opens the door. His expression tells her exactly what he thinks of Kevin. It's as if he knows she's the only one who can read the look on his face. She's forced to lower her eyes.

People usually say they get butterflies in their stomach when they're in love. That's not how it is for her. First her wrists tingle. Then her arms go limp and she turns into a rag doll.

The first time she saw Max an electric shock shot through her hands. How incredibly pathetic to get a crush on a teacher. Especially one like Max: good-looking in the obvious way that girls like Vanessa Dahl find attractive – greenish-brown eyes, curly dark hair and sinewy forearms.

It's a double period and Minoo dives headlong into the work she has in front of her. She loves math. Clear rules. Crystal-clear answers. Right or wrong, no gray areas.

Now and then she looks up to catch a glimpse of Max.

She remembers what her mother said, that it isn't good to bottle up your feelings. But there's no way she's ever going to tell anyone how she feels about Max. Least of all him.

When the first period is almost over, Max empties his coffee cup, closes his briefcase and leaves the room.

There's a ten-minute break. Ten minutes with nothing to do, but be alone and pathetic for everyone to see.

They're on the third floor. There's a hall that leads up to the attic. It's a dead end and Minoo has noticed that no one uses the bathroom up there. It's the perfect place to be left in peace. She hurries up the stairs and turns the corner.

When she opens the door to the bathroom, she is struck by the smell of cigarette smoke. A mirror is smashed. Shards of glass are strewn across one of the sinks. The window is wide open and a girl is huddled on the ledge, smoking.

She's wearing a black tank top, a flared knee-length skirt with pink skulls on a black background, and long white socks. A notepad is propped up on her knees. She's writing in it intently with a felt-tip pen.

Only when the door slams behind Minoo does she look up. Her bangs almost cover her eyes, which are rimmed with thick black liner. The rest of her hair is gathered into two wavy pigtails.

It's Linnéa Wallin.

They were in the same class in seventh grade. Everyone knew that Linnéa's father was an alcoholic and that her mother was dead. Linnéa was constantly skipping school, until one day at the beginning of eighth grade, the teacher had announced that she wasn't coming back. Rumors floated around that she had gone to live with distant relatives or was dead. Later it turned out that she had been in a home. That sparked more rumors: she had tried to kill herself, her father was a pedophile, she was dealing drugs, she was selling sex on the Internet, she was a lesbian. Since then, Minoo has seen her only with others from the alternative crowd.

And now she's staring at Minoo with disappointment in her eyes.

'Hi,' Minoo says.

'I thought you were somebody else,' Linnéa says.

Minoo glances at the smashed mirror.

'It wasn't me,' Linnéa says.

'I didn't think it was,' Minoo lies. Her ears turn red as always when she gets embarrassed. She tries the handle to one of the stalls as coolly as she can. The door's locked.

'That one seems to be out of order,' Linnéa says.

Minoo doesn't answer. Instead she opens another stall.

She locks the door and rests her forehead against the cool

tiles. Through the thin door she hears Linnéa light another cigarette.

Minoo lets an appropriate amount of time pass before flushing the unused toilet and coming out again. She looks at herself in the mirror as she washes her hands. She glances at Linnéa, and feels a sudden pang of envy. Linnéa is cute and thin but, worse, her skin is clear. Minoo has suffered regular outbreaks of acne since she was thirteen. In eighth grade, Erik Forslund had asked if she'd been hit in the face with buckshot. Grown-ups always tell you it goes away when you get older. But, like so much of what they say, that doesn't seem to be true.

Linnéa interrupts her thoughts: 'You don't need to pretend.'

Minoo's ears turn bright red again. 'What?'

Linnéa has laid aside her book. 'You only come here to hide, don't you?' she says.

'I like to be on my own,' Minoo mumbles.

Linnéa smiles inscrutably. They look at each other for a moment.

'You won't tell anyone, will you?' she says, waving the cigarette.

'What you do is none of my business.'

'Exactly.' Linnéa tosses the cigarette into the sink. It fizzes as the lit end extinguishes against the wet enamel. She jumps down from her spot by the window. The pen rolls off her notepad on to the floor, past Minoo and under the locked stall door.

Minoo bends down and looks for the pen beneath the door.

The pen is lying in something dark and sticky. Further inside she sees a black cloth bag and a pair of black boots. There's someone sitting on the toilet seat.

Minoo stands up so suddenly that she feels faint.

'What is it?' asks Linnéa.

'I think there's someone in there . . .' It occurs to her that it might be some kind of joke. Maybe the whole thing is being filmed and her ridiculous reaction will be put up on the Internet. 'But I'm not sure . . .'

Linnéa goes into the adjacent stall and stands on the toilet seat. She peers over the partition. Minoo waits for a reaction but it doesn't come. The seconds pass, one by one.

'What is it?'

Linnéa climbs down from the toilet seat and disappears.

'What did you see?'

No answer. The open window swings in a sudden gust of wind. Minoo goes over to Linnéa. She is leaning with her back against the wall, staring ahead vacantly.

'It's Elias,' she says finally.

Elias Malmgren? Minoo has seen him in town with Linnéa several times. She must mean him. 'What's happened? Is he okay or what?' Minoo asks even though she knows the answer.

Linnéa drops to her knees and throws up into the toilet bowl. She keeps retching until only thick, clear saliva is left. Minoo stands there, stunned, until Linnéa turns around. Her thick eyeliner has started to run. Their eyes meet and Minoo realizes that Linnéa is falling apart. 'Come on,' she says, and holds out her hand.

Linnéa grabs it and scrambles to her feet. She looks around wildly.

'We have to get somebody,' Minoo says.

Linnéa stares at her. She shakes her head. 'We can't leave him.'

'I'll stay,' Minoo says, immediately regretting it.

'We have to get him out.'

'We're going to,' Minoo says, and wonders how she's managing to stay so calm.

Linnéa runs out the door and the window slams shut in the cross draft. For a brief moment, Minoo becomes aware of the *smell* before the window blows open again. It's a smell she's never come across before, but she instantly realizes what it is. It's the smell of death. But she can't think about it. Not now.

She looks toward the stall. So much blood.

She feels the panic creeping up inside her when she sees the razor-sharp shards in the sink.

Minoo jumps when the door is thrown open. The school janitor enters, holding a toolbox. He's in his forties and has a shock of graying hair. His ice-blue eyes are wide open and staring straight at her. He mumbles something unintelligible, sets down his toolbox, and rummages around in it.

Linnéa returns and goes up to Minoo and takes her hand again, gripping it convulsively. A moment later the principal arrives.

Minoo has seen Adriana Lopez only once before, when the new students were welcomed to the school. She looks between thirty and forty, with a short bob and bangs. She is wearing a knee-length black skirt and a white blouse with all of the buttons done up. Attractive but stern. Not a principal to whom you would take your problems, Minoo senses.

'Girls, you can't stay here,' she says.

'I'm staying,' Linnéa says.

The principal meets her gaze. 'Leave, now,' she says.

'We're staying,' Minoo says.

The janitor takes out a screwdriver. It's easy to open these doors from the outside. Presumably they were designed to be that way. Linnéa moves closer to Minoo and squeezes her hand even harder. 'Don't look,' she whispers.

And Minoo wants to shut her eyes. She wants to leave. But instead she stands there wide-eyed as the door swings open.

The janitor turns away and the principal gasps. Minoo can't move. The shock is like ice surging through her body.

Elias's head is pitched back and his eyes are open, staring at the ceiling. His arms are hanging limply at his sides. His right hand is still holding a big shard of the shattered mirror. There is a wide gash in his left arm.

Minoo and Linnéa put their arms around each other. It just happens. Minoo isn't the type to hug people, and senses that Linnéa isn't either. Right now, all they need is to feel the closeness of somebody else, someone alive.

Far away, in the real world, she hears sirens approaching.

CHAPTER 4

Nearly all the students are gathered in the playground. They're crowded together, jostling for space. The conversations are animated but hushed. No one knows who's died, but there are rumors floating around that it's Elias Malmgren. The teachers have sent everyone home, but clearly nobody's planning to leave until the corpse is carried out.

The corpse. Rebecka shudders. She and Gustaf are standing outside the front entrance. He's standing behind her with his arms wrapped around her.

'Promise that nothing will ever happen to you,' she says, in a low voice.

Gustaf hugs her a little harder and puts his lips to her ear. 'I promise,' he says. He kisses her cheek.

Sometimes Rebecka still can't believe they're together. Gustaf has always been the most popular boy in school. The one whose name gets scribbled in the margins of girls' notebooks over and over again in class. Rebecka had been one of those girls, but she'd never thought he'd notice her. She's never stood out as anything special. It had almost given her a sense of security to be so sure that she would never get Gustaf. Local soccer star. A year older. Handsome as a Hollywood actor and almost as far out of reach.

But then at the ninth grade spring ball, everything had changed. They'd kissed. And a week later, the night after the school year had ended, they'd kissed again. Rebecka had had two bottles of beer and was just drunk enough to have the courage to ask, 'Are we together now?'

'Of course we are!' he'd answered, and flashed his wonderful smile. 'Of course we are!'

Over the summer, her life had changed completely. Everyone knows who Rebecka is now. But, above all, *she* has changed. It almost scares her, how dependent she's become on Gustaf. He's so beautiful. She never tires of looking at or kissing him.

She is more torn over having become 'someone'. She feels as if the rug could be pulled out from under her at any moment. She can see it so clearly in front of her – how one day everyone will realize that she's not particularly smart, funny or pretty. More than anything, she's afraid of the day Gustaf realizes that.

A collective gasp runs through the throng of students as the school doors open and the paramedics emerge, carrying a covered stretcher. As they move toward the ambulance, the crowd closes in behind them. Students crane their necks, trying to catch a glimpse of the person lying under the sheet. The paramedics lift the stretcher inside and close the doors. Then they walk calmly to the front of the ambulance and climb in. The sirens whine. Presumably to clear people out of the way, Rebecka guesses. There's no reason to hurry when you're transporting a body.

'It's him,' says a panting voice.

Ida Holmström is with her constant shadows, Julia and Felicia. Together they form a blonde version of the Three Musketeers.

'It's Elias Malmgren,' Ida continues.

'How do you know?' asks Gustaf.

'We heard some teachers talking,' Julia says.

Ida gives her a murderous look, clearly upset at being interrupted. This is her moment. She looks at Gustaf with puppy dog eyes. 'Sad, isn't it?'

Before Rebecka and Gustaf got together, Ida treated her like she didn't exist. The day after the last day of school she had called and asked Rebecka if she wanted to go swimming in Dammsjön Lake. As if they had been friends forever. Although Rebecka realized the absurdity of the situation, she didn't dare refuse – because she's terrified of Ida.

'I don't understand how anyone can just kill themself,' Felicia mumbles.

Ida nods. 'It's so incredibly selfish. I mean, like, think of his parents.'

'He must have been depressed,' Rebecka says, feeling an instant urge to smack herself for sounding so wimpy.

'Of course he was depressed,' Ida says. 'But everyone has problems. It doesn't mean you have to kill yourself. If everyone felt that sorry for themselves, there wouldn't be anyone left.'

'I think he was gay,' Felicia says.

'Yeah – I read they often commit suicide,' Julia adds.

'He was being bullied, for fuck's sake,' Gustaf cuts in.

Ida meets his gaze and flashes her most charming smile. 'I know, G . . .'

Rebecka struggles to suppress a grimace. 'G' is a nickname Ida came up with. No one else uses it.

'. . . but seriously,' she continues, 'nobody was forcing Elias to dress like that and *wear makeup* to school.' Julia and Felicia nod as Ida continues, encouraged by their support. 'I mean, he could have made more of an effort to fit in and act more normally. I'm not saying it was his fault he was bullied, but he didn't do much to stop it either.'

Rebecka stares at Ida, whose expression seems full of anticipation as she looks at Gustaf.

'Jesus Christ, Ida,' he says. 'Don't you ever get tired of being a bitch all the time? Take a day off once in a while while.'

Ida flutters her eyelashes. Then she lets out a forced laugh. 'God, you're so funny, G,' she says and turns to Julia and Felicia, who look at each other uncertainly. 'Men have such a raw sense of humor.'

Rebecka grabs Gustaf's hand. She's proud of him, but it's gnawing at her that she didn't say anything.

Minoo and Linnéa are sitting in the principal's office on the threadbare dark-green sofa. The principal is in the next room, where the assistant principal usually sits, and is speaking to a uniformed police officer.

Linnéa flips her phone in her hand as if she's waiting for a call. Minoo tries not to stare at her. Linnéa's body language is screaming that she doesn't want to be bothered.

The room is surprisingly small. A shelf is packed with different-colored binders. A few tired-looking potted plants stand in the window. The white and green checked curtains are stained and the windows need washing. Papers are stacked in neat piles on the desk next to an ageing computer. The chair is ugly but, no doubt, ergonomic. The only thing that stands out is a lamp with a dragonfly-patterned glass mosaic shade.

It's the first time Minoo has ever been to the principal's office. You're only ever called there if you're in trouble or if something terrible has happened.

When Minoo was in elementary school, she used to day-dream about something dramatic happening – that the school would catch fire, or that everyone would be taken hostage by a bank robber on the run. The older she got, the more she saw how childish that was. But it is only now that she knows how far from reality her fantasies were.

The things that are awful in reality are nothing like the things that are awful in movies. It's not exciting. It's just scary, horrible and dirty. Above all, you can't turn it off. Minoo already knows that the image of Elias will haunt her for the rest of her life.

If only I'd shut my eyes, she thinks.

'I've seen a dead person before,' Linnéa says suddenly. Her eyes are fixed on her phone, which she's still flipping between her ink-smudged fingers. Each nail is neatly painted neon pink.

'Who?' Minoo asks.

'I don't know what her name was. It was an old lady. A drunk. She had a heart attack and died. Just like that. I was, like, five.'

Minoo doesn't know what to say. It's so far removed from her own life.

'You never forget something like that,' Linnéa mumbles.

Her eye makeup is a mess. It strikes Minoo that she herself hasn't cried. Linnéa must think she's the most insensitive person in the world. But Linnéa just looks at her. 'We were in the same class in seventh grade, weren't we?'

Minoo nods.

'What's your name again? Minna?'

'Minoo.'

Linnéa doesn't say her name. Either she can't be bothered or she takes it for granted that Minoo knows it. And why wouldn't she? Everyone was always talking about Linnéa Wallin.

'Girls,' they hear the principal say, and Minoo looks up. Adriana Lopez's clean features show no sign of emotion. 'The police want to speak to you,' she continues.

Minoo glances up and is shocked when she sees the hatred with which Linnéa looks at Miss Lopez.

The principal seems to have noticed it, too, because she stops short. 'You were Elias's friend, weren't you?' she asks.

Linnéa stares at her in silence until the principal turns away and mutters something to the police officer now entering the room.

'You can stay,' he answers, and they sit down.

The police officer, whom Minoo recognizes as Vanessa Dahl's stepfather, struggles to find a comfortable position on the folding plastic chair. Eventually, he swings one leg on to the other with his foot perched on his knee. It doesn't look especially dignified.

'I'm Niklas Karlsson. I'll start by taking your names.'

He pulls out a little notepad and pencil – Minoo notices that the end is chewed. A police officer who chews pencils. A rodent in uniform.

'Minoo Falk Karimi.'

'I see. You, of course, I recognize,' he says to Linnéa.

It may have been meant in a friendly way, but it didn't sound like it. Minoo's whole body tenses when she sees Linnéa squeeze her phone until the plastic cracks.

Don't say anything, she thinks. Please, Linnéa, don't do anything stupid. You'll only make things worse for yourself.

'I realize this must be terrible for you,' Niklas says, and goes back to playing the sympathetic police officer, 'and crisis counseling is available.'

'We're bringing in a team of psychologists,' the principal says. 'You can see one straight away.'

'I'm already seeing a psychologist,' Linnéa says.

'I see. Well, that's good,' the officer says. 'Did you know Elias?'

'No,' Minoo mumbles.

Niklas looks at Linnéa. It's obvious he's trying to hide his contempt for the black-haired girl with streaked eyeliner. 'But you two were friends?' he says to her.

'Yes,' Linnéa answers, and lowers her gaze.

'Elias had problems, I understand.'

A nod is her only answer.

'And he'd tried to commit suicide before.'

'Once,' Linnéa says, her voice little more than a whisper.

'I see,' the officer says. 'Then perhaps there's nothing more to say about it. Naturally the pathologist will examine him. But the situation does seem fairly straightforward.'

There is something so condescending about his voice that Minoo wants to scream. If Elias had been murdered, and the murderer had made it look like suicide, the police would miss it. Because that's how things are in this stupid town. You're only what everyone thinks you are.

'I see,' the policeman says again, and stands up. 'Can you get yourselves home?'

Minoo hasn't thought that far ahead. 'I'll call my mom,' she says.

'How about you?' the principal asks Linnéa.

'I'll manage.'

But the principal hasn't finished. Minoo can see that she's groping for words. Even before she starts talking, Minoo knows she'll say something about Elias, and that it will be so terribly wrong.

'Linnéa,' she begins. 'I'm so very sorry about Elias. He seemed like a very special person.'

Linnéa's voice is hoarse and tense when she answers. 'Then why didn't you tell him that?'

The principal is rooted to the spot. Her mouth is half open, but nothing comes out.

'Now, let's keep calm, all right?' the police officer says, glancing at the principal protectively.

Linnéa gets up and leaves the room without a word.

Minoo looks at the principal uncertainly.

'You can go now,' Miss Lopez says.

Minoo walks back to her classroom to get her bag. The chairs have been put on top of the desks. Specks of dust swirl in the light falling through the window. She walks up to her desk, but her bag isn't there.

'Minoo?'

She turns.

Max is standing in the doorway with it. 'I held on to this for you.'

'Thanks.'

When he hands her the bag, their hands brush against each other, and Minoo nearly drops it. Her arms have gone limp again.

How can I feel like this when I've just had such a horrific experience? she wonders.

'How are you doing?' Max asks softly.

'I don't know,' Minoo says, surprised by the effortless honesty of her answer.

He nods understandingly. 'When I was your age, someone close to me committed suicide.'

His voice is calm, but he clenches his fist. A certain kind of pain never goes away.

'I didn't know Elias,' Minoo says, 'but Linnéa did.'

Suddenly she feels Max's hand on her shoulder. The heat burns right through the fabric of her shirt. 'If you ever want to talk,' he says, 'you know where to find me.'

'Okay.' She doesn't dare say any more. She isn't sure that her voice will hold up.

'I'm really sorry. No one should ever have to see what you saw. Look after yourself now,' he says, and gives her a little squeeze before he lets go.

Suddenly Minoo notices that she's shaking. Panic takes hold of her, digging its sharp claws into her chest, making it hard to breathe. 'I have to go,' she says. 'Thanks.'

She rushes out of the classroom and down the stairs. The sunlight blinds her when she throws open the doors and runs out into the playground. Linnéa is sitting cross-legged, smoking, by the front entrance.

Minoo's heart is pounding and she's so short of breath she has trouble speaking. She looks toward the street and sees her mother's red car. She can make out her familiar profile through the windshield.

'Do you want a ride?' she finally manages to say.

'No.'

'Are you sure?'

'Why were you running?'

'I – I don't know. I just felt I had to get out of there.'

Linnéa flicks her cigarette away. 'He didn't kill himself,' Linnéa says.

'What do you mean?'

'I spoke to him just before it happened. He was going to come over to my house later that night. He wanted to talk—' She stops herself. 'We'd had an argument. But we weren't . . . There was something he wanted to tell me . . . He wouldn't have just . . .' Linnéa doesn't finish her sentence.

She can't admit to herself, Minoo thinks, that her best friend abandoned her. 'Why didn't you say anything to the police?' she asks instead.

'*The police.*' Linnéa snorts. Suddenly her gaze is hard and unforgiving.

'Well, shouldn't you tell them?' Minoo says.

'What the hell would you know about anything? You've always lived in your cozy house with your cozy family.'

Minoo meets her gaze. She's ashamed because she knows it's true. At the same time, she thinks that perhaps Linnéa's truth isn't the only truth. If Minoo has mainly experienced the lighter side of life, Linnéa has mainly experienced the darker side. Is the one truer than the other?

Linnéa smiles scornfully. 'Aren't you going to run to Mommy now?'

Minoo feels a sudden flash of anger. 'I feel sorry for you,' she says, and walks toward the car.

'Well, fucking don't!' Linnéa shouts after her.

CHAPTER 5

Anna-Karin gets up, staggers down the aisle of the lurching bus and resolutely aims for the door. She is so tired of being afraid that someone is going to say something nasty to her as she walks past. Or, even worse, that she'll hear a stifled snigger. When neither happens, she hears echoes of previous insults in her head. Voices that whisper how fat she is and how she stinks of manure.

But today no one even looks up. Everybody on the bus is whispering, but not about her. Today nobody's talking about anyone except Elias.

The bus takes a final curve and stops with a jolt that causes her to stumble. She feels her stomach drop in the tenth of a second when she thinks she's going to fall and make everyone laugh, but she regains her balance without anyone noticing. The doors open and she steps down on to the soft shoulder.

She takes a few deep breaths as the bus disappears down the road. As soon as she sees the cow pasture, her lungs double in size. She can breathe freely.

The gravel crunches beneath her feet as she walks up to the house. When she reaches the field she goes over to one of the big, brown-eyed animals. 'Hello, my beauty,' she mumbles, as Grandpa always does.

The cow's big tongue licks her hand when she holds it out. Flies are buzzing around its warm coat. Yes, it smells of manure, and she loves it. Anna-Karin is a completely different person at home. Her back straightens and her fear of sweating disappears. She can think about other things than whether or not the angle of her head gives her a double chin, or if her breasts are jiggling beneath her shirt in a way that might invite comment.

She reaches the front garden. Two red-painted wooden houses, one with two floors and the other just one, built at right angles to each other. The barn and a few smaller buildings stand further away.

Anna-Karin goes up to the two-story house and opens the front door. She takes off her shoes and plucks Pepper out of her pocket. He's fallen asleep and moves a little as she gently lays him in a basket in the hallway. She's made it nice and cozy with the remains of an old carpet.

Loud peals of laughter can be heard coming from the living room. Anna-Karin looks in and sees her mother lying on the sofa. She's fast asleep, with her mouth wide open. There's an American living room on the TV screen. Anna-Karin considers taking the remote and turning down the volume, but she doesn't want to risk waking her mother and being yelled at.

Instead she tiptoes into the kitchen. She takes out a box of chocolate balls from the refrigerator and a bag of French rolls from the breadbox on the counter. She hollows out the little white rolls, places a chocolate ball in each one and flattens them into patties. She eats them standing at the counter, with gulps of milk. The full sensation in her stomach makes her feel nicely drowsy.

Anna-Karin looks toward the kitchen window through which she can see Grandpa's house. She spots the hunched figure inside and waves. Grandpa gestures for her to come over. Anna-Karin eagerly leaves the house with the hysterically laughing TV personalities.

Grandpa's front door leads into a tiny hall where one of his work overalls hangs on a hook. To the left you can see into the kitchen. Nearest the door stands a bluish-gray wooden bench. This is where Grandpa's friends usually sit when they visit, before it's time to move to the kitchen table for coffee. That's where Grandpa is sitting now, looking out of the window as he slurps a cup of coffee.

Anna-Karin doesn't like coffee, but she loves the smell. Grandpa's little house always smells of coffee, newly chopped firewood and animals. Today it also smells of the freshly ironed clothes that lie folded neatly in a basket by the bedroom door.

'Hello, sweetheart,' Grandpa says.

'Hello,' answers Anna-Karin. She sits down at the table.

Grandpa is wearing a red and green checked shirt and corduroy pants. He always takes off his overalls before he comes inside. He doesn't want to bring dirt inside.

He gazes at her inquisitively. 'Back already?'

'They let us out early.'

'Really?'

It's an opening to say more, but Anna-Karin's throat tightens. She doesn't want to talk about Elias, doesn't even want to think about him.

Suddenly she wishes she were a little girl again. When she'd fallen and hurt herself, it was always in Grandpa's lap that she'd wanted to sit. Now she wants to go back to that time. Then maybe she'd have the courage to cry, to let out all the stuff that has stuck and hardened in her chest. Anna-Karin hasn't cried properly since elementary school. There's just too much to cry about. Now it's as if a manhole cover is blocking her tears.

'Has Mama been out today?' she asks.

'Don't think she was quite up to it.'

'She's out of bed anyway,' Anna-Karin says, and feels the hard, bitter anger inside her.

'Mia doesn't have it easy,' Grandpa says.

Anna-Karin regrets having brought it up. Officially her mother has taken over the farm, but Grandpa still does most of the work. Some days she loads everything on to him. Still Grandpa never has a bad word to say about his daughter.

Sometimes Anna-Karin is seized by terrible pangs of guilt because she's so angry with her mother. She understands that she's probably depressed, that she didn't want to take on the farm and is stuck with it. But at the same time it seems as though she lives to complain. Because what would she do without it? She's always the one who's most wronged, who suffers most, is the most deserving of sympathy in the whole world. That's how it's been for as long as Anna-Karin can remember.

Anna-Karin looks at Grandpa as he gazes out of the window. He can sit there for hours. She often wonders what he's looking for.

Grandpa was seventy-seven last spring, but it's only over the past year that he's really started to look old. Anna-Karin doesn't want to think of what will happen when he's gone.

Vanessa lays her towel on the lawn in front of Jonte's house. It has a washed-out pattern of yellow and brown flowers and doesn't seem completely clean. Who cares? She just wants to lie down and forget everything. Without getting grass stains on her clothes.

She glances up at the red two-story house, which also looks washed-out – the paint is sun-bleached and flaking. She hears a bass line throbbing inside. It's making the windowpanes rattle. Through the living room window, she sees the gigantic TV and the silhouettes of Wille, Jonte and Lucky against the explosions on the screen.

She lies down, pulls her shirt up to her bra and lets the sun warm her stomach.

Wille had been in a bad mood when he'd picked her up from the school. 'I'm not a damn taxi,' he'd mumbled.

'Well, go fuck yourself then!' she'd shouted, and had thrown open the door while the car was moving.

Wille had jammed on the brakes and the car behind them had come close to crashing into them.

Vanessa had stared at him, fear pulsating through her.

'Shut the door,' he had said, in a low voice, and she had done so immediately.

'Fucking old man.'

That had hurt, she could tell. Wille is twenty-one and she knows he finds the age difference between them embarrassing.

When they had gotten together she had just turned fifteen. By then she had already heard a lot about Wille. Vanessa recognized something of herself in him. He wanted more – to feel more, experience more. She had thought that life with him would be an adventure.

And now she's lying here while he's playing video games with his slacker friends.

But he's still the best-looking guy she knows. And he kisses her in that firm way she likes.

Vanessa angrily swats at a fly that refuses to understand it's unwelcome on her face. The sun is warm, but she can detect the first hint of autumn chill. Big clouds have started to gather on the horizon.

'Nessa?' Wille calls.

She raises a hand and waves.

'Vanessa?' Wille says again.

'Yeees!' she shouts back. 'What do you want?'

No answer. She sits up on her towel. Wille is standing at the open window, staring at her.

No. He's staring *right through me*. It's happening again. 'Wille!' she shouts, panic-stricken.

No reaction. Wille cranes his neck and scans the lawn.

'Where the hell are you?'

'I'm here!' Vanessa shrieks, waving her arms.

But he can't see or hear her. She grabs her towel and waves it. He doesn't react, so she tosses it aside in frustration.

Wille almost falls over. He's still not looking at her but at the towel on the lawn. 'What the . . . What the fuck?' he gasps.

'What is it?' Jonte asks, as he comes up to the window. Lucky tries to squeeze between them.

'That towel,' Wille says. 'It just appeared out of nowhere. I swear! It wasn't there before.'

Jonte and Lucky stare at him. Then they stare at the towel and back again. They burst out laughing.

'Chill, Wille. You're tripping!' Lucky bellows.

Jonte says something and closes the window with a bang.

Vanessa stands in the sunshine for a moment. She sees her own hands clearly in front of her. Her tanned legs. But something's missing. Something doesn't feel right.

She almost starts crying when she realizes what it is.

She's not casting a shadow on the lawn.

The sweet-smelling smoke hits her as she sneaks into the house. Wille is sitting in an armchair, staring at the TV and smoking a joint. He's lit from behind by the sun – his blond hair looks like a halo. Vanessa's heart somersaults. Sometimes she's taken by surprise when she looks at him.

She wants to go up and touch him but she's too scared to

try. She has to keep hidden the strange thing that's happening to her. At least until she knows what it is.

'Vanessa?' Jonte asks.

She whirls around. Jonte scans the room but sees nothing. His eyes are unusually alert and focused beneath the dark blue woolen hat he's pulled down over his eyebrows.

'You're being paranoid, dude,' Lucky mumbles pointedly.

'There's somebody here,' he says. 'I'm fucking sure.' Lucky is lying half upright on the couch gripping the PlayStation handset. His fat belly is poking out beneath his T-shirt, which reads *Pride of Engelsfors*. Lucky, whose real name is Lukas, was in Vanessa's class in ninth grade, but he never made it to tenth. Instead he spends his days as Jonte's errand boy, going out for beer, ordering pizza and helping with the cultivation in the basement.

'Did you hear about the priest's kid?' Lucky says, frantically punching away at the handset.

Vanessa sees how Jonte tenses, just slightly. Wille slowly releases the smoke he's been holding in his lungs. 'What?' he asks.

'Elias Malmgren. The priest's son. He killed himself. At school. They found him today.'

'Are you sure it was him?' Wille asks. He tries to sound blasé, but Vanessa hears the unease in his voice.

Of course, she thinks. They knew each other. Elias used to come here to score weed. But that was ages ago, like Christmas break in ninth grade.

'Positive,' Lucky says.

'Shit,' Jonte says. 'He was here yesterday, buying weed.'

'You think he had a bad trip or something?' Lucky asks.

'*A bad trip?*'

Jonte and Wille burst out laughing. Lucky smiles in his ingratiating way that makes Vanessa's skin crawl.

'He tried a few times before,' Jonte says. 'Probably wanted to be completely out of his skull when he did it.'

But he's feeling guilty, Vanessa can tell. She wonders why. Jonte doesn't usually care about anyone except himself.

'He was, like, a total loser,' Lucky says. 'Cutting his arms and shit. I thought only chicks did that kind of thing.'

'Shut up,' Jonte says suddenly.

Both Wille and Lucky tense and stare at him.

'There's someone in the house,' he whispers.

The others glance around. Vanessa holds her breath.

'Maybe it's Elias's ghost, come to haunt us,' Lucky says, and gets a smack on the back of the head from Wille's open hand.

Vanessa feels the hairs on her arms stand up. Suddenly it's as if the air billows around her, like a gust of wind. Jonte stares straight at her.

'Where the hell did you spring from?'

Wille looks around and laughs nervously. 'You shouldn't sneak up on us like that, Nessa. You're going to give your uncle Jonte a heart attack.'

Lucky laughs as well, for a bit too long. Vanessa does her best to smile indulgently.

She goes and sits on Wille's lap. She needs to feel his arms around her. Needs to feel that she's *here*. He nuzzles her neck. She presses herself hard against him.

Outside it starts to rain.

CHAPTER 6

Rain is pattering against the kitchen window. Minoo likes the sound, the feeling it gives her of being cocooned inside a secure house. Billie Holiday's voice is filtering through the speakers in the living room. The low-hanging kitchen lamp casts a warm glow over her parents' tired, anxious faces.

'How are you feeling, darling?' her father asks.

That's the third time he's asked since he came home. 'Okay,' she answers briefly.

More than anything, she just feels incredibly tired and drained. She's talked to her mother for a few hours, but she doesn't know how she's 'feeling'. All she knows is that she's too exhausted to think.

'Are you going to write about it?' she asks.

Her father scratches the bridge of his nose, making his glasses bob up and down. 'We've discussed it. If the poor boy had killed himself at home, of course we wouldn't. But as it happened at school . . . The whole town already knows about it.'

Her mother shakes her head. 'You'll be criticized for writing about it.'

'We'll be criticized if we don't.'

Minoo's father is the editor of a local newspaper. It only comes out a few times a week and mostly offers up exciting headlines like 'New Traffic Circle Installed on Gnejsgatan Street'. Three-quarters of the town's households subscribe to the *Engelsfors Herald*. Everyone knows who Minoo's father is.

'Cissi has written an article,' he continues. 'I had to cut half of it, of course, get rid of all the gory details. You know what she's like. But suicide is a sensitive topic, no matter how we tone it down.'

Minoo stares at her plate. She has barely touched her food and the meat sauce suddenly looks repulsive. 'Are the police sure it was suicide?' she asks.

'There's no doubt about it,' her father answers. 'But – and this stays between us, all right? Not a word about this to anyone at school?'

'Of course not.' Minoo sighs. She has never given him reason to doubt her ability to keep quiet. Minoo learned early on that most people collect information so that they can pass it on, but that the only way to get your hands on *really* interesting information is to be trustworthy.

'Elias died yesterday some time after four thirty. He had just been to see the principal. He'd been missing school and the principal wanted to "nip it in the bud", as she put it. They spoke for half an hour.'

It suddenly dawns on Minoo what Linnéa had meant when she accused the principal. What had happened at that meeting? 'What did the principal have to say?' she asks.

'She's shocked, of course.'

60

'And she saw nothing to suggest he was suicidal?' her mother asks.

'Of course that's the question that'll be asked. Why didn't she?'

'Poor woman. She's barely been there a year and this happens.'

'Naturally the school's responsibility is going to be questioned. Especially since the way he did it seems to have been intended as a kind of message to the school itself.'

'Erik,' her mother says, 'maybe you don't want to remind Minoo of . . . '

'That wasn't my intention, for God's sake,' her father hisses.

'Can't we talk about something else?' Minoo asks.

Her parents stare at her anxiously and exchange looks.

'I can't bear to listen to any more about Elias,' she mumbles.

'I understand,' her mother says calmly.

While they finish their meal, they talk about cutbacks at the paper. Occasionally Minoo makes a comment. Yet she doesn't remember a word of the conversation once dinner's over.

Anna-Karin's mother lights a cigarette while she's still chewing her last mouthful, always eager to fill her lungs with nicotine and tar. The food is something she wants to get out of the way so she can have that delicious after-dinner smoke. Anna-Karin gave up complaining about it a long time ago. Her mother feels that cigarettes are the only luxury she allows herself, and that's why she intends to 'damn well smoke without feeling guilty about it'.

Rain is pelting the window. Puddles are forming in the garden in front of the house.

The potato salad and smoked pork loin swells in Anna-Karin's mouth. It doesn't feel like there's room for anything in her stomach except stress. She tried to study for a while before dinner, but found herself reading the same paragraph over and over again.

She's afraid she won't be able to handle her natural science classes. If she wants to become a vet, she'll need excellent grades. She can't fall behind so early in her first semester of tenth grade.

'I got a phone call,' Grandpa says, all of a sudden, and looks at Anna-Karin, 'from Åke. His son works as a paramedic. Åke was wondering how you were. If you knew the boy.'

'What's this?' Mama asks, between puffs.

They stare at her. Might as well get it over with.

'A boy died at school today. Elias. He killed himself.'

Mama takes a long drag from her cigarette, then shrouds the table in ultraviolet smoke with a single exhalation. 'And you're only telling me now?'

Anna-Karin looks at Grandpa helplessly.

'It wasn't Helena's son Elias, was it?' Mama continues.

'Helena who?'

'The priest! What was Elias's last name?'

It's easy to forget that Mama once had another life. It's only when she starts talking about old friends and acquaintances that Anna-Karin remembers.

'Malmgren,' answers Anna-Karin.

'Good Lord, it *is* him.' Mama puts out her cigarette and immediately lights another one. She looks elated. She's always like that when there's a tragedy or an accident. It's the only time she ever stops wallowing in her own misery. 'Poor Helena,' she says. 'Isn't that typical? She works as a spiritual guide to others, but I suppose you can still be blind to what's going on in your own home. How did he do it?'

'I don't know.'

'But he did it at school?'

Mama is excited now. For once she's alert and bursting with energy. She leans toward Anna-Karin as if they were two friends gossiping over coffee.

'Who found him?'

'Two girls. One of them is in my class. Minoo.'

'The newspaper man's daughter,' Mama says.

Grandpa has been sitting there without saying a word. Now he reaches across the table and pats Anna-Karin's hand. 'Was this Elias a friend of yours?'

'No. I just knew who he was.'

'When you're young you think the world revolves around you and that every little setback is a catastrophe,' Mama says. 'You don't understand how good you've got it. All the responsibility you're spared.'

'Young people don't have it easy these days,' Grandpa remonstrates.

'No? They expect to have everything done for them.' Mama snorts.

Anna-Karin has trouble swallowing again. Her anger is

stuck, like a lump, in her throat. She puts down her knife and fork.

'With his whole life ahead of him,' Mama continues. 'I can't understand it.'

But I can! Anna-Karin wants to scream.

She's thought so many times how easy it would be to end it all. The first occasion was when she was eight and had told her teacher about her living hell. He tried to talk to the kids who were bullying her, but they responded by stripping her down to her T-shirt and underwear and leaving her in the playground in the middle of winter. 'Next time we'll kill you, farm girl,' said Erik Forslund. When her mother came and picked her up, Anna-Karin said that they had been playing. If Mama had probed a little, she would have told her the truth. But instead she had scolded her for making her drive all the way to school to pick her up.

Yes, Anna-Karin knows how it feels to want to die. For eight years she'd thought about it almost every day, then put it out of her mind. Because Grandpa's here. And the animals. And the holidays when she doesn't have to go into town. And sometimes, when she dares to think that far ahead, the dream of another life takes form – a life in which she's a vet and can buy a farm of her own, in the middle of the forest, far away from Engelsfors.

'There's probably a lot we don't know about how the boy was doing,' Grandpa says to Mama, in his diplomatic manner.

'It can't have been easy, of course, with those parents.' Mama nods, misunderstanding Grandpa as usual.

Sometimes Anna-Karin doesn't know which of them annoys her most: Grandpa, who won't judge anybody, or Mama, who judges everyone except herself.

'I mean, Helena's always worked a lot, and Krister – don't get me started on him. The great government boss – I don't suppose he has time for anything as mundane as his family. Oh, yes, things aren't always as perfect as they appear.'

Mama relishes the misfortune of successful people and makes no attempt to hide it.

'Of course, I don't want to say that it's somehow the parents' fault, but you can't help wondering. When children enter this world, they're like blank pages. It's we adults who fill them. And when your father left us, I said to myself, "Anna-Karin shouldn't have to . . ."'

Mama continues to talk, but Anna-Karin can't bear to listen any longer. *You're fucking evil*, she wants to scream. *You don't know anything about Elias's family, you don't even know anything about your own family, and still you sit there judging them. You don't have the right to say anything.*

JUST SHUT UP!

Anna-Karin's heart is pounding in her chest. Suddenly she notices the silence.

Mama has stubbed out her cigarette. The butt lies in a crumbled V-shape on the edge of her plate, but is still smouldering. She's staring at Anna-Karin, wide-eyed. She clears her throat and tries to say something, but all that comes out is a hiss.

Anna-Karin glances at Grandpa. He looks concerned.

'Are you all right, Mia? Is there something stuck in your throat?' he asks.

Mama reaches for her glass of water and gulps. She clears her throat loudly, but still can't speak.

'Mama?' Anna-Karin says.

'I've lost my voice,' she mimes.

She gets up and shuffles out of the kitchen holding her cigarettes. Soon afterward the TV comes on in the living room.

Grandpa and Anna-Karin stare at each other. Anna-Karin starts to giggle uncontrollably.

'It's nothing to laugh at,' Grandpa reproaches her, and she goes quiet.

But it is, she wants to say. It's hilarious.

Minoo spits out the toothpaste, rinses her brush and wipes her mouth with a towel. She looks at herself in the mirror and feels a shiver down her spine. The glass surface is hard, shiny. Would she be able to smash it with her hand? Is that what Elias did?

She's got to stop thinking about it.

She leaves the bathroom and goes into her room. The little round lamp with the green shade is casting a warm glow from the bedside table. Minoo is wearing her pajamas, bathrobe and slippers, but she's still shivering. She goes to the window to check that it's closed properly.

She remains standing there.

The tops of the trees and bushes are swaying uneasily in the wind. It's stopped raining. The paved street is glistening in the light from the streetlamps. A bush casts a strange shadow.

No. Someone's standing there. In the darkness, just beyond the reach of the streetlamp.

She draws the curtains and peers through the narrow gap between them. She is absolutely sure now. A person is standing in the shadows, looking straight at her house.

Minoo sees the figure move away. When it reaches the next lamppost and passes through the cone of light, she sees the person's back. A black sweater with the hood pulled up.

Minoo stands stock still until the figure has disappeared.

Suddenly she hears the creak of footsteps behind her, and the panic she has been carrying all day explodes. Minoo screams in terror. When she turns, her mother is in the doorway.

'Minoo . . .' she says.

The tears come. In the next moment, she feels warm arms around her and breathes in her mother's scent. Minoo sobs until she has no more tears.

'*Bashe azizam,*' her mother says comfortingly.

That night her mother sits on the edge of the bed until Minoo has fallen sleep.

Vanessa is dreaming about Elias. He is standing in front of the dead trees in the playground, watching her. When she sees him, she feels sad. Elias Malmgren is dead and will only be remembered as the boy who killed himself in the school bathroom.

She is woken by Wille's phone vibrating hard against the

floor. Damn it. They had fallen asleep on a mattress in Jonte's house. Is it the middle of the night? It's hard to tell with the blinds pulled down.

Wille's phone is still ringing when she lifts it to see what time it is. She rejects the call, but registers the name on the screen.

Wille has taken all the covers as usual and she shivers. She lays her hand on Wille's midriff and feels the warmth of his skin. He's moving around uneasily – he looks so different when he's asleep. It's as if she can see him as a boy and as a very old man at the same time. Vanessa spoons against him and pulls the covers over them.

'Linnéa W,' it had said on the screen.

Linnéa Wallin.

Elias Malmgren's best friend.

Wille's ex.

CHAPTER 7

The cart bounces and lurches along the road. She's on her knees and has managed to free herself from the sack they pulled over her head. The morning air cools her sweaty face. She glances at the driver's hunched back and floppy black felt hat.

She straightens up a little and struggles with the ropes. They are tied too tightly.

A forest stretches along one side of the road, dark and silent, and on the other, a wide expanse of open fields. Little gray huts lie scattered here and there, huddled beneath the clear sky. In the east, the morning star glows above the pink streak of dawn.

She tries to muster the courage to jump from the cart. But how far would she get with her broken body and fettered feet? Would she even survive the fall? She wouldn't be able to catch herself with her bound hands.

But what holds her back more than anything else is despair.

What sort of life would await her if she escaped into the forest?

Alone and cast out. Hunted by those she had thought she

could trust. Forsaken by those who had promised always to protect her.

The red sun will clear the horizon at any moment.

They are nearly there.

Rebecka opens her eyes. The smell of smoke stings her nose, more pungent than it was yesterday morning.

The floor feels cold beneath her feet. She pulls on her socks from yesterday, a sports bra, an old T-shirt and baggy sweatpants. Then she sneaks out of the room and quietly closes the door behind her.

She peeks into her little sisters' room. Alma and Moa are still asleep. Rebecka can hear their breathing, and is filled with the love she often feels for them. It takes away the sadness and fear she experienced in her dream.

Only when she steps out into the hall does she realize that it is only six o'clock. She can hear her mother's gentle snoring from behind the closed bedroom door, the humming and clicking of the refrigerator. Not a sound from her brothers' room. Rebecka laces up her running shoes, grabs her gray hoodie from the chair and leaves the apartment.

As she's running down the stairs she can feel the endorphins pumping into her bloodstream. By the time she steps out on to the street, euphoria is bubbling inside her. It's a beautiful day again today. The sun bathes the dull three-story brick apartment blocks in a warm glow.

Rebecka pulls out her battered MP3 player from the pocket of her hoodie and puts in the earbuds. She jogs down the street and turns left at the end. She quickens her pace.

The only time she loves her body is when she's running, when she can feel the blood surging through it. It's a machine that burns calories and oxygen.

She wishes she could see her body the way Gustaf claims to see it. But to her all reflective surfaces are like fairground mirrors. It started in sixth grade when she and a few friends went on a diet together. The others gave up after just a few days, but Rebecka discovered she was good at it. Way too good. Since then not a day has gone by without her thinking about what she eats and how much she works out. Several times a day she calculates it in her head: small breakfast, small lunch, slightly bigger dinner in exchange for an extra long run – how many calories does that make?

The autumn of ninth grade was the worst. That was when she ate least and was best at hiding it. On weekends she would sometimes stuff herself with sweets and chips, so that her mom and dad wouldn't get suspicious. Then, to compensate, she ate even less the following week. It was during one of those weeks that she fainted in the gym, and the teacher sent her to the nurse where she made a partial confession that she might have been a bit 'lax' about eating. But only for a few weeks. 'I swear.' The nurse believed her. Rebecka was such a sensible girl, not at all the type to develop an eating disorder, the nurse thought.

Things had been a bit better during the spring semester. And then she had met Gustaf. Now she doesn't starve herself, but the thoughts are still there. Even if the monster keeps to itself most of the time, it's always there, whispering, waiting.

The town houses give way to detached homes. In front of her rears Olsson's hill where the big May bonfire is lit each year. She sprints up the long steep incline. When she reaches the top, she slows down and stops.

Her heart is pounding in her chest. Her face is flushed. The music is exploding in her head. She removes her earbuds.

Down below the canal runs past. Beyond it lies the church. The cemetery. And the parsonage. Where Elias lived. Where his room is now empty. Where two parents have lost their son.

They'll see his grave whenever they look out of the window, Rebecka realizes. Suddenly she's crying.

She didn't know Elias, and doesn't want to revel in someone else's misery, like Ida Holmström and her friends, yet she feels a great sadness weighing on her chest. Because what happened was so senseless. Because he could have been happy if he'd held out a little longer. And because of something else that she can't put into words.

She wipes her tears with her sleeve and turns.

Someone is standing at the foot of the hill, gripping the handlebars of a bicycle. He or she is wearing a black hoody, similar to the one she has on, with the hood up. Rebecka can't see the person's face, but she knows they're looking straight at her.

It feels like an eternity before the figure in black hops onto its bike and pedals off. Rebecka lets a few more minutes pass before she runs home.

◎

When Rebecka comes in, Alma and Moa are stirring. It is nearly seven o'clock, and Rebecka starts to get breakfast ready, quietly so that she doesn't wake her mother who came home in the wee hours of the morning after her night shift at the hospital.

She puts milk, cereal, a loaf of bread and butter on the table. Since her father started commuting weekly to Köping, there have been many such mornings when she helps Anton and Oskar get off to school and takes Alma and Moa to daycare. Most of the time it's okay. But sometimes she feels like Cinderella before her transformation. Now, with the figure in the black hoodie still haunting her, she's glad to be doing something so mundane.

Rebecka goes into her brothers' room. Oskar wrinkles his nose and groans as the light from the hallway falls across his bed. He has just turned twelve and has become taller and thinner over the summer. Even though his face is still that of a child, Rebecka has a sense of how he'll look when he grows up. Anton, just a year younger, isn't far behind. But when they're asleep they look so small. Helpless.

She goes to the window and opens the blinds.

There are a thousand possible reasons why the figure in the black hoodie might have been standing on the hill; he wasn't necessarily stalking her. Rebecka doesn't believe a single one of them.

'Are you sure you should go to school today?' her father asks, over breakfast.

He and Minoo are alone since her mother is at the

hospital. Radio voices are reporting on world events. Her mother can't stand having to listen to the radio in the morning, so her father takes the opportunity to do so when she's not there.

'The longer I wait, the harder it'll be.'

He nods as if he understands, but he has no idea. If she were to stay at home today, rumors would immediately start to circulate. Maybe people would say she'd gone crazy. Or committed suicide herself. Then when she finally came back to school, everyone would stare at her a thousand times more than they would if she went in today.

'Might as well get it over with,' she adds.

'Want a lift?'

'No, thanks.'

Her father looks at her with concern, and Minoo feels compelled to change the subject. 'Have you made up your mind whether or not to write about it?'

'We're going to wait and see how things develop. There might be an investigation into the school's responsibility in the tragedy. The boy's parents might demand it. Then we'd find ourselves in a completely different position.'

Minoo is relieved. Mainly for selfish reasons. The sooner everyone forgets about it, the sooner she can go back to being anonymous.

She brushes her teeth and goes into her room to fetch her bag. She glances out of the window and shudders when she thinks of last night. Of the figure standing out there.

Her father waits for her in the hall, his hands clasped over his stomach, which has grown considerably over the last few years. 'Are you sure you want to go?'

'*Yes*,' she answers, instantly regretting the irritation in her voice. She gives her father a hug.

Minoo often worries about him – he sleeps too little, works too hard, and eats too much junk food. Her grandfather, whom she never met, died of a heart attack when he was just fifty-four. Her father is fifty-three. Now and then he and her mother argue about it. These 'discussions', as they refer to them, are conducted in low, heated voices that Minoo isn't supposed to hear, but sometimes her father loses his temper. 'Save your diagnoses for your patients!' he snaps.

At those moments Minoo hates him. If he won't look after himself for his own sake, he ought to for theirs.

'Call me if you need anything,' her father says. Minoo nods and hugs him again, extra tightly this time.

Minoo doesn't need to hear the hushed voices in the playground to know that they're all talking about the same thing: Elias. How he did it. The girls who found him.

'Look, there she is,' a few older kids whisper, as she walks past.

She pulls her backpack hard against her as she goes into the school. She lowers her head, trying to make herself invisible as she pushes her way through the bustling entrance hall. The entire school has been told to assemble in the auditorium to observe a minute of silence for Elias.

The looks and whispers follow her. Her ears grow redder with each step she takes. Minoo can't take it any more. She runs down the stairs to the cafeteria in the basement. At this time of the morning, no one is there except the kitchen staff. She heads for the girls' bathroom.

Only once she has shut the door can she breathe normally. She looks at her watch. If she waits a few minutes, sneaks into the auditorium as the ceremony is about to start and sits at the back, perhaps no one will notice her.

She walks up to a mirror and stares at her face. Is this how Elias was standing before he . . . did it? She shuts her eyes and opens them again. She tries to see her face from outside, as Max would see it.

It's become an obsession every time she looks at herself in the mirror.

If my zits cleared up, I might be pretty, she thinks. Or okay at least.

Then she's unsure again. How is it possible to spend so much time in front of the mirror every day and still not know what you really look like?

She thinks of when she was alone in the classroom with Max. The warmth from his hand. She feels it again and it spreads throughout her body. Why did she run away? What would have happened if she'd stayed?

The door is thrown open with a bang. Minoo spins around. Linnéa's standing there.

'Hi,' Minoo says, wondering if what she was thinking might be printed across her forehead.

'Hi,' Linnéa answers, and walks in.

She's wearing black jeans and a long black hoodie. She looks Minoo up and down. 'Hiding again?' she asks, with a hint of a smile.

Minoo should be angry with her, but she can't be. The harsh words that were said yesterday don't count: too petty in view of what happened.

'Can we forget what I said yesterday?' Linnéa asks, as if she had just been thinking the same thing.

'Sure.' Minoo tries to shrug with a degree of indifference. 'How are you doing?' she blurts out. Not the most sensitive question to ask someone who had found their best friend dead in a bathroom.

Linnéa looks as if she's about to say something sarcastic, but then her face softens. 'I wasn't going to come in today,' she says quietly, 'but I felt like I had to, for Elias's sake.'

Minoo thinks of her own selfish reasons for not staying at home, and is happy that Linnéa isn't looking at her. Her gaze is directed somewhere else, almost as if she's looking inside herself. She nibbles the tip of her bright pink thumbnail.

'I wish more people had known him,' she says. 'He could be so funny. And considerate.'

Minoo is uncertain how to answer. 'Shall we go?' she says, after a moment's hesitation.

Linnéa nods and walks out ahead of her.

The entrance hall is now empty, except for a few stragglers hurrying toward the auditorium.

'Are you all right?' Minoo asks, before they go in.

The murmuring from the auditorium sounds like a gigantic beehive.

'No,' Linnéa answers, with her hard little smile. 'But I never am.'

Chapter 8

Rebecka and Gustaf are sitting next to each other in the second-to-last row. The auditorium has remained essentially unchanged since the school was built: a big hall with a sloped floor leading down to a wood-paneled stage. The sun falls in through the high, dirty windows and casts a shadow pattern on the opposite wall. A lectern has been placed on the stage, and the rows of seats are packed with students.

Rebecka turns her head and sees Minoo Falk Karimi and Linnéa Wallin slip in and sit in the row behind her. She smiles at them uncertainly. Linnéa doesn't appear to see her, but Minoo smiles back.

Rebecka has always liked Minoo but it's difficult to get close to her. She comes across as so grown-up that she makes Rebecka feel childish and at a disadvantage. Besides, Minoo is so damn smart. She was unstoppable during class discussions last year. She would put forward one crystal-clear argument after another. No one stood a chance against her, not even the teachers. Once class was over, Rebecka sometimes saw holes in Minoo's reasoning. But when Minoo had presented her arguments they'd sounded so feasible that you just had to accept them.

It must be nice to be like that, Rebecka thinks. To never doubt yourself.

'The whole school's here,' Gustaf says, in a low voice.

'It's so awful,' Rebecka whispers. 'Everyone cares all of a sudden.'

'I guess they all want to show they weren't one of the people who were bullying him,' Gustaf says.

Rebecka looks at his serious expression, his straight profile and ruffled blond hair. A lot of people see Gustaf just as a good-looking soccer hunk. But they don't know anything about him. He's smart – smarter than almost anyone else Rebecka knows. And by that she doesn't mean academically: he knows about life. She takes his warm, dry hand and squeezes it tightly.

The chatter in the hall dies down as the principal walks up to the lectern. 'Tragedy has struck our school,' she begins.

The first sniffles start in the front rows, but Rebecka can't see who's crying.

'Yesterday Elias Malmgren was found dead here. We cannot begin to understand what his family and friends are going through, but it affects us all when a young person chooses to take his own life.'

More sniffling. Suddenly Rebecka feels dizzy. The air is heavy and it's difficult to breathe.

'Rebecka?' Gustaf whispers.

The principal's voice sounds increasingly distant, as if she were speaking under water.

'I have to . . .' Rebecka murmurs.

Gustaf understands. As always. He helps her up and leads

her discreetly toward the door. She notices heads turning in their direction, but she doesn't care. She needs air.

As soon as they emerge from the auditorium the dizziness subsides. She takes a deep breath.

'Do you want to go outside?' Gustaf asks. 'Shall I get you a glass of water?'

'Thanks,' she says, and gives him a hug, pressing her nose against his neck and taking in his smell. 'It's better now. I just felt a bit light-headed.'

'Have you had anything to eat today?'

'Yes,' she answers. 'Why do you ask?'

They've never talked about her problem, but Rebecka is sure that Gustaf senses something. It comes across in glances and pauses, as if he's building himself up to ask but doesn't know how to.

'I just thought . . . You said you were feeling light-headed.'

She shouldn't be annoyed. He's just showing he cares.

But can't you ask me straight out? she thinks. Can't you just ask what you've been wondering for months? Is it true what they say about Rebecka? That she throws up after lunch? That she passed out during PE at the beginning of last year because she hadn't eaten?

And why can't *you* tell him about it? a little voice asks. He's your boyfriend. You love each other.

Rebecka already knows the answer.

She's afraid he'll disappear. How could he stand to be with someone who's such a pain? Who's so disturbed she won't eat, then eats too much, throws it all up and goes back to not eating. Someone who lives in constant fear of falling apart. Boys don't want girls with hang-ups. They want girls who are relaxed, cheerful and laugh a lot. It's not hard to be like that with Gustaf because he makes her happy. She's been able to conceal the other side so far.

Why wouldn't he be able to love that side, too? the voice asks. Let him in and you'll see. Tell him what you've never told anyone else.

Rebecka savors those words and the relief she knows she would feel. Then she remembers the anxiety that would return as soon as she'd told him. To confide is to make oneself vulnerable. She remembers how in the past secrets were used as weapons in the endless personal wars that broke out. How even the most innocent things could be turned into poison in other people's hands.

But Gustaf wouldn't do that, would he?

Not knowingly. But all it takes is one careless comment to someone during football practice – how he's worried about her – to get the gossip mill churning.

No, she decides. Better to keep it inside. Only then can she be sure where her secret is.

'I probably had too little breakfast,' she says. 'I was out running this morning so I should have had a bit extra.' Surely that's not something you'd say if you really had a problem?

Gustaf looks relieved, if not completely convinced. 'You have to look after yourself,' he says. 'You mean so much to me.'

Rebecka kisses his unbelievably soft lips. 'You mean *everything* to me,' she whispers, thinking that that wasn't quite true because the others mean something, too – her mom and dad, her brothers and sisters – but it feels nice to say it. Somehow it captures the immensity of what she feels for Gustaf, which she finds impossible to put into words.

'Want to go back inside?' he asks.

She nods. It would be wrong to leave.

When they step back into the auditorium, the principal is still at the lectern. Now students of all ages are crying, people who didn't even know Elias existed. No one looks at Rebecka and Gustaf as they take their seats.

'Now we're going to listen to a poem, after which we'll observe a minute of silence for Elias,' the principal says softly. 'Then we'll go out into the playground and watch as the flag is flown at half-mast.'

The principal makes way for a fair-haired girl, who has mounted the stage.

Rebecka's mouth is instantly dry. It's Ida Holmström.

'I don't believe this . . .' Gustaf mumbles.

But no one else seems to react. And why would they? Most of them probably didn't know how mean Ida could be.

Nobody was forcing Elias to dress like that and wear makeup to school.

The words echo in Rebecka's head. Ida leans forward and accidentally breathes too close to the microphone, generating a blast of feedback from the loudspeakers. The sniveling fades out.

'My name is Ida Holmström and I've been in Elias's class since I was nine. He was really nice and we tried to be there for him when he was down. It feels so empty now he's gone. I'd like to read this poem on behalf of his friends.'

Rebecka glances at Gustaf, who is clenching his teeth so hard that his jaw muscles tense visibly.

> 'When I am dead, my dearest,
> Sing no sad songs for me;
> Plant thou no roses at my head,
> Nor shady cypress tree . . .'

Ida clears her throat as her voice quivers. Is she moved? Or faking it? The sniffling has started up again. It's a beautiful poem, but nothing could be more wrong than Ida Holmström reading it to Elias.

I mean, he could have made more of an effort to fit in and act more normally.

Rebecka turns discreetly and glances at Linnéa, perhaps Elias's only real friend in this packed auditorium.

Linnéa isn't trying to hide her hatred. Rebecka has never seen a look like that before, and she knows instantly that something is going to happen.

> 'Be the green grass above me,
> With showers and dewdrops wet;
> And if thou wilt, remember,
> And if thou wilt, forget.'

Ida looks at the audience as if she's expecting applause.

Then she adds: 'Now let us observe a minute of silence for Elias.'

The hall is silent, but only for a few seconds. Rebecka hears the spring-loaded folding seat snap shut against the backrest when Linnéa stands up. 'You're such a fucking hypocrite!' she says loudly.

There is a rumbling in the auditorium as several hundred students turn around.

'You stand there pretending you cared about Elias. You're one of the people who used to bully him, for Christ's sake!'

Ida stares back from the lectern like a deer caught in headlights.

The principal gets up. 'Linnéa . . .'

But Linnéa steps out into the aisle, approaches the stage and raises her voice above the principal's: 'In eighth grade Erik Forslund, Robin Zetterqvist and Kevin Månsson cut Elias's hair off . . .' She continues speaking as she heads resolutely toward the stage, where Ida is standing, gripping the lectern. 'There were only a few tufts left when they'd finished with him. And his head was bleeding. You gave them the scissors, Ida. It was you! I saw it! And so did the rest of you, you sick fucking hypocrites!'

Shouts of support are heard from the back where a few more outcasts are sitting.

Ida leans toward the microphone. 'It was really sad that Elias was bullied,' she says, her voice sounding unusually shrill, 'but that's not true.'

The whole thing happens so quickly that no one has a chance to react. Suddenly Linnéa is on the stage bearing down on Ida, who lets go of the lectern and backs away.

'Linnéa!' the principal shouts, a note of panic in her voice.

And Rebecka thinks, Something terrible's going to happen. Someone has to stop this – now!

The next moment there is a creaking sound from the ceiling. The metal beam to which the stage spotlights are attached shudders. Then it collapses on to the lectern with a crash, landing on the floor between Linnéa and Ida. Shards of glass explode across the stage from the lamps as they shatter.

Ear-piercing feedback screeches from the speakers, and everyone claps their hands over their ears until the janitor pulls out the plug. Then everything is quiet. Deathly quiet. People drop their hands, but no one says a word.

Linnéa and Ida stare at each other, stock still. Eventually Ida loses the wordless battle. She flees the stage and runs for cover in the front row among her friends.

The murmuring begins again. The principal tries to speak to Linnéa, but she steps down from the stage and runs toward the exit.

Rebecka looks at the dust that is still floating in the air, at the glass scattered across the floorboards.

I did that.

It's an insane notion, but she doesn't doubt it. She had caused it to happen. It was impossible and yet it had happened. It had happened in front of everyone.

'Keep calm,' the principal shouts from the stage. 'The front rows leave first, then the rest of you. We'll assemble outside in the playground.'

Rebecka can't take her eyes off the metal beam. She's never believed in the supernatural, never been able to take ghost stories and horoscopes seriously.

Now she doesn't just believe. She *knows*.

Anna-Karin is among the last to leave the auditorium. She's been sitting at the very back, as far away as possible so that no one will notice her. It felt especially important to do so on a day when she had decided to leave Pepper at home. Or maybe Pepper had made the decision: just as she was about to pick him up, he had shot under the sofa and holed up in there until she had to leave for the bus.

She had felt hurt – and frightened. Anna-Karin has always had a way with animals. They love her.

But now reality seems to have gone haywire, when she considers Pepper's behavior and her mother losing her voice mid-sentence – it hadn't come back by the time Anna-Karin had left – her strange dreams and the fact that she'd woken up two days in a row with her hair smelling of smoke. Somehow the chaos on the stage is connected with all of that.

She moves robotically down the stairs and outside. Through a gap in the throngs of students, she sees the janitor go up to the flagpole. In the background she glimpses the principal. Her face is taut.

The flag is slowly raised, and then lowered again. It comes to rest two-thirds of the way up the pole, hanging limply.

They stand there for a few minutes, uncertain what to do. A few start crying again, but it all feels a little half-hearted after the drama in the auditorium. The principal says something and those closest to the flagpole start to disperse and head inside to where classroom discussions await them with teachers and psychologists. 'It's important to gather up all the emotions experienced when something like this happens,' the principal said in her speech. As if negative emotions were as easy to clean away as litter on the playground.

Anna-Karin gazes at the flag. Poor Elias, she thinks. But at least he had some friends like him.

Anna-Karin has never been part of a group. She's never liked any particular kind of music or had any particular style. There's nothing to distinguish her at all.

'That little bitch Linnéa . . .'

The voice to her right is all too familiar. She turns. It's Erik Forslund, with Kevin Månsson and Robin Zetterqvist. The boys Linnéa said attacked Elias with a pair of scissors.

'We should teach that fucking dyke a lesson,' Robin hisses.

The others nod.

Anna-Karin's anger starts to build. She stares at them until Erik Forslund notices her. Anna-Karin realizes that this is the first time she's looked him in the eye since elementary school. Back then she hadn't learned to stare at the ground wherever she went, that that was how you got through life in one piece.

'What the fuck are you looking at, *B.O. Ho?*' he jeers.

It's as if all those years of rage wash over her. Only this time she doesn't direct it at herself. She's not angry with herself for being ugly, worthless, fat, disgusting and pathetic. She's angry with Erik instead. She hates him – a nice feeling: it fizzes up through her like soda.

Piss in your pants!

She's gazing straight into Erik's eyes when it happens. Something shifts in them. Suddenly a dark spot expands across the crotch of his jeans.

He glances around in a panic. So far no one has noticed. There's still time for Erik to save himself.

And that's when Ida walks by, with Julia and Felicia in tow. She has just been humiliated in front of the whole school and now sees an opportunity to deflect the attention to somebody else. She looks at Erik, then glances down. She can't hold back a smile. 'Oh, baby, what have you done? Have you wet yourself?' she bursts out, in a fake-caring voice. She says it just loudly enough that the people closest to her swing around. And then the people closest to them. Everybody laughs. One of those real tension-releasing belly-laughs and it's just what they need.

'Oh, gross!' a voice says.

Anna-Karin relishes every passing instant as her dream comes true before her eyes. Erik looks at Robin and Kevin in desperation, but they just laugh with everyone else. In the confusion he meets Anna-Karin's gaze again. 'Erik Piss-pants,' she says calmly.

Erik runs away. At each step his shoes squelch. Anna-Karin watches him hurry off with a growing feeling of exultation. It's as though a thousand angel choirs have burst into song.

All her life she's listened to Grandpa's tales of ghosts and supernatural phenomena. About dowsing, the Sami *noaidi*, the old man who could stem the flow of blood with his mind. Why shouldn't it happen to her? Who is more deserving of magical powers than Anna-Karin Nieminen, the eternal victim? Isn't this perfect justice?

CHAPTER 9

Slowly Vanessa takes off her clothes, one item at a time. Her body is aglow in the light from the campfire. Lucky lets out a raunchy whistle, and Wille punches his arm, a little harder than necessary. Vanessa smiles.

God, she loves being drunk. All the sharp edges disappear and problems fade into insignificance. The freaky shit that happened in front of the mirror and at Jonte's house – none of it matters. The fact that Linnéa Wallin still calls Wille doesn't matter. Soon nothing will matter at all. In two years she'll be an adult. In two years she'll leave school. Then she'll get into a car, leave this town and never look back, not once. Until then she plans to enjoy life to the max.

Vanessa is down to her bra and underwear now. She snatches the bottle of home-brew and Coke from Wille's hand and has a few gulps. Then she starts dancing, slowly, as if she can hear some sexy melody inside her head and just has to move to it. She wishes Michelle and Evelina were here, but on the other hand it's fun being the only girl.

'Christ! Do you have to put on a strip show in front of everyone?' Wille mutters.

She ignores him and turns to the others. 'Anybody got a cigarette?'

All five dig in their pockets. Mehmet, good-looking but too short, holds out a lit one. As she takes it from him, she accidentally brushes his fingers. He sniggers nervously. She can almost hear his erection.

'Isn't Jonte coming?' Lucky asks, without taking his eyes off Vanessa.

'He didn't feel like it,' Wille tells him.

'Good,' says Vanessa. 'I'm so *fucking* tired of Jonte.'

Scattered laughter among the boys. Wille looks irritated.

'I'm going for a swim,' she says, and heads for the water. The full moon is lit up like a huge spotlight above the lake. The nights have taken on a deep autumnal blackness and the air smells of earth and fungi.

Vanessa flicks away her cigarette, which fizzles when it hits the water. Then she pulls off her bra and underwear, tosses them behind her and dips her foot into the water. It's colder than she expected, but she wades out. When the water reaches her waist, she dives in.

Dammsjön Lake swallows her. The coldness of the water clears her head a little, and she swims a few strokes. It's dark and silent. The water caresses her body as she glides toward the surface and breaks through it.

Vanessa takes a deep breath. She treads water and runs her fingers through her hair, pressing it flat against her head. Then she looks back at the beach. The campfire is a little speck of light in the encompassing darkness. The forest is a compact mass swaying slowly in the wind.

Wille's white T-shirt glows in the dark as he walks toward the water's edge. 'Come back!' he shouts.

'You come here,' she shouts back, and fends off the mosquito buzzing around her head.

'It's fucking freezing!'

She doesn't answer, and instead dives again. Her body is used to the cold now. She does underwater somersaults, tumbling over and over until she barely knows which way is up. When the air in her lungs is almost exhausted, she launches herself upward and almost feels the first twinge of panic before she finally breaks the surface. She was deeper than she'd thought. She looks toward the beach again.

Wille has stripped to his underwear, and is standing knee-deep in the water.

'For fuck's *saaake*!' he shouts, and Vanessa laughs.

'You're such an old woman,' she yells back.

Wille wades out further and sinks down till the water reaches his shoulders. He keeps on swearing.

'It'll feel really good once you're in, I promise,' she calls teasingly.

'You always make promises you can't keep!'

That makes Vanessa think of Linnéa. How Wille had promised they weren't in touch any more.

Vanessa isn't the jealous type, except when it comes to Linnéa. Because she knows that it was she who dumped him. If she hadn't, maybe they'd still be together. But Vanessa has no intention of mentioning the phone call. She won't let anyone see that Linnéa makes her feel insecure.

Besides, she despises girls who secretly check their boyfriends' cell phones.

Wille takes big strokes. She can make out his features now. Soon he reaches her and puts his arms around her. Their wet faces meet and she kisses him. Their bodies glide easily toward each other beneath the surface.

'You're so fucking sexy,' Wille whispers, in that voice. The one that makes her feel warm inside.

'Look who's talking,' she murmurs, running her finger along the elastic waistband of his briefs. 'Go and get a blanket.'

'The usual spot?' Wille asks, with a drunken smile.

She nods and they kiss again.

'Hurry up,' she whispers, then kicks away, doing a few strokes on her back.

Wille teases her for always wanting sex, but he loves her for it, she knows. He thinks it's all his doing, that he's so incredible in bed she just can't get enough of him. But Vanessa has always loved sex. Even the first time, when everyone said it was supposed to hurt. Having sex for her is like being drunk. It makes her forget everything she doesn't want to think about. It makes her feel like the center of the universe.

Vanessa shivers as she steps out of the water. Her body feels heavy on land. She hasn't sobered up nearly as much as she'd thought. She staggers as she bends to pick up her underwear and pulls it on.

When she looks up she sees the moon again. It's blood red. She's never seen anything like it.

Wille is lying on the blanket, waiting for her, as she enters the little cluster of trees. Their spot.

'Have you seen the moon?' she asks.

Wille doesn't answer, just pats the blanket next to him. She lies down and he immediately rolls on top of her. Suddenly she feels the earth move beneath her. 'I feel sick,' she says and shoves him away.

A moment's dizziness, and then she feels something take control of her body. She sits up involuntarily.

'What are you doing?' Wille asks, far away.

Vanessa feels dizzy again. Her perspective is askew. It's like looking through the wrong end of a telescope. She feels her body rise and yanks at the blanket so hard that Wille rolls off it. Then she wraps it around herself and starts to walk. Her feet find their way, in spite of the darkness and the ground, which is littered with rocks and holes. Her legs are steady.

Wille grabs her shoulder and spins her around. He looks worried and she wants to calm him, but she can't speak. She pulls free of him and walks out into the night. Somewhere nearby a raven caws.

'Well fucking forget it then!' Wille shouts after her.

I must be really hammered, Vanessa thinks.

Anna-Karin is sitting in her room in front of the computer. She's staring at the screen, at the posts being made.

In middle school, she had created a profile on one of the most popular sites. She still gets angry when she thinks about it, angry that she could have been so stupid as to imagine she could make friends. Of course they'd found her. Erik Forslund and Ida had tricked her into revealing her password. She'll never forget the pictures they put up. The things they wrote.

The profile is still there. Naturally they had changed the password so that she couldn't delete the account. Sometimes she goes in and looks at it, just to remind herself that she can never trust anyone. It's a scab she can't stop picking at.

Often she reads other people's blogs where they write about their lives. People who think that what they've just eaten for dinner or what they're wearing is so important that they have to share it with the world.

When somebody complains too much about their non-problems, she gets so annoyed that she has to write something nasty. Then she lies awake for hours, terrified that the blogger will manage to track her down.

Now she's checking a blog by Evelina, Vanessa Dahl's friend. In her latest entry she's written how sad it is that a guy in her year just committed suicide. In the entry below it she's posted a picture of herself with Jari Mäkinen. Their faces are pressed together so tightly it must have hurt. It looks as if she's holding on to his back. Anna-Karin thinks she looks like one of those hot music video girls.

Me and my boy Jari . . . 2 hot 4 school!!!:P

Anna-Karin's cheeks feel hot in the glare from the screen. It's so fucking ridiculous the way Evelina clings to the senior boys. But Anna-Karin would like nothing better than to be Evelina in that picture.

Alone in her room, she studies every pixel in Jari's face.

She's looked at him often over the years. Looked, peeked, even stared, when she's been sure no one could see her. Jari's father helps her mother and Grandpa on the farm sometimes, and when Jari was younger he used to come too. Each time Anna-Karin would hide in her room until he'd gone home.

She is about to write something nasty to Evelina in the comment box when her legs tingle, as if they've fallen asleep.

Then she stands up so forcefully that her chair skitters across the room. That wasn't me, she thinks, in horror. That wasn't me.

When Minoo wakes up she's standing in the garden in her pajamas. She's wearing her slippers. The last thing she remembers is lying on her bed, studying. She must have fallen asleep.

Panic bubbles inside her as her feet begin to move with a will of their own. She walks through the garden and out onto the street.

Is this a dream? No. She's sure it isn't. She tries to stop, turn around, run the other way, but her body moves forward inexorably.

The streets are empty, the night silent. All she can hear is the plastic soles of her slippers scraping along the asphalt and the sound of her breathing. She tries to scream, but can only produce a whimper.

It feels bizarre to try to think logically in a situation that is so completely absurd, but that's all Minoo can do to quell her panic. She tries to remember if she's read about anything like this, but her thoughts keep heading off in directions that terrify her even more. Mental illness. Possession.

In the end she tries to stop thinking altogether.

Minoo reaches the interstate and sees a truck hurtling toward her from the left. Her body doesn't slow down but steps onto the asphalt. The truck blasts its horn. Minoo screams inside herself. The ground vibrates beneath her feet as they continue marching resolutely forward. She steels herself for the moment of impact, when her body will be crushed and smeared across the road.

But it never comes.

She can't work out whether it's the metal monster or just its backdraft that buffets her. The vehicle lets out a prolonged blast of its horn without slowing, but Minoo is safely on the other side of the road.

Her feet start climbing the steep embankment that runs alongside the interstate. She slips on the damp grass and loses a slipper. The ground feels cold against the sole of her foot as she continues her ascent. The moon is glowing in the black sky. It is an unnatural red.

That can't be right, she thinks.

When she reaches the top, she starts walking along the train tracks. After a while she loses her other slipper.

The forest closes in around the railroad, the harsh moonlight illuminating the tracks. Minoo thinks it's strange that the moon is red, but its light seems normal.

She listens nervously for an approaching train.

The tracks are seldom used at night, but sometimes long freight trains come through that she can hear from her house.

She catches sight of a little stream and alongside it the old dirt road. It's almost never used now because the interstate was built through Engelsfors. Only a few stray mushroom pickers or horse riders ever make their way out here.

Suddenly Minoo changes direction. She slides down the embankment and onto the dirt road. Her legs are stiff, but they continue moving forward.

The gravel hurts her feet. She hears wings beating above her. Ahead she sees Kärrgruvan, the long-since-closed fairground. The wire fence that surrounds it is broken in several places. The tall bushes, once carefully trimmed into all sorts of imaginative shapes, have been allowed to grow wild.

Minoo walks through the arched gateway with KÄRRGRUVAN mounted above it, and past the old ticket office, which has been boarded up with rotting planks. She sees the round dance pavilion with the pointed roof that makes it look like a circus tent. Further away there is a dilapidated red stall with HOT DOGS in white lettering across the top of the closed service window.

Somehow this place seems even more desolate and threatening when you know that it was once full of life, laughter and eager anticipation.

But it's not completely deserted, Minoo now notices.

Someone is standing in the shadows by the dance pavilion. Minoo's feet stop. The figure breaks away from the shadows and takes on solid form. Minoo immediately recognizes him.

It's the school janitor.

CHAPTER 10

'My name is Nicolaus,' the janitor says solemnly.

He's wearing an old-fashioned black suit, a white shirt, a red and blue striped tie and freshly polished shoes. As if he's dressed up for the occasion.

'Welcome, O Chosen One,' he continues, 'you who have come to this sacred place on the night of the blood-red moon!'

He raises his hands toward the sky. When she instinctively takes a step back, Minoo discovers she has regained control of her body. It becomes clear that the man is completely out of his mind when he virtually howls, 'Behold! The prophecy has been fulfilled!'

'Excuse me?'

He drones on, taking no notice of her question. 'You and I have awoken from our slumber. And now our eyes have been opened! Anon shall we witness the moment when our destiny shall be fulfilled!'

He looks at Minoo expectantly.

'You must have mistaken me for someone else,' she says weakly.

His intense gaze pins her to the ground.

'Tell me, did you come here of your own free will, or were you brought here by a mysterious force, something beyond the realm of human understanding?'

Minoo doesn't know what to say. How could he know that?

Nicolaus nods in satisfaction.

'Who are you?' she asks.

'Nicolaus Elingius is my name. I am your guide. You are the Chosen One.'

'Chosen for what?' Minoo asks.

'I don't know yet,' says Nicolaus impatiently.

'So you don't know any more than I do about what's going on?'

He looks around furtively. 'No. I mean . . . We have to be patient. I'm trying to grasp my memories, but that's like trying to catch a sunbeam. Like the newborn lamb that opens its eyes to the light and is blinded, we shall—'

'I'm going home now,' says Minoo.

Nicolaus shushes her. His eyes are fixed on a point behind her. A cold wind finds its way underneath her pajama top. 'Someone is lurking in the shadows,' he whispers.

Minoo thinks of the figure in the light of the streetlamp and shudders.

Now she hears the gravel crunching under someone's feet at the entrance to the fairground. She turns slowly.

At first Minoo doesn't recognize her because Vanessa's hair is wet and pasted against her skull. Her makeup, always so perfectly applied around her big brown eyes, has run down her cheeks. She is wrapped in a gray woolen blanket and is irritatedly plucking away some leaves that are caught in her hair. Minoo glimpses a pair of leopard-print underpants and a matching bra under the gray wool.

'I don't understand . . .' Nicolaus mumbles, staring at Vanessa in horror.

'What's going on and who the hell are you?' Vanessa asks.

It's obvious she doesn't want to show that she's scared to death.

'I'm Nicolaus. I'm supposed to . . . guide the Chosen One,' he says, with what little authority he can muster.

Vanessa is rocking back and forth to keep her balance. She must be drunk. Why else would she be running around half naked in the forest?

'Wait a minute,' says Vanessa. 'You're the creepy school janitor.'

Nicolaus grimaces stiffly.

Vanessa looks at Minoo as if she's only just realized she's there. 'What the hell are you two doing out here?'

Minoo feels silly for being offended that Vanessa has lumped her with Nicolaus. Can't she tell that she and Minoo are in the same situation?

Vanessa's blanket slides down to reveal her bra.

'Dear child, cover yourself!' Nicolaus is aghast.

'*You* stop staring, pervert!' Vanessa pulls up her blanket.

He backs away, clearly shocked. 'No one holds the fairer sex in higher esteem than I. Please tell me, did you come of your own free will, or were you brought here by a mysterious force, something beyond the realm of human understanding?'

The same question, but he had asked it differently this time. It's obvious to Minoo that Nicolaus is hoping she'll say she came of her own accord.

'I'm going to kill you if you did this,' says Vanessa.

Nicolaus is visibly deflated.

'It happened to me, too,' Minoo tells Vanessa. 'It was as if something took control of me.'

At that moment they hear the gravel crunching again.

It's Anna-Karin. The hem of her flannel nightgown hangs in shreds. Her feet and calves are covered with mud and God knows what else. She's panting heavily and her cheeks are flushed.

It is indeed Anna-Karin, but there's something different about her. She looks exhilarated in a way Minoo has never seen before.

Nicolaus's eyes widen. 'God help me,' he mumbles. 'There are three of them.'

'Four,' says Vanessa, pointing at Rebecka Mohlin, who suddenly appears behind Anna-Karin.

Rebecka is wearing her baggy sweatpants and a fleece. She stands there, huddled up, looking at the others.

Something grasps against Minoo's arm, and she spins around with a pathetic little shriek. Linnéa is standing behind her. She's still wearing her black hoodie. Her eyes are bloodshot and her gaze unsteady. 'Minoo, what's going on?' she asks. 'Is this really happening?'

'It looks like it,' Minoo answers.

'I'm losing my fucking mind,' she whispers, glancing at Vanessa and Nicolaus.

'No, you're not.'

Linnéa doesn't listen. Her grip on Minoo's arm tightens when she catches sight of something behind her.

Minoo turns and sees Ida Holmström walking toward them, her blonde hair cascading over her shoulders and a white lace nightgown fluttering around her. She seems to have stepped out of some black-and-white horror film, with the silver heart at her throat glinting in the moonlight and her eyes staring vacantly like a zombie's.

Minoo looks at Nicolaus, who mumbles to himself as he runs his fingers through his grizzled wavy hair.

'There's only supposed to be one of you!' he exclaims. 'As it was written, "The Chosen One shall come to the sacred place in the glow of the blood-red moon." There I am to meet and guide her . . .' His voice drops to a whisper. 'There can be only one of you. How am I to know which?'

He falls silent. Minoo realizes that someone has to start asking the right questions. 'Was everyone brought here like some kind of radio-controlled robot?'

The resulting silence speaks volumes. Minoo feels an enormous sense of relief. Whatever's happening, it's not just happening to her.

'Okay. That means we've all come here "in the glow of the blood-red moon".'

'Wait,' says Nicolaus. He sounds breathless.

Minoo can see that he's struggling to clear the banks of fog in his head.

Suddenly the words are pouring out: 'We have been awoken from our torpor for a reason. The Chosen One shall lead the fight against evil, and I shall guide her. The Chosen One possesses enormous powers, and she alone can save us all from destruction.'

Anna-Karin brushes her hair away from her face and looks at Nicolaus. 'The rest of you can go home,' she says. 'I'm the Chosen One.'

Anna-Karin's heart is pounding so hard that she thinks it'll explode when everyone looks at her. Even though Nicolaus has mentioned evil and destruction, it's more frightening for her to speak in front of the girls. But she has to be brave. She knows that what she's about to say is true. 'I can make people do things. It happened yesterday and today,' she says. She's speaking too quickly – she knows she sounds stupid.

'Maybe someone should call the psychiatric hospital,' Ida says, with a cackle. She seems to expect the others to join in, but no one does. No one laughs at Anna-Karin. Just Ida. Vile, despicable Ida.

It happens again. Anna-Karin's fear melts away, exposing a bedrock of raw hatred, incredibly powerful and hard. She is the Chosen One. And she's going to show them.

Speak the truth, she commands. *Speak the truth about why you read that poem in the auditorium today.*

Ida turns pale when her lips start to move. She tries to force them together, to stop the words, but they spew out of her like vomit.

'I read that poem because I wanted everyone to believe I cared. But I don't care. I think it's just as well that people like Elias commit suicide.'

Minoo and Rebecka just manage to grab Linnéa before she hurls herself at Ida.

'I didn't mean . . .' Ida whispers, and clasps her throat. She looks at Anna-Karin. 'You made me say that, you fucking freak!'

'You!' Nicolaus exclaims in relief, and turns to Anna-Karin. 'You are the Chosen One!'

'Excuse me,' says Vanessa, 'but I became invisible the other day.'

Anna-Karin gets angry again. Doesn't Vanessa realize it's Anna-Karin's turn to be the center of attention?

'I didn't do it on purpose,' Vanessa continues, 'but it happened. Twice.'

Nicolaus looks at her in horror. He can't dismiss her yet.

'I can't explain it,' says Rebecka, slowly. 'But the accident in the auditorium today . . . it was me who did that.'

It's harder for Anna-Karin to be angry with Rebecka. She likes her.

'Have the rest of you experienced anything out of the ordinary?' Minoo asks. 'I mean, besides the fact that we're all here.' No one answers, so she continues: 'I dreamed I was locked up in some kind of dungeon in another time. And in the next dream I was on a cart. And when I woke up my hair smelled of—'

'Smoke,' Linnéa cuts in.

'Otherwise I haven't noticed anything special,' Minoo mumbles.

Minoo is used to being the best at everything, and Anna-Karin can see she's disappointed that she doesn't have any amazing new powers. She thinks she can hide it, but Anna-Karin sees right through her. She's an expert. You become a very keen observer when you're always in the background.

'Neither have I,' says Linnéa.

Everyone looks at Ida.

Please don't let her have any powers, Anna-Karin prays silently. If she does, there's no justice at all in this world.

'I'm going home,' says Ida.

'Wait a minute,' Rebecka says.

'No! I don't want anything to do with you, you fucking freaks!'

'You haven't had any strange dreams?' Rebecka asks.

Anna-Karin can't understand why Rebecka is wasting time on Ida. Nobody wants her here.

'So what if I have?' Ida screams. Then her gaze hardens. 'Rebecka, we can still be friends if you come with me now.'

Rebecka doesn't hesitate. 'I'm staying,' she says.

'Just wait till I tell G about this,' Ida says, and walks off.

But she doesn't get far.

Ida looks like something from a cartoon, when she stops mid-step, as if she's just walked into a wall. Rebecka can almost hear the *boing* you hear when Wile E. Coyote runs into a door that's been drawn on a cliff face. She almost expects to see a cloud of little birds twittering around Ida's head.

Ida staggers and remains standing there, her back still turned to the others.

'Ida?' Rebecka says.

Ida doesn't answer. She just stands there, motionless.

And then she's not motionless.

Her body is dragged back toward them, dangling limply a few inches off the ground as if by some unseen hand. Her toes brush against the ground as she moves through the air.

Rebecka slides closer to Minoo. Vanessa looks frightened and Linnéa backs away. Anna-Karin sneaks up to Nicolaus.

Standing together they form a loose circle, with Ida hovering in the middle.

Her head is hanging down and her face is slack. Steam is coming from her half-open mouth, as if it is very cold where she's hovering. Everything becomes still again. A strange shudder spreads through Rebecka's body. Her skin is covered with goose bumps and the hair on her arms stands up. It's as if the air itself is charged with electricity.

Ida slowly lifts her head.

No, Rebecka realizes. Someone or something has raised Ida's head.

A string of white mucus oozes from the corner of Ida's mouth and dribbles slowly down her chin, remains suspended there, then drips to the ground. Her mouth closes and she opens her eyes. Her pupils widen and stare vacantly in front of her, yet it feels as if her gaze pierces right into Rebecka, sees things inside her that not even she knows about.

'Do not be afraid. You are in a protected place.'

It's Ida's voice, yet not. It's soft and warm.

'The enemy cannot find you here. It is only here that you are safe. It is only here that you may meet together. You must hide your friendship from everyone else.'

'At school, too?' asks Anna-Karin.

Ida's·face contorts into a grimace. 'Especially at school. That is a place of evil.'

'I could have told you that,' Linnéa mumbles.

Ida looks around. 'The Circle is seven,' she says. 'One of you is missing.' A lone tear runs down her cheek. 'Then the battle has already begun.'

'Who's missing?' Nicolaus asks.

'Elias,' Linnéa whispers.

Ida nods. Nicolaus looks dismayed and Rebecka thinks she understands how he feels. A piece is missing. The puzzle will never be complete.

'If evil prevails, the flames will engulf the world,' says Ida. 'You cannot afford to doubt. Evil is closer than you think. It is searching for you. You must train your powers, become stronger together. You need each other.'

Rebecka thinks she hears whispers of agreement coming from the forest. Like the concurring voices of invisible creatures all around them. In the next moment Ida looks straight at Rebecka, and a voice fills her head, a warm, loving whisper.

You must lead them, Rebecka. They won't like it, but they need you. It is your task to deepen the bond between you. But it is our secret. No one else must know that I have given you this charge. Do you understand?

Rebecka can only nod. Ida looks at her gratefully, then turns to the others. 'Trust each other. Trust Nicolaus. Soon he will remember more and be of help to you,' she says.

Ida gazes sadly at Nicolaus. His ice-blue eyes are glistening. 'Trust no one,' Ida continues. 'Neither your parents, nor your brothers and sisters. Not your friends. Not even the love of your life. And remember, the Circle is the answer.'

Ida sinks toward the ground. Minoo runs up to her. Rebecka and the others follow. They all gather around Ida.

'Who are you?' asks Minoo.

'I am you. You are me. We are one. The Circle is the answer.'

'What kind of evil are we to fight?'

No answer. Ida's eyelids flutter as the foreign presence leaves her body. Everything becomes still. A faint smell of smoke hangs in the air.

'Is she . . . is she dead?' Vanessa asks.

Minoo cautiously lays her fingers against Ida's neck. 'No.'

'So it's possible,' says Nicolaus. 'You are the Chosen One. All of you.'

Rebecka looks at the others. Six people with nothing in common have been brought together by something huge and incomprehensible. All of a sudden it feels completely natural that they should be here together. As if it had always been meant.

Ida opens her eyes and stares at them.

'How do you feel?' Rebecka asks anxiously.

'If you don't let me go now, I'll scream,' says Ida.

CHAPTER 11

There wasn't enough room for them all in Nicolaus's old mustard-yellow Fiat. Since Rebecka and Minoo were closest to home, they had offered to walk.

Minoo glances at Rebecka out of the corner of her eye. Neither has said a word since they left Kärrgruvan. The silence is starting to become uncomfortable. Unless it's Minoo's imagination. Sometimes it's hard to tell the difference between fantasy and reality. Tiny, almost imperceptible signals can become so easily amplified in her head.

In school she's never afraid to raise her hand because, there, she knows what she's talking about. But now, alone with a pretty and popular girl like Rebecka, she is silent.

It shouldn't be so difficult to find something to talk about after everything that's happened tonight. But the more she struggles to think of something to say, the more stuck she gets. Everything sounds so lame, so dull. How do they do it, all those people who babble on seemingly oblivious to the fact that most of what they say is meaningless?

'I hope we don't meet anyone we know,' says Rebecka.

Minoo nods, relieved that the silence has been broken. 'Yeah. Good thing it isn't the weekend. Not that there's all that many people out then either, but the chance of us bumping into someone would be greater. It should be quiet now – it's very early still, and most people are probably asleep. Unless someone's out walking their dog . . .'

Minoo feels like hitting herself. It's so typical of her. At first she can't get anything out because she analyses every word. Then she removes the filter and blurts out whatever comes into her head.

'Yeah, I guess it would have to be that, then,' Rebecka says with a smile.

They've reached the interstate.

Minoo makes very sure that no trucks are coming before she crosses.

'Did you know Elias?' asks Rebecka.

'No. You?'

'No. But I feel as if I did . . .' Rebecka stops and turns to Minoo. Her face is framed with loose coils of reddish-blonde hair. Her eyes shift between gray and blue. Her skin and features are so perfect that she almost looks Photoshopped. It's impossible to stop staring.

'I don't know how to explain it,' Rebecka continues, 'but it wouldn't have made any difference if we had all been best friends before this. We still wouldn't have known each other like we're going to get to know each other now. You know what I mean? That we belong together in a way that has nothing to do with who we were before tonight.'

Minoo hesitates. She sort of understands what Rebecka's getting at. Tonight has been strange to say the least. But Minoo has no mysterious new ability to make things move or people tell the truth. She doesn't feel especially transformed.

'I'm just babbling,' says Rebecka, with a dismissive wave of her hand.

They start walking again.

'I wonder what sort of power Elias had,' Minoo says, when the silence starts to feel uncomfortable again.

'Maybe he didn't have one. Neither you, Linnéa nor Ida had noticed anything unusual, apart from your dreams.'

'So you didn't think there was anything special about Ida tonight?' Minoo asks.

As she hears her words, they sound petulant in a way she hadn't intended. But Rebecka just giggles.

'To be honest, I'm a bit jealous of you,' says Minoo. 'I've always wanted to have a superpower.'

'Well, maybe yours is your brain,' says Rebecka. 'You're so incredibly smart. Maybe that's why we need you.'

'So you can make things fly through the air, and I can . . . think?'

Rebecka laughs. It's not a nasty laugh. Minoo has apparently been funny again without realizing it. That's promising: she never makes people laugh when she tries to.

'I just mean that there have to be answers to our questions. And if anyone can find them, it's you. We can't wait for Nicolaus to remember things. We have to look for ourselves,' Rebecka says. 'Besides, maybe you and Linnéa have powers you don't know about yet. Mine just came out of nowhere.'

What Rebecka says is logical. Minoo may as well be

patient. And if, in her familiar role as *studius maximus*, she can make a contribution, well . . .

Then it hits her. It might not be the end of the world, but pretty close to it. Minoo stops mid-step.

'What is it?' asks Rebecka.

'We've got a chemistry test tomorrow,' says Minoo, 'and I haven't finished studying for it.'

Linnéa lives in an eight-story apartment block near Storvall Park. It's one of the many buildings in town in which half of the apartments are empty and boarded up.

The front entrance stinks of urine. Vanessa wrinkles her nose and Linnéa smiles wryly. 'Welcome to the Engelsfors Hilton,' she says.

She opens the elevator door and they step inside. It's easily big enough for ten people and rattles loudly as it trundles slowly upward. Vanessa catches sight of her face in the mirror. She looks like a horror-movie victim who's been chased through a forest: leaves caught in her tousled hair and makeup streaked down her face.

Suddenly she realizes she has to speak to Wille, but it feels wrong to borrow Linnéa's cell to call him. She is starting to regret that she accepted Linnéa's offer to swing by her house to borrow some clothes. But she can't possibly go home wrapped in a blanket.

Linnéa opens the elevator door and they step out. Vanessa instantly notices the name on the letterbox: 'L. Wallin'. 'You've got your own apartment?' she asks, as she follows her.

'Yeah,' Linnéa answers, unlocking the door, as if it were

the most natural thing in the world. She kicks off her shoes in the hall, continues into the living room and switches on a few little lamps on the floor. They've all got red and pink shades and bathe the room in a soft red glow.

It's a shabby two-room apartment with linoleum floors and white wallpaper with little blue flowers. You can hardly see the walls for all the paintings, posters and pages ripped from magazines. In the living room a big sofa is draped in a large piece of red fake velvet. Placed in front of it, a painted black wooden crate serves as a coffee-table. A big ceramic panther perches next to the sofa. Tiny cracks form a white net covering the black body.

'Cool, huh?' Linnéa says. 'Can you believe someone threw it out?'

'Threw it out?'

'I get almost all my stuff off the street.'

Vanessa takes a closer look at the pictures on the walls. There's a series of creepy photographs of animals in clown outfits, and an oil painting that at first glance seems to depict an idyllic landscape until you notice the silhouette of a woman in a white dress hanging by her neck from a tree; standing nearby, two smiling figures, with pupil-less eyes, hold hands. Vanessa likes the pictures, but draws a blank on the band posters. Most are Asian, with names that she's never heard of before.

Linnéa's cell phone rings. She pulls it out of her pocket, looks at the screen and grimaces before she sets it aside.

Vanessa's gaze falls on a big black wooden cross on the wall. It's covered with small bits of silvery metal.

'Nice,' she says, mostly just to make conversation.

Linnéa comes and stands next to her and runs a finger over the cross. Her nails are painted with bright pink polish that is starting to wear away. 'Elias gave it to me. It's from Mexico. See these little symbols? They're all the things that this cross is supposed to protect against. Here's a broken leg, for example. Crying eyes . . . and a sick horse.'

Vanessa laughs nervously and pretends to look, but the only thing she's aware of is how close to her Linnéa is standing, so close that Vanessa can feel the warmth of her body through the blanket. Linnéa's phone rings again. 'What the fuck,' she hisses. She goes back to it and rejects the call.

'Who keeps calling?' Vanessa asks.

'Just a guy who refuses to understand when to stop.'

Vanessa sees a flash of something in Linnéa's eyes. Something that looks like . . . pity? She feels queasy and has to look away. She's suddenly realized who's calling, but won't humiliate herself by asking. 'Oh, yeah?' is all she says.

'Go and see what you can find in my wardrobe,' says Linnéa, pointing toward the bedroom door.

The blinds are down and Vanessa fumbles along the wall till she finds the light switch. The bed is wide and unmade. But what catches Vanessa's eye is the sewing machine on the floor next to a workbench stacked with different fabrics and jars of thread and buttons.

'You sew?' she asks Linnéa, who's just coming into the room.

Linnéa gives a quick nod, and Vanessa sees it was a stupid question. What else would she do with a sewing machine? What is it about Linnéa that makes her feel like everything she says comes out wrong?

'There's a mirror inside the wardrobe door,' says Linnéa, and hands her a packet of wipes.

Vanessa opens the wardrobe. Everything in there looks like something from a Japanese horror version of *Alice in Wonderland*. No matter what she puts on she'll look as if she's on her way to a costume ball dressed as Linnéa.

'Take whatever you want,' Linnéa says, and walks out.

The phone rings four times in the living room. Linnéa doesn't answer it.

The clothes hangers clatter as Vanessa flips through the outfits. Eventually she picks the most neutral one she can find: a black skirt, a white top and a knitted black sweater made of a fluffy yarn. She gets dressed, wipes off her makeup and removes the bits of forest from her hair. She looks almost half decent now .

'I'll give you back your clothes at school tomorrow. Today, I mean,' Vanessa says, as she goes back into the living room, holding her blanket.

Linnéa is lying crashed out on the sofa, her feet draped on one of the armrests.

'I'm going to stay at home today. But it's cool, we can do it another time,' she says drowsily.

Another time, Vanessa thinks. Yup. From now on we'll be forced to spend time with each other.

She and Linnéa, Minoo and Anna-Karin, Rebecka and Ida. If the salvation of the world depends on their ability to work together, well, unfortunately things look pretty fucked. Sorry, billions of people living on earth, Ida Holmström is all that stands between you and destruction.

'Christ, I hate her,' Linnéa mumbles.

'Who?'

'Ida. If evil is coming after us, I hope it takes her first,' says Linnéa. A little smile plays at the corners of her mouth. Vanessa catches herself grinning back. They look at each other for a moment.

'It's Wille who keeps calling you, isn't it?' Vanessa asks.

'Yeah.'

'Have you . . . have you started seeing each other again?'

Seconds pass. Linnéa sits up slowly.

'No.'

'So what does he want?'

Linnéa drops her gaze.

'Just tell me, okay?' Vanessa asks, making her voice as hard and fierce as she can to hide her fear. Is Wille angry with her for running off? Is that why he's calling Linnéa now? Is that what he usually does when they've had a fight? If he's still in love with Linnéa, I'll die, she thinks.

'He's angry with me,' Linnéa says.

Vanessa stares at her. 'What?'

'It's hard to explain. We fought all the time when we were together. Sometimes he gets it into his head that we've still got things to sort out. Like, why I said whatever it was that time a hundred years ago. Silly stuff.'

It's unlike Wille to get so caught up in the past. He doesn't even spend much time thinking about the present.

'We fought all the time. It can be addictive. You want to win once and for all.'

Vanessa doesn't know what to say. If Evelina or Michelle tries to lie to her she picks up on it instantly. But Linnéa makes her feel unsure of herself. And she won't find out the truth from Wille. She can't confront him with this information because no one can know that she and Linnéa are talking to each other.

If only she could think clearly. She's been awake for so long that her drunkenness has given way to a hangover.

They head for the front door. Vanessa borrows an old pair of shoes, and ties them – it seems to take ages, with Linnéa's eyes burning into the back of her neck.

The latch on the front door sticks. Vanessa tugs at the doorknob, twisting it in different directions. Linnéa opens the door for her, and Vanessa practically flies down the stairs.

CHAPTER 12

Rebecka is still wide awake when she hears the key in the front door, then her mother hanging up her jacket and taking off her shoes. The door to her brothers' room opens, then to her sisters'.

Rebecka has already looked in on them. It was only once she and Minoo had parted company that she realized the children had been at home on their own all night. What if there had been a fire? Or one of them had woken up, not found either Rebecka or their mother, gone out on to the balcony, fallen off—

She ran home as fast as her tired legs could carry her. Everything was quiet and calm, just as she'd left it.

Her mother's footsteps approach in the hall and Rebecka forces herself to breathe normally. Her door doesn't open. Instead she hears her mother go into the kitchen.

Rebecka stays in bed, feeling an odd mixture of relief and melancholy. It's obvious that her mother doesn't see her as a child any more. Even when Rebecka was five or six, she had made sure that Anton and Oskar stayed out of trouble and behaved themselves, then later with Alma and Moa. She was constantly told what a wonderful babysitter she was.

She sits up in bed and thinks of her new family, the one she'd met tonight. Now she's expected to play the same role there: the one who leads, mediates and keeps the group together. Will she be able to pull it off? Will she have the energy?

She goes into the kitchen where her mother is preparing breakfast. 'Up already, Beckis?' she asks, and gives Rebecka a hug.

Rebecka cheers up a little. It's not often she and her mother got to spend time alone together.

As they set the table together, her mother tells her about an eventful night in the ER. A fight had broken out at Götvändaren, the only hotel in town, which had left a man needing seven stitches. Another man had beaten his wife with a hot frying pan because she had burned the pork chops. An older woman working the nightshift at the saw mill had accidentally cut off her left hand. And a little child had been so terrified of the dark he had become almost psychotic. He was utterly convinced there were monsters wandering along the street below his window.

'You could sure tell there was a full moon last night,' her mother says and sets out the breakfast bowls.

Her mother has a theory that people behave differently during a full moon. If it affects the tides then it has to affect people, too, since they consist primarily of water. In her mother's world, anything from an unusual number of births to outbreaks of violent crime or insomnia can be attributed to a full moon.

'Maybe things are especially crazy when the moon is red,' Rebecka suggests.

Her mother looks at her questioningly. 'What do you mean?'

Rebecka becomes uncertain. 'It was red. Blood red.'

'Strange you should say that,' her mother says. 'A few of the patients were talking about how red the moon was. But when we nurses looked outside it seemed completely normal.'

Her mother pours herself some more coffee.

Rebecka looks out of the window to where a transparent moon lingers in the light morning sky. It's still red. Her mother follows her gaze without reacting. Obviously she sees nothing strange about it.

'I must have dreamed it,' Rebecka says quietly. She thinks for a moment. 'Mom, have you ever heard anything strange about Kärrgruvan?'

'What do you mean?'

'I don't know – has anyone ever said something weird happened there?'

'What are you talking about?'

'The fairground.'

'What fairground?'

'Kärrgruvan!'

Her mother's brow furrows. 'It sounds vaguely familiar. Where is it?'

'Here, in Engelsfors.'

Her mother used to go to Kärrgruvan a lot when she was young for concerts and dancing. She's spoken about it nostalgically. Now she just laughs. 'You must have had some really strange dreams last night,' she says.

'I guess I must,' Rebecka mumbles.

It feels strange to be sitting at the kitchen table eating breakfast as if nothing's happened, Vanessa thinks. Chewing, swallowing, chewing, swallowing, drinking some juice, then starting again. As if it was just another day.

Her mother emerges from the bedroom and puts an arm around her. Vanessa closes her eyes. It feels nice. But her mother lets go almost immediately. Their hugs are so brief, these days. It's mostly Vanessa's fault. She's sighed too often over her mother's attempts at closeness. How's she supposed to know that Vanessa would like nothing more just now than a hug?

'A new shop's opened up at the mall, the Crystal Cave,' her mother says.

'And they sell, let me guess . . . crystals?'

Her mother doesn't pick up on the sarcasm. 'Yes, and essential oils, all sorts of stuff. Apparently you can have your palm read, too. The owner's name is Mona Moonbeam.'

'Mona Moonbeam? Well, that doesn't sound made up, does it?'

Her mother laughs and pours water into the coffee-maker. As it starts to sputter she stretches and yawns. 'Nicke called while you were in the shower. Apparently things got pretty lively in town last night,' she says, and starts slicing a loaf of bread.

'Define lively in Engelsfors.'

'There was a big altercation over at Götvändaren, and several drunken brawls across the town. Nicke said he'd never seen anything like it. He was just about to head home after work when they had a call about a woman who had hanged herself from the roof of a house in Riddarhyttan, on the road to the elementary school. He was on his way there when he called and thought he wouldn't be home for another few hours.'

'Oh, God, how awful to be deprived of Nicke's presence. That's going to ruin my whole day,' Vanessa says. She instantly regrets her comment when she sees her mother's hurt expression.

'For God's sake, Vanessa, how long are you going to keep this up? Nicke is Melvin's father. You have to accept him.'

'I'll accept him when he accepts me.'

'Why can't you just grow up?'

Vanessa's bout of conscience evaporates. She has to bite her lip to stop herself from screaming.

Her mother had only been dating Nicke for a few months when she'd gotten pregnant and cheerfully announced that Vanessa was going to have a sibling. Secretly Vanessa had hoped that Nicke would shirk his responsibilities but, no, he wanted to be a father, and they'd moved in together in time for the birth.

She can't help but love Melvin, even if it was tiresome at the beginning to be woken all the time by a crying baby, but she's hated Nicke from the start. He doesn't make any effort to be nice to her – she's the one who has to adapt. And her mother doesn't see that. She's blind to Nicke's faults and lets him make the rules.

'Grow up yourself,' Vanessa snaps, and storms out into the hall.

'Don't speak to me like that!' Her mother follows her.

Vanessa slams the front door in her face.

'Did you hear the cows last night?' Grandpa asks, when he and Anna-Karin's mother enter the kitchen after the morning milking.

'What do you mean?' Anna-Karin asks, through a mouthful of cheese sandwich.

'They were bellowing in the barn as if they'd all gone crazy,' her mother croaks. Her voice has returned but it's not quite back to normal yet. 'Thanks to them, I didn't sleep a wink. Not that I ever get any sleep with my back.'

'I must have been out for the count,' Anna-Karin mumbles.

'Really?' Grandpa says. 'You still look tired.'

'I hope you're not coming down with the cold I've had,' her mother says, as she lights a cigarette.

Grandpa comes up to the table and lays a hand on Anna-Karin's forehead. 'You don't have a fever anyway.'

The old Anna-Karin would have been happy to feign illness and stay in the security of her room. That's changed. For the first time in her life she's longing to go to school.

'I'm fine,' she says.

Grandpa gives her a hard pat on her shoulder; his version of a hug. 'It was that blood moon, it kept the cows awake. Maybe it disturbed you, too, in your dreams.'

'Blood moon?' Her mother snorts. 'You and your nonsense. I didn't see any blood moon.'

Anna-Karin glances at Grandpa. She's aching to tell him about all the incredible stuff that's happening, about how her life is changing, but she can't forget the warning: *don't trust anyone.*

When Anna-Karin enters her room, she goes up to the mirror. She knows she's no beauty, but she has nice eyes – they're large and an unusual green – and her mouth has a pretty shape, especially when she smiles. She tests it out in front of the mirror. Her teeth are white and even. That's something at least.

She grabs a regular bra instead of the one she usually wears to make her breasts look smaller. Most girls want bigger breasts, she reminds herself.

But when she buttons up her jeans, her self-confidence falters again. She must have the most disgusting rolls of stomach fat in the whole school. She chooses a T-shirt that is several sizes too big and pulls her jacket over it. She feels secure again.

Anna-Karin smiles hesitantly into the mirror. From now on she's going to smile more often.

Minoo is approaching the school just as one of the school buses pulls up outside the front gate with a loud hiss. From a distance she sees Anna-Karin among the students that pour out of it. Their eyes meet for a brief moment. Anna-Karin smiles, so fleetingly that Minoo almost thinks she imagined it, then looks at the ground again, her face hidden behind her veil of hair.

'Minoo!' Rebecka shouts, walking toward her.

Amazing to to think they'd seen each other just a few hours ago. In such extraordinary circumstances.

'I thought we weren't supposed to let on that we know each other,' Minoo says in a low voice when they meet.

'But we're in the same class.'

'That doesn't mean we should be talking to each other, does it?'

Rebecka gives her a strange look and Minoo realizes she's being silly. 'Sorry. That was excessive,' she says, when they start walking together. 'Everything just feels so strange.'

'I know, my mom said that the ER was full of people last night, that a lot of weird things had happened. Did your father hear anything? From the newspaper, I mean.'

'He'd already left for work when I got up. Or when I pretended to get up.'

'You haven't slept either?'

Minoo shakes her head. She almost blurts out how she threw herself at her chemistry book as soon as she got through the door, but stops herself in time.

'The weirdest thing is that some of the patients said the moon was red,' Rebecka continues, and stops at the playground entrance, 'but when my mom and the other nurses looked outside, none of them saw it. And when we looked at the moon together this morning I could see it was still red, but she couldn't.'

'So, not everyone could see it?' Minoo asks.

'Looks like it. And my mother didn't know what I was talking about when I mentioned Kärrgruvan. It was as if she'd forgotten it even existed.'

A shiver runs down Minoo's spine. 'Maybe that's what makes it a protected place. I read a book once where there was this tree you couldn't see unless you knew it was there. Maybe it's the same sort of thing—' Abruptly Minoo stops and blushes. She's been babbling again. 'Of course, it was just a children's book.'

'Can you believe we're talking seriously about this?' Rebecka asks.

Minoo laughs. No, she can't. They continue to walk and pass Vanessa, who follows them with her gaze but says nothing.

'It looks like something's happened,' Rebecka says.

Only now does Minoo see how many people have congregated in the playground.

Gustaf comes up to them and kisses Rebecka so intimately that Minoo has to look away. Luckily it's over quickly. Gustaf and Rebecka are like one of those perfect couples you see on TV, and try to make yourself feel better by deciding that no one looks like that in real life.

I wonder what the first boy who kisses me will look like.

That thought flutters through her mind in various forms almost every day. Late at night, as she's about to fall asleep, she sometimes allows herself to believe that it will be Max. But in the clear light of day that idea seems childish and absurd.

'Have you seen it?' Gustaf asks.

Minoo and Rebecka exchange a look.

'Seen what?' Rebecka asks.

'If you had, you wouldn't be asking. Come on!'

He takes Rebecka's hand and gestures to Minoo to come too. Minoo follows them. The students are standing in two loosely formed groups, with a fair distance between them, while the middle of the playground is empty.

'There,' says Gustaf, and points.

A crack has cut right through the middle of the play-ground. It's not very wide, but it winds from the soccer field to the dead trees.

'There's a rumor going around that some old mining tunnels have collapsed,' says Gustaf.

'I can't imagine they'd build a school on top of old mining tunnels,' says Minoo. 'Plus the mines were pretty far away from here.'

'Maybe they did some test drilling around here back in the day,' Rebecka suggests.

She casts a knowing glance at Minoo when Gustaf isn't looking. Rebecka doesn't believe that explanation either. But it'll do for now. The crack must have had something to do with all the other stuff that happened during the night so they shouldn't be encouraging questions.

The front doors to the school open and the principal strides out on to the steps. She stands there calmly as the chattering slowly dies away. When she speaks, each word she says is as clear as if she were using a microphone.

'You must all leave the playground. The school will be closed while the crack is investigated.'

Scattered cheers and applause. Minoo looks around. Rebecka and Gustaf are standing in front of her. Vanessa is by the goalposts with Evelina and Michelle. Ida is sitting on the railing beside the front steps with Felicia. Oddly, Anna-Karin is next to them, talking to Julia.

Max is with a few of the other teachers. He's got his jacket over one arm, his briefcase in his hand, and looks incredibly hot. Behind him she can just see Nicolaus. We're all chess pieces on a board, Minoo thinks, set up for a decisive match.

'The fire department has been here to inspect the gas and water pipes, but they want to carry out further checks,' the principal continues. 'Tomorrow we'll make up the work we miss today.'

She goes back inside the school. The playground empties.

'See you tomorrow then,' Rebecka says, and smiles at Minoo.

'See you Minoo,' Gustaf says.

They walk off entwined in each other's arms. Minoo looks after them for a moment, then turns toward the school again. She gazes at the drab building – the rows of identical windows, the bland brickwork – and tries to picture it as a place of evil. But it's difficult. It's not a place she likes, but she knows who she is here and what she's good at.

In the rest of the world she has no idea.

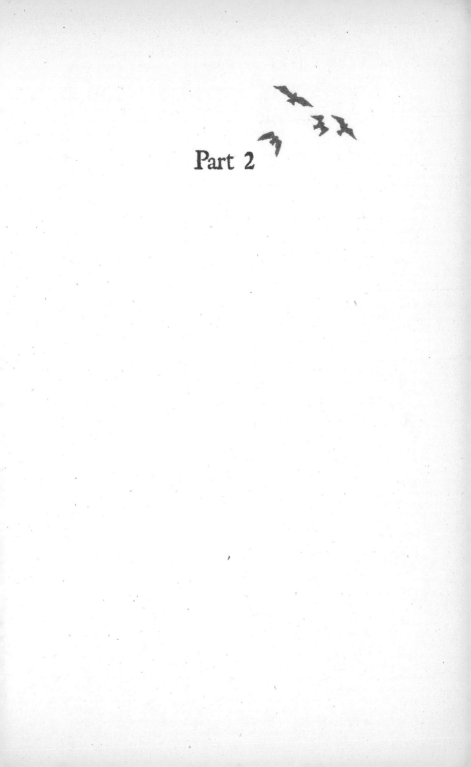

Part 2

CHAPTER 13

As she runs down the steps to the cafeteria, it's as if her entire body is carried forward in one fluid movement. She doesn't need to look where she's putting her feet. The fear of tripping is gone, as if it never existed.

The lunch line winds out into the stairwell. The girls standing at the back turn, see her and break into fawning smiles that spread like a wave as she passes. Several of the boys look away sheepishly when their eyes meet. She knows they're infatuated.

She continues all the way up to Kevin Månsson and Robin Zetterqvist, who are standing by the cutlery and plates. She notices that Erik Forslund isn't with them. He's barely been seen at school since he wet himself in the playground.

'Here.' Kevin hands her his tray and lets her go ahead of him.

She doesn't answer, simply takes the tray and serves herself.

It's so different now, living in her body. She feels at home in it. She has control of it. She's sure-footed. Her back is straight. Her ponytail bobs with every step she takes. Her entire being feels light, free and natural. She's happy.

'You look so hot today!' Felicia says, when she comes up to their table.

They're sitting in a side room just off the main seating area – a sort of appendix with no windows and just enough space for six tables. According to the unwritten law, this is where the popular crowd sits.

'Thanks,' she says, and sits down.

Both Felicia and Julia look at her expectantly. They're like a couple of eager puppies hopping around their master's feet. If Felicia and Julia had tails, they would definitely be wagging them.

'Felicia and I were just saying it feels like we've been friends with you for years,' Julia says.

'Yeah, I can't believe it's only been a few weeks,' Felicia says.

Anna-Karin smiles. 'Nor me.'

Kevin and Robin are walking toward them; they have always been considered the coolest and funniest boys in their class, perhaps even in the whole school. Anna-Karin wonders who decided that. When had everyone got together and crowned them kings?

But it doesn't make any difference now. Those days are gone. Anna-Karin has seen to that.

Robin and Kevin have reached their table now. She turns to Julia and Felicia and rolls her eyes dramatically. They roll theirs back.

'We were thinking of sitting with you, if that's okay,' Robin says.

Kevin pulls out the chair next to Anna-Karin. She stares

at him as Julia and Felicia hold their breath. 'I don't think so,' she says flatly, and Kevin lets go of the chair as if he'd just burned himself on it.

'Maybe some other time,' Robin says.

'Maybe not,' she says.

Robin is disappointed. He thinks no one can tell, but she picks up on everything.

'Bye,' she says, and waves at him exaggeratedly.

'Yeah. Bye, Anna-Karin.' Robin sighs and shuffles off with Kevin in tow.

Felicia and Julia giggle behind their backs.

'They're such losers,' Felicia says, just before they've moved out of earshot.

'*Soooo* immature,' says Julia.

Anna-Karin picks up her spoon and starts to eat the brownish-green pea soup. It looks disgusting but, these days, she eats everything. Her body is crying out for nourishment. She wonders how much energy her powers are sucking out of her. She can hardly stop herself from emptying the bowl into her mouth and swallowing it all in big gulps.

'Where did you guys disappear to after history?' Ida sets her tray down opposite Anna-Karin but ignores her. She sits down and glares accusingly at Julia and Felicia.

'We just went ahead,' says Julia.

'To get a good table,' Felicia adds.

Ida snorts. 'You could have asked me if I wanted to come instead of running off like that.'

'We didn't run,' Felicia retorts.

'Well, ex*cuuuse* me,' Ida says, then looks at Anna-Karin. Her eyes are full of hate. But what can she do? Ida knows what Anna-Karin can do to her if she confronts her. Anna-Karin can make her reveal her darkest secrets, make her strip naked on the tables, whatever she wants. Ida drinks some water and looks away. She knows she can never win.

Felicia and Julia are clearly ill at ease. They seem to be searching for something to say, anything, to break the uncomfortable silence. Anna-Karin doesn't offer any help. The awkwardness of the situation makes Ida seem even more of an intruder. The person nobody wants around.

Felicia's eyes search for something to comment on. They land on Vanessa, who's standing by the salad bar. 'What the hell is she wearing?' Felicia snorts.

Julia and Ida start giggling hysterically. Vanessa is dressed in a pink shirt and a skirt that is so short it's essentially a belt.

'I don't know what she's doing here,' says Ida, staring at her almost covetously. 'I mean, what's the point of her being at school now? It's not as if she's going to do any more with her life than squeeze out a few kids.'

Vanessa turns and looks straight at them. Julia and Felicia almost collapse in a fit of laughter. Vanessa doesn't bat an eyelid. She pins her gaze on Anna-Karin, who has to look away.

Her expression has said everything. Anna-Karin may be able to trick everyone else, but she's a fraud. Vanessa knows it. And so does Anna-Karin.

The old insecure Anna-Karin wants to let down her hair and hide behind it. But she's someone else now. She's in control. 'Vanessa's cool,' Anna-Karin says. 'She does her own thing.'

'Exactly. She's definitely got her own thing going,' Felicia agrees quickly.

Anna-Karin looks at Ida. Her lips are pressed together in a thin line. She gets up. 'This food is so disgusting – I can't eat it. Are you two coming, or what?'

Julia and Felicia stare demonstratively into their bowls. As she waits a few seconds too long for an answer, Ida takes the silver chain hanging around her neck, wraps it around her finger and then lets go, setting the little silver heart spinning. There's a hint of uncertainty in her eyes that Anna-Karin has never seen before. And when she walks away, nobody watches her go.

The red and yellow leaves in the forest around Kärrgruvan seem to glow in the afternoon sun. Minoo is sitting on the edge of the stage looking at Rebecka, who is standing in the middle of the old dance floor. A small tower of brightly colored wooden blocks, borrowed from Rebecka's siblings, stands next to Minoo. A rectangular green one hovers in the air above the tower before landing gently on top of the others with a faint click.

Rebecka rubs her forehead. Then she blinks and trains her eyes on the plastic box. A bright yellow cube rises up from it. It hangs in the air, then moves slowly toward the top of the tower.

Halfway up, it bumps against a blue block. The construction wobbles, then collapses. The blocks are strewn across the stage. Rebecka curses.

'But you're improving,' says Minoo.

'You have no idea how difficult it is,' says Rebecka.

Minoo feels a twinge in her gut. No, she doesn't. She still has no idea how it feels to have a super-power. And her brain hasn't been much use either. She's spent hours online and in the library, but it's hard, if not impossible, to sift through all the information. Most of what's been written about supernatural phenomena is muddled, contradictory or gibberish.

Rebecka's power seems to come under the heading 'telekinesis'. But Minoo doesn't know where to start looking for something that might give them a hint of the connection between herself, Rebecka and the others. How do you go about finding a mysterious prophecy? Where are the parchments and ancient books when you need them?

Nothing has happened since that night in the fairground. No mysterious nocturnal excursions, no strange dreams, no stench of smoke in the morning. Instead of putting Minoo's mind at rest, it's made her even more uneasy. She feels as though she's walking around with a safe dangling over her head.

And their so-called guide seems unable to shed any light on anything.

A few days after the night with the blood-red moon, Minoo had gone to school early to talk to Nicolaus. He was sitting in his office, surrounded by slips of paper and documents, and sweating in his dark blue cardigan and bright red tie.

When Minoo shut the door behind her he jumped as if she'd set off a firework in the room.

He stood up and she saw that he was wearing a pair of maroon corduroy pants that clashed with his tie. 'Go away!' he said, in a stage whisper. 'We're not protected here!'

'Could we meet tonight, then? At the fairground? We've got a few things to talk about.'

Nicolaus looked troubled. 'I can't . . . I mean . . . I don't know anything . . . I don't even know who I am.'

Suddenly Minoo became aware of a dark shadow gliding along the floor. She looked down and saw a pitch-black cat staring at her. Where one eye should have been there was an empty socket with jagged edges. Minoo didn't want to look at the animal. She felt as though she'd get scabies in her eyes from looking at its scruffy coat with the scattered patches of bare skin.

Nicolaus recoiled when the cat jumped onto his desk and strolled across his papers.

'I don't understand what's wrong with this creature,' he complained. 'It follows me wherever I go.'

The cat, which had lain down next to the telephone, turned its head and looked straight at Minoo again with its one eye.

'What did you mean, you don't know who you are?' Minoo asked, as the mangy cat started to lick its tangled fur.

Nicolaus sighed deeply. 'My name is Nicolaus Elingius. That's what it says on my employment contract, and on the deeds that prove I've owned my humble dwelling for a year.' His voice trembled as he continued: 'But I don't remember buying it. I don't remember anything of my life here as the janitor. I don't remember my mother or father. I don't remember who I've loved or hated, if I've had any sons or daughters . . . I don't remember where I've lived . . . or why I came . . .' With his head in his hands, he mumbled a few archaic phrases that Minoo barely understood.

'Well, you do know one thing – that you're supposed to guide us,' she said cautiously.

Nicolaus raised his head and looked at her with profound sadness. 'I've forfeited that privilege. I was here, at the school, when Elias was put to death yet I did not prevent the atrocity that took place.'

'You didn't know.'

'Dear child,' Nicolaus interjected, 'would you ask a blind man to lead the blind?'

Since then Nicolaus has seemed more and more confused each time Minoo has seen him. Once he stood in the hallway staring into a light as if he were under hypnosis while the students laughed behind his back. Now nobody's seen him for several days.

Rebecka comes to the edge of the stage and nimbly heaves herself on to it. Together they gather up the toy blocks and put them back into the plastic box.

'It feels wrong that we're not all here,' says Rebecka.

She's said that a number of times over the past few weeks. Minoo drops the last block into the box. Rebecka has tried to get everyone to meet at the fairground, but the only one who has shown any interest is Minoo. 'They'll probably understand eventually,' she says.

'What'll make them understand?' Rebecka asks, sounding almost angry. 'Does someone else have to die? Wasn't Elias's death enough?'

Minoo wishes Rebecka hadn't said his name. It conjures up the image she's been trying hard to forget: the pale face, the slashed arm, the blood all over the floor and tiles. 'But what can we do?' she asks, trying to shake off the memory. 'Out of nowhere we're told we're supposed to fight against evil and the destruction of the world. And then – nothing. We should at least have been given a task.'

'But that's the whole point,' says Rebecka. 'This is our task. What we're doing now. We have to get to know each other. And we have to practice our skills. That's what Ida said. When she wasn't Ida, I mean.'

'We know Anna-Karin's "practicing",' says Minoo.

'I have to make her understand how dangerous it is. I'm going to talk to her again,' Rebecka says, and rubs her forehead.

'Are you all right?' Minoo asks.

'I'm fine. I can do it for a lot longer now. In the beginning it was only a few minutes before I'd have a headache. I recover much quicker, too.'

Minoo pulls her jacket more tightly around herself. The air is raw and damp, and the cold penetrates deep beneath her skin.

'Something else has happened,' says Rebecka. She takes

out one of the blocks again and lays it on the floor between them. 'Although I'm not sure if I can do it now,' she says.

Rebecka's eyes narrow from the strain. Minoo looks at the block and wonders what's going to happen. It doesn't budge – Rebecka must be very tired. Then she sees it. The wisp of smoke is so thin that a soft breeze disperses it. But then more smoke billows up and a corner of the block catches fire.

Rebecka looks up at her. For a second Minoo worries that she'll accidentally set fire to her too. She has to resist the temptation to cover her face with her hands.

'Freaky, right?' Rebecka says quietly.

Minoo can only agree. At first the little flame is edged with blue, but it soon turns solid yellow. Now it's spreading along two sides of the block. Rebecka bends forward and blows it out.

'When did this start?' Minoo asks.

'Yesterday. There was a lit candle on the table and I got it into my head that I'd try to put it out. It wasn't hard. It was like . . . pinching the flame with your fingers. So then I tried lighting it. I had an awful headache afterward. Gustaf was really worried.'

'He didn't see, did he?'

'No, of course not,' Rebecka answers. Her gaze is distant. She pulls her hands inside the sleeves of her jacket. 'It's becoming almost impossible not to say anything to him. This is so huge.'

'You *can't* tell him!' Minoo's voice sounds shrill. She didn't mean to shout. But she feels panicked by Rebecka's admission. Doesn't she remember? *Trust no one . . . Not even the love of your life.*

'I know,' Rebecka says. She's quiet for a long moment. 'It's just that there's so much else we don't talk about.'

Minoo realizes that this is one of those defining moments when two people may be on the verge of becoming really close friends.

'There have been rumors about me,' Rebecka continues.

Minoo hesitates, unsure whether she should admit she's heard rumors about Rebecka since middle school. She was one of the girls everyone said had an eating disorder. 'Was it true?' she says.

'Yeah. I suppose it still is. I know it can come back. But it's been better since last spring. Though I do still think about it. Often.'

'What does Gustaf say?'

'We've never talked about it, but he probably knows.' Rebecka meets Minoo's gaze. 'I'm just afraid that if he finds out he won't want to be with me any more. You're the first person I've ever told.'

Minoo wants to say something clever. She wants to show she's worthy of such trust, wants to help Rebecka with lots of good advice and promise her that everything's going to be fine. But she realizes at once that it's better to stay quiet. Let Rebecka say whatever she needs to.

'When I think back to how I was before I got together with Gustaf, it's like looking at an old black-and-white movie. He sort of brought in all the color. But I feel as if I still belong to that black-and-white world, and that he's going to realize it at any moment. That I'm not . . . in color. If he sees that, everything's going to come crashing down.'

'But he loves you. That's obvious. Maybe you just have to trust in that.'

'I wish it was that simple,' Rebecka says.

'Don't you love how I'm sitting here giving you advice, me with my huge experience with boys and relationships?' Minoo says, and Rebecka laughs.

'Okay, now it's your turn. Don't you have any deep dark secrets you want to get off your chest?'

Minoo hesitates. 'Well, I've got a crush on someone I can never be with,' she says. 'How immature is that?'

'Come on. Who is it?'

'You have to promise not to tell anyone. I mean, I know you wouldn't say anything, but I have to say, "don't tell anyone," so that I've said it. It makes me feel better about it.'

Rebecka laughs again. 'I promise,' she says.

Minoo can barely make herself say his name. She's so afraid of sounding like the silly little virgin she is. 'Max.'

It comes out of her like a gasp. She'd like the floor to open up and swallow her, for someone to nail fresh planks over her and forget her for all eternity.

'Do you think he feels the same?' Rebecka asks, as though it wouldn't be strange if he did.

'Of course not,' Minoo answers. 'Sometimes he sort of looks at me, but that's probably me reading things into it that aren't there.'

'Why don't you talk to him outside school some time? If you feel there's something between you, you're probably right.' She makes it sound so easy.

'Thanks. But I think the best thing for me to do is just to stop being in love with him.'

'Good luck,' Rebecka says ironically, and Minoo can't help but smile.

CHAPTER 14

City Mall is the epitome of everything Vanessa hates about Engelsfors. It's deserted, ugly and, above all, an embarrassing failure.

It opened six years ago to a great fanfare and free balloons for all the children. Now there's nothing there but shuttered stores and the Sture & Co. bar, hangout of choice for all the local drunks. The entire building sits in constant gloom because no one can be bothered to replace the light bulbs in the ceiling. The Crystal Cave is the first new addition to the place for more than two years.

A bell dings as Vanessa opens the door. There is a strong smell of incense. The walls are a warm yellow and it's packed with shelves, tables of books, dream catchers, dolphin paintings, scented candles and mysterious jars. And, of course, there are crystals in all colors and sizes.

An older woman is sitting behind the counter flipping through a gossip magazine. Her skin has been battered by the sun, and her straggly blonde hair is a mess mangled from endless perms. Her lipstick is a frosty pink, and her eyelids droop under a heavy coat of turquoise shadow. Her denim outfit has small golden butterflies embroidered here and there.

So, this must be Mona Moonbeam. Vanessa doesn't know what she was expecting, but not someone who looks as if she's stepped out of an eighties music video. As she approaches the counter she smells stale smoke and sickly perfume. 'Hi . . .' she begins.

'What do you want?' Mona croaks, without looking up from her magazine.

Vanessa is annoyed. This shop probably needs all the customers it can get. Mona Moonbeam ought to cheer and scatter rose petals at her feet. 'Am I disturbing you?'

Mona Moonbeam lowers her magazine slowly and looks at her. 'What do you want?' she repeats.

'My mother was in here and had her palm read. Jannike Dahl? She said you had some kind of two-for-one offer.'

She lays the receipt on the counter and Mona picks it up slowly, as if she wants to emphasize that she's not going to hurry on Vanessa's account. She puts on the glasses she has hanging around her neck and examines the slip of paper closely and fastidiously. Then she looks at Vanessa and lets out a long, deep sigh.

Vanessa is about to turn and leave. But she's already put this off for several weeks and the offer expires today. Her mother would be disappointed. She wants Vanessa to share her interest in dream interpretation, affirmation and aura photography. 'Is there a problem?' she asks.

Mona snorts, gets up and comes out from behind the counter. A dark red velvet curtain hangs between a cabinet filled with books on the occult and a copper dragon that comes up to Vanessa's waist. Mona pulls it aside and goes in, waving for Vanessa to follow her.

The room is small and stuffy. Inside, more velvet curtains are nailed haphazardly on the white walls, but the peach-colored linoleum flooring ruins any attempt at creating an atmosphere of mystique. In the middle of the room two chairs are upholstered in red plush, and a table is covered with a dark purple gold-fringed cloth. Mona gestures her over, and Vanessa takes that to mean she should sit down. A sharp metal spring inside the seat cushion cuts into her buttocks as she sinks into the chair.

'What the fuck?' Vanessa squirms to find a comfortable position. 'This chair's broken.'

'You're too bony,' Mona mutters, and sits down opposite her.

Vanessa is about to respond with something about Mona's well-padded rump, but bites her lip.

Mona's bracelet rattles as she fumbles under the table. Then she rubs something into her hands. Vanessa has time to wonder if it's magic oil, then sees the bottle of hand sanitizer.

Mona holds out her hands. 'Let's see your mitts,' she says.

Warily Vanessa lays her hands in Mona's. The moment their skin touches, Vanessa gets a strange feeling. It reminds her of how she feels when she's about to become invisible. A bit like a wind gusting inside her.

Over the last few weeks she's become increasingly adept at controlling her invisibility. She can feel it coming and stop it. She has also started to learn how to bring it on when she chooses. That's considerably more difficult, and the first time she tried to do it her nose bled.

Mona examines her hands and Vanessa is suddenly nervous. After all, she doesn't know anything about the woman. Her heart beats a little faster when she counts the weeks backward in her head and realizes that Mona must have arrived in the town just before Elias died.

This was a bad idea, Vanessa says to herself, a very bad idea, in fact.

'I see that you're an independent young woman who wants to go her own way,' says Mona.

'Really? Impressive guesswork,' says Vanessa, as her pulse subsides.

'I'm not in the business of guessing!' Mona gives her an irritated look. 'You want to go out into the big wide world and have a look around.'

'Gosh! I must be so special.' She's got nothing to worry about. Everything Mona says would be true of any girl Vanessa's age. Mona is a charlatan, just like the rest of her mother's gurus. Now the charlatan scrunches up her mouth so that every nicotine wrinkle on her upper lip shows. Then she appears to make a decision.

'All right. Let's do this properly.'

She grabs Vanessa's hands more tightly. A new feeling surges through Vanessa. She feels as she did when Ida levitated at the fairground: as if the air were charged with electricity. The hairs on her arms stand up. She holds her breath.

'I see a man,' says Mona. 'You have a complicated relationship.'

'Oh?' says Vanessa, trying to sound indifferent.

'It won't last.'

'You can't just come out and say something like that!'

Mona smiles wryly. 'Do you want me to stop? Can't you handle the truth?'

Vanessa grits her teeth.

Mona peers intently into her right palm and follows a line with her index finger. It tickles. 'See this? These two lines are intertwined all the way to the end. The love of your life isn't the one you think, but it's someone you've already met. Oh dear, oh dear . . . It'll be no picnic, but you're tied to each other.' Mona laughs – no, that's the wrong word. Mona *chuckles*.

'What's so funny?' Vanessa asks.

'You'll see.' Mona lets go of Vanessa's right hand and grabs the left one. 'You feel very let down by someone. I see a parent who . . .' Suddenly Mona leans so far forward that the tip of her nose almost brushes against Vanessa's palm. 'Aha!' she cries.

Vanessa's mouth goes dry. Her tongue is glued to the roof of her mouth and she can't speak.

Mona glances at her triumphantly. 'I knew it,' she says. 'Wait a minute.'

Mona gets up and walks over to a black-painted chest of drawers. The top drawer gives such a shrill squeak when she pulls it open that Vanessa starts. Mona rummages around noisily until she finds what she's looking for.

Vanessa catches a glimpse of a plastic bag containing yellowish-white stones before Mona disappears out of the room. She returns with a lit cigarette in the corner of her mouth, holding a red marble ashtray in one hand. The bag dangles in the other.

'I need bigger guns,' she says. She unties the bag and pours the contents on to the table. Vanessa goes cold when she sees they aren't stones.

They're teeth. Human teeth.

'You see these inscriptions?' says Mona, and holds up two front teeth.

Vanessa recoils.

'Oh, don't be such a wuss,' says Mona. 'Just be glad I'm not using animal droppings or entrails.'

Vanessa's gaze glides down to the table. The gleaming teeth have strange lines on them that intersect in various ways. Each tooth has an inscribed pattern.

'These are Ogham characters,' says Mona. 'The druids used them thousands of years ago. Some people believe that the characters are even older and originate from the ancient moon-goddess cults of the Middle East.'

She gathers all the teeth in her cupped hands and shakes them several times. They rattle and click. Then she opens her hands and they scatter out across the table. Vanessa feels that charged sensation in the room again. It's as if someone was gently drawing a grater over her skin.

Mona turns a few teeth over so that their inscribed characters are visible. She studies the result and sucks in a few drags from her cigarette, which is still lodged in the corner of her mouth. 'This character, *úath*, stands for terror or fear,' she explains, pointing at a molar. 'And this one . . .

No. You probably don't want to know.' She looks at Vanessa provocatively.

'Of course I do.'

'*nGéadal* stands for death. Death is hanging over you.'

Mona takes another drag, making the column of ash at the end of her cigarette grow so long that it might break off at any moment. She takes off her glasses.

Vanessa is having trouble breathing. The room seems to be getting smaller, as if at any minute the walls will close in on her and crush her.

'You don't have to take everything literally,' says Mona, as if what she had said was nothing out of the ordinary.

Vanessa gets up suddenly, grapples with the mass of velvet hanging in the doorway, and finally gets through it to the other side, back into the normal world where the air is breathable.

'Hi,' someone says, and Vanessa looks around.

Linnéa is standing behind the shelves. She's holding a pearlescent porcelain figure of a cherub. 'So ugly it's wonderful,' she says.

Vanessa looks at the chubby angel playing the harp. Nobody but Linnéa would be able to take that grotesque thing home and make it look cool.

Mona steps into the shop and casts a sweeping glance over Linnéa's leopard-print fake fur. The shirt underneath has been cut to shreds and put back together with safety pins. She's paired it with a super-short skirt made of pink tulle, and the knee-high combat boots.

'Empty your pockets,' Mona croaks.

'Why?' Linnéa asks.

'I know a thief when I see one.'

'I don't have any pockets,' Linnéa says. She spins around, a full turn, and smiles smugly.

Mona grabs a handful of the imitation fur, examines it closely and decides she's telling the truth.

Vanessa decides that Linnéa is just what she needs right now, after this chain-smoking old fruitcake with her death characters. They leave Mona Moonbeam and her stuffy little shop.

'What the hell were you doing with that old bat?' Linnéa asks, and fishes a packet of cigarettes out of her boot as they emerge from the mall. She lights one and holds it out to Vanessa, who takes it even though she usually only likes the taste when she's drunk. Linnéa lights another for herself and they start to walk.

'My mom insisted I come,' Vanessa answers. She doesn't want to talk about her fortune – she'd prefer to forget about it. 'What were *you* doing there?' she continues, before Linnéa gets the chance to ask any more questions.

'Just picking up some stuff,' Linnéa says, with a grin, and shows her a packet of incense she'd hidden in her other boot.

Vanessa's impressed.

When they reach Storvall Park they stop beside the fountain.

'Have you been back to the fairground?' Linnéa asks.

Rebecka has tried to get Vanessa there several times, but she's always said she's seeing Wille or Michelle and Evelina.

She doesn't want to think about what happened that night. Doesn't want it in her life.

'No. Have you?' she asks,

'No,' Linnéa says, barely audibly. 'I want to know why Elias died, but I don't know what to do'

'Maybe we should meet up with the others,' Vanessa says, after a while. 'Try to find out what's going on.'

'If I do anything, I'm going to do it by myself,' Linnéa answers curtly.

Vanessa takes a drag and tries to hide how disgusting it tastes.

Behind Linnéa she sees one of the drunks who usually hang out in the park. He's dancing an odd little jig on the grayish-brown grass. Totally and permanently wasted. But nice, Vanessa knows that because she used to get him to buy booze for her from the liquor store before she met Wille.

Linnéa tosses her cigarette on to the ground and painstakingly grinds it out with her boot. Suddenly she looks annoyed. Is she afraid that Vanessa's going to ask to come home with her?

'I've got to go,' Vanessa says, to make it clear she's not trying to become best friends.

Linnéa doesn't answer.

Behind her the drunk is shaking his head. He staggers forward unsteadily, approaching them with jerky movements. 'Hello!' he calls.

'Hi,' Vanessa shouts back, and hopes he'll be satisfied with that.

But he continues toward them. 'Linnéa, the light and joy

of my life!' he calls, in the slurring, broken voice that all drunkards seem to acquire sooner or later.

'Friend of yours?' Vanessa asks, with a little laugh.

Linnéa doesn't answer. She just walks away.

'Linnéa!' the drunkard shouts again.

He stops short in his bizarre dance, rocking back and forth, looking after Linnéa with empty eyes and gaping mouth.

Linnéa speaks to him so softly that Vanessa barely catches what she says.

'Bye, Dad.'

CHAPTER 15

When Anna-Karin opens the front door she is met by the smell of freshly baked bread. A smile spreads across her face.

'Hi, sweetheart, are you back from school?' her mother calls from the kitchen.

'Yes!' Anna-Karin shouts back, as she hangs her jacket on the hook in the hall. She's barely had a chance to take off her shoes before her mother rushes up and gives her a warm hug. She doesn't stink of cigarettes because she's stopped smoking. And the house smells of bread, soft soap and fresh air.

'How was school today?' her mother asks, letting go.

'Good. I got everything right on the history test.'

'My smart girl!' her mother says proudly.

Anna-Karin doesn't feel guilty that she guessed everything, then used her power on the teacher. She has some rules: she avoids manipulating her teachers as far as she can, and never uses her power on the science teachers, only on those who teach unnecessary subjects, like history, German and PE. None of that's going to be of any use to her as a vet. And what would be the point of learning a bunch of meaningless stuff just to forget it afterward?

'I was baking some scones, and then it occurred to me that I might as well make some cinnamon buns, too.' Her mother laughs, wiping a floury hand on her bright apron.

Her mother's smile doesn't reach her eyes, but Anna-Karin doesn't mind. Soon her mother will discover how good it feels to *live* life. Then that smile will become genuine, she's sure.

Pepper slinks down the stairs and stops at the bottom.

'Hello, sweetie,' Anna-Karin says, crouching and holding out her hand. Pepper's eyes glisten yellow-green. His tail ticks guardedly back and forth. He doesn't come any closer. She can't understand what's come over him. Little Pepper, who used to lie in her pocket and purr. 'Come on, Pepper.' Anna-Karin beckons. 'Kss, kss, kss . . .'

He doesn't budge.

Come here, Anna-Karin thinks, as she looks deep into Pepper's eyes. *Come here now. I just want to cuddle you.*

Pepper hisses at her and bolts back up the stairs.

'Forget it, then,' Anna-Karin hisses back at him.

Just then her cell phone rings. It's Rebecka's number. Can't she let it go? None of them understands how much Anna-Karin deserves her new life. And she's not going to apologize for it.

This will never work, Rebecka thinks. I'll never manage to bring them together.

She sticks her phone into her pocket and looks around for Gustaf in the deserted City Mall. He left his scarf at Leffe's kiosk when he was in there buying chocolate. 'Wait here, and I'll run back for it,' he said.

He's been away for a long time. Far too long.

Rebecka is shifting from one foot to the other, wishing she had something to read. Something other than her biology textbook. She scans the darkened shop windows in which her reflection appears as a shadow. She looks like a ghost inside the empty units. The only light is coming from the newly opened Crystal Cave.

Rebecka moves closer. The window is crammed with brass pyramids, tarot cards, incense, small angel statuettes and, of course, crystals in every conceivable size, shape, and color. There is also a display of jewelery, a glittering mass of silver and cheap stones. Most of it looks like junk. But her eyes are drawn to a silver necklace with little red stones. Like tiny drops of blood around the neck. She rests her fingers on the glass. The necklace isn't her style yet she wants it. She wants to buy it now, at once, and wear it all the time. If only she had the money . . .

Rebecka doesn't know how long she's been standing there looking at the necklace, when she feels the skin crawl on the back of her neck. Someone's watching her, she's sure.

She focuses her eyes on the reflection in the window. A blurred figure is standing behind her. She can only just make it out in the faint sunlight filtering through the front entrance to the mall, but she instantly recognizes it.

She doesn't dare turn. A few seconds pass but it feels like eternity. The figure is still standing there.

She sees someone moving around inside the Crystal Cave. A woman in a denim suit with a shock of blonde hair. She's walking around, muttering to herself. If she would just look up and see Rebecka. But the woman disappears behind a curtain, and Rebecka realizes there wouldn't be a single witness if that figure were to come after her now. This dark shopping mall is the perfect place to attack someone, even though it's the middle of the day, in the middle of the town. Her back tenses with fear.

Rebecka struggles hard to gather her courage. Nothing can be worse than standing there, waiting for something to happen. She tries to convince herself that she's strong. She has a power she hadn't known about last time the figure had stalked her.

She takes a deep breath and turns. Just then she hears the automatic doors open with a faint whisper. The figure has vanished. Gustaf is running toward her, his footsteps echoing against the stone floor. 'Sorry it took so long,' he says. 'Leffe takes his job a little too seriously. I had to describe the scarf to get it back. I'd never thought about what colors the squares were—'

He breaks off and stares at her probingly. 'Are you all right?'

'It's nothing. Did you see anyone on your way in?'

Gustaf looks at her quizzically. 'No. Why do you ask?'

She forces a smile, cheerful and unconcerned. 'I thought I saw someone I knew, that's all.' She turns to the Crystal Cave's window. 'Have you seen this new shop? Mostly horrible stuff, but a few nice things.'

'Anything in particular you like?'

She points at the necklace.

'I knew it,' says Gustaf, and grins in satisfaction.

'What?'

'Nah, I was just thinking . . . It's your birthday soon . . . I shouldn't have mentioned it.'

He laughs and she senses he's already bought the necklace for her as a present, or at least planned to. He's like a child. You can see everything in his face. It's as if he's never had to hide anything.

'Just don't go buying me anything too expensive,' she says quietly, and hopes she hasn't hurt his feelings.

They've tried to discuss the money issue, but it's difficult. Gustaf's parents have plenty and are happy to share it. By contrast, there's never anything to spare in Rebecka's big family. Gustaf always says her family is generous, too, that you give according to your means, which sounds sensible. If she had a lot to give she would. But when you don't have much, it's difficult to receive anything.

'You're so quiet,' Gustaf says.

She realizes she hasn't said anything for a while. 'I was thinking.'

'Sometimes I wish I could see into your head,' he says, and smiles.

'You'd get bored pretty quickly,' she answers, and puts her arm around his waist.

Rebecka studies the photo of her and Gustaf on the wall beside his bed. He had taken it – he had held the camera up to them during a walk by the sluice gates during the first week they were officially going out together.

She rests her head on his arm, lies close to him and feels the heat of his body.

'I love you,' he whispers, and his breath is warm against her ear.

'I love you, too.'

Gustaf's parents are having dinner at his mother's boss's house. But he and Rebecka had been as quiet as always while they had sex. It sticks with you, the knowledge that you have to be careful because someone might hear you or walk in at any moment.

'Are you comfortable like that?' he mumbles.

'M-hm,' Rebecka answers. She wriggles a little closer to him. She loves feeling his skin against hers, wants to press every square inch of her body against his. Gustaf puts his other arm around her and kisses her forehead.

The wind is picking up. The town house where Gustaf lives is on the last street before the forest takes over on this side of the town. There's a mass grave from a cholera epidemic out there. They walked past it last summer: a few large blocks of stone mark its location. They felt cold even when the sun was on them and each stone was linked together by a thick black chain.

The memory of the grave brings with it other unwelcome thoughts. In her mind's eye, Rebecka sees the figure reflected in the window, and feels again how her muscles tensed, as if she were preparing to defend herself. She tries to relax again, to hold on to the bliss of just a moment ago.

'What is it?' Gustaf asks.

'What do you mean?'

Gustaf leans away from her slightly so he can look at her. 'It's like you're . . . I don't know how to put it . . . like you're always somewhere else, these days.'

Rebecka opens her mouth to protest, but Gustaf asks, 'Has something happened?'

She wriggles closer and presses her forehead to his chest. She'd rather not be looking at him when she lies to him. 'No.'

'Are you sure?'

'There's a lot going on at school,' she says.

She hears Gustaf's heart beating inside his ribcage and wonders how it feels to be him, so calm and confident in all situations.

'You spend a lot of time with Minoo now,' he remarks.

Rebecka is surprised yet relieved by the change of subject. 'Yes. I really like her. She's so smart. And nice. She can be funny, too – sometimes I think she doesn't realize it.'

'We should do something, the three of us, some time.'

'M-hm.'

'Do you think she'd like any of my friends? Rickard, maybe?'

Rebecka imagines Rickard and Minoo together and has to giggle. Rickard is sweet, but he only ever talks about football. That couldn't be more wrong for Minoo.

'Why not?'

'Minoo's in love with someone.' It just slips out of her.

'Who?'

She's promised not to tell anyone, and now she's on the verge of doing so. It would feel so good to share a secret with Gustaf, to compensate for all the others she's keeping from him.

But, no, she thinks. It's not my secret to tell, and Minoo would never forgive me. 'I'm not allowed to say.'

'Of course you are.'

'No, I promised.'

'Oh, come on.'

'Why are you so curious? Are you hoping she's in love with you?'

She laughs when Gustaf pretends to scowl at her. Then he throws his leg over her, pins her to the mattress and tickles her. She lets out a shriek and starts to laugh.

'Tell me.' He's laughing too.

All she can do is shake her head – she can barely breathe.

Eventually they calm down. He starts kissing her but now everything he does tickles. His stubble against her neck makes her cry out again, and she pulls up her shoulder to protect her sensitive skin.

And as she's lying there, she can't understand how she could ever have doubted that he'll love her no matter what happens.

Chapter 16

Rebecka comes home at midnight and stays up for another two hours with her French homework. Then she can't sleep. Her thoughts are drawn constantly to the figure at the mall. And when she does fall asleep, it follows her into her dreams.

I have to tell Minoo, she thinks, as she gets up the next morning.

Immediately she feels lighter inside. She isn't alone, after all.

Music is filtering softly from the radio when she comes into the kitchen. Anton and Oskar are still asleep. Alma tries to lift Moa out of the high chair, and Moa lets out a high-pitched shriek that hurts Rebecka's ears. Her mother is standing by the window with her battered cell phone pressed to her ear, mumbling gravely.

Rebecka takes the carton of buttermilk out of the fridge and glances at her.

'No, I can't do that,' she says. 'You'll have to tell her yourself.' She holds out the phone to Rebecka. 'It's your father.'

Rebecka takes the phone, sensing that she's about to hear bad news. 'Hi, Beckis.' Her father sounds tense. 'I've got bad news. I have to be at a conference over the weekend so I'll miss your birthday.'

She shouldn't care about something as childish as a birthday without her father, but she does. 'Oh,' she says, and stares at the fridge, focusing on a magnet that looks like a smiling bumble bee. She feels her mother watching her.

'It's very important that I'm there for it. Otherwise you know I wouldn't—'

'I understand,' Rebecka breaks in. 'Talk to you later. 'Bye.'

Her father tries to say something else, but she hangs up.

'Beckis,' her mother says, in the soft voice that makes Rebecka's skin crawl.

Her mother wants to comfort her, but she doesn't know that her tone and her pitying expression make everything worse. Rebecka just wants to pretend that nothing happened so she can forget about it.

'It's okay,' she says, and avoids her mother's eye.

She puts the buttermilk back into the fridge. She's hungry but decides to suppress it, which gives her that hard, powerful sense of control. The one she knows is dangerous.

'How about we go out to eat? At the Venezia, maybe?'

'I'm celebrating with Gustaf,' says Rebecka.

'Ask him to come with us.'

'Maybe. Do we have to decide now? I'm so stressed out . . .'

Her mother lays a hand on her cheek, and she has to stop herself flinching so she doesn't hurt her feelings.

'Okay. We'll talk about it later,' her mother says.

'I have to take a shower,' Rebecka mutters, and walks toward the bathroom.

'Wait a minute,' her mother calls. 'The principal called, too. She wants to speak to you after school today.'

'About what?'

'A routine chat, she said.'

'All right,' Rebecka says, in as detached a tone as she can muster.

She goes into the bathroom, takes off her nightie, turns on the shower and waits for the water to warm up.

There's no such thing as a 'routine chat' with the principal. It has to be about her eating disorder. She's sure of it. It couldn't be anything else.

She steps into the shower and lets the water gush over her. There's only one person she's ever confided in about it. And that's Minoo.

There are five minutes to go before first period starts. Minoo is sitting at the back of biology class waiting for Rebecka.

They don't sit next to each other in every class they have together, but it happens more and more frequently. Minoo knows they should be more careful, but human contact is addictive. Before she'd gotten to know Rebecka it was as if she had put part of herself into deep freeze – the part of her that longed for friends and companionship. But then Rebecka had come along and thawed her. Now Minoo understands that it's one thing to be alone when you don't have any friends, but being without them once you have them is a lot more difficult.

She looks at Anna-Karin, who is sitting on a desk at the front talking to Julia and Felicia. They're not even in this class. Minoo had felt sure that Anna-Karin would eventually stop brainwashing Julia, Felicia and half of the school. She thought it was so wrong, so dangerous, that Anna-Karin would come to understand it sooner rather than later.

Now she sees that maybe she isn't going to stop. After all, she herself would never consider going back to being alone. Why should Anna-Karin be any different?

Rebecka enters the classroom a few seconds before the biology teacher appears. It's not like her to be late. She's not wearing any makeup and has dark circles under her eyes. Yet she's still so pretty. Minoo never gets tired of looking at her. There's such variation in her features, so many different Rebeckas from one moment to the next, yet she's clearly herself all the time.

Rebecka sits next to Minoo but barely returns her smile. Instead she is preoccupied with putting fresh lead into her mechanical pencil.

Mr. Post, the biology teacher, goes to his desk and turns to the class. He's wearing the same red sweater with egg stains – at least, that's what Minoo hopes it is – that he's had on every time she's seen him.

'Well,' he says, 'we're going to talk about the fascinating world of plants.'

He's sucking a cough drop as he starts drawing a plant cell on the board. Someone lets out a muffled giggle. He went through exactly the same subject last time. Everybody knows why he sometimes falls asleep at his desk and why he's always got a cough drop in his mouth. How else would he hide the smell of booze on his breath.

Minoo writes in her notebook and slides it over to Rebecka. *How are you?*

Rebecka stares at it as if it were a riddle. She spins her pen in her hand. Hesitates. Then starts writing.

'Can anyone give me a synonym for cryptogam?' says Mr. Post and Minoo automatically raises her hand. 'Milou?' he says.

Someone laughs. Minoo has stopped trying to remind him of what her name is.

'Cryptogams are spore plants. Phanerogams are seed plants,' she says.

Kevin groans, and she regrets having answered the question more thoroughly than was called for. Why does she always have to be such a know-it-all? Why is it so important for her to see the teacher's contented little smile when it makes the rest of the class hate her?

Rebecka slides the pad back to her and Minoo reads it. Rebecka has written several things and erased them. The only thing that was allowed to remain is: *Have you told anyone what I said to you at the fairground?*

Minoo goes cold inside. She meets Rebecka's gaze and blushes. She's innocent but becomes so nervous that she probably looks like the world's biggest liar. She grabs the pen. *No! Why do you ask?*

I've been called to the principal's office for a 'routine chat'. She looks at Minoo probingly and writes *Sorry I doubted you.*

Minoo meets her eye and whispers, 'It's okay.'

It's more than okay. She feels as she did when she narrowly escaped being run over by that truck. Rebecka nods and starts writing again. *Someone was following me yesterday. Don't know who but I've seen them before, the day after Elias.*

Minoo thinks of the figure outside the house that night. She scribbles down that she thinks someone's been following her, too. When Rebecka finishes reading she looks up. Minoo knows they feel the same: relieved not to be alone. Afraid now that it is doubly real.

Rebecka writes:

We have *to meet.* All of us. *At midnight. I'll text the others and tell them. They* have *to understand now. I don't know what we're going to do but we have to* help *each other.*

Minoo nods. She wonders if Rebecka understands that she's the only one who can hold them together. She's the only one that everyone likes. The combination of Vanessa, Ida, Linnéa and Anna-Karin is like a minefield, and Rebecka is stopping the whole thing from blowing up.

CHAPTER 17

'I'm sure it's nothing,' says Gustaf.

They're standing on the stairs. Rebecka is one step higher so, for once, they're the same height. They're speaking softly so their voices won't echo.

'She said it was a routine chat, right?' he continues.

'Have you ever had a "routine chat" with the principal?' Rebecka asks.

Jari Mäkinen, a senior, is running down the stairs with a pink bag that looks completely out of place in his arms. He and Gustaf greet each other with a nod.

'Well, have you?' Rebecka repeats, once Jari has disappeared.

'No. Maybe it's something new she's starting. After Elias and everything. She wants to speak to students who—'

He breaks off. Rebecka swallows. This is it. This is the moment they're going to talk about it.

'Students who what?' she asks.

Gustaf presses himself close to her and breathes in the scent of her hair.

'You smell nice,' he mumbles.

She almost shoves him away.

He looks at her anxiously. 'What's wrong?'

'What was it you were going to say about students like Elias and me?'

Why don't you say it yourself? she hears a little voice inside her say. Don't wait for him. Tell him the truth. Minoo's right. You have to trust him.

'I just mean that maybe she wants to check up on all the tenth grade students,' Gustaf says.

Her disappointment in him and herself for their cowardice weighs on her chest.

'I'll wait for you outside,' he says.

'Okay,' Rebecka mumbles.

'I love you,' he says. 'You won't forget that, will you?'

They look at each other, and Rebecka discovers how close she is to tears. She can only shake her head in response.

It's dark in the principal's office. The blinds are down and the only light is from the desk lamp. The shade is a glass mosaic, a circle of dragonflies standing wingtip to wingtip. There are no papers on the desk, not even a pen. The computer is switched off.

The principal is wearing a dark-gray suit with a large silver brooch on the lapel. It looks old. Her bone-white blouse is buttoned up to the neck, and her black hair is perfectly in place. As usual her face is well made-up. It strikes Rebecka that many people would describe the principal as beautiful.

'Sit down,' the principal says, with a stiff smile.

Rebecka takes the armchair placed in front of the desk.

The principal looks her steadily in the eyes, but suddenly she is distracted.

'Excuse me,' she says, and reaches for a strand of hair caught on Rebecka's knitted sweater.

Rebecka doesn't know what to say.

'You're probably wondering why I wanted to speak to you,' the principal says, and drops the hair into the wastebasket.

'I think I know why.'

The principal has dark, intelligent eyes.

'Yes?'

The weight is still pressing on her chest. Rebecka has to force herself to speak. 'Who's been talking to you?'

'Talking to me?'

'Was it Julia or Felicia? Ida? Or was it the school nurse? Is she allowed to talk about that kind of thing? Was it Minoo?'

She regrets adding Minoo's name. She wants to trust her – she has to if they're going to be friends. But why did she look so guilty?

'What would they have said about you?' the principal asks.

She'll start crying if she doesn't close her eyes. She squeezes her eyelids together.

Suddenly Rebecka knows what a relief it would be to let go. To let herself fall and see if they catch her. Let go of the fear that her secret will be exposed. Expose it herself instead.

'We'd better start at the beginning,' the principal says.

Part Two

Rebecka opens her eyes. The bewilderment on the principal's face seems genuine and Rebecka realizes she may have been mistaken. Perhaps this really is a routine chat?

'Rebecka, what did you think this meeting was about?'

Now she feels incapable of telling her anything. The secret has regained its hold over her. She gets up and grabs her bag.

'Excuse me, I have to go,' she says.

'Wait!' she hears the principal say as she shuts the door behind her.

She runs down the hallway to the main staircase. Gustaf is waiting for her at the front entrance. Waiting to make everything good again. But she can't see him now. Not with the panic still throbbing inside her. She needs to be alone.

Rebecka continues up the main stairs and down a hallway. Then it's as if her strength gives out. She leans against a wall and glides down on to her haunches.

Only now does she become aware of how fast her heart is beating.

Only now does she realize where she is.

She's sitting opposite the door leading to the bathroom where Elias died.

Ever since he was found it's been locked and blocked off. It's covered with notes and inscribed messages.

R.I.P.
We miss you!!!!!
It's better 2 burn out than 2 fade away
Sorry

Live fast, die young & leave a good-looking corpse
Sorry for everything, Elias
Forgive me

And, scratched deeply into the wall, clearly legible despite someone's attempts to cross it out:

The only good faggot is a dead faggot

Rebecka reads the messages one after another. Down by the floor, something is written in beautiful black lettering:

The good die young

The fluorescent ceiling lights flicker with a tinny electrical sound. Then they go out.
That's how it is.
It's a voice that isn't really a voice, more like one of her thoughts, and yet not. It sounds nothing like the voice that had filled her head that first night, when she was given the task of leader. That voice had been a guest. This voice has *forced* its way into her consciousness.
What's written there is true, it continues. *The good can't survive in this world. You're too good, Rebecka.*
She recognizes the fear that takes hold of her. It's the same as the fear she felt when she was being stalked on the morning after Elias's death. The same fear as she felt yesterday when she knew she was being watched.

It's you, she thinks. Her pulse is throbbing in her ears. *Who are you?*

Get up.

Rebecka's body stands up immediately, as if she herself had issued the command. *Open the door to the attic and go up the steps.*

Her feet start moving automatically. The attic door is ajar. She tries to focus her powers on closing it. But suddenly there is resistance: something is blocking her with a power much stronger than her own.

Her vision blackens and she feels a trickle of blood run from her nose to her upper lip and into her mouth. It tastes of metal, earth and sweetness.

Don't fight it, the voice says gently. *There's no point.*

She mounts the narrow stairway leading to the attic.

What do you want? she asks, but she knows the answer all too well. This was how Elias died.

She's reached the top of the steps. There are two doors: a rickety wooden one leading to the attic storage room, and a metal one leading outside. On to the roof. She sees her hand reach out and press down the handle of the metal door. The wind buffets her face when it swings open. The sky is blue, with white clouds chasing each other.

Elias was suffering. I released him from pain. I'm doing you a favor, Rebecka.

Please, she begs. *Please, I don't want to die. I have four little brothers and sisters. My parents . . . Gustaf . . . Minoo . . .* Panic makes it hard for her to formulate her thoughts.

177

They'll get over it. Better to disappear now and remain perfect forever in their memories.

Rebecka's feet step over the threshold. The roof is laid with glittering black tar paper that crackles under her feet as she walks toward the edge.

You won't have to suffer any more.

The voice inside her head is seductive now. It sounds like the only voice in the whole world that really cares about her, and she has to force herself not to listen to it.

But I want to suffer! she shouts inside herself. *I want to live! I want to live!*

Her feet stop just one step from the edge. She can see the playground down below, the dead trees and the black asphalt that has been used to fill in the long crack. From up here it looks like a scar. She sees the road where the bus has just driven past, a few students running for the stop. If one of them could just look up . . .

Please, she begs. *Please, let me live.*

Suddenly she feels the presence hesitate in her body. Her legs are no longer rigid. If she tries a little harder she can turn away from the edge. If she concentrates . . .

Rebecka clenches her fists. She's regaining control.

No. I have to do it.

The voice is there again. The hesitation is gone. She feels it trying to regain control of her. She feels the pressure of the intruding will. But this time she has two advantages. She has hope, because she's seen a weakness in the enemy, and she's ready.

She pushes back. Her head is in excruciating pain, as if her brain is expanding to bursting point. Tension builds inside her skull. She puts her hands to her head, as if to stop it exploding. Yet another line of blood trickles from her nose.

The intruding presence is buckling and Rebecka is teetering on the edge of the roof. Her stomach clutches when she looks down to the playground far below.

She backs away from the edge and crumples to the roof. She doesn't have the strength to stand up, much less walk down.

Rebecka fumbles in her bag for her cell phone. At first she thinks of calling Gustaf, but she'll never be able to explain what she's doing up there. She has to call Minoo.

She hears footsteps coming up the stairs and turns. The sun blinds her and she has to shade her eyes with her hand to see who's standing in the doorway.

Rebecka smiles uncertainly. 'Hi,' she says. 'How did you know I was up here?'

CHAPTER 18

A cold wind is blowing across Storvall Square. Minoo is thinking about Rebecka's words, scribbled on her notebook: *Someone was following me yesterday.*

She shoves her hands into her pockets and hunches her shoulders. She hurries toward the light yellow house on the other side of the square. *Engelsfors Herald* shines across the façade in big neon lettering.

Ever since Minoo started school, she has been dropped by her father's office at least once a week. Usually he barely has time to say hello, but it's still nice to sit at the table in the coffee room, do her homework, browse through the magazines and feel the energy of the editorial desk.

Minoo turns before she opens the front door. There's not a single person on the square.

Nope, not a single *person*.

One of the town's three banks stands next to the *Engelsfors Herald*. The building is one of the most impressive in town: a heavy nineteenth-century construction with marble columns at either side of the entrance. A mangy cat is lying on the steps leading up to the entrance. It is staring straight at Minoo with its one green eye. It climbs awkwardly to its feet – not cat-like in the least – and walks up the steps. Then it walks back down, up and then down, before it returns to its original spot and lets out a single meow.

When Minoo enters the lobby, she is met by the smell of coffee from the news desk. Her father often says that if the *Engelsfors Herald* were ever to close down, the town's consumption of coffee would be halved. That's probably true. Sometimes Minoo wonders if her mother and father could survive on coffee alone, like cars and gasoline.

Cissi and her father are standing and gesticulating at each other inside his office. It's obvious that they're in the middle of an argument. Cissi's big blue eyes are wide and her short ash blonde hair is sticking up more than usual, like a hedgehog's quills. Minoo can't see her father's face, but his neck is bright red. He's furious.

Cissi is a recurring topic of conversation at the dinner table. On the one hand, she's quick and expresses herself well. On the other, she's far too prone to sensationalism and lazy fact-checking. Her article about Elias's suicide wasn't the first that Minoo's father had had to pull.

Minoo stands outside the office. She can hear their voices, muffled by the glass, and can just make out what they're saying.

'You're out to sabotage me!' Cissi says. 'I have a unique opportunity to be first on the scene. The paramedics called it in just two minutes ago.'

'You can do whatever you like, but I won't print a word of it.'

Her father is incensed. Minoo doesn't think she's ever heard him so angry before.

'This concerns the entire community,' Cissi says.

'It concerns no one but the girl's family!'

Minoo sees how Cissi changes her tactic.

'I can understand how difficult it is for you to look at this objectively,' she says, in a softer tone. 'You've got a daughter the same age—'

She breaks off when she catches sight of Minoo.

Her father turns. 'Minoo . . .'

Something has happened. Something awful. She can see it in their faces. Her father moves to the door and opens it. 'Come in,' he says.

Cissi looks at her with an expression that is intended to convey pity and compassion, but her greedy curiosity shines through. Minoo's father lays a hand on her shoulder. He casts a pointed glance at Cissi, who leaves the office.

'There's been an accident . . .' he begins, then looks around furtively.

It's hot in the office, Minoo thinks. Hot and stuffy. Cissi's perfume hangs in the air.

'Your friend Rebecka . . . has died.'

'*What?*'

'She's dead.'

Instantly Minoo wants to reassure him. It's just a misunderstanding. Someone has died, and that's terrible, but it's not Rebecka. She'd said goodbye to her friend just before she went to her meeting with the principal. 'It can't be her,' she says, and smiles to prove that there's nothing to worry about, that he's wrong.

'I know it's difficult to take in—'

'No. It really can't be her. It's impossible. We saw each other just a few moments ago.'

'It's only just happened,' her father says.

Minoo's smile is making her jaw ache.

'I didn't want you to find out like this,' her father says. 'I thought . . .'

Minoo shakes her head. 'It can't be her.'

'It seems she . . . was depressed. As if she'd made up her mind that she didn't want to go on living.'

Minoo remembers what Linnéa said that day in the playground: *He didn't kill himself*. She hadn't believed her. She had thought Linnéa just couldn't accept the truth. 'What happened?'

Her father hesitates.

'I'll find out anyway,' Minoo adds.

'She jumped. From the school roof. I'm so dreadfully sorry.' Her father grabs hold of her shoulders and looks into her eyes.

And Minoo knows it's true.

'Sweet child.' Her father hugs her hard and long. At first all she can do is stand there motionless, but then she clings to him. She's suddenly so close to breaking down and telling him everything. About Elias. About Rebecka. About the Chosen Ones. About how they're all going to die, one by one.

But what could her father do about it? What could

anyone do? Nobody can help them. Except, perhaps, one person.

She feels a switch flip inside her, and all her emotions are turned off. She has to act, solve the problem, warn the others. 'Is there a computer I can use?'

Her father gives her an odd look. 'This has to be kept secret until her family has been informed,' he says. 'You understand that, don't you?'

She nods and he takes her to a work station. She does a quick search for a home address, memorizes it, then erases the history from the browser.

'I have to go to the ladies' room.' She feels her father's eyes on her back as she heads for the bathroom.

As soon as she's out of sight, she opens and closes the door without going inside and continues along the hall toward the emergency exit. She emerges onto the street through a side entrance.

Minoo casts a quick glance toward the windows but can't see her father. He'll worry once he realizes she's disappeared, but that can't be helped.

She starts to run.

She crosses Storvall Square and turns down Gnejsgatan. Her heart is pounding. She runs faster and almost passes number seven, a three-story building with a green stucco façade. The door swings open at a gentle shove.

It says 'Elingius' beside the only door on the ground floor.

She rings the bell and hears shuffling footsteps inside. The security chain is unfastened. The door opens and Nicolaus appears in a black bathrobe. He's so pale that his skin seems almost transparent and his ice-blue eyes seem to have faded a little. He looks like a nocturnal animal that has never seen daylight.

'I have to talk to you,' Minoo says, and walks in without waiting for an answer.

The apartment is simply furnished. It has only been fitted out with the bare essentials. No carpets, no curtains. The living-room walls are light brown; a beautiful silver cross hangs beside an old framed map of Engelsfors, just like the one in Minoo's bathroom.

'Minoo?' Nicolaus says in surprise.

She turns to meet his questioning look. 'Rebecka is dead,' she says. She has no time to dress it up.

Nicolaus is rooted to the spot. He blinks once. Minoo is about to explode with impatience. She has to make Nicolaus understand at once so they can decide what has to be done. 'They're saying she committed suicide,' she says, 'but, of course, we know that wasn't the case.'

Nicolaus sinks down onto a spindle-back chair. 'Another one,' he says.

'What are we going to do?' Minoo asks.

'The fault is mine,' Nicolaus mumbles. 'I should have protected her.'

Minoo is about to fall apart. The only way she can hold herself together is to keep moving forward. She can't think about what has happened to Rebecka, no matter what. 'You know as little as we do about whatever is hunting us down,' she says, and forces herself to sound calm. 'You can't blame yourself.'

'I've failed.'

'Stop it!' Minoo shouts. 'I came here because I need your help.'

'How can I help when I don't—'

'I know,' Minoo cuts in. 'You don't know who you are. But who does when it comes down to it?'

Nicolaus stares at her.

'You can't run away from this,' she says. 'None of us can.'

He blinks again suddenly, as if he has just woken from a deep sleep. 'You're right. I've allowed myself to be consumed by self-pity. I've allowed my heart to become filled with black bile—'

'Exactly,' Minoo says quickly, to shut him up. 'We have to gather the others together and draw up a strategy. But I can't do it alone. I need you. *We* need you.'

CHAPTER 19

'Hello?' Anna-Karin steps into the hall. She can hear a faint humming coming from the kitchen. Her mother is singing some golden oldie about catchy melodies and rockin' rhythms.

Anna-Karin's cheeks flush, but Julia and Felicia smile as ingratiatingly as ever.

'What a beautiful place you've got here,' says Julia.

'It's *soooo* cool that you live in the countryside,' Felicia adds. 'And I love your cows. They've got, like, such intelligent eyes. As if they knew all sorts of things.'

Anna-Karin has thought the same thing so many times, but when Felicia says it, it sounds moronic.

Not once since she's been at school has Anna-Karin ever brought a friend home. Even though she knows she's in full control of the situation, her heart is pounding and when her mother steps out of the kitchen, her heart thuds even harder.

'Hello, girls! Is this Julia and Felicia?'

Julia and Felicia greet Anna-Karin's mother, smiling and sucking up to her.

'I've baked cinnamon buns,' her mother says. 'Come into the kitchen.'

They sit around the table and her mother puts out a plate of buns straight from the oven, with a jug of blackcurrant juice. 'I'll leave you girls to it,' her mother chirps. 'The cows need feeding, too.'

When she leaves the kitchen the singing picks up again.

'Help yourselves,' says Anna-Karin, and slides the buns toward Julia and Felicia.

They each take one and bite into it obediently.

'You know, I think Jari's in love with you, Anna-Karin,' Julia says, when the front door slams behind her mother.

Anna-Karin smiles. 'I think so, too,' she says, and they giggle with their mouths full of half-chewed bun.

Until today she hadn't dared to use her power on Jari. She'd watched him for so many years from such a great distance. After the last lesson, though, she had mustered the courage when he happened to walk past her locker. 'Jari, I left my bag in the art room. Could you get it for me?' she asked.

Julia and Felicia were standing a few feet away. They giggled far too loudly.

For an awful moment Anna-Karin thought he would respond with a scornful smirk, that her power would have no effect on him. But then he smiled as everyone smiles at her, these days, cheerfully and sort of surprised that she wanted to speak to him. 'Of course,' he answered. Three minutes later he was back with Anna-Karin's bag. His forehead was a little sweaty.

'But I'm not sure,' she says now. 'We barely know each other.'

'It's obvious he's interested,' Julia insists.

'*Soooo* obvious,' Felicia joins in.

Anna-Karin is starting to understand how it works. She enjoys hearing her friends promise things they can't possibly know anything about. *No, of course he likes you. It's obvious he wants you. Everything's going to be fine.*

They hear a cough from the kitchen door.

'Hello, girls.'

Anna-Karin hadn't noticed Grandpa coming into the house. Now he's standing there, smiling warmly.

'Hi,' Felicia and Julia say, with one voice.

'This is Julia and Felicia,' Anna-Karin says.

'Nice to meet you,' Grandpa says, and glances at Anna-Karin before he heads out again.

There was a question mark in his eyes. He's wondering what's going on with Anna-Karin – and with her mother. She's been getting looks like that for the past few weeks.

'Was that your grandfather?' Julia asks.

Anna-Karin nods distractedly and recalls that Grandpa noticed the moon was red. Perhaps he knows.

'He's *soooo* cute. I wanted to go up and hug him,' Julia continues.

'Me too,' Felicia agrees, and wolfs the last of her second cinnamon bun, swallowing it so eagerly that it makes a disgusting sound deep in her throat.

They fall silent.

Julia and Felicia look about nervously. When a text message dings on Anna-Karin's phone it's a welcome distraction. She picks up her phone. It's from Minoo. At first she doesn't understand it. It's as if it were written in another language. She stares at the words. Then she says, 'You've got to go,' to Julia and Felicia. 'Now.'

Everyone is assembled for the first time since the night it all began. Even Ida has come. She's leaning against the curved railing that surrounds the dance floor twirling her silver necklace around her fingers. She's wearing beige riding pants, a dark green knitted sweater and black boots. A riding helmet is sticking out of the bag sitting next to her on the floor. Minoo had no idea Ida was into horses. It strikes her how little she knows about Ida's life.

There are just five Chosen Ones left. Rebecka's absence is so marked that she seems more present than ever. Minoo can tell that the others feel the same. It's as if an actor has suddenly vanished in the middle of a performance: the rest of the ensemble is still there, not knowing what to do.

Minoo turns her head and sees the mangy cat saunter on to the dance floor. It sits by the steps and starts licking one of its paws. The green eye seems to be watching them.

'Shoo,' Nicolaus barks, but the cat doesn't budge.

'Leave it alone,' says Anna-Karin. 'It's not doing any harm.'

The cat returns the favor by hissing at her.

Minoo meets Nicolaus's gaze. He nods once. She turns to the others. 'So, whoever killed Elias has now killed Rebecka.'

'How do you know she didn't kill herself?' Ida asks. 'It's possible, you know. She was totally anorexic – everyone knew it.'

Anger bubbles inside Minoo. 'Shut up,' she says slowly.

Ida's eyes open wide. A few tears trickle down her cheeks. 'I refuse to believe this shit!' she shouts. 'I don't want to die! I don't want to be here with you!' Her voice cuts through the clear autumn air.

'So what's it to be?' Linnéa asks coldly. 'You'll have to choose.'

A wave of gratitude sweeps through Minoo: at least Linnéa understands.

'What are you talking about?' Ida snaps.

'We can be sure of only one thing,' Minoo says. She pauses for effect and looks at the others one by one. They have to understand, and they have to understand now. 'If we don't stick together we'll die.'

Ida wipes her tears on the sleeve of her sweater, so hard that her cheeks redden.

'We've been behaving like idiots. We were warned and we didn't listen,' Minoo says. 'Rebecka was the only one who really got it. She said time after time it felt wrong that we weren't together, and now that she's . . . gone . . . it's proof that she was right.'

The others look sad and ashamed. They ignored all of Rebecka's attempts to bring them together.

'I don't understand,' Ida says softly. 'How can she be . . . dead?'

Minoo swallows the hard lump in her throat, the one that is making it hard for her to breathe and get out the important things she has to say. 'We have to start working together,' she says. 'That's what Rebecka would have wanted. Does anyone have a problem with that?'

Ida stares demonstratively at her boots.

'Can we count on you, Ida?' Minoo asks.

'Yes,' she snarls.

'I'm in,' Linnéa says.

'Yes,' Vanessa says.

'Me, too,' Anna-Karin says.

'And I'll do my utmost to assist you,' Nicolaus says.

Minoo remembers what Rebecka said:

What'll make them understand? Does someone else have to die? Wasn't Elias's death enough?

No, it wasn't. But she mustn't blame the others. That'll get them nowhere.

'Rebecka told me today that someone was following her,' she says. 'I think I saw the same person standing outside my house. Have any of you noticed anything?'

'Something was wrong with Elias before he died,' says Linnéa. 'He was afraid, but he never got the chance to tell me why.'

Minoo nods. Linnéa is struggling noticeably to hold back tears, and Minoo's impulse is to comfort her. But to yield to emotion now would break the illusion: Minoo has to pretend to be the leader of the group, at least for the moment. She must seem to be in control so the others don't lose hope. She feels incredibly small and frightened, but it would be selfish to let it show. Their fragile sense of unity could vanish in an instant. 'Has anyone else noticed anything?' she asks.

The others shake their heads, one after another. Minoo swallows again. If it was only Elias, Rebecka and her . . . Does that mean she's next? 'We have to find out who's stalking us,' she says.

'Or what,' Nicolaus adds.

'And we have to be a lot more careful. Anna-Karin . . .' Minoo pauses. This is unexpectedly difficult to say. Suddenly she realizes she's a little afraid of Anna-Karin, even though she looks harmless in her duffle coat and knitted hat.

'What?' Anna-Karin asks irritably.

'You know,' Minoo says.

Ida snorts but doesn't say anything.

'Nobody knows what I'm doing. That's the whole point,' Anna-Karin says. Her jaw juts, making her look like a grumpy child.

'Can you really be sure?' Nicolaus says calmly. 'It's possible, of course, that we're the only ones who can see behind the scenes of your performance. But if someone else at school is searching for the Chosen One, you're putting yourself at great risk.' All of a sudden his voice is full of authority. 'We've already learned that the school is a place of evil. That was where Elias and Rebecka were killed.'

Anna-Karin's face is bright red. 'How do you know I've used my power? Is it so impossible to imagine I could become popular without it?'

Ida rolls her eyes, but still says nothing.

'Yes,' Vanessa says matter-of-factly. 'Nobody becomes popular overnight. It doesn't work like that.'

'You have to stop it,' Minoo says.

Anna-Karin shoots her an angry look.

'What the hell are we going to do? Do we have any leads?' Vanessa asks.

Minoo glances at Nicolaus. They've discussed one theory. Now that she's about to present it, it seems far-fetched, but it's the only one they've got.

'Before Rebecka died, she had a meeting with the principal,' she says.

Minoo looks at Linnéa, hoping she'll understand. She does. 'So did Elias,' she says.

'Adriana Lopez became the principal of Engelsfors School about a year ago,' Minoo continues.

'Wait a minute,' Ida interrupts. 'You think *the principal* did it?'

'I haven't come up with much information,' Minoo says, ignoring Ida, 'but I did manage to dig up some stuff about her on the Internet. Before she came here, she was the assistant principal at a school in Stockholm. Before that, she worked as a teacher. There's nothing strange in any of that. We have to find out more about who she really is.'

'It makes sense,' says Vanessa. 'I mean, the school is a place of evil and she's in charge of it.'

Minoo nods, relieved that they hadn't laughed at her.

'It's all we've got to go on,' she says. 'But we have to keep our eyes and ears open. Vanessa, your stepfather's a policeman. He'd probably mention if there was anything strange going on, right?'

'Maybe,' Vanessa says briefly.

Part Two

It's at that moment that exhaustion hits Minoo. She shuts her eyes, tries to shut out the world, tries to tap back into the inexplicable strength that has kept her going until now. But there's nothing left.

Rebecka is dead. The realization hits her full force and she almost buckles.

'Minoo?' she hears Nicolaus say.

'I think I have to go home.'

Soon after Nicolaus and Anna-Karin have dropped Minoo near her house, it starts to rain, pummelling against the roof of the car as they drive out of the town.

Nicolaus parks at the bus stop and insists on accompanying Anna-Karin quite a way down the road leading to the farm. He's got a big black umbrella that he holds over them as they squelch through the mud. Anna-Karin tenses, prepared to defend herself if he criticizes her again. But he doesn't say a word.

When they're almost at the house, he stops. The rain patters on the umbrella and draws out the sweet smell of earth.

'Anna-Karin, this can't go on,' he says. 'Someone could get hurt.'

He doesn't look stern, more concerned, like a father who's worried about his daughter. Anna-Karin doesn't care what the others think, but she doesn't want to disappoint Nicolaus.

'I'll think about it,' she promises.

'Good.'

He pats her shoulder and turns away.

Anna-Karin runs through the rain and stands under the little roof that covers the steps leading to the front door.

She doesn't want to go inside yet. She watches Nicolaus disappear into the darkness with his umbrella. She knows he's right. That Minoo's right. That what she's doing is dangerous. She's known it all along. Deep down.

In ninth grade an ex-junkie had talked to the class. He'd said that when he'd tried the drug for the first time it had felt like coming home. Now Anna-Karin knows what he'd meant. Her power makes her feel intoxicated, high. It fills the enormous void she's been carrying around with her almost all her life. And now they're expecting her to give it up.

All right, she decides. It's not worth the risk. It's not worth more people dying.

Anna-Karin looks out into the autumn darkness. She feels satisfied with her decision. It feels grown-up.

As soon as I've got Jari, she thinks, I'll stop.

CHAPTER 20

Minoo doesn't remember how she got home, just that her mother opened the door and that she almost collapsed on the steps in front of her.

When they helped her to bed she knew she wouldn't be able to stand up again for a long time. The thought of food made her feel sick. Warm tea and lightly buttered toast are all she can face. Her mother sits on the edge of the bed and tries to get her to talk, but she's too exhausted to respond, barely has the strength to even look at her. Eventually her mother gives up. Before she leaves, she opens the window to let in some fresh air. Minoo can't even muster the energy to get up and close it when she starts to feel cold, so her father does it when he comes in. He lingers for a moment at her bedside, mumbles something about how anxious he is about her, that she just has to shout if she needs anything. Minoo shuts her eyes. She wants to be left in peace. She's too tired even to cry. All night she slips in and out of sleep, and in the morning she feels more drained than ever.

Vanessa calls to tell her they're holding a minute of silence at school for Rebecka. Minoo has no intention of going. A minute for a life is insulting.

The rest of the day passes in a blur. Some of the time she's sleeping. Some of the time she's awake. It makes little difference. Her father comes home during his lunch break to look in on her and makes her another slice of toast. She can't manage it all, and flushes the rest down the toilet once he's gone back to work.

When darkness falls she lets the shadows take over the room. Now she falls into a deep sleep.

They're standing on the dance floor. The leaves on the trees are glowing an unnatural red. Rebecka is wearing a long white nightgown, identical to the one Ida had on that first night. Minoo is in her underwear, embarrassed because she feels naked.

'You're late,' Rebecka says.

Something is wrong with her face. Something small is moving around under the skin, causing it to bulge and come loose from the muscle wherever it passes.

Rebecka takes a step toward her and Minoo sees the thing start to break through the skin. A little sore appears on Rebecka's cheek and widens. Something glistening yellow-white forces its way out. It's a maggot.

'Help me,' Rebecka whispers, holding out her hands. The tips of her fingers are black. 'Help me,' she whispers again, and comes closer.

Minoo tries to back away, but there's resistance in the air, as if she's wading through deep water. The maggot is hanging out of the wound and wriggles until it drops to the floor at Minoo's feet. Then the skin of Rebecka's face breaks open in several more places. Underneath it a glistening yellow-white mass is writhing through her dead flesh.

Rebecka puts her hands on Minoo's bare shoulders. 'Do you see what you've done?' Rebecka says. Her cold fingers move up to Minoo's throat and squeeze, just as her face falls off altogether.

When Minoo wakes up, her throat is sore, as if she's been screaming. She's drenched in sweat. Her sheets are damp, her covers soaked, and her pillow is as wet as a sponge.

But she's gained new strength. For every hour she lies there she's letting Rebecka down. She has to find her murderer – the monster who killed her and Elias.

Minoo gets up, showers and brushes her teeth. The thermometer indicates a few degrees below freezing and she pulls on a pair of dark jeans and a black knitted cardigan over a black T-shirt. Then she has to lie down for a moment to catch her breath.

Her mother and father are at work and she texts them to let them know she's going to school today. She stops in front of the refrigerator, but the thought of food still makes her feel sick. Better to get out while she still has the will to do so.

The sun is blinding, but offers no warmth.

When she cuts across the field, the frosted grass rustles under her boots.

She can see the school in the distance. Her gaze moves automatically to the roof. How long was Rebecka in the air? A second? Two? Did she have time to scream?

As she passes a gas station she stops short. Black words against a yellow background. All capitals, as if the letters are shouting.

REBECKA'S BOYFRIEND TALKS ABOUT SUICIDE PACT

Minoo steps into the harsh fluorescent lighting of the gas station and buys a copy of the national tabloid. Three full-page spreads. All the articles are by Cissi, except one, which talks about 'similar pacts' around the world.

Minoo's eyes run back and forth across the pages. A passport photo of the principal, who has refused to comment. A picture of Elias. A picture of the school against a gloomy cloud-filled sky, with a dotted arrow indicating where Rebecka had fallen from. A close-up of candles, flowers and handwritten cards with hearts that students have left on the spot where she died.

There is also a picture of Rebecka's mother, sitting at her kitchen table with her hands clasped in front of her. And taking up an entire page: Rebecka's school photo from ninth grade. Minoo knows she hated that picture. She touches Rebecka's face gently. It's a nice photo. She should've liked it.

Minoo flips to the interview with Gustaf as she walks toward the school. He is also depicted in a ninth grade photo. He's smiling into the camera with a confidence you only have if people have told you all your life how great you look. He seems not to have a care in the world. In contrast with the headline is a heart-wrenching quote from him: 'I'll never forget her.'

But when Minoo skims the article, she becomes angry.

It describes Rebecka as one of the school's most popular students, but it portrays her as a person who was 'actually' introverted and depressed. Gustaf describes how he always felt she was thinking about things she didn't want to talk about. He comments on the rumors about her eating disorder. ('I think it was true') and makes himself out to be the perfect boyfriend, who tried to help her in every conceivable way. Then he washes his hands of it: 'But you can't help someone who doesn't want to be helped.' What angers Minoo most of all is the last sentence. 'She's probably better off where she is now.' As if what happened is a good thing.

Minoo crumples the newspaper and throws it into the trash can outside the school gates.

'Excuse me, may I ask you a few questions?'

Minoo looks up and meets the glinting lens of a black TV camera. A microphone is shoved under her nose. The reporter introduces herself and the channel she works for. Several other journalists are standing behind her. Their faces exude a combination of impatience and eager anticipation. They come from radio stations, local papers, national tabloids and TV news channels.

'I understand that you were one of Rebecka's closest friends,' the reporter says.

Her hair is so perfect and shiny that it looks fake. Minoo has never seen hair like it in real life. The other journalists approach. Some have their pads and pens at the ready, in case Minoo says anything of value.

Minoo's brain gets stuck. The camera inches closer.

'You are Minoo, yes?' the woman asks.

Minoo sees a school yearbook in her hand. She sees herself circled in thick red marker; Rebecka is circled too.

'It's just awful what happened. What do you know about the suicide pact she was part of?'

'There was no suicide pact,' Minoo says.

The camera lens sniffs around her face. It's a like an open maw, ready to swallow her.

'Are you in the pact, too?' the woman asks.

Minoo stares at her. Didn't she hear what Minoo said?

'How many have joined?'

Her heart is beating fast and her dizziness has come back. Minoo lowers her gaze and walks through the gates, closing her ears to the woman calling her name.

'What disgusting behavior,' a man she's never seen before says to her.

Minoo looks him over. He's young, tall and fashionably unshaven, probably good-looking, if you like that type.

'It's people like her who give us journalists a bad name,' he says.

Minoo's gaze falls on the flowers and candles that mark the spot where Rebecka died. She continues toward the front entrance to the school. The guy with the beard follows her. He says he's from one of the tabloids. The one that Cissi hasn't sold her tall tales to. 'Can you tell us about your friend so I can do her justice in the paper?' he asks.

She wonders if these reporters will come back to ask other students whether they knew Minoo, the latest victim of the suicide pact.

'Can't you at least tell me what you know about the pact? You do realize it has to be stopped! Or do you want more kids to die?'

Minoo stops at the foot of the steps and turns. The guy with the beard looks at her eagerly, as if he were a Labrador and she was holding a tennis ball. He's almost drooling.

'Come on, Minoo. You can talk to me. I only left school myself a few years ago. I remember what it was like.'

Minoo takes off her backpack and holds it. She feels so tempted to throw it at him. Her chemistry book is heavy. It would hurt. 'There was and is no pact,' she says, and heads up the steps.

Vanessa is standing just inside the door, talking on her cell phone. Their eyes meet for a moment. Vanessa lowers the phone from her ear, but Minoo doesn't stop. She marches down the hallway to her locker, passing Anna-Karin on the way. She's perched on a table, surrounded by admirers who seem to worship her. She breaks off in mid-sentence when she catches sight of Minoo, seems to lose her train of thought, but then turns back to the others and continues talking. Julia and Felicia laugh loudly.

Minoo pulls out her math book and notebook, stuffs them into her backpack and shuts the locker.

When she turns, Anna-Karin is standing there. 'How are you doing?' she asks.

Minoo shrugs her shoulders.

'I'm going to investigate the principal's office today,' says Anna-Karin, in a low voice. 'Nicolaus said she's with the town council all afternoon. I'll get the assistant principal to let me in.'

Minoo hesitates. Anna-Karin shouldn't expose herself to any more risk. On the other hand, what's the alternative?

'I'll do it during my free period after lunch,' says Anna-Karin, and returns to her court.

Minoo walks down the hall. Sweat runs down her back and inside her jeans as she goes up the stairs.

When she reaches the second floor she's too tired to go any further. She has to sit down and catch her breath. She stares at the stone steps, at the white fossils trapped inside them for eternity. Orthoceratites. That's what the little creatures are called, she remembers. Out of the corner of her eye she sees jeans-clad legs running past her up the steps, hears shouts and laughter and disconnected sentences – *I think he likes me, he just doesn't know how to show it . . . No way! No fucking way! Are you kidding? . . . Always says she hasn't studied, but she got, like, twenty-eight out of thirty on the test* – and when she gets up it's as if her heart is too weak to pump the blood all the way up to her head. Her knees give way and she is amazed to find that the cliché is actually true – that they really do give way. Darkness closes in so she seems to be peering through a tapering tube. Then she falls.

But someone catches her. When she opens her eyes she's looking straight into Max's concerned face. She's sitting on the steps, leaning against the wall, and he's so close to her that she's breathing in his exhalations. And he hers? She has a strange taste in her mouth, which probably means she has bad breath.

'Are you all right? Should I get the nurse?' he asks.

She turns away so that she can breathe again. 'I'm all right, I just haven't eaten anything,' she mutters.

At once she becomes aware that people have gathered and are staring at her.

Max opens his briefcase and pulls out a banana. She takes it and tries to stand up, but black spots swirl in front of her eyes.

'Eat this first,' Max says.

'Thanks,' she says. 'I can manage now.'

But Max stays where he is.

Minoo starts to panic. She can't imagine eating anything in front of Max while he's watching her so closely, especially not some phallic fruit. She starts peeling it, so slowly that she hopes he'll get bored and wander off. But he doesn't budge.

She raises the banana to her lips. No, she can't do it. She breaks off small pieces instead, pops them into her mouth, hopes her hands aren't too dirty. Can't he just go away?

'I'm so sorry about what happened to Rebecka. You were friends, weren't you?' Max asks.

'Yes,' Minoo says, her mouth full of banana.

Max looks as if he wants to say something else, but instead he sits down next to Minoo and puts an arm around her.

There's something about the way he does it, so totally

natural, that makes her cry for the first time since Rebecka died. The warmth of his arm melts the lump in her throat and releases the tears. Someone catcalls at them. She doesn't care. She doesn't care that she probably looks like a depressed baboon as she scrunches up her face and sobs, holding a half-eaten banana.

Please don't say anything, she thinks. There's nothing to say and if you try it'll just ruin the moment. This is the only thing that helps.

And Max remains quiet. The bell rings and the students around them disappear into their classrooms. Max's arm stays put. His breathing is calm and steady.

After a while she wipes away the tears with her sleeve. She's probably got mascara all over her cheeks. 'I have to wash my face,' she says.

'Take as much time as you need,' Max says, and gets up.

He heads up the stairs. Just as he's about to walk out of sight, he turns and flashes Minoo a small smile. She nods, as if to say she's okay. Once he's out of sight she sniffles and stands up on her weak legs.

CHAPTER 21

When the assistant principal, Tommy Ekberg, returns from lunch, Anna-Karin is standing outside his office, waiting for him. He starts when he sees her. Then he smiles warmly. 'Well, hello there,' he says.

Adriana Lopez's closest subordinate is a short man with a shiny bald head and a bushy mustache. He's wearing a loud shirt with a psychedelic pattern. His stomach hangs over the top of his slightly too-tight jeans.

'I thought maybe you could let me into the principal's office,' Anna-Karin says.

He looks at her in astonishment. He opens his mouth to say something.

Just do it, Anna-Karin commands.

Tommy Ekberg gives a little sigh of resignation. He takes out the huge set of keys that has permanently distended the back pocket of his jeans. 'Now?' he asks, rattling them.

Anna-Karin nods. He walks ahead of her toward the principal's office.

And then go back to your desk and think about something completely different until you've forgotten that you ever did me this favor, she commands, staring intently at the back of his neck. A few flakes of dandruff bob in the fluff that encircles his bald spot.

'Okey-dokey, whatever you say. Your wish is my command!' he answers jauntily, as he unlocks the door. He throws it wide and gestures invitingly. 'I'll go back to my desk now and think about something else.'

Anna-Karin shuts the door behind her. Then she walks up to the window and pulls down the blinds. The room darkens and she turns on the desk lamp with the dragonflies on the shade.

The desk is bare and polished. She turns on the computer – a prehistoric PC. The screen flickers to life. A sluggish humming starts from its interior and the image of a sunset fades into view. As does a window requiring a password. Anna-Karin knows too little about Adriana Lopez to hazard a guess at what it might be. She switches it off

She walks over to the bookshelf, takes down a few binders at random and flips through them. They're full of class schedules, financial reports, letters of application and payslips. Nothing of interest.

Suddenly she hears footsteps outside the room. Panic hurtles toward her like a runaway freight train. But she steels herself, thinks of Rebecka. Rebecka, who only wanted the best for everyone, who was one of the few who were always nice to Anna-Karin. Who had tried to hold the group together. Anna-Karin feels guilty when she thinks of how she ignored her calls and messages. She's going to make up for it now.

She catches sight of a black handbag in an armchair. It's the one the principal usually has slung over her shoulder when she arrives at school in the morning.

Anna-Karin's hands are sweaty. So sweaty that her fists would probably drip if she clenched them. *The B.O. Ho.*

She walks up to the handbag, as if she were afraid it might bite her. She lifts it by the shoulder strap. It's heavy.

Anna-Karin pours the contents carefully on to the coffee table. Among the makeup, Tampax and Kleenex there is a black date book, and a key-ring with 'Hermès' inscribed on it. Anna-Karin looks around the room. It seems almost too simple. What if Adriana Lopez isn't attending council meetings today?

Maybe she's walked into a trap.

Anna-Karin resists the impulse to run out of the office. Instead she wipes her hands on her jeans and opens the clasp on the date book.

The principal's handwriting reflects her character: restrained and perfect. Anna-Karin flips through it. Her meetings with Elias and Rebecka have been entered. But she finds no pentagrams, no notes about killing them.

Anna-Karin holds her breath as she flips to today's date. Sure enough, this afternoon she has a meeting at the town hall between one and four p.m.

She continues flipping through the pages. On Friday there is a single entry: *Train to Stockholm 5.42 p.m. Booking reference XPJ0982U.* And on Sunday: *Train to Engelsfors 1.18 p.m.*

That means the principal will be away all weekend. That her house will be empty. And that's where they have to look if they're to stand any chance of finding something that explains who Adriana Lopez really is.

Anna-Karin fishes up the key-ring from the table. It jingles a little as she puts it into her pocket.

Vanessa is curled up on the sofa. Wille's laptop is so hot against her thighs it almost burns her.

'Christ, you really pound away at those keys – you're going to break it,' Wille says.

'Your computer's already broken,' says Vanessa. 'The fan's bust.'

'Since when did you become a computer expert?' Wille scoffs.

Vanessa grits her teeth. Just let me save the world in peace.

Minoo has gotten them all to set up alternative email addresses that they can use when they chat. Vanessa isn't sure how necessary that is. Would an ancient evil really have learned how to use the Internet?

But who's to say which security measures are necessary? Rebecka had died. Each time Vanessa remembers, it's like a slap in the face.

'What are you doing that's so secret? Are you looking at porn?' Wille asks.

He moves closer to her on the sofa.

'Can't you leave me alone for five minutes?' She shoves him away.

Ida has taken over the discussion on the screen with her constant nitpicking. She's demanding they take a vote on whether or not to break into the principal's house this weekend. When she doesn't get an answer within half a second, she resends the question, over and over again, like a disruptive five-year-old.

I'm in favor, Vanessa types, and is met with everybody else's agreement.

Wille crawls closer and tries to put his head in her lap.

'Stop it, you jerkwad! Can't you let me breathe?' Vanessa says.

'But what's so important?' Wille whines.

'It's private!'

Wille crawls back to the other end of the sofa.

'You're IMing your other boyfriend,' he says.

He tries to sound like he's kidding, but she isn't fooled. She can't be bothered to answer. He starts prodding her thighs with his sock-clad toe. On the screen Minoo asks if they should take Nicolaus with them. The thought of having him there during a break-in makes Vanessa smile. Wille misinterprets it, of course, and thinks she finds him funny despite herself.

'Come on, tell me who it is!' he pleads. 'Tell me, tell me, tell me!' His big toe prods her thigh so hard that the computer bounces in her lap. She logs out of the chat and slams it shut with a bang.

She tries to glare at Wille, but he's looking so good right now that she loses her train of thought. His hair is all over the place and his smile exuberant. He's wearing the gray sweatpants she likes, even thought they're ugly and baggy.

'Vanessa?' Wille's mother, Sirpa, calls from the kitchen. 'Would you like to stay for dinner?'

'Yes, please!'

Sometimes Vanessa wishes Sirpa were her mother. Sirpa is always kind and considerate and she makes the best food Vanessa's ever tasted. She doesn't nag or criticize.

'What's for dinner, Mom?' Wille shouts.

'Spaghetti Bolognese.'

Wille looks at Vanessa and whistles.

I love him, Vanessa thinks. None of that other stuff matters. We're going to be all right.

Because there is 'other stuff', a downside to Wille's childish charm. He still lives with his mother. He has no job. Of course, there are hardly any jobs to be had in the town, but that's not the point: the point is that he seems happy with things as they are. He makes a bit of money dealing for Jonte in Engelsfors and the even smaller backwaters hidden in the surrounding forest. He squanders it on clothes, computer games, and presents for Sirpa. Wille likes to buy nice things for his mother. And Sirpa is always happy and teary-eyed when he gives her an expensive perfume or a new radio for the kitchen. The notion that he ought to be contributing to the rent or buying food instead doesn't occur to either of them.

But when Vanessa sees Wille in moments like this, she feels there's hope for him. She just has to get him to realize he's too good to be hanging out with the likes of Jonte and his gang of losers. Too good to get stuck in Engelsfors forever.

Minoo logs out and puts the computer to sleep.

She had been expecting Ida to cause trouble but she still feels frustrated.

Minoo's mother had taught her that all people have their 'explanation': a combination of chemistry, inheritance, child-hood experiences and learned behavior. Even when Kevin Månsson was terrorizing everyone in preschool, her mother was explaining that there was probably a reason for it.

Minoo wonders if Ida can be explained. Did her parents bully her in the way she bullies other people? Or does she think she's being funny when she's mean? Does she know how much she hurts people? She must – right?

It dawns on her that she's never really talked to Ida one-on-one. Only when the whole group's been together, and it's obvious that nobody likes her. Maybe it's not so strange that she had become instantly defensive. Perhaps they hadn't given her a chance to be anything but a bitch.

Minoo picks up her cell phone and calls Ida. The phone rings at the other end. Minoo's relieved: Ida isn't going to answer. But then a ring is cut short and there's rustling in the receiver.

'Hello?'

Minoo considers hanging up.

'Hello?' Ida repeats impatiently.

'Hi, it's me . . . Minoo.'

'Yeah, so?'

'Am I disturbing you?'

Ida groans. 'No. I'm thrilled to hear from you.'

Minoo regrets having called her on the spur of the moment. She should have prepared herself, laid out a strategy.

'Are you just going to huff into the phone or what?' Ida sighs.

'Can't we stop this?' Minoo says.

'What?'

'I know we can never be friends – the five of us, I mean – but do we have to argue all the time?'

'If someone argues with me, I argue back.'

Talking to Ida feels like banging your head against a wall. A particularly hard one.

'But it isn't getting us anywhere,' Minoo responds.

'Why don't you say so to Fatso, the slut and the junkie?'

It's as if a bolt of lightning just struck her head. 'Can't you stop being so fucking immature?' Minoo shouts.

Ida giggles and Minoo knows she's lost.

'I'm speaking the truth,' Ida says calmly. 'If people can't take it, it's not my problem.'

'You know what?' Minoo says. 'I hope you're next. The world would be a much better place if you were dead.'

She hangs up and comes close to smashing her phone against the wall. Instead she throws it on to the bed where it bounces. She wishes she was the kind of person who could rip down curtains, throw glasses and plates, topple book-shelves, tear down entire houses to vent her anger.

She was trying to hold the group together for Rebecka's sake, and instead she had said the worst thing she could possibly say. Not even Linnéa or Anna-Karin, both of whom have much more reason to hate Ida, have said anything like that to her: the one thing no one should ever say to another person.

CHAPTER 22

Minoo's body is pumping with adrenaline as she makes her way to Adriana Lopez's house, which is about ten minutes' walk from school in an area known as Lilla Lugnet.

Here, the houses are spaced further apart and there are more empty plots. The blackened ruin of a burned-down house is waiting to be demolished. It looks eerie in the moonlight. Rumor has it that there was an underground swingers' club in the basement. Supposedly married couples used to meet up there at night to share partners and bodily fluids. A jealous woman was said to have set the place on fire. Apparently a few people had died in the flames, and their spirits can be heard some nights, moaning and sighing with pleasure and pain.

Minoo shivers and zips her jacket to her chin. When she passes the charred remains of the house, she realizes she's pricked up her ears but she can't hear any horny ghosts.

Her heart nearly stops when a black-clad figure steps out of the shadows at the edge of the property. Minoo is about to run when the figure raises its hand in greeting.

It's Linnéa.

They walk down the street together. Minoo is painfully conscious of each and every window they pass, the curious eyes that might follow them. She's starting to regret having agreed to break into the house with invisible Vanessa.

The general understanding was that Minoo would come along since she's the 'smartest' of them. Flattery had won over fear. How desperate for affirmation can you get? she wonders. She becomes aware that Linnéa is smiling. 'What's so funny?' she whispers.

'I was just thinking that this probably isn't your kind of weekend activity.'

Minoo knows she's a bit of a goodie-two-shoes, but she hates other people to point it out. 'Is it yours?'

'Relax – we know she won't be back until tomorrow,' Linnéa whispers. She looks excited. As if she were on an adventure.

They turn onto another road and glimpse Ida crouching in the bushes as look-out. If she sees anyone coming she'll warn Anna-Karin, who is standing guard closer to the house. Anna-Karin is invaluable since she can get passers-by to choose a different route. But they hadn't dared count on Ida, which is why she's been given a task that's somewhat redundant.

Minoo is relieved she can't see Ida's face in the shadows. She hasn't been able to look her in the eye since the phone call.

'Couldn't she have stayed at home?' Linnéa mumbles.

'We have to do this together,' Minoo says, and feels like a massive hypocrite.

The street they walk along is narrow, the houses fewer and older. Anna-Karin is standing on a little stretch of public land between two high fences. She looks at Minoo and Linnéa nervously as they pass.

'Look,' Linnéa murmurs, nodding at Nicolaus's car, which is hidden in the shadow of a big tree.

He's waiting there in case they have to make a quick getaway. He doesn't like the plan, but he knows there's no other way.

They continue for another ten yards and there, at the end of the street, is the principal's house.

The property is surrounded by a freshly painted white wooden fence, which almost glows in the dark. The garden is overgrown in a way that seems intentional. A flagstone path starts at the gate, continues under a tall birch tree and leads up to the front door. The white wooden house has two floors and is adorned with elaborately carved cornices. Two of the upstairs windows are set with an abstract pattern of stained glass, like church windows.

The handle on the gate presses down and the gate opens by itself. Minoo's heart nearly stops before she realizes Vanessa is standing beside it, invisible.

'Can you hear me?' Vanessa whispers. She's trained herself to be heard but not seen for tonight. Minoo nods, facing the spot where she thinks Vanessa is standing.

They stop at the front door and Minoo pulls on a thin pair of latex gloves she stole from her mother's office. 'Do you think she has an alarm?' she whispers, as she pulls out her flashlight.

'I guess we're about to find out.' Linnéa smirks and takes out the key.

Minoo has to admire Anna-Karin's courage. She stole the principal's key, ran to the locksmith a few blocks from the school, made a copy and managed to return the original without anyone noticing.

Linnéa turns the key and the lock opens easily. She presses down the handle and makes an ironically inviting gesture.

'Welcome to the House of Horrors,' she says. 'I'll stay here and keep watch,' she adds in a more serious tone, when she meets Minoo's gaze.

Vanessa fades into view on the other side of Minoo and gives her an encouraging nod. Then she vanishes again as she slips inside the darkened house.

Minoo thinks of Rebecka and follows her.

Minoo switches on her flashlight and aims it at the floor to minimize the chance of anyone seeing the light through the window. A row of coats hangs in a large alcove in the hall. They sneak across the creaking floorboards – Minoo hopes they're not leaving footprints.

'Does she actually *live* here?' Vanessa murmurs, as they enter the living room.

Minoo knows exactly what she means. The place looks too perfect. The furniture is heavy and dark, and looks as if it belongs in a castle. Old portraits and landscape paintings in somber colors hang on the walls. The open fireplace seems never to have been used, despite the basket of neatly stacked uniform-sized logs. There are no books lying around. No magazines. It smells spotlessly clean. Too clean. As if the air has never been sullied by human presence.

They walk along a hallway and look into the kitchen, a bathroom and a guestroom. Everything is furnished in the same manner. Opposite the stairway leading to the second floor there is a little room used as an office. A shelf is filled with ordinary books – literature, biographies and poetry. No old parchments or Latin manuscripts.

'Let's go upstairs,' Minoo whispers.

No one answers.

'Vanessa?' she whispers, louder, panicked at the idea of being alone in this big, dark house.

'Sorry. I forgot you can't see me. I nodded,' Vanessa says, beside her.

They sneak up the stairs, which creak beneath their feet. Minoo realizes that if the principal were to come home now they would be trapped upstairs. Unlike Vanessa, she would never get outside unseen.

The landing is bathed in moonlight pouring through a skylight so Minoo switches off her flashlight. Shadows lurk in every corner.

'Want to start with the rooms on the right?' she whispers.

Silence.

'Vanessa?'

'Sorry. Yes.'

A long carpet deadens their footsteps. Minoo opens the door at the far end of the hall, where the shadows are at their thickest. She steps into the room and switches on her flashlight again. At the far end, there is a neatly made bed and a simple floor lamp. Fitted cupboards line one wall. But there's no indication that anyone sleeps here.

'She must be a psychopath,' Vanessa whispers.

One of the cupboard doors opens. Something black and shapeless flies out, like a desperate bird released from its cage. Minoo lets out a muffled cry. When the black shape stops moving she sees an elegant evening dress floating in the air.

'A rich psychopath,' Vanessa whispers, and hangs the dress back in the cupboard. 'This is Prada.'

Minoo opens the door to the adjoining bathroom. Thick towels hang over a bar of brushed steel. The shelves and cabinets are filled with an immaculate array of exclusive cosmetics and skincare products, all with the labels facing forward.

'Wow! What a lot of makeup. Do you think she'd notice if something went missing?' Vanessa asks.

There's an unmistakable eagerness in her voice that causes Minoo to shake her head in terror.

'Just kidding,' Vanessa says.

Yet Minoo doesn't dare move away from the front of the cabinet until Vanessa has left the bathroom.

The next door leads into an empty room.

As does the next.

The third is locked.

Minoo pulls at the handle. If there's anything of interest in this house, you can bet it'll be in the locked room. 'What do we do now?' Minoo asks.

She hears a strange noise, a faint metallic scraping coming from the door. Like little claws scratching. Minoo takes a step back. If the principal is some kind of evil queen, maybe she has nasty little minions hidden about her palace, silent sentinels ready to defend her secrets.

The handle presses down and the door opens a crack.

Something materializes in the corner of her eye, and Minoo whirls around.

Vanessa grins at her.

'Did you hear that . . .' Minoo begins, then notices the hairpin Vanessa is holding. And she understands that the door wasn't opened by someone inside the room. Vanessa, wonderful Vanessa, had picked the lock. She could have hugged her, but Vanessa has vanished again.

They enter the room. Minoo hardly dares to breathe. The moonlight filters in through the stained-glass windows, creating a dreamy effect. The colored panes project irregular shapes across the floor. Unlike the rest of the house, there is a faint smell of life in here, of dusty paper and old leather. There is also a hint of burned wood and a pungent smell that Minoo can't identify.

The room is the biggest one upstairs. There is a fireplace in here, too, but it appears to have been used frequently, judging from the blackened brickwork. A bookcase runs the full length of the opposite wall, with three stuffed birds perched on top – two different owls and a pitch-black raven with a razor-sharp beak. The contents of the shelves are protected by glass doors secured with big padlocks.

Most of the spines of the books are so worn that the titles are unreadable, but Minoo's gaze lands on one – *Unaussprechlichen Kulten* – and she shudders, as if she had touched something ancient and thoroughly evil.

'Where are you?' she whispers.

'By the desk. Look,' Vanessa whispers, and a hand appears out of thin air to point at something.

Underneath a stack of books, in various stages of disintegration, lies an old map of Engelsfors. Next to it there is a strange iron object with a big screw in the middle. And two photographs, blown up from last year's school photo. One of Elias. And one of Rebecka.

'I'm going to take a picture of this so we can show the others,' Vanessa whispers. She sounds tense.

Minoo goes to the shelf next to the fireplace. It's stacked with brown glass jars, each labeled with a Roman numeral. She picks one up at random, with the number XI, and unscrews the lid.

At first she can't tell what the small desiccated spheres are.

Eyes.

She screws the lid back on tightly and puts the jar back where she'd taken it from.

Small flashes light up the room when Vanessa photographs the desk with her phone camera.

Suddenly Minoo glimpses movement near the ceiling. Her gaze falls on the birds. She stands motionless, waiting for a beak to open, a wing to flap. But they don't budge. Of course not.

She forces herself to focus on the task at hand. Find clues. Evidence. She mustn't let fear get the better of her. She has to think of Rebecka and Elias. She's here for their sake.

She walks up to a little wooden table standing next to a well-worn leather armchair. A circular, dark red wooden box is lying on the table. Minoo shines her flashlight on it. The lid is divided into two halves by a vertical line. Depicted on one half is an ingeniously carved city with strange architecture that looks like nothing Minoo has ever seen before, and on the other, swirling galaxies and unidentifiable slithering shapes. In the middle a man holds his hands straight out at his sides as if he were forming a bridge between the two halves. The line cuts his body in two. His eyes are closed.

'Minoo . . .'

Vanessa's voice comes from just behind her. Minoo turns. Vanessa is visible again.

'Look down,' she says.

How had she missed those lines when she entered the room? Or have they appeared while she and Vanessa have been in there?

A big white circle is drawn on the floor. In the middle of it there is a smaller circle, approximately a foot in diameter. Inside the smaller circle, there is a strange symbol. Minoo and Vanessa are standing inside the bigger circle.

Minoo bends down and runs her finger across the outer line. It feels greasy and warm. She snatches her hand away.

'We have to get out of here,' Vanessa mutters.

The air above the smaller circle starts to shimmer, as it does over asphalt on a hot summer day. Minoo tries to run, but she can't move. She hears a dull pulsating sound in the ceiling above them.

A wave of hot air shoots through the room. The heat makes it difficult to breathe. The muffled pounding grows louder, causing a vibration in their chests like a heavy bass line.

'I can't move,' Vanessa squeals.

Minoo struggles, but it's as if her feet are glued to the floor. The heat causes sweat to trickle from her hairline over her forehead. Vanessa stretches out her hand. 'I can't fucking move!' she shouts, over the din.

The moment they touch the pressure pinning their feet to the floor eases – enough for them to move.

'Run!' Vanessa yells.

As they race out of the room Minoo glances back and sees something unbelievable before she flees toward the stairs.

The muffled pounding grows in intensity as they race along the hall, down the stairs and through the lower rooms. The windowpanes are rattling and a painting crashes to the floor in the living room. Vanessa throws open the front door and they burst out into the night air. Minoo tears after her toward the open gate.

Out of the corner of her eye she spots Linnéa, who doesn't ask questions, just joins them.

The three girls stumble into each other as they throw

themselves into Nicolaus's car.

'Did you see it, too? In the light?' Vanessa says to Minoo, when they're sitting in the back seat.

Minoo nods. She knows what Vanessa saw: a human form taking shape from a pillar of light.

CHAPTER 23

When Minoo and Vanessa tell the others what they saw at the principal's house, Anna-Karin feels unexpectedly closed off. It's as if she had to see it to believe in it. She should be the last person who needs convincing that the supernatural exists. But their account of what happened sounds like an old ghost story she's heard a million times.

She's sitting on the stage, looking out across the dance floor. Her parents had met here many years ago. She doesn't know much more than that. Her mother usually describes her father as a handsome man and a good dancer. But she ends the story with a bitter laugh, saying, 'If I had known how bad he was at everything else, I would have run away as fast as my legs could carry me.' It sounds as though her mother wishes she had run away, even though that would have meant Anna-Karin had never been born.

A mild rain has started to fall and is thrumming gently against the dance pavilion's roof. It's leaking and little pools are forming on the wooden floor. The one-eyed black cat has puffed itself up at Nicolaus's feet. He seems to have grown used to it and has even given it the imaginative name of Cat.

'So now we know that the principal is the killer,' Vanessa says.

'Not quite,' Minoo adds.

'How much proof do you need?' Linnéa asks.

'Excuse me,' says Ida, 'but you three are, like, missing the point here.'

'Which is what exactly?' Linnéa snaps.

'Well,' says Ida, her voice dripping with sweetness and venom, 'the point isn't that we know it's her. It's that she knows we've been there.'

'We don't know if she saw us,' says Vanessa. 'Even if it was her.'

Ida rolls her eyes.

'We're not completely helpless,' says Minoo, sounding unconvinced.

'Against her you might very well be, I'm afraid,' says Nicolaus.

He'd been flipping silently through the photos on Vanessa's phone. Now he was staring vacantly into space. 'I suspect that the principal is in league with the demons.'

Minoo takes out a little notepad and starts scribbling feverishly.

'Demons? Where the hell did that come from? Do you, like, know something all of a sudden?' Vanessa says.

'God have mercy on your souls,' Nicolaus mumbles, and staggers.

Minoo lowers her notepad. 'Are you all right?'

The confusion is back in Nicolaus's eyes. 'What was it we were talking about?'

Part One

'The principal,' Anna-Karin answers. 'And something about demons.'

'Ah, yes! Demons. The principal.' His gaze moves back to the photos. 'I've seen this device before. God help us.'

'Okay . . .' says Vanessa.

Anna-Karin gets up and walks closer to him when he holds up the phone to display one of the photos: the one of the iron object with the big screw in the middle.

'I thought I recognized it. It's a tongue tearer,' Nicolaus continues.

'A what?' Ida asks shrilly.

'You force the victim's tongue through this opening, screw it fast, then pull out the tongue like this . . .' He demonstrates by sticking out his tongue as far as it will go. 'Then you turn a crank so that the tongue is pulled out further and further. You continue until the root splits and the tongue comes off. The human tongue is surprisingly long.'

Anna-Karin looks at the image, unconsciously pulling her tongue as far back in her mouth as she can, as if to protect it. Now she has no trouble in believing the ghost story.

'She saw us,' Minoo says faintly. 'I'm pretty sure of it. Do you think she'll do something at school?'

'That was where Elias and Rebecka died,' says Linnéa.

'I suppose we'll just have to wait and see which of us it is on Monday,' Vanessa says.

Perhaps it was an attempt at a joke, but nobody laughs.

CHAPTER 24

On Monday morning, Vanessa briefly considers not going to school. The events of Saturday scared her, but the prospect of sitting alone at home and waiting for something terrible to happen seems far worse.

She hasn't heard Nicke mention any break-ins at Lilla Lugnet. If the police had been called out for something that exciting he would definitely have talked about it at the dinner table. Of course, that doesn't mean they're in the clear. Vanessa can't imagine that a person who's in league with demons would bother calling the police if someone broke into her secret torture chamber.

Her mother is reading a thick book about how to cast your horoscope. It's her day off and she's humming as she sits there, taking notes while flipping through the book. Her face is calm, which makes her look younger. She was only seventeen when she had Vanessa, and thirty-three is still pretty young. Sometimes Vanessa thinks her mother has thrown away her life. She wears herself out, and for what? Mother of two and a care assistant at an old people's home. Is that all she's going to do with her life? Doesn't she have any ambition? Vanessa isn't going to make the same mistake. She's going to be young for as long as possible. She wants to savor life. Real life. The one that exists away from Engelsfors. If she survives long enough.

'I'm going now,' she says.

Her mother smiles. For someone who's thrown away her life, she looks very content. 'Hey, I almost forgot,' she said. 'How did it go at Mona's?'

Why does her mother have such a knack for bringing up the very thing Vanessa doesn't want to talk about? 'Good,' she mumbles.

'I was really impressed,' her mother says. 'What did she say to you?'

'It's private.'

'That's okay, Nessa. I understand if you don't want to tell me everything. Maybe I don't want to know.'

She says it with a knowing smile, as if she knows what Vanessa's going through, that she understands what it's like to be a teenager. But her mother has no idea what Vanessa is going through. And Vanessa can never tell her.

'No, you don't,' she says quietly, and gives her mother a quick hug.

The first thing Vanessa sees when she arrives at school is Jari. He's standing with Anna-Karin, who is tossing her hair and laughing exaggeratedly.

'You're crazy.' Anna-Karin giggles at something Jari has said, and Vanessa quickens her pace so she doesn't have to hear any more.

She sits through her morning classes on pins and needles,

flinching at every movement in the classroom. Evelina and Michelle look at her as if she should be strapped into a strait-jacket and pumped full of tranquilizers. They're probably right.

When she comes down to the cafeteria she sees the principal at the salad bar. Adriana Lopez is piling a mountain of grated carrot on to her plate. All of a sudden everything seems silly and unreal.

Maybe the principal is a demon. But an entire morning marks the upper limit of how long Vanessa can feel afraid – especially of a demon who loves carrots.

Monday drags on into Tuesday, then Wednesday, Thursday and finally Friday. Nothing happens. They meet at the fairground once to decide on a strategy. Linnéa wants them to use Anna-Karin's powers to get the principal to expose herself. Minoo objects: Rebecka had some pretty potent powers, which didn't save her.

Vanessa wants to scream with frustration. There's nobody they can ask for help or advice. Now they're just waiting their turn to die, like animals to the slaughter, without even *trying* to fight back. One afternoon when she watched the principal getting into her car, she felt like running up, yanking open the door and shouting, 'Go on, do it! What are you waiting for?'

She had intended to spend the weekend with Wille, to try to forget everything, but he'd said he had to help Jonte with 'this thing'. Michelle and Evelina are in Köping for a concert, and Vanessa can't afford to go too.

Part Two

On Saturday the storm hits. The last of the autumn leaves are torn from the trees, and there's a howling wind that pummels the town with rain.

Vanessa is a prisoner at home. By the afternoon claustrophobia is creeping in. It feels as though Nicke is everywhere. If she goes into the kitchen, he's there making coffee. If she wanders into the living room, he's lying on the sofa, reading a crime novel, muttering about bad research. In the end Vanessa starts tidying up her room for something to do.

'Can you do the rest of the apartment, while you're at it?' her mother says, in a way that suggests she's being funny.

But Vanessa actually does it. If nothing else, it's fun to irritate Nicke with the sound of vacuuming. He can hardly complain.

Afterward, Vanessa sits in front of the computer. Nobody's logged in. She tries calling Wille. No answer. She walks up to the window.

Engelsfors is best viewed in darkness, from a bit of distance, when all you can see is streetlamps and lit windows. Vanessa catches sight of the church spire. That's where Rebecka is going to be buried on Monday. Vanessa wishes she could be there, but it's out of the question. Nobody can know that she and Rebecka were friendly.

Frasse scratches at the door and she lets him in. He lies down on the bed and sighs contentedly. Vanessa glances at her cell phone on the desk. Then she picks it up.

Linnéa sounds out of breath when she answers. 'Has something happened?'

Vanessa is a little confused. Then she realizes that Linnéa was hardly expecting an 'ordinary' call from her. 'No, I just wanted . . .'

'I'm busy.'

'Forget it,' says Vanessa, and hangs up.

Unease wells up in her chest. She calls Wille. The phone rings at the other end. He doesn't answer.

Frasse yawns so widely that it looks as if his jaw is going to pop out of joint. Vanessa puts down her phone and downloads a horror movie. It'll be nice to look at some imaginary monsters. Anything to stop her thinking about the ones already living inside her head, whispering that her boyfriend is cheating on her at this very moment with Linnéa Wallin.

The windowpanes rattle in the wind.

Minoo is searching online for information about demons. Again. As usual she gets nowhere. The stories she finds are more like fairy tales. She tries to compare them with each other, but draws no useful conclusions other than that evil creatures figure in most religions and cultures. But originally the word demon had nothing to do with evil. It stems from the Greek word *daimon* which simply means 'spirit', 'god' or 'being'. Evil demons didn't appear until the arrival of Christianity.

Minoo sighs in frustration. She's sure that the people who put up the information on these sites know as little about it as she does. A lot of it is obviously nonsense; other stuff is wishful thinking from wannabe Satanists, but most of it is the senseless rambling of religious nuts. And they frighten her as much as any demons.

Minoo gets up and massages her stiff shoulders. Her gaze falls on the black dress hanging on the wardrobe door.

They had bought her funeral outfit after school yesterday. Minoo had put it off as long as she could until her mother had forced her to go shopping with her in Borlänge. Minoo feels sick just thinking about the funeral. It's the day after tomorrow, and she wishes she could get out of it. But her mother keeps insisting: 'You have to go. It's part of the grieving process. You'll understand what I mean afterward.'

Rebecka's parents don't want the funeral to become a big spectacle, and have invited only the closest family and friends to attend.

Minoo doesn't know if she'll be able to handle it. What will she say to Rebecka's mother? How will she cope with seeing Rebecka's little brothers and sisters? Is Gustaf going to be there? She hasn't spoken to him since Rebecka died. Not since she read Cissi's interview with him in the paper.

Minoo takes her outfit and hangs it inside the wardrobe, out of sight.

Then she picks up her dog-eared copy of *The Secret History* and lies down on the bed. But she can't concentrate on the familiar words. Instead her thoughts wander from the principal to demons, to school, to Max.

Max is a refuge from the darkness, and she lingers on his face. Her thoughts give way to dreams of longing, the kind of dreams that have filled so many lonely Saturday nights.

Chapter 25

The trees are silhouetted against the gray-white sky. It is one of those non-weather days – neither wet nor sunny. A vast grayness sits like a lid over the town.

Minoo walks along the path to the door of the church, the gravel crunching under her feet. Her new dress feels tight around her chest, making it hard for her to breathe. A few old ladies in black coats are standing on the church steps, talking in low voices. Minoo stares at their grizzled hair and wrinkled faces: Rebecka will never look like that.

Her parents had offered to take time off work and go with her, but Minoo said no. Now she can hardly remember why. She regrets it.

She tortures herself with various nightmare scenarios. What if she does something wrong – cries too much, giggles hysterically, faints or trips? What if she ruins the funeral for Rebecka's family? Does she have the right to be there? She had known Rebecka for such a short time.

Slowly she climbs the steps and passes the old ladies, entering through the open doors. People are already sitting in the pews. Everyone has their backs to her. No one would notice if she turned and left.

Then she sees the white coffin. Next to the altar there's an enlarged photograph of Rebecka on an easel. It's a nice picture. She's sitting at Dammsjön Lake, squinting a little in the sunlight, smiling at the person taking the picture. And Minoo knows she has to stay.

She is the only one there who knows why Rebecka died. The only one who knows it wasn't suicide. Somehow that makes it her duty to be present. At least one person at Rebecka's funeral knows the truth.

As she walks up the aisle, she remembers that this is also how bridal couples and parents christening their children enter the church. Minoo's parents aren't religious, but suddenly she understands the point of church; here, birth, life and death occupy the same space.

Minoo sits somewhere in the middle and tries to make herself invisible.

The bells start to toll.

Several people are sniveling.

She looks at Rebecka's picture again, at her smiling face, which looks so alive, and it's as if she realizes for the first time that Rebecka is never coming back. Never. It's like staring into a bottomless pit. It's impossible to get your head around. Forever. Eternity. Suddenly tears are streaming down her face. She becomes afraid of losing control completely. She hides her face in her hands and thinks about everything Rebecka was and everything she might have been, all the things she'll never feel, see and hear, love, hate, yearn for and laugh at. An entire life. Gone.

Helena Malmgren, Elias's mother, isn't conducting the

service. Of course not. How could she bear it, so close to Elias's death? Instead it's a young priest. He's uncertain, stumbling and mumbling his way through the sermon. Minoo hears the words slip past: . . . *so young* . . . *God has a purpose* . . . *after death* . . . but none provide comfort. When the priest talks about Rebecka, he sounds as if he's talking about someone else, and Minoo wants him to shut up. Leave them in peace. She hates him for being so ill-prepared. She hates the psalms about souls going to Paradise. How can anyone pretend there's something beautiful and meaningful about Rebecka's death?

The organ music plays. Cautious tones rise up through the church.

Rebecka's parents stand and walk to the coffin. Rebecka's father, a tall, broad-shouldered man whom Minoo has never met, is red-faced from crying. Now and then his sniffs echo through the church, penetrating through the organ music. Her mother has the closed-off expression of the deeply shocked. They are leaning on each other for support. Behind them come Rebecka's two little brothers; they are so like their elder sister that it's painful for Minoo to look at them. They're wearing black suits and holding each other's hands as they follow their parents toward the coffin. She wonders how much they understand of what's going on. An older man is behind them, resting his hands on their shoulders.

The young priest nods respectfully to the family and there is genuine empathy in his face. Minoo's anger toward him disappears. He tries to comfort them: an impossible task, but at least he's trying.

When the people sitting in the pew in front of Minoo get up, she follows them. Her legs feel unsteady as she walks toward the coffin. The tears well up again as she gets closer and it feels right and proper. It's fitting that she should cry with Rebecka's family and everyone else who knew her. She cannot take away their grief, but she can share it.

Minoo catches sight of a big wreath of lilies with white ribbons on which is written: REST IN PEACE – YOUR FRIENDS. They had chosen the most generic inscription they could come up with so as not to arouse curiosity. But Minoo knows who the senders are and that gives her strength.

One by one the funeral guests go up and lay a flower on the coffin. Minoo doesn't have a flower. She didn't know she was supposed to bring one with her. When she reaches the coffin she instead lays her palm against it. She almost expects to feel something – a sign, an electric shock – but the wood is cool against her skin. It's impossible to imagine that Rebecka is lying inside.

Rebecka, Minoo says to herself, I promise I'll find the person who did this. And they will never have a chance to do it again. I promise you.

Following the ceremony coffee is served in the parsonage but Minoo can't bear to stay any longer. She can't imagine what it must be like for Rebecka's parents to cope with all the questions and guilt, the rage and sorrow. It's awful not to be able to tell them that their daughter didn't commit suicide.

She steps out onto the church steps and looks out across

the new section of the cemetery, which extends to the other side of a long box hedge. Elias, the seventh Chosen One, lies somewhere over there.

She walks down the steps and continues along the gravel path. She thinks about the room in the principal's house, the frightening things inside it. How can they defeat such an enemy?

'Hi.'

She looks up. Gustaf is leaning against a tree. He seems a little lost in his black suit. Their eyes meet and Minoo quickens her pace. Gustaf is the last person she wants to talk to.

'Minoo . . .'

She doesn't answer, just walks faster. He follows her.

'Please – can't I just talk to you?' he calls out.

'No!' she hisses.

'It's not how you think.'

Minoo stops so suddenly that Gustaf almost cannons into her. Seeing him close up causes some of her anger to dissipate. He's no longer the golden boy who's never faced any hardship. His eyes are red and his skin is ashen.

'What's not how I think?'

'That interview. That's why you don't want to talk to me, right?'

'What do you think?'

Gustaf looks at her, searching for words that don't come.

'You said she was better off dead!' Minoo reminds him.

Gustaf shuts his eyes. When he opens them, they're wet with tears. 'I was standing at the front entrance waiting for her,' he says, 'I saw her fall and hit the ground. I couldn't do anything—' He chokes up. Tears run down his cheeks. Minoo is crying, too. A lone raven flies above their heads and lands on a tree.

'Cissi came over to my house that night,' Gustaf continues, more composed. 'Of course she said she was a journalist, but it didn't feel like that when we talked. She really seemed to care. And I said lots of things I shouldn't have. I barely even *remember* what I said. My mother's filed a complaint against the newspaper, but now it's been printed . . .'

Minoo knows what Cissi can be like – she ought to have understood what had happened at the interview. And there's no trace of deceit in Gustaf's face. He's speaking the truth, she's sure.

The remnants of the anger she's felt toward him evaporate, leaving just their grief. Minoo can hardly bear hers, and she can't begin to conceive of the emptiness Rebecka must have left behind in Gustaf.

'I just have to know,' he says. 'Did she say anything to you about being unhappy? Did you notice anything to suggest she didn't want . . . to go on living?'

'No,' she answers. 'But I do know one thing. You made her happy.'

Gustaf looks away. 'Not happy enough.'

'You can't think like that.'

'Sure I can. I knew something was wrong. Sometimes I sensed she wanted to talk about it. If only I'd asked her . . .'

'She could just have told you,' Minoo says gently.

'But instead she jumped off the school roof.'

There's nothing Minoo can say. She can't tell him the truth.

'Her parents must hate me,' Gustaf continues. 'I didn't dare go to the funeral. I didn't want to ruin things any more than I have already.'

'Go and talk to them. Maybe they understand more than you think.'

Gustaf shakes his head. 'I can't.' He looks at Minoo and his face breaks into a smile that is full of pain. 'She was the best thing that ever happened to me. I'm so fucking alone without her. I don't recognize my own life any more.'

He sobs, and Minoo does the only thing she can: she puts her arms around him. From the corner of her eye, she sees the raven flap its wings and fly off into the gray-white sky.

CHAPTER 26

Vanessa has been standing in the darkness outside Linnéa's door for more than an hour. Linnéa is playing hard grindcore inside her apartment. The singer is alternating between singing and screaming. Vanessa has always thought that kind of music sounds like a really bad headache, but now that she's forced to listen to it, she gets the point of it. At first it stressed her out, but when she let go and allowed herself to be carried away by it, she found it became strangely relaxing. It's as if all the stress and fear are transformed into rage, which the music resolves.

I shouldn't be here, she thinks.

But she can't leave. Not until she knows for sure.

Late last night she'd gotten a text message: 'Tired as hell. Sleep well ☺'. When she tried calling, the phone rang but nobody answered. She didn't sleep a wink all night.

She knew it would piss Wille off if she woke him at seven in the morning demanding he drive her to school. She had to play her full register – scornful, facetious, sexy, angry, helpless – before he gave in. And then it didn't feel like a triumph. On the contrary. She was humiliated.

She'd thought that if she could just see him she'd know

whether he'd been with Linnéa. That was why it was so important to meet him first thing in the morning. And at first Vanessa took Wille's silence in the car as a sign that he hadn't cheated on her. Because if he had, surely he would have tried to suck up to her. But then she wondered instead if the silence meant he was tired of her.

When they reached the school she threw open the car door and slammed it behind her. She didn't care if people stared at her as she crossed the playground, ignored Evelina and Michelle when they called to her. As soon as she got inside, she ran to the girls' bathroom by the cafeteria.

All the cubicles were empty. Vanessa made herself invisible and began to cry quietly and furiously.

Just then Linnéa entered.

Vanessa held her breath. She hardly even dared think. But Linnéa had her phone pressed to her ear and seemed preoccupied. She sighed deeply at whoever was talking to her. She stood in front of the mirror, ran one hand over her black hair and bared her teeth as if to check whether any food was caught in them.

'Stop it. I can't talk about shit like this when I'm at school,' she said. 'No, but I'm here now . . . I don't want to know anything about it. That's your problem. Okay . . . I realize that . . . M-hm . . . I don't know . . . Okay . . . Come over tonight, then. At nine. And don't call me again today.'

The clock on Vanessa's phone reads 9:34. She needs to pee. A telephone number appears on the screen. Minoo. She must have tried to call her, like, seven times already this evening, but Vanessa decides she'll have to wait. Linnéa hasn't rushed off to the fairground so it can't be all that important.

At 9:46 she tells herself that if no one's appeared by ten she'll leave. At ten she decides to give it fifteen more minutes, even though she's about to pee her pants.

At 10:09 the front door to the building opens and a light comes on in the stairwell. The cables in the elevator shaft creak, and Vanessa keeps her eyes fixed on the little window. The elevator rises into view and stops. She glimpses a figure standing inside.

The doors open.

It's not Wille.

It's Jonte.

He walks up to Linnéa's door and rings the bell.

The music cuts off in the apartment. He rings the bell again.

Linnéa opens the door. She's not wearing any makeup and has on a pair of running shorts and a tight black T-shirt with a bat on the chest and DIR EN GREY written across it. She gives Jonte a hard look. 'You're late.'

'Sorry,' he says, but doesn't sound as if he means it.

Linnéa steps aside to let him in.

Vanessa follows him. It just happens, without her realizing. She has just enough time to press herself against the wall before Jonte closes the door and locks it.

Now she's standing in Linnéa's hall and has no idea why she came in, or why she follows Jonte and Linnéa into the living room.

Fuck, she thinks. Fuck, fuck, fucking fuck.

Linnéa stops suddenly and gives Jonte a strange look.

'What?' he asks.

'Why do you smell like coconut?'

Jonte snorts with laughter and throws himself on to the sofa, which gives a loud crack. He's wearing a washed-out black hoodie and baggy jeans. He picks up a little bag of weed, pulls a packet of Rizla papers from his pocket and deftly rolls a joint. Linnéa sits next to him and leans her head on his shoulder.

Vanessa grimaces. Jonte isn't bad-looking but he's so . . . unsavory. And almost as old as Vanessa's mother.

Linnéa suddenly stares piercingly into the room. It's as if she's looking straight at Vanessa. But that's impossible. Isn't it?

Jonte lights the joint and takes a deep toke.

'What are you so fucking uptight about?' he says to Linnéa, as he hands her the joint.

Linnéa smokes it as she stands up and walks over to her laptop, which is open. She puts on a slow song. The female vocalist sounds sad and frustrated.

'Come here,' Jonte says, and Linnéa goes to him, lays the glowing joint on an ashtray and sits close to him. She kisses him and Vanessa winces. But she can't take her eyes off them as Linnéa tugs off her T-shirt, and Jonte unfastens her black bra, then runs his hands over her back to her breasts.

Linnéa eases back on the sofa with a hand around Jonte's neck. He glides down on top of her and reaches for the joint. They continue kissing each other, alternating with drags from the joint. Linnéa slips off her shorts in one slick movement. Her underpants are bright pink with little black hearts. Jonte lets his hand slip inside them. Linnéa starts to smile. Suddenly she raises her head and looks at Vanessa. 'Had enough yet?' she says.

'No way,' Jonte mumbles, and kisses her neck.

Vanessa is so shocked that she stumbles out into the hall and accidentally knocks over one of the little lamps.

'What the fuck was that?' she hears Jonte say.

'I'll go and have a look – I need to go to the bathroom anyway,' says Linnéa.

Vanessa is fumbling with the lock when she feels something soft hit the back of her head. She turns. Linnéa's T-shirt is lying on the floor. She's standing there with her arms crossed over her naked breasts. Her face is in shadow. 'I know you're there,' she whispers, barely audibly.

Vanessa opens her mouth to say something but no sound comes out.

Linnéa marches toward her and Vanessa presses herself against the wall, trying to stop herself from staring at Linnéa's breasts as she unlocks the door.

'Get out,' Linnéa hisses, and Vanessa bolts.

Linnéa slams the door so hard that the sound carries throughout the building. Vanessa runs down the stairs and out through the front entrance.

The first thing she does is squat in some bushes to pee. Only then can she begin to think clearly. She's behaved like a lunatic and it was her weekend of isolation that did it.

She mulls it over as she walks briskly homeward. What

should she say next time they meet? 'Hi, I'm sorry I'm a sick pervert who likes to watch my friends having sex. Well, I mean we're not even friends, really, you and me, but still, it was a lot of fun. How was it for you?'

What she'd really like to ask Linnéa, though, is why she's with a loser like Jonte. And, while she's at it, she'd like to ask herself why she cares. As long as Linnéa isn't sleeping with Wille she should be happy.

There's something about Linnéa that makes her behave unpredictably. Why did she follow Jonte into the apartment? She has no answer to that. The only reasonable explanation might be that she really is a sick pervert.

It's almost eleven thirty when Vanessa sticks her key into the door. She hopes her mother has gone to bed. Nicke is away in Borlänge, at a conference, so she doesn't have to worry about him.

But when she goes into the hall she hears voices in the kitchen. She takes off her shoes and coat as quietly as she can. Frasse saunters into the hall and licks her hand. Thank God he doesn't bark. She's so focused on being quiet as possible that she doesn't notice Melvin's toy car on the floor in front of her. She steps on it, sending it flying into the wall with a bang.

'Nessa?' Wille appears in the kitchen doorway. 'I've been waiting for you all night. Where have you been?' There's no hint of rebuke in his voice, just concern.

'Over at Evelina's,' she says, and makes a mental note to warn her alibi. 'Why didn't you call?'

'Can't we go to your room and talk about it?' Wille asks.

Part Two

Vanessa peers into the kitchen. Her mother is reading her horoscope book, studying it conspicuously to show that she isn't eavesdropping.

Vanessa nods and they go to her bedroom. She shuts the door. When she turns around Wille puts his arms around her. She moves close to him, feels the warmth of his body and catches the smell that is uniquely his.

He's mine, she thinks. Mine and nobody else's.

'Sorry for being such an idiot this morning,' she murmurs.

'I know why you were pissed off with me. I disappeared all weekend.' He lets go of her. 'I wasn't at Jonte's place . . . I was at his father's cabin.'

'Alone?'

'I needed to think. I've been a bit depressed.'

Suddenly Vanessa is frightened. 'About us?'

'About everything,' Wille answers. 'I've got no job. I'm living with my mother. I haven't done anything since I left school.'

Vanessa bites her lip. She'd been hoping he'd realize he needs a life. The question is whether there's room in it for her.

'I tried to think of what I like about my life and what I don't. And I saw that there isn't much I do like.'

Vanessa's eyes fill with tears. Here it comes. Now he's going to break up with her. This is where everything ends.

'Except you,' Wille says. 'You're the only good thing in my life. You and my mom. Shit – that sounds weird.'

Vanessa laughs and starts crying at the same time.

'Nessa?'

'I thought you were going to dump me.' She sniffles.

'No, no! Far from it! It's just . . . I want to be the man you deserve. You're so incredible. I love you. And I was wondering . . . Can we get engaged?' Wille digs in his pocket and pulls out a thin silver ring. 'We can wait to get married, of course. Ten years, if you like. I just want everyone to know that we belong together.'

Vanessa's head spins. She doesn't know how she feels any more.

'Do you want to?' Wille asks.

Yes. There's one thing she knows she feels: she loves him, whether she likes it or not. And she wants everyone to know they belong together. That they've chosen each other. That they've decided against everyone else. He slides the ring onto her finger. Then he digs out another, thicker ring from his other pocket and hands it to her so that she can put it on his finger. 'It's you and me now,' Wille says.

'It's you and me,' Vanessa echoes. 'I love you.' She kisses his warm mouth and presses her body against his. His hands work their way under her top and down toward the small of her back.

There is a knock at the door. 'Vanessa!' her mother's shrill voice calls.

Wille tries to break free but Vanessa clings to him. 'Forget her,' she mutters.

A moment later the door opens a crack. 'Wille, Vanessa's got school tomorrow.' Her mother is using her serious voice, the one that brooks no resistance.

'Oh, for fuck's sake!' Vanessa bursts out.

'It's okay,' Wille says. 'I've got to go home anyway.'

She follows him to the front door. She tries to kiss him, but Wille finds it embarrassing in front of her mother. Instead he gives her a hug. 'I'll pick you up after school tomorrow,' he promises.

She shuts the door behind him. When she turns, her mother looks worried. Vanessa holds up her left hand.

'Aren't you a bit young for a ring?'

Her mood sinks. Her mother can't even pretend to be happy for her sake. 'It's not like we're getting married tomorrow,' she snaps. 'It's a symbol that we belong together.'

'I just don't understand why you're in such a hurry to commit yourself to someone when you're so young.'

'You got pregnant with me when you were sixteen, for Christ's sake! With someone at a conference in Götvändaren! You were so drunk you couldn't even remember his name.'

'Don't you use that tone with me,' her mother says.

'Don't you use that tone with me,' Vanessa mimics. She realizes instantly that that was the wrong approach if she wants to seem mature enough to get engaged.

Her mother glares at her. 'Go ahead then, play grown-ups. Maybe you and Wille should move in together so we have a bit more space here.'

It was like a stab in the gut. 'You'd like that, wouldn't you? So you and Nicke can *fuck* in peace. Or have you found someone else to have an unplanned pregnancy with? This time you might want to keep a pen and paper handy so you can write down his name.'

For a moment Vanessa thinks her mother is going to hit her. It's never happened before, and it's never been this close to happening. Her mother turns abruptly and marches off into the kitchen.

'You can have what you want!' Vanessa shouts. 'I'll move in with Wille!'

'You do that!' her mother shouts back. 'We'll see how long you can stand it!'

'I hate you! Sirpa's a much better mother than you've ever been!'

She goes into her room and slams the door, expecting to hear her mother storm after her, open the door and shout at her to remember the neighbors, or does she want them to be evicted?

But nothing happens.

Vanessa is standing in the middle of her room. She feels empty inside. All day she's been like a pinball, bouncing back and forth between extremes of emotion. All she wants now is to sleep. She reaches for the covers to pull them aside.

There's a knock on the door. Vanessa tries to decide if she has the energy to make up with her mother. But her mother doesn't come in. Instead she calls through the door. 'I got a phone call at work. You don't have to go to your first class tomorrow. The principal wants to speak to you. A routine chat.'

◎

Part Two

Late that night Minoo finally hears back from Vanessa and can confirm that all five of them have been called to the principal's office first thing in the morning.

Half an hour later, she opens the door to her room. The house is quiet. She sneaks down the hallway, past her parents' closed bedroom door. She hears a sound from inside their room and stiffens. But it's just her father snoring.

Only once the front door is shut behind her can she breathe normally. A thick fog has enveloped the garden, making any shapes appear vague and indistinct. There's no wind, and her footsteps seem to echo across the entire neighborhood.

Nicolaus is waiting for her in his car, hidden in the fog, a hundred yards down the street. She climbs into the passenger seat. He is shivering in his thin coat, and his breath steams out of his mouth when he speaks.

'Good evening,' he says. 'Or perhaps that's the wrong choice of words on such a fateful night.'

For a moment they sit in silence. Minoo looks at his hands resting on the steering wheel. They're red and chapped. 'You've got to buy some clothes,' she says. 'A down jacket, gloves and a hat. It'll be winter soon. You'll get sick if you don't.'

Nicolaus looks at her gratefully. 'You're far too kind, far too considerate. I don't deserve it. I wish I could help you. I know there's a solution but I . . . can't remember . . .' His brow furrows. 'It's like a moth fluttering at the very edge of my vision. All I catch is a glimpse of its flapping gray wings.'

He sighs and turns to Minoo. 'I can't allow you all to walk straight into the lion's den,' he says.

'We have no choice. The lion has spoken to our parents.'

'You could . . . skip school. Isn't that what you call it?'

'We can't skip school forever. Besides, she can hardly have planned to kill us if she wants to meet us in her office during the day when the school is full of people.'

'Maybe that's what she wants you to think.'

CHAPTER 27

'Please come in,' the principal says.

Adriana Lopez is wearing a dark green, knee-length Sixties-style dress with black pumps in some kind of reptile skin.

She sits down in the armchair next to the little coffee table. Two folding chairs have been brought out. Minoo sits on the sofa, between Vanessa and Anna-Karin. Ida and Linnéa take the chairs. Once they're seated, silence settles over them.

There is a clock hanging above the door to the assistant principal's office. It ticks the seconds loudly, one by one. It reminds Minoo of a time bomb. At any moment the world may explode.

'I know you were in my house,' the principal says.

Minoo feels the blood drain from her face.

'Did you find what you were looking for?' she continues.

Ida gets up so suddenly that she knocks her chair over backward. 'I've got nothing to do with this,' she says.

The room is deathly quiet. Nothing but *tick, tock, tick, tock.*

'I've got nothing to do with *them,*' Ida continues, her voice cracking with desperation.

'Sit down,' the principal says.

Her voice is the exact opposite of Ida's: controlled, confident, impossible to disobey. Ida picks up the plastic chair and sits down obediently.

Lopez crosses one leg over the other and clasps her hands over her upper knee. 'I know who you are,' she says.

'And we know who you are,' Linnéa retorts.

Minoo holds her breath.

The principal's eyes bore into Linnéa. A little smile tugs at the corners of her mouth. 'Excuse me?'

'I said that we know. Who. You. Are,' Linnéa says, meeting her gaze without blinking.

The principal laughs. Not a real laugh, but the indulgent kind that grown-ups produce when they don't take you seriously.

'Do you now? This should be interesting. Tell me, Linnéa. Who am I?'

Minoo wants to stop everything. Strike the set and start again. It's a bad mistake to attack Lopez.

'You're the one who killed Elias and Rebecka,' says Linnéa.

And now there's no going back. It's too late to retract anything. Exactly three seconds pass. *Tick, tock, tick.*

'That's not true.'

'You're lying,' Linnéa says coldly.

'I just want to make it clear that I've got *nothing* to do with them,' Ida says.

The principal ignores her.

'But you're right about Elias and Rebecka not having committed suicide,' she says.

It takes a while for her words to sink in.

'If we were to believe you didn't kill them, do you know who did?' Anna-Karin asks.

'Excuse me,' Linnéa interrupts, 'but I think you're accepting this a little too easily. Have you forgotten that we found torture instruments at her house?'

'I collect medieval artifacts,' the principal says calmly. 'Tragically, instruments of torture fall into that category. It may be a rather macabre hobby, but it doesn't make me a murderer.'

'You were the last person Elias and Rebecka saw before they died,' Linnéa says.

'And I'm about to tell you why I saw them,' the principal says, and turns to Anna-Karin. 'But to answer your question, Anna-Karin, no, I don't know who killed them. My primary mission was to find you.'

'What do you mean "mission"?' Vanessa asks.

The principal smoothes an invisible crease in her dress. Her face is expressionless. Minoo gets the feeling it's a mask she could remove at any moment.

'I work for the Council. My task was to come here and investigate the level of truth in the prophecy regarding this place.'

'A prophecy? About Engelsfors?' Minoo asks.

'Engelsfors is a very special place,' the principal says. 'It's close to other . . . I suppose you might call them dimensions. We don't know why, but the boundary separating the different realities is thinner here. The prophecy speaks of a Chosen One, who will be woken to protect the world when an unearthly evil tries to break through that boundary into our reality. I was sent here to find the Chosen One. My search was made more difficult because there are so many of you. I was looking for one person. I had just picked up Elias's trail when he passed away.'

'Elias didn't "pass away". He was *murdered*,' Linnéa says.

'Yes,' the principal agrees.

'Why didn't you protect him if you knew it was him?' Linnéa asks.

'Firstly, the Council investigates on average 764.2 prophecies each year, all over the world. Only about 1.7 percent of them come true. I wasn't sure if this particular prophecy had any basis in reality. In fact, the statistics spoke against it. And I didn't have time to confirm whether or not Elias was in fact the witch I was looking for.'

Vanessa turns her head so fast her ponytail whisks across Minoo's face, leaving behind it a faint scent of coconut.

'Wait, wait, wait,' Vanessa says. 'Did you say *witch*?'

The principal nods impatiently.

'Is that . . . what we are?' Anna-Karin asks.

'I'm afraid it's a term that carries with it some unfortunate baggage. It has come to be falsely associated with all sorts of crazy nonsense. But, yes, you are witches. As am I. Some are born with special powers, which usually become apparent during puberty, but most people can learn at least some simple magic through diligent study.'

Magic. Minoo gets goose bumps up her arms when she

hears the word. Of course there's a word for everything that has happened. It's a word she's read a thousand times in fairy tales and fantasy stories, yet it sounds new and unfamiliar when the principal utters it. Frightening, yet enticing. The fantastical is possible.

'As Linnéa quite correctly pointed out, I had a meeting with Elias just before he was murdered,' the principal continues. 'The purpose of that meeting was to find out whether he was the Chosen One. I could have waited for the blood moon to appear, but I already had certain indications. Anyway, I took a strand of his hair and sent it to our laboratories. The following morning I received the test results, which confirmed my suspicions, but by then it was already too late. I thought it was all over. As I said, I was sure I was just looking for one person. But during Elias's memorial service, I noticed magical activity in the auditorium. That was when I realized there could be more of you.'

'But how did you know it was us?' Minoo asks.

There is a second part to Minoo's question that she doesn't dare voice. If the principal could find them, does that mean the evil that is after them can, too?

'Some of you have been less discreet than others,' says Lopez, looking at Anna-Karin, who squirms uncomfortably on the sofa next to Minoo. 'Let me take this opportunity to inform you that there are laws that must be obeyed even where magic is concerned.'

'Laws?' Anna-Karin asks weakly.

'Three simple rules. You may not practice magic without

the Council's express permission. You may not use magic to break non-magical laws. And you may not reveal yourselves as witches to the non-magic public.' She turns to Anna-Karin again. 'The Council might turn a blind eye to any transgressions you may have committed up until now because you didn't know the rules. But I advise you to refrain immediately from practicing any magic at school.'

'What is the Council, and why should we submit to it?' Linnéa asks.

'For the same reason that you submitted to society's laws before your powers were awoken,' the principal says. 'You are part of the magical society, and in that society the Council enacts the laws and governs. We should all be thankful for that.'

Linnéa snorts.

The principal ignores her and continues: 'But getting back to how I discovered you. Part of the prophecy refers to purely calendrical events, among other things that the Chosen One would be woken on a night with a blood moon. Most people can't see the blood moon – I myself can't see it with the naked eye – but it follows a particular cycle and there were signs I could interpret. I sent out my familiar—'

'Your what?' Vanessa interrupts.

'Through a complex process, a witch can create a connection with an animal. Most often it's a cat, a dog, a frog or a bird. I chose a raven. Or, rather, it chose me. Simply put, we share a part of each other's consciousness. My familiar can act as my eyes or ears when my own aren't up to the task. I sent him out and he saw you gather by Kärrgruvan. I reported it to the Council, which ordered me to arrange meetings with you, one at a time. I started with Rebecka. I sent a strand of her hair for analysis to be a hundred percent sure she really was Chosen. Unfortunately she passed away, too, before I received the answer.'

'She was murdered!' Linnéa shouts. She has stood up. She's so worked up that she's shaking. 'They were murdered! They were murdered and you couldn't stop it! You could at least have warned them!'

'After Rebecka's death, I got in touch with the Council for permission to take action, not just to observe. My request set off an intense debate –'

'We could have died, too!' Linnéa cuts in.

'– but after your break-in, the process was speeded up. Now we can draw up a mutual action plan,' says the principal.

'*A mutual action plan?* That's what the idiots at Social Services always call it,' says Linnéa. 'Only their idea of "mutual" is that they make the decisions and we do as they say. Isn't that what you had in mind, too?'

'That attitude will get us nowhere,' the principal answers.

'Go to hell!' Linnéa shouts. Everyone except the principal jumps. 'We don't need you! We never asked for your help!'

The principal looks at Linnéa coldly. Then she stands up, walks to the door, heels clicking, and pulls it wide open. Nicolaus almost falls into the room. 'You may as well come in,' she says frostily.

'I . . .' Nicolaus seeks out Minoo's gaze.

'She's not the murderer,' Minoo says quietly. 'At least, it doesn't look like it.'

Nicolaus takes a few steps into the room. The principal shuts the door behind him and returns to her seat. Nicolaus looks a bit lost standing there. His eyes wander to Anna-Karin. 'Is it true?' he asks. 'Is she . . .'

'She's a witch,' Anna-Karin says. 'We all are.'

'Witches,' Nicolaus mumbles. 'Of course. Witches.'

'So, you claim to be the girls' guide?' the principal says, crossing her legs again.

'That is my sacred duty, yes.'

'That's strange,' the principal muses. 'The prophecy says nothing about a guide. You're an interesting phenomenon that we must examine more closely. But for now I have to ask you to keep away from the girls. From now on I am their guide and teacher.'

'No,' Nicolaus protests feebly. 'No, I can't allow that . . .'

'By order of the Council I release you from your duty. You are welcome to offer any suggestions or information but, from now on, everything must go through me.'

Minoo can see that Nicolaus is struggling to understand. 'But this isn't an assignment,' he manages. 'It's my *calling*.'

'You care about the girls, don't you?' the principal says, with forced composure. 'You want what's best for them?'

'Of course.'

'We have knowledge and resources, Nicolaus. What can you offer?'

Nicolaus lowers his gaze. 'Nothing,' he mumbles. 'Except my life.'

Minoo's heart almost breaks.

'I apologize.' He gives a shallow bow and disappears into the hallway with his head lowered.

'Nicolaus!' Anna-Karin shouts. 'Wait!'

The door slams shut. Minoo looks at the principal, who is completely placid. It seems to be all in a day's work for her.

'You must begin your training at once. We'll determine exactly what powers you possess and how we can best make use of them.'

'Make use of them?' Linnéa says.

'In the coming battle,' the principal responds. 'Alongside your training, the Council will intensify its research into the prophecy and do everything it can to find whoever is guilty of murdering Rebecka and Elias.' She peers intently at them, one by one. 'And you mustn't, under any circumstances, experiment with your powers on your own.'

Ida stands up again. This time the chair remains upright. 'I can't take this any more! You can't force me to take part. I won't!'

The principal looks at her without batting an eyelid. 'Are you sure?'

'Yes!'

'Then you'll get an F in every subject.'

'You can't do that!' Ida bursts out.

'I'm the principal of this school. And I'm a witch. What do you think?' Adriana Lopez peers unflinchingly at Ida, who sits back down. Then she turns back to the group. 'That's enough for today. I realize it's a lot for you to take in. Before you leave I must ask you each to leave behind a strand of your hair in the pre-printed envelopes, and fill in this form about which magical powers you have developed. We'll meet at nine o'clock on Saturday morning in the fairground.'

CHAPTER 28

Vanessa is drumming her nails on the worn tabletop at Café Monique.

Click-click-click-click. Click-click-click-click. Click-click-click-click.

An elderly couple looks at her with irritation. Vanessa glares at them.

Click-click-click-click. Click-click-click-click. Click-click-click-click.

They dig into their pastries. God, she hates the idea of getting old. But the alternative is worse. Not getting old. Vanessa's fingers stop. She empties another packet of sugar into her coffee. She'd had a part-time job here until last summer when Monika said she couldn't afford to keep her on. But she still treats her to free coffee.

A glass cabinet contains piles of several-year-old gossip magazines. Perched on top of the cabinet are dusty bouquets of dried flowers. And then of course there's Monika, with her pert dresses and perpetual frown. She's not very nice, but Vanessa respects her because she struggles on with her café in a town where most people feel they can drink coffee at home.

Vanessa takes a sip. The coffee is lukewarm. She hears the bell tinkle and a chilly gust of wind blows through the café. Linnéa walks in and sits down opposite her.

'Hi,' Vanessa says.

Linnéa doesn't answer. She smells of fresh air, and Vanessa realizes it's probably stuffy in there.

'Do you want anything?' Vanessa asks.

'No.'

Linnéa's black eyes flare, and a series of unwelcome images pops into Vanessa's head: Linnéa's naked skin, Jonte's hand groping her breast.

'Well?' Linnéa says. 'What did you want?'

Vanessa had prepared herself for this meeting, tried out different things to say until she had composed a whole speech in her defense. It's not her style and now she understands why. When the time comes to deliver it, her mind is blank. 'Sorry,' she says.

'For what?'

'You know.'

'I want to hear you say it.'

Vanessa is so embarrassed she wants to run away.

'I just wanted to be sure that you and Wille weren't . . .'

'And that's why you followed Jonte into my apartment? Or were you there already?'

'No. I waited outside. I don't know why I followed him in.'

Linnéa leans back in her chair and folds her arms. 'Okay,' she says finally. 'I can understand it might have been tempting. But if you spy on me like that again, I'll kill you.'

Vanessa nods. She'll never put herself through something like that again.

They look at each other for a moment. The windows behind Linnéa are fogged up. Vanessa twists her silver ring a few times. Linnéa says nothing, just stares at the ring.

Vanessa wonders if she understands. 'Wille and I are engaged.'

'Congratulations. Really,' Linnéa says.

Vanessa gets angry. 'Why the hell are you sleeping with Jonte?'

'What?'

'I just don't understand it. Seriously. He's so old. And you're so pretty.'

'Thanks . . . I think,' Linnéa says. She grins widely.

Vanessa can't help smiling, too. 'You know what I mean,' she says.

'It's hard to explain the thing with Jonte. Or maybe it's too obvious.' She leans forward across the table. Vanessa does the same. 'When I was eleven I got drunk the first time,' Linnéa says, 'Jonte sold me the booze. When I was thirteen, I started getting stoned. By then he was selling weed. When I moved on to harder stuff, he sold me that, too.'

Vanessa has heard much worse rumors about Linnéa, but she's surprised that she's talking so openly about it.

'Then I stopped. But Elias . . . couldn't stop. I got Jonte and Wille to promise not to sell to him any more. Then I found out they'd broken their promise just before . . . Elias died.'

'I know,' Vanessa says quietly. She'll never forget that afternoon. *Did you hear about the priest's kid? . . . He probably wanted to be completely out of his skull when he did it.*

'That first night at the fairground,' Linnéa says, 'I'd been over at Jonte's place to give him a piece of my mind. But I never got the chance.' She shakes her head. Her eyes are glistening, but she grits her teeth. She won't show more than she has to. Vanessa knows how that feels. No one takes a crying girl seriously.

'I was so lonely after Elias died,' Linnéa says quietly. She blinks away her tears. 'I'm so fucking disgusting.'

'No, you're not.'

'You don't know anything about me,' Linnéa says harshly. 'And you don't know anything about Wille either. He calls me sometimes, wanting me back. I'm sorry I lied to you before. I didn't want to hurt you, but now that I've seen that ring . . . You can't trust him.'

For once Vanessa is dumbstruck. She feels empty, now that it's been confirmed.

'I don't want him,' Linnéa says, softer now. 'Just so you know. And I don't think he wants me either, really. He just wants to know he's got a chance. For his ego's sake.'

'Maybe that's how it was before, but he's changed. He loves me,' Vanessa says.

'You deserve someone better.'

'So do you.'

They look at each other, and Vanessa thinks she ought to feel depressed. What Linnéa has said should have laid waste to everything. Instead she feels relieved in some strange way. And, as so often where Linnéa's concerned, she has no idea why she feels the way she does.

Anna-Karin stares intently at her math notebook in which she's solving problems on Pythagoras's theorem. Grandpa is sitting on the other side of the living room, browsing through the newspaper. Now and then he glances at the kitchen. A frenetic rattling, clattering and pounding is coming from it. 'What's she doing?' he says.

'She was going to boil the silver,' Anna-Karin says, 'to sterilize it.'

Grandpa folds the newspaper neatly and lays it on the little table by the armchair. 'I know I should be happy that she has all this new energy,' says Grandpa.

Anna-Karin pretends to be absorbed in the relationship between the hypotenuse and the opposite side.

'It's just so odd,' Grandpa continues. 'Before she barely had any energy at all. Now you can't get her to stop.' He sighs and takes off his reading glasses. 'But there's no point in complaining,' he says. 'It's like in winter we go around complaining that it's cold, wet and dark, but when summer comes we complain that it's too hot.'

Now you can't get her to stop. Anna-Karin could get her to stop. As soon as she's got Jari she'll stop everything. What the principal had said about the Council had made up her mind for her.

If only her mother didn't look so healthy. There's strength in her footsteps. She laughs, and is filled with energy. Wouldn't she like to be that person rather than the woman who lay glued to the sofa every night, chain-smoking? Anna-Karin doesn't want to go back to being the person she was a few months ago.

'Was this what Mom was like before Daddy left?' Anna-Karin asks.

'What do you mean?'

'That maybe she's finally happy again. And that this is the person she was before Daddy . . . ruined everything.'

Grandpa gets up slowly from his armchair. He comes over to the sofa on which Anna-Karin is half lying. She pulls her legs underneath her to make room for him.

'I sometimes forget that you don't remember how things were before,' he says, and pats Anna-Karin's knee. Then he looks at her, a little too probingly. 'I've never seen Mia like this before. Not even when Staffan was still around.'

For a moment she considers forcing him to tell her more about her father. It would be so easy, in the same way that it was easy to make Ida tell the truth about her Elias speech. But Anna-Karin feels sick just thinking about it. She could never, ever do that to Grandpa. 'I don't even remember what Daddy looked like,' she says. She's seen photographs of him, of course. She's looked at some so often that she feels as if she can remember the moment they were taken, but she knows that's just her imagination. Beyond the frame of the photo, there's nothing. She can't see her father's face move, can't hear his voice.

'I just don't understand how someone can simply up and leave their family, like he did,' she says.

Grandpa opens his mouth to answer, but her mother breaks into song in the kitchen.

Anna-Karin and Grandpa look at each other.

It's as if her mother has heard them talking and wants to reassure them that everything is wonderful, just wonderful. She pronounces each word with exaggerated crispness, singing in a loud, chirpy and somehow far too young voice.

Suddenly the kitchen is silent. No singing. No clattering.

A scream cuts through the air. It's shrill and full of pain, and reminds Anna-Karin of something she's heard before.

Grandpa leaps up from the sofa, but she sits there petrified. That scream. When Anna-Karin was little they'd had pigs on the farm. When they were going to be slaughtered . . .

Grandpa flings open the kitchen door and Anna-Karin finally jolts out of her paralysis. She runs after him.

Her mother is standing at the stove, and turns to them with a smile. She's wiping her hands frantically on her apron.

'What, in God's name . . . ?' Grandpa says.

'Bah! I've been a clumsy fool,' her mother says cheerfully. She holds out her hands. The skin is a deep dark red, almost purple. Her fingers are so swollen that her rings are digging into her flesh. 'I was just trying to take the silver out of the boiling water,' she says, with an embarrassed laugh.

Grandpa's frailty has disappeared. He grabs his daughter's hands and shoves them under the tap to run ice-cold water over them. Anna-Karin looks at the pot on the stove and only now becomes aware of the bubbling sound coming from it. The steam.

I'm going to stop, she thinks. I'm going to stop it. Soon. I swear.

But, deep down, she doesn't know if she can.

Part 3

CHAPTER 29

Minoo is walking briskly along the dirt path toward Kärrgruvan. There is a layer of frost on the ground and the air smells of snow. She's wearing overalls, a down jacket, hat and mittens, and feels like a Sumo wrestler.

She normally sleeps until at least ten, sometimes twelve, on weekends. This morning she came down to breakfast at seven thirty. Her mother was at the kitchen table with her life-giving cup of coffee, and a magazine that was incomprehensible to anyone who didn't know at least ten thousand Latin terms. She'd raised her eyebrows when she saw Minoo. 'Is your clock not working properly?' she asked, and turned the page.

'I'm trying to develop some better habits,' Minoo answered, and almost puked at how chirpy she sounded.

'Minoo. You don't always have to work so—'

'We're rehearsing a play today,' Minoo said, to put a stop to the lecture.

'God, I'd do anything for some culture up here,' her mother said, pushing away the magazine. 'Which play is it?'

Minoo wanted to turn the clock back. Idiot, she thought. *Romeo and Juliet.* It's for English.'

'You're putting on *Romeo and Juliet*?'

'Just a few scenes.'

'But, still, Shakespeare in tenth grade English. Ambitious teacher. What part are you playing?'

'We haven't decided yet. Probably a tree.'

'You'll make a wonderful tree.' Her mother smiled.

She got up and gave Minoo a quick hug. 'Break a leg sweetie.'

As soon as her mother had left the kitchen, Minoo went to the coffee machine and filled a Thermos mug with coffee and milk.

Now she's sipping it but the caffeine isn't kicking in. When she reaches the fairground she's so tired she could lie down on the dance floor and go to sleep. And maybe she would have, if Linnéa hadn't already been there. She looks even more tired than Minoo, sitting on the stage, writing in her diary. She's wearing a dark blue down jacket that is several sizes too big and a far cry from her usual style.

Minoo walks up the steps into the pavilion. Linnéa doesn't look up.

'Hi,' Minoo says.

'Hi.' Linnéa carries on writing.

Minoo drinks her coffee, forcing herself not to start babbling. Instead she leans quietly against the railing.

Not that it's ever quiet inside Minoo's head: to-do lists, obligations, possible and impossible scenarios play out constantly. And there's always a stupid remark she made or some embarrassing thing she did to obsess about. Sometimes she contemplates embarrassing things she did a hundred years ago and is overwhelmed by shame. Like when she and her cousin Shirin were pretending that their Barbie and Ken dolls were having sex and Aunt Bahar came in. Shirin had said immediately it had been Minoo's idea. Which it had. Bahar had laughed, but Minoo still wants to crawl under a stone every time she thinks of it.

Linnéa giggles suddenly.

'What is it?' Minoo asks.

'You looked funny, that's all.'

Minoo smiles hesitantly.

'Is that coffee?' Linnéa asks.

'Do you want a sip?' She walks over to Linnéa, who takes the mug and gulps. 'Oops. I think I took the last of it,' she says, smiling weakly.

'That's okay,' Minoo answers.

Linnéa stuffs her notepad in one of her oversized jacket's pockets. 'This group's starting to have a few too many people I hate. I don't know how I'll be able to listen to that woman without strangling her.'

Minoo doesn't know how to respond.

The days after the meeting in the principal's office have in some ways been the nicest for a long time. Finally they have someone to show them the way. She hasn't had to brood over demons, and instead has been able to focus on doing her homework and pining for Max.

Minoo knows that Linnéa thinks the principal let Elias and Rebecka die, but she herself is not so sure. There must be reasons they don't know about. She can't believe that anyone would let two people die without intervening just because some rules have to be followed.

She wants to give the principal a chance. There is no alternative and she's longing for knowledge. And she's hoping that the principal will discover that Minoo, too, has a power.

'Do you think you have a power you don't know about?' she asks Linnéa.

Linnéa meets her gaze. 'Why? Do you?'

'No. But I was thinking that since everyone else seems to . . . Have you felt anything?'

Linnéa's eyes wander to the fairground entrance where Vanessa is arriving. She's wearing a jacket that's far too light, as if she doesn't want to accept that winter's set in. Vanessa probably thinks the seasons ought to adapt to her, not the other way around. Minoo smiles to herself.

'Christ, I've got such a hangover.' Vanessa groans, as she trudges onto the stage. When she catches sight of the Thermos mug, her eyes glint. 'Is that coffee?'

'It's empty,' Linnéa says.

Vanessa rolls her eyes. 'Christ, what a wonderful fucking morning,' she says, and sinks down next to Linnéa.

Minoo notices how close to each other they're sitting. Perhaps they're becoming friends.

'Where's Her Witchiness?' Vanessa sticks a piece of gum into her mouth. 'I thought she'd be waiting here, whip in hand.'

Linnéa giggles. She and Vanessa start talking about friends they have in common. Soon they're completely absorbed in their conversation. It's not that they're shutting Minoo out, but they do nothing to include her. As usual she doesn't know how to break in without sounding either like a precocious know-it-all, or an annoying younger sister.

Minoo sits on the dance floor and pulls out her biology book. She pretends to read, but all she can think is how much she misses Rebecka.

The bus shelter is built of red-painted corrugated iron. Someone had come up with the idea of painting small windows on it with a view of a garden. Later the word SLUT had appeared in black marker across the flowers. Anna-Karin has always felt it was directed at her.

Only two buses run past here on Saturdays, but the principal said she could pick her up. She hadn't dared to refuse. The principal scares the shit out of her. She worries that Adriana Lopez will divine at a glance what she's done to her mother.

She hasn't slept a wink all night. As soon as she closed her eyes she saw the pot of boiling water and her mother's hands. She certainly hadn't meant her to get hurt. Of course not.

Most frightening of all, she's not sure how her power influences her mother. In the beginning she used it so intensively that she lost control of it. It started to work on its own, like a snowball sent rolling down a slope. It's the same with Julia, Felicia and the others at school, except Jari. She still has to use it actively on him.

An expensive-looking dark blue car is driving toward her.

The principal is sitting behind the wheel. Anna-Karin's insides twist, as if someone had grabbed them with a pair of pliers.

Pull yourself together, Anna-Karin.

The car pulls up to the curb. Anna-Karin gets up and opens the passenger door.

'Hello,' the principal says, with a cool smile. 'Sorry I'm late.'

'That's okay,' Anna-Karin mumbles, and gets in.

'I need to talk to you,' the principal says, as she accelerates.

The pliers twist again. Anna-Karin can't look at the principal so she stares out through the windshield, at the gray sky, the black trees and the white road markers rushing past.

'You are abusing your powers,' the principal says, 'as you're well aware.'

'I haven't—'

'It's not a question. It's a fact. There may be extenuating circumstances, since there was no one to guide you, but rules are rules. It's my job to inform you that the Council has launched an investigation.'

'An investigation?'

'You're committing a crime, Anna-Karin.'

Anna-Karin turns to her. She's sitting there with her perfect profile, in her perfect winter coat, in her perfect car. She's judging Anna-Karin.

'You don't understand anything, you and that Council.'

The principal lets out a long sigh. They drive in silence as they approach Engelsfors's most exclusive area. The principal parks the car outside a big green house. 'You haven't been found guilty yet, but you have to stop immediately.'

'I'll do as I please.' Part of Anna-Karin is fascinated by how rude she can be to someone who terrifies her.

The principal looks probingly at her. 'Anna-Karin,' she says. 'Answer me honestly. Do you think you can stop?'

'Of course. But I'm doing nothing wrong,' she says stubbornly.

The principal scoffs. 'We'll talk more about this later,' she says. 'Here's Ida.'

Anna-Karin sees a blonde figure hurrying toward them. She hunches in her seat and stares at her hands. She's not going to let Ida see how frightened she is.

CHAPTER 30

At nine thirty they hear a car approaching, the gravel crunching under its tires. Minoo puts away her biology book and gets up as a dark blue Mercedes pulls into the fairground.

As soon as the car stops, Anna-Karin climbs out and marches angrily toward the dance pavilion. She stands at a distance from the others, arms folded.

'Hi,' Minoo says, but Anna-Karin just stares at the floor.

'Good morning,' says the principal, who is walking toward them with Ida in tow.

Ida is clenching her teeth, so hard that Minoo wonders if she can still open her mouth at will.

'Must have been a pleasant drive,' Linnéa says.

Vanessa giggles, but Minoo is irritated. Can't they take this seriously?

Adriana Lopez walks to the middle of the dance floor, her ankle-length winter coat sweeping around her feet. She's wearing leather gloves and an elegant fur hat. Minoo thinks admiringly that she looks like a character in some nineteenth-century Russian novel. She's holding a black leather bag that she sets down beside her.

'I'm sorry I'm late,' she says. Then she says to Ida, who has stopped on the steps leading up to the dance floor, 'Step inside the circle.'

Minoo wonders what circle the principal is talking about. When she works it out, she's annoyed at her own stupidity. The round dance floor is itself a circle.

Ida walks onto it with evident reluctance.

'Let's turn up the heat, shall we?' the principal says. She glances at Vanessa and Linnéa. 'I suggest you get off the stage.'

Linnéa and Vanessa get up slowly. Minoo decides they're just as curious as she is, even if they're trying to hide it.

The principal takes a little black cylinder, like a tube of lipstick, from her pocket and pulls off the top. When she draws a circle in the middle of the dance floor, Minoo recalls the symbols in her house. She tries to make eye contact with Vanessa, but she's watching the principal.

Intensely focused, Adriana Lopez draws a symbol in the center of the circle. When she straightens up she removes a few sticky white threads from the marker and puts the top back on.

'What's that?' Vanessa asks.

'Ectoplasm,' the principal answers curtly.

Minoo wonders if that means any more to the others than it does to her.

The principal takes out a book. It has a worn black leather cover and is the size of an ordinary paperback. She opens it and fishes out a shiny object she has hidden beneath her coat. It looks like a silver loupe and is attached to a long chain that she wears around her neck. She twists the loupe's eyepiece, as you might adjust the focus on a pair of binoculars, and puts it to her eye.

Minoo is waiting for her to start incanting a spell, but she mumbles quietly to herself. At once a flame erupts inside the circle.

It's no ordinary flame, shimmering in varying shades of blue from cobalt at the bottom to light sky blue. It takes Minoo a moment to grasp what makes the flame so eerie. It's not that it's blue, and is burning a few inches above the ground, but that it's completely silent. After a few seconds she feels her face warming up.

The principal takes off her coat, hat and gloves and lays everything in a neat pile on the floor next to the railing. Underneath she has on a well-tailored dark gray suit.

Minoo also removes her outer garments and lays them on the floor. Now she notices that the air around the pavilion is glimmering. She cautiously reaches out her hand and meets a slight resistance, as if she's touched an invisible membrane.

'Try,' the principal says.

Minoo turns. The principal nods at her encouragingly. Minoo reaches further – and breaks through the membrane. On the other side the air is cold.

'An outer circle,' the principal says, and makes a sweeping gesture around the circular dance floor, then she points toward the smaller circle where the flame is burning. 'And an inner one. The outer circle binds. The inner circle holds the power source.'

'What *is* the power source?' Vanessa asks.

'The symbol in the inner circle.'

'But what kind of symbol is it?'

'We'll take it one step at a time. And you must trust me.'

'Of course,' Linnéa says sarcastically. 'We'll just get murdered in the meantime.'

'I've already explained the situation to you. And there's another issue that the Council has asked me to clarify.'

Minoo pulls out her notebook and the pen she always has with her. Yes, she's a true nerd.

'According to the prophecy, the Chosen One is supposed to be impossible for evil to trace, at least until the great battle is upon us. And that won't be for several years. We thought you had some kind of magical protection, that you were immune to evil.'

'You said the great battle won't come for several years,' Minoo says, taking notes. 'How many?'

'It's unclear. At least two, but probably closer to ten, according to our calculations.'

'So we could be facing Armageddon when we're leaving school. Not much of an incentive to get good grades,' Linnéa says.

'This has nothing to do with the Biblical apocalypse,' the principal says dryly.

'Can you tell us what we're going to be fighting in this battle? Isn't it about time we heard this prophecy?' Vanessa urges.

'It's not that simple.'

'Why did you bring us here if you're not going to answer any questions?' Linnéa asks.

'That's enough.' The principal raises her hand. 'Perhaps Nicolaus let you push him about, but you won't get anywhere if you try it with me. I'm here to teach you to master and develop your powers, but you're behaving like children. I can't teach the fundamentals of magic to children.'

No one says anything.

'Your powers are a wonderful gift,' the principal continues, 'but they can also be very dangerous to yourselves and to others. Your abilities are in their infancy, but as they develop, you'll find it harder to control them.'

She turns to Vanessa. 'One day you'll make yourself invisible and discover you can't reverse the process. You might be forced to spend the rest of your life as a shadow.'

Abruptly Vanessa stops chewing her gum.

That must be the worst nightmare for someone who's so much in love with her own reflection, Minoo thinks.

'The same goes for the rest of you,' the principal says. She lets her gaze linger on Anna-Karin, before she moves on to Ida, Minoo and Linnéa. 'Even those of you who have not yet developed any powers.'

Perhaps Minoo should feel frightened, but that 'yet' has made her happy. Perhaps she has a power after all. The principal seems to think so.

'There has always been a certain amount of magic in the world. And the barriers separating our world from others has varied in strength over time.'

'What "other worlds"?' Vanessa interrupts.

'Our world isn't the only one. There are countless others. Don't interrupt me again,' the principal says sternly. 'During the last few centuries we've lived through a magical drought with occasional local flare-ups. One such flare-up took place here about three hundred years ago. Your dreams might be channeling what happened then.'

'How do you know what we've been dreaming?' Vanessa asks.

'My raven saw and heard everything that was said on the night of your awakening. It's the opinion of the Council and myself that the one who spoke through Ida that night was the Chosen One from the 1600s.'

'Who was she?' Minoo asks. 'And what happened to her?'

'We don't know. The church and parsonage burned down in 1675, and a great many important documents were lost.' The principal regards them gravely. 'If I compared the last two thousand years to a magical drought, then what's coming is more like a flood. Individuals with powers like yours have been incredibly rare, but now they're appearing in a number of places across the world. The battle that is coming may affect our entire reality.'

'That's why Nicolaus spoke of our destiny,' Anna-Karin says.

Adriana purses her lips. 'I'd prefer to call it your task,' she says.

'So you mean that the fate of the world will be decided in Engelsfors?' Vanessa asks.

'I know it's hard to imagine,' the principal says, with a hint of a smile, 'but that may well be so. This place has a high level of magical activity, which will continue to grow.'

Minoo listens, fascinated. 'So magic doesn't exist everywhere?'

'No.' The principal looks at Minoo approvingly, as if she thought it was a good question. 'We believe that the energy will eventually spread over ever larger areas, but just now we're looking at local phenomena.'

Vanessa says thoughtfully. 'Does that mean our powers won't work everywhere? For instance, if I went to Ibiza on vacation, could I become invisible there?'

'Ibiza, as it happens, has a very high level of magical activity,' the principal answers, 'but you've understood correctly. The power doesn't just come from within you. You have to be hooked up, as it were, to a power source. And that's here. You need Engelsfors, just as you need each other, and Engelsfors needs you. We still don't know why there were . . . seven of you. But together you form a circle. Witches have worked in circles throughout the ages. You won't get anything important done if you don't learn to work together.'

She's wrong to reduce it to a 'task', Minoo thinks. 'Destiny' is a much better word.

Rebecka had understood that. This is much bigger than they are and they are destined to carry it out. But in any case they are tied to Engelsfors. And to each other.

'Any more questions?' the principal asks.

Part Three

Everyone remains quiet.

She smiles, satisfied. 'Right,' she says. 'Let's talk about magic. Theory and practice.'

CHAPTER 31

'Forget everything you think you know about magic and the supernatural,' says Miss Lopez. 'I guarantee it's wrong. We make sure of that.'

'How?' Linnéa asks.

'Among other things, the Council has a special department that goes through whatever information is on the Internet. There may be kernels of truth in what you find there. Some magical facts are hidden in folklore and traditions, but they're so inextricably intertwined with nonsense that it's virtually impossible to distinguish one from the other. We remove anything that gets too close to the truth, and leave all the misleading junk. The lunatics and amateurs actually do us a big favor.'

'So you're engaged in censorship as well?' Linnéa says contemptuously.

'We're entering a new magical age so we have to be in control of whatever knowledge there is. You can't imagine what damage it could cause if it were to fall into the wrong hands.'

But Linnéa won't back down. 'And who decides whether

it's in the wrong hands? You and the Council? Who keeps an eye on *you*?'

The principal smiles mirthlessly. '*Quis custodiet ipsos custodes*? "Who protects us from our protectors?" The ancient philosophers asked that question, and I'm not going to discuss it right now.'

Minoo looks pleadingly at Linnéa and gets a grimace in return. She longs for order, not more chaos.

The principal opens her bag. She hands out five identical black books and silver loupes. Minoo weighs her book in her hand. It's incredibly heavy for something so small. She examines the loupe. It's segmented into eight parts of which six are very thin, ribbed and adjustable.

'This is the *Book of Patterns*,' the principal says. 'And this' – she holds up a loupe – 'is one of two tools at your disposal for interpreting it. This is the other,' she says, and taps her temple.

Vanessa groans.

'Open your books,' the principal says.

Minoo opens hers. Six symbols are lined up on the first page.

She turns it. Then another and yet another.

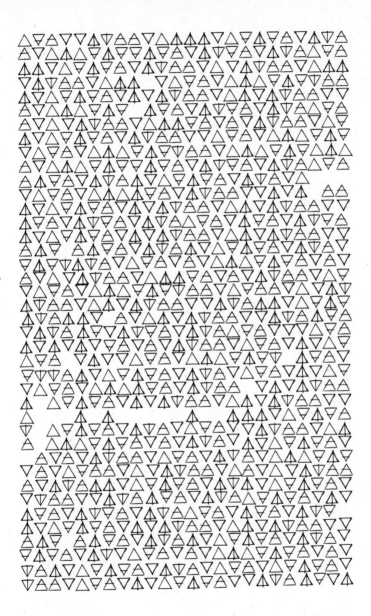

The Circle

294

'I don't see any patterns,' Ida says. It's the first thing she's said all morning.

Minoo doesn't say so, but she agrees with Ida. The pages are covered with incomprehensible symbols of various sizes. Some may look as if they're in some kind of order, but others are scattered everywhere. Some pages are blank. It looks like the most difficult IQ test ever, and Minoo is stumped.

'Six symbols,' the principal says, 'arranged in magical constellations. You can only learn what they mean through deep and sustained reflection and with the help of this.'

She holds up the loupe again. 'The Pattern Finder.'

'What's in this book anyway?' Anna-Karin asks.

'That depends on who's looking,' the principal responds. 'No two witches see the same thing. The *Book of Patterns* acts as transmitter and receiver. The witch reading it has to know what she's looking for. Then the book will show her what she needs. It's like tuning into the right frequency on an old-fashioned radio.'

'And the thing you use to tune in with is . . . that?' Ida asks.

'Yes. But it's useless if your senses aren't focused on the search.' The principal's eyes are dreamy. 'The book often knows what we need better than we do. It's as if it can see right into our souls.'

'Cheesy,' Vanessa says in a sing-song voice.

The principal glares at Vanessa. 'On the contrary,' she says. 'This book contains all the knowledge that a witch will ever need. What you see depends in part on how well developed your powers are, and in part on what symbol you belong to. It contains magic formulas and rites, prophecies and tales from the past.'

'Does that mean our prophecy looks like this?' Linnéa says, and points at a page on which the symbols look as if a tornado has passed through the book.

Adriana Lopez nods. 'That's why it's not easy just to read out the prophecy to you. When the time is right, you'll be able to see it, but you won't all see it in the same way.'

'Then how do *you* know what's in it?' Minoo asks. 'If everyone sees different things, I mean.'

'Generations of witches have read the prophecy and written down exactly what they've seen. The texts overlap at a number of points. It's a question of pure statistics.'

'So the majority is always right?' Linnéa asks.

'I see you're the philosopher here,' the principal answers mordantly.

Minoo sees Linnéa's eyes darken and realizes she must intervene. 'What was it you said about the symbols before?'

Adriana holds up the books.

'There are six different symbols in this book, arranged in different constellations. They resemble Asian pictograms in that they can mean many different things, and each symbol stands for an entire concept. But, for the sake of simplicity, you could say that they represent the six elements.'

'Four,' Ida cuts in, as she spins her necklace. 'There are four elements.'

The principal sighs irritably, and Minoo is relieved she hadn't beaten Ida to it.

'As I said just a moment ago, you must forget every-thing you thought you knew. The concept of the four elements was put forward by the pre-Socratic philosopher Empedocles. In China and Japan they talk about five elements. But the true number is six. And every witch is closer to one element than the others.'

Six elements but seven Chosen Ones. What does that mean? That two of them have the same element? Or could one of them be left with none? Minoo feels the nagging fear that it might be her.

'Do you know which ones we are?' she asks.

The principal gives her a look that's difficult to interpret. 'Yes. The results of the analysis arrived today. That's why I was late. I'd like to start by saying that the powers you have are typical of your respective elements. But that doesn't mean a given power can't be found in several different elements. For example, air and water witches can learn how to control storms. Metal and fire witches can generate lightning, but not rain. There's a whole science to it.'

'Can I guess?' Vanessa asks. 'I'm air?'

'Correct,' the principal answers.

'Does it mean I can learn how to fly?'

'That depends on how your powers develop,' the principal answers, a little impatiently.

Five elements left, Minoo thinks.

'Excuse me, but can I guess now?' Ida asks. 'Is Anna-Karin earth?'

'Yes.'

Ida gives a scornful laugh that stops abruptly when the principal stares at her disapprovingly.

Four left, Minoo thinks, and concentrates on taking notes.

'Earth is associated with a strong connection to nature and living creatures,' the principal continues, looking at Anna-Karin. 'And strength. Physical as well as mental. You, Ida, are metal.'

Three left.

'Ida's connection to the metallic element makes her a perfect medium, which you saw on the night of your awakening. The art of fortune-telling and visions are also natural abilities.'

For a wonderful moment the principal lets her gaze move toward Minoo before she turns to Linnéa.

'You, Linnéa, are water. You should be able to learn how to control your element in various forms—'

'What was Elias?' Linnéa breaks in.

'Wood,' the principal answers. 'A typical wood quality is being able to shape and control different kinds of living material. And Rebecka was fire, like me,' she concludes.

Minoo often has nightmares in which she's at school and suddenly discovers she's naked. That's exactly how it feels now when everyone turns to her. She's the only one left.

'Am I the same?' she asks. 'I mean, do I have the same element as someone else?'

The principal looks at her for what seems like eons before she answers. 'No. Unfortunately I can't see that you're close to any of the elements. Technically, you shouldn't be here.'

It's worse than the nightmares of being naked. She looks

up at the ceiling, as if someone up there could save her. The only thing she sees is the faintly shimmering air that lies like a dome under the roof of the dance pavilion. More magic. Magic she will never master.

'That's bullshit,' she hears Linnéa say. 'Minoo had the same dreams as the rest of us. She came here on the same night as us.'

'Minoo,' the principal says.

Minoo lowers her eyes reluctantly to look at the beautiful dark-haired woman, so confident in her knowledge and authority.

'I can't explain it. Just as I can't explain why there were seven of you and not one, or Nicolaus's role. But I'm sure we shall find out more.'

Nicolaus, Minoo thinks. It's me and Nicolaus. The failures. The ones who don't belong anywhere.

And Minoo does something she's never done before. She gathers up her things in the middle of a class and walks away. She ignores everyone calling to her and doesn't stop walking until she gets home.

All through school, Minoo has waited to be exposed. And now it's happened. Minoo Falk Karimi is a fraud. She's nothing. It's been confirmed once and for all.

Lasagna – make every day a party! it says, at the top of the sheet of paper Vanessa is holding.

'Ugh – gross! It says you're supposed to put chicken liver in the meat sauce,' she says.

Evelina makes a puking sound and pretends to stick her

fingers down her throat. Normally Vanessa would have laughed, but now she's far too nervous. There are so many steps to keep track of. Her normal cooking repertoire consists of pasta and ketchup or fried eggs.

'You must be able to leave it out without it making much difference,' she says, in dire need of back-up. 'Or do you have to add more ground beef?'

'How should I know?' Michelle says, as she sits on the floor scratching Frasse's stomach.

You're a big help, Vanessa thinks, and lowers the heat so that the béchamel sauce won't stick to the pan.

'Excuse me,' Evelina says, 'but are you pissed off with us because we didn't buy chicken liver? You didn't put it on the list.'

'I know,' says Vanessa. She has to try hard not to lose her temper at Evelina's whining. 'But celeriac was there.'

'I don't even know what it *is*, for Christ's sake.'

Vanessa doesn't either, but she has no intention of admitting it. The frying pan sizzles as she tosses in the onions. 'Never mind,' she says. 'It'll have to work without it.'

'Where did you find the recipe?' Evelina asks. 'In the Middle Ages?'

'Can't you give me a hand?'

Evelina's eyes widen. 'Excuse me. But we did the shopping for you while you were cleaning up. Or have you forgotten that?'

'Why don't you shut up?' Vanessa blurts out. When she sees Evelina's angry face, she adds: 'Sorry! I'm so nervous.'

Evelina's expression softens into sympathy, while

Michelle gets up and comes over to them. 'Tell me what to do,' she says.

'It'll be fine,' Evelina says.

Vanessa feels enormous bubbling love for her friends – her *real* friends, whom she barely has time to see any more – before stress takes over again and she picks up the recipe. 'Michelle, could you "peel the carrots and the celeriac", only not the celeriac obviously. Evelina, could you "chop every-thing very finely"?'

Like good little soldiers they position themselves along the counter with their implements and the carrots.

'So, how do you think it'll go?' Michelle asks.

She peels as slowly as she talks, one rasping pull of the peeler at a time. Vanessa wants to snatch the carrot out of her hand, but instead stirs the sauce slowly and carefully, trying to breathe at the same pace.

'Nicke hates Wille. He thinks Wille's, like, a total criminal,' she says. 'And my mother believes everything Nicke says. Plus she hates the idea of my getting engaged.'

It's become clear that her mother has only tolerated Wille up till now because she thought things wouldn't last. But since the engagement she's been in a total panic and has become intensely anti-Wille. She goes on about how Vanessa's too young to be making momentous decisions, as if *she* hadn't made an even more momentous decision when she was sixteen and got pregnant with the first drunken screw that came along.

Vanessa hopes this evening can be the start of something new. She's going to make this goddamn lasagna. It's going to taste great, and everyone will be impressed that Vanessa is much more grown-up than they'd realized. And Wille is going to charm her mother. He's promised to make an effort.

'Well, Wille *is* a drug dealer,' Michelle points out. 'Nicke, like, arrested him.'

'That wasn't for dealing drugs. It was for smoking dope in Storvall Park,' Evelina objects.

'My mother thinks that if you smoke once, you turn into, like, a crack-whore the very next day,' Michelle says. 'She always thinks I'm doing drugs. I mean, like, if I happen to be a bit tired it's "Are you doing drugs?" Or if I'm annoyed or too happy, "Are you on drugs?" She's on me whenever I behave in a way she thinks a normal person shouldn't.'

'My parents are exactly the same,' Evelina says.

'They must have been made in the same factory as my mom,' Vanessa says.

Michelle grins. She starts talking about a new haircut she's thinking of getting, then she and Evelina launch into a deep discussion about the pros and cons of bangs. Vanessa works hard not to scream with boredom.

Ordinarily, Michelle's hair would have been a normal topic of conversation, not all that exciting but acceptable. Now it's difficult for Vanessa to show any interest in such things when there are so many more important things on her to-do list: She has to (1) save the onion that's in danger of burning in the frying pan; (2) save her future with Wille by making a perfect lasagna; and (3) save the world.

The latter really ought to be her main focus but, compared to the other things, it doesn't seem quite as urgent at the moment.

CHAPTER 32

Frasse runs down the hall barking when the doorbell rings. His tail beats against Vanessa's legs as she opens the door. Wille is outside with a bunch of flowers. His hair is combed back, and he's wearing black jeans and a black shirt under his jacket. He looks mature, clean-cut and a little dressed up. Her heart melts. He really has made an effort for her. 'You brought flowers?'

'They're for your mother,' Wille says, and lets Frasse lick his hand.

Vanessa kisses him blissfully on the lips. 'You're the best,' she whispers, and almost trips over the dog on the way back to the kitchen.

Her mother and Nicke are sitting at the table, waiting. Their faces are locked in rigid disapproval, which doesn't change when Wille comes in. Only Melvin, sitting on the floor playing with his blocks, smiles.

'Hi there, squirt.' Wille ruffles his hair. Then he holds out the flowers to Vanessa's mother. 'Thank you for inviting me to dinner,' he says.

'Vanessa did the inviting . . . Thank you,' she adds

mechanically, and removes the wrapping with an explosion of rustling.

Wille shakes hands with Nicke, who leans back in his chair and looks at him with a condescending smirk. Vanessa hates him for it, but says nothing. With this dinner she's going to prove she's an adult, no matter what her mother and Nicke think.

Her mother rummages in the cupboard for a suitable vase. She fills it with water and puts the flowers into it. They're gerberas, Vanessa's favorite. They look like the flowers you see in cartoons. 'They're very nice,' her mother says, and puts the vase on the table, which Vanessa has laid for dinner.

'I'm glad you like them,' Wille answers.

There is an awkward silence and Vanessa is glad to have something to do. She pulls on a pair of oven mitts. Hot air hits her face when she opens the oven door. The lasagna dish is so hot that it almost burns through the mitts. She bites her lip to stop herself letting out a string of swear words and sets the dish on the stove with a little bang.

'Smells great,' Wille says.

'Vanessa's been in the kitchen all day,' her mother says, 'and the girls were here to help earlier.'

'I didn't know you could cook,' says Wille to Vanessa.

'Me neither,' she says, as she cuts the lasagna into individual sections.

It is bubbling and sizzling at the edges, and the cheese on top is dark brown, but the knife meets with unexpected resistance. She hopes it's just that it's blunt. The lasagna has been in the oven for a very long time.

She takes the salad servers out of the drawer and sticks them into the salad.

'You have a lovely apartment,' Wille says.

It's such a typically grown-up thing to say. Vanessa is moved by his attempt to start up a conversation, but her mother and Nicke don't try to help him.

'Well, at least we have a roof over our heads,' is all her mother says.

'But it's really nice. Beautiful wallpaper . . .' His voice peters out.

Luckily Melvin starts whining that he's hungry. Vanessa's mother lifts him into the high chair and tells him that dinner's ready. He claps his hands and everyone laughs, a little stiffly.

At last, the lasagna is steaming in the middle of the table. Salad, bread and butter are within reach of everyone. Vanessa takes her seat. She serves the first piece to Wille. He's the guest, after all.

'It looks delicious,' her mother says, when Vanessa hands her a plateful.

'Aren't you on a diet, Jannike?' Nicke says, and Vanessa suppresses another impulse to shout at him.

She looks at Wille nervously as he forks some lasagna into his mouth. To her horror, she thinks she hears a crunch as he chews. He makes a strange face and Vanessa can't work out whether it's because the food is too hot or disgusting.'I thought we could drink a toast to Wille's and my engagement,' she says. 'I know everyone here isn't as happy about it as Wille and I are, but I hope you'll come around.'

Her mother raises her glass. She smiles quickly, as if she wants to get it over and done with. 'Cheers,' she says.

Nicke gives his beer a quick wave in the air, takes a big gulp and suppresses a burp, which he instead releases silently through his pursed lips.

Wille is drinking cola, like Vanessa, everything to emphasize that he's a well-behaved young man. She takes a sip and meets his gaze across the table. He chews carefully and smiles at her. The atmosphere is more tense than ever. Even Melvin seems to notice. He's poking at his food with his little fork.

Nicke and Vanessa's mother are eating, staring at their plates as if there was something incredibly interesting on them, like a spyhole leading all the way to China. The clinking of the cutlery seems unnaturally loud. *Clink. Scrape. Squeak. Clink. Scrape. Squeak. Scrape. Clink.*

Vanessa doesn't have much appetite, but cuts a little piece of lasagna and puts it into her mouth. It's hard and tough and has absolutely no taste. It's the gustatory equivalent of gray. Or beige. 'This is inedible,' she says and pushes away her plate.

'What are you talking about? It's great,' Wille says.

'M-hm,' her mother says, with her mouth full.

'I'll want seconds,' Wille says.

Nicke walks over to the refrigerator and returns with a bottle of ketchup, which he almost empties onto his plate.

'So,' he says, 'where are you working, these days, Wille?'

Wille glances at Vanessa. Nicke knows he doesn't have a job. 'It's difficult to find anything in this town.'

'Yeah, I can imagine. You left school without any qualifications, didn't you?' Nicke says.

'I passed my exams,' Wille says. He sounds embarrassed because he did it by the skin of his teeth. Vanessa wishes he was sitting next to her so she could squeeze his hand under the table.

Her mother clears her throat. 'How's Sirpa?'

'She's fine. She's had some trouble with her neck.'

'I'm sorry to hear that,' her mother says.

Vanessa wonders if her mother is thinking the same thing. That she'd said she'd rather have Sirpa as a mother.

'She's got a tough job,' Vanessa's mother says now. 'Sometimes I think she lives at that supermarket. No matter what time I go there, she always seems to be sitting at the checkout.'

'It's harder than many people realize,' Wille says.

The whole time Nicke has been gazing at Wille with open contempt. Now he turns to Vanessa's mother and says, in a completely normal tone: 'Of course she's working all the time. She's got a grown-up son to support. A strong, healthy young man she's breaking her back for.'

The silence that settles around the table is so tense that even Melvin looks up from playing with his food. His eyes are wide and take in everything.

'That was uncalled for,' Vanessa's mother says to Nicke. But she doesn't sound upset. She doesn't say it as though she means 'That was unfair and I don't agree with you,' but more 'That's not the sort of thing you say when the subject can hear you.'

'As I said,' Wille mutters, 'jobs are difficult to come by in this town.'

'There's nothing stopping you moving somewhere else,' says Nicke. 'Is there?'

He glances at Vanessa, but she refuses to meet his eye. She looks at Wille. They belong together. She's never truly felt that until now. It's the two of them against the world. And why, she asks herself, should she sit here quietly, all polite and grown-up, when the so-called adults at the table are behaving like a couple of playground bullies?

The flowers that Wille brought suddenly look pathetic in the middle of the table.

Vanessa turns to Nicke. 'Can't you behave like a normal human being for once?'

'Please don't start arguing now,' her mother says, as if Vanessa were the one causing the trouble.

Rage explodes inside Vanessa. She can't hold it back any longer. It's too unfair, beyond belief. 'Excuse me, but haven't you by any chance noticed how Nicke's been behaving throughout dinner? And as soon as I say something it's me who's acting up?'

'Vanessa—'

'You always take his side! You're such a great team, you and Nicke. You can never do anything wrong. And I'm just causing trouble all the time and being a pain in the ass.'

'We've got a guest here,' her mother says.

'Now all of a sudden you notice we've got a guest! But when Nicke's harrassing *my fiancé*, that's okay, is it?'

'I didn't say that.'

It's one of her mother's catchphrases, normally coupled with that sad look. She thinks she's being so fucking clever: she doesn't say anything straight out so she can play the innocent victim when you confront her with it.

'Fucking hell!' Vanessa shouts. 'I don't know what gave me the idea I could cook a celebratory meal, invite Wille over and think it was going to make any difference. You've already made up your minds.'

Her mother looks at her with big, offended eyes.

'All you do is just sit there feeling so fucking sorry for yourself,' Vanessa continues, 'but I'm the one who's been forced to live with the fact that you've dragged home a succession of losers. Wille is better than any of the men you've ever been with. He's a thousand times better than that one!' She points at Nicke without looking at him.

'Nessa mad,' Melvin says.

'Yes, I am,' Vanessa says, looking at her little brother. 'And you're going to be mad, too, when you grow up and realize what kind of parents you have.'

'Maybe I should go,' Wille says.

'Stay where you are,' Vanessa says. 'This is my house, too.'

'I agree with Wille,' Nicke says. 'It would be better if he left.'

'No, it would be better if *you* left!'

'That's enough, damn it!' Nicke shouts, and pounds his fist on the table.

Melvin bursts into tears and Vanessa rushes to pick him

up, but her mother beats her to it. She lifts him out of the high chair, turns his face to her chest and pats his little head. The crying gives way to bawling, drawn-out, heart-wrenching – and ear-piercing.

'There, there,' his mother coos, as she glares accusingly at Vanessa.

'I'm not the one who frightened him!'

'That's enough, Vanessa,' her mother says. 'Wille, it's probably better if you go now.'

'See you around,' Nicke says, with a smug smirk. 'Down at the station, no doubt.'

'Thanks for dinner,' Wille says. He pushes in his chair and puts his plate on the counter.

'I'm coming with you,' Vanessa says.

'You're not going anywhere until we've talked this through,' her mother says loudly, over Melvin's howling.

Vanessa meets her gaze and feels a wave of pure hatred shoot through her. 'Go fuck yourself,' she says. She walks out into the hall, where Wille is already putting on his shoes, steps into her own and wriggles into her jacket. She grabs her bag.

'If you leave now, don't bother to come back!' her mother shouts.

'I'm not going to!' Vanessa screams back.

'Nessa not go!' Melvin shrieks.

She wants to put her hands over her ears. She doesn't want to hear him now. She loves him too much. Instead she makes herself cold and hard.

She runs down the steps after Wille, looking at the

back of his neck. She may be leaving her home for the last time. She convinces herself that it's worth it – that *he's* worth it.

CHAPTER 33

Minoo has often fantasized about taking this route. But the realization of how pathetic it would be has always prevented her. Tonight, though, it feels right – she's already so pitiful that she may as well humiliate herself even more. She has no pride left to lose.

On either side of her there are identical single-story buildings in which a few residents have attempted to defy the uniformity by putting up decorative fans and brightly colored lamps. She is walking along the even-numbered side, looking at the odd numbers. She stops beneath a streetlamp, opposite Uggelbovägen number thirty-seven.

Minoo looks at the yellow house. It has a tiled roof with a tall black chimney. A pair of windows flanks the front door: to the left, a square bathroom window with frosted glass, and to the right, a bigger one with the blinds lowered. It's dark inside.

She tries to imagine what Max looks like when he comes home in the evening, how he strides up to the door, unlocks it and goes inside . . . But it's as if her imagination has stopped working. She can't picture him living in this house. It's too ordinary. Anyone could be living there.

Minoo remembers what Rebecka said that autumn day. *If you feel there's something between you, you're probably right.*

She could use Rebecka beside her right now. She's never felt more alone.

Minoo gasps, and seconds later, tears are welling in her eyes. They run down her cheeks and wet her scarf. She snivels, digs out a crumpled handkerchief from her jacket pocket and blows her nose.

'Minoo?'

She turns to see Max walking toward her.

Deep down this was what she'd been hoping for. That something would happen with Max tonight, good or bad, it doesn't matter. So what if he laughs at her, pities her? It doesn't matter, just so long as he sees her.

'Hi,' she says.

Max stops in front of her. His breath shrouds his face in clouds of steam. 'What are you doing here?'

His eyes probe her. It's impossible to read his expression. 'I was out for a walk,' Minoo answers. 'I felt shut in.' That isn't a lie at least.

'Is anything the matter?'

Minoo shrugs.

'Is it Rebecka?' Max asks.

'M-hm.'

She doesn't dare say any more.

Max nods thoughtfully. Then he casts a quick glance at the house opposite. 'I live there.'

'Really?' Minoo lowers her gaze and hopes he hasn't

realized that she came here in stalker mode.

'Would you like to come in?' he asks.

She nods.

They walk across the street together. She can hardly believe she's on her way to Max's house. With him.

He unlocks the door and turns on the light in the hall. 'Shall I take your jacket?' he asks.

She pulls down the zipper and he helps her off with it. It ought perhaps to make her feel like an adult, but she feels more like a toddler at preschool. While he hangs up her jacket, she removes her shoes and hopes he doesn't notice they're an abnormally large size 9.

'Would you like some tea?'

'Yes, please.'

Max goes to the kitchen. Minoo catches sight of the bathroom door and slips inside.

When she turns on the light she's met by gray tiles and a blue linoleum floor. It's just an ordinary bathroom, yet she's in an enchanted place because it's Max's. It's full of clues about who he is. He brushes his teeth with an electric toothbrush, but shaves with a manual razor. He washes his hands with unscented soap from a pump bottle. He buys toothpaste in huge economy-size tubes. Perhaps she'll crack some important code if she stares at these things long enough. But then, of course, he'd wonder what on earth she was doing in there.

Minoo turns toward the mirror and sees her unmade-up face. It's as red with acne as her eyes are with crying. If only she didn't look so grotesque she'd dare to imagine that Max wanted her here. That he isn't just taking pity on her for being so pathetic.

'Stop it,' she whispers to herself. 'Get out of here!'

She unlocks the door and steps into the hall. Music comes on further inside the house. A moment later Max appears with two cups of tea. He looks so warm and friendly standing there like that. Not to mention hot. So hot she can feel her ears flushing. She wonders what it would be like to kiss him. To kiss anyone, for that matter. She feels a tingling in her wrists and the strength drains from her arms.

I have to go, she thinks, before I make a total fool of myself.

'Are you coming?' he asks.

She follows him into the living room. It's tastefully furnished yet homely. There is a sofa against the far wall. To the right of it stand shelves filled with books, films, and a few old LPs. A framed poster of a woman with dark, curly hair in three-quarter profile hangs on the opposite wall. She's wearing a draped blue silk dress. Her head is angled slightly downward and her expression is serious and introspective – suffering. In one hand she's holding a pomegranate, while the other grasps the wrist. There's something angst-ridden about the pose. Minoo takes an instant liking to the painting. She feels somehow as if she knows the woman.

She glances at the books. An assortment of Swedish and English titles. She's glad they aren't the tired old selection of novels that you see in *everyone*'s bookshelves and will flood the flea markets ten years from now.

'See anything you like?'

Her gaze falls on *The Lover* and her cheeks heat.

'This one's great,' she answers and fingers the spine of *Steppenwolf*. *Great*? She could hit herself. *Interesting, fascinating, fantastic*. Any other superlative would have sounded better. But Max seems pleasantly surprised.

'It's one of my favorites,' he says.

'And I really like those,' she continues, and points, hoping it isn't too obvious how hard she's trying to impress him. Sure, she's read those books and she likes them. But she reads other stuff, too. Fantasy and science fiction. Max would probably find that immature. Wouldn't he?

'*The Stranger* and *Notes from the Underground*,' Max says, when he sees which titles she's pointing at. He laughs. 'You're not a fan of happy books, are you?'

'Happy books depress me,' she answers, which is true. But she hears how it sounds and smiles sheepishly. 'And *that* didn't sound pretentious in the least.'

'It's okay,' Max says, returning her smile. 'Especially for a sixteen-year-old.'

The comment about her age stings a little, but she's still intoxicated by the attention. She sits down on the black sofa. Max puts the cups on the table and sinks down beside her. There are just a few feet between them. She could reach out and touch him. At least, she could if she were a different, much braver and better-looking person. Vanessa, for example.

'What a nice place you have,' she says.

'Thanks.' He doesn't say more. He just looks at her with

his greenish-brown eyes.

Minoo's gaze wanders toward the steaming cups on the coffee table. 'Do you like it here?' she asks. 'In Engelsfors, I mean.'

'No.'

When she looks at him he smiles. Minoo can't help but smile, too. 'Are we so terrible?'

'It's not the students but the other teachers. They want everything to be as it's always been. In the beginning I thought they might be more open to change. But now it's been almost a whole semester . . .'

Minoo had always thought teachers stuck together. That they agreed on everything. He's speaking to me like he would to a grown-up, she realizes. 'What are you going to do?' she asks.

'I don't know. I'll stay till the summer anyway. Then we'll have to see.'

Minoo reaches out for her cup and hopes she can wash down the desperate cry of *Don't go!* that's trying to erupt from her throat. Tea spills over the rim of the cup as she lifts it, and droplets of boiling liquid spatter her skin.

'Careful,' Max says, taking it from her.

His hand touches hers and she's happy that he's holding the cup or she would have spilled it over both of them. 'Thanks,' she mumbles.

He dries the cup with a napkin, then hands it back to her. Minoo's damp fingers slip on the smooth porcelain handle. She raises the cup slowly to her lips again and sips.

'How about you?' he asks.

Part Three

'What?'

Max pulls up his leg slightly so that he's facing her. His arm is resting on the back of the sofa. If she moved a little closer he'd be able to put it around her, like he did when they were sitting on the steps at school. She'd curl up against him, rest her head on his chest.

'I suspect you and Engelsfors don't mix very well either,' he says.

Minoo gives a silly, nervous laugh and puts down her cup. Her hand is far too unsteady. 'I hate this town,' she says.

'I can understand that,' he says. 'You don't fit in here.' He must have seen the anxious look in her eyes because he reaches out and lays his hand on hers. 'I meant it as a compliment,' he says.

His hand is so warm and soft against hers. And he doesn't take it away.

'I grew up in a little backwater, not far from here, that's just like Engelsfors,' he says. 'I remember how trapped I felt. How lonely and claustrophobic. But later you see that there doesn't have to be anything wrong with you because you don't fit in. Could even be the other way around.'

'Rebecka fitted in,' Minoo says. 'At least, nobody thought she was strange. But she was still different.'

'She meant a lot to you,' Max says softly.

That was an opening, as if he'd said, 'It's okay to talk if you want to.'

'Not just to me,' she says. 'Everybody loved her. Especially Gustaf, her boyfriend. They were such a nice couple.'

Minoo manages to stop talking and leans back into the sofa. His hand is still on hers. She wonders if the back of your hand can sweat. She turns her gaze toward the woman on the wall. 'Who painted that? The original, I mean.' Good thing I pointed out I knew it was a poster and not an original, she thinks to herself.

Max removes his hand. 'Dante Gabriel Rossetti,' he says, sounding a little like his teacher-self. 'He belonged to an English art movement – the Pre-Raphaelites. The model's name was Jane Morris. She was Rossetti's muse. In this one he painted her as Persephone, who was carried off by Hades, god of the underworld. She became his sad queen.'

Minoo gazes at the woman's milky-white skin and thinks that she must look like a monster by comparison. 'It's beautiful,' she says, and turns back to Max. 'She's beautiful.'

'Do you remember the friend I was telling you about? The one who committed suicide?' he asks softly.

Minoo nods.

'Her name was Alice. She showed me that picture . . . She looked so much like her, it was uncanny. She used to joke that she was Jane Morris's reincarnation.'

'You loved her.' Minoo doesn't know where those words came from.

Max looks at her in surprise, as if she's woken him up. 'Yes,' he answers. 'I did.'

She meets his gaze and holds it.

'You're a very unusual person, Minoo,' he says quietly. 'I wish . . .'

He falls silent.

'What?' she asks, in a voice that is no more than a whisper.

She moves closer to him – just a hair's breadth – but she feels as if she's just thrown herself off a cliff. It's now or never. Let it happen, she thinks. Please, let it happen.

Max's hand, which just a moment ago was resting on the back of the sofa, finds its way to her shoulder and lies there.

It's as if they've become each other's reflection. When he moves toward her, she moves toward him, until they're so close that their lips meet.

Minoo has always worried that she'd do something wrong the first time she kissed someone. But Max is kissing her now and it's not difficult at all. It's simple, it's perfect. His lips are warm and soft and taste a little of tea. His hands are on her back, then on her waist, and she moves in closer to him.

Then he stops himself. His lips pull away from hers and he straightens, takes away his hands. He presses the tips of his fingers to his forehead and shuts his eyes tightly, as if he had a splitting headache. 'I'm sorry,' he says finally. 'This is wrong. You're my student . . . And I'm way too old for you—'

'No,' she interrupts. 'You don't understand. I may be sixteen, but I don't feel sixteen. I can't even speak to people my own age.'

'I understand you might feel like that,' he says, 'but when you're older you'll realize how young you actually were.'

It hurts so much that she can't understand how she can still be alive. She gets up from the sofa. 'I have to go.' She rushes out into the hall and pulls on her jacket, shoves her feet into her shoes and staggers toward the front door.

'Minoo,' she hears Max say behind her.

She presses down the handle and almost falls out of the house. She continues straight across the street and runs as fast as she can, back the way she came, without turning once.

She doesn't slow down until she reaches Storvall Park. The few scattered streetlamps spread pools of light in the dense darkness. Minoo sinks onto a bench. Snowflakes begin to fall and more come in quick succession. The first real snowfall of the year.

If I just sit here without moving I'll soon be hidden under a layer of snow, Minoo thinks hopefully. I can thaw in time for spring, completely dead.

A low doleful meowing drifts through the park. She listens into the darkness. It's impossible to tell which direction it's coming from. The wind blows through bushes and the trees' bare branches. A shadow glides into the light of the streetlamp.

Cat.

All at once she feels enormous pity for the poor creature. We're both wretched, you and me. 'Pss, pss, pss,' she says, trying to get its attention.

The cat stops, looks at her and moves closer. Then suddenly it lets out a *blurk* and bends its neck as if something were stuck in its throat. *Blurk*. Minoo is glad she didn't pet it – who knows what diseases it has?

Blurk, it croaks again.

And suddenly she realizes what the animal is doing: it's trying to cough up a hairball.

'Goodnight, Cat,' she mumbles, and stands up. 'Good luck.'

Blurk, Cat responds, and something lands on the ground in front of it with a tinkle. A small object that glitters in the light of the streetlamp.

Cat looks at Minoo urgently and she moves closer.

There, in a little pool of cat puke and hair, lies a key.

Minoo hesitates for a long moment, then picks it up.

Like some kind of affirmation, Cat rubs against her once, then disappears into the darkness.

Chapter 34

On Monday morning Minoo gets up half an hour earlier than usual. The weekend feels like a long and strange dream. The blue flame. The six elements. The book of patterns. Cat and the key. And Max. Above all Max.

Max had kissed her.

There's no denying that.

He had kissed her and it had meant something to him. However much she doubts herself, she could see it in his eyes.

He wants her. Her heart sings when she thinks about it. Max wants her, and she's going to make him understand that it's okay. There's no reason to fight what they feel for each other.

Minoo puts on a black top she bought last year but never dared wear. It's tighter than the ones she usually wears and is a bit lower cut. Normally she doesn't wear much makeup, except for concealer on her acne, but now she takes out her barely used eyeliner and frames her eyes. When she examines herself in the mirror, she immediately dislikes the result. Her eyes look smaller.

She washes it all off and starts from scratch – covers her

acne with concealer, applies a little more beneath her eyes, and finishes off with mascara on her upper lashes. She uses the concealer on a few more pimples just beneath her collarbone and on her shoulder. Why content yourself with pimples on your face when you can have them all over your body?

Minoo puts her makeup bag on the bedside table and catches sight of the little key. She's washed it several times and rubbed it with disinfectant, but still she can barely make herself touch it.

She has a theory about where it leads. Before the weekend, Minoo would immediately have shown it to the principal. But she has no intention of doing that now. Not after what happened at the fairground. Adriana Lopez hasn't been in touch since Minoo left – obviously she doesn't consider her a Chosen One any more, so why should Minoo be loyal to her?

She puts the key into her pocket and glances at herself in the full-length mirror.

She doesn't look bad. If she squints she can almost pretend she's pretty.

It's snowing and an inch-thick layer of snow has settled over the playground. Minoo is early. Only a few pairs of footprints wind their way up to the entrance.

When she enters the school she's hit by the pungent smell of cleaning fluid. The graffiti that had adorned one of the walls is still visible, despite attempts to scrub it off:

IF U WANNA SAVE THE PLANET
KILL UR FUCKIN SELF

Minoo doesn't know if it's the smell or the message that makes her feel sick. She looks away and continues toward Nicolaus's office at the far end of the hall. Her footsteps echo desolately beneath the buzz of the fluorescent lighting.

She hears something else: a muffled scraping sound behind her. Like something dragging itself along the floor.

Minoo spins around.

The hallway is deserted.

'Minoo?' someone whispers.

She turns back. Nicolaus has appeared in the doorway of his office. She casts a glance over her shoulder before she heads into his room.

Nicolaus is dressed in a threadbare gray suit. He looks threadbare and gray too. As if he has aged a few decades since the principal dismissed him.

'Hi,' Minoo says. 'I have to show you something.'

'Oh?' Nicolaus says, raising one eyebrow. 'Has *that woman* given her permission?'

'No,' Minoo answers gravely. 'I haven't said anything to her. And I'm not going to either, if you don't want me to.'

A little smile spreads across Nicolaus's face before he catches himself and switches to a more dignified expression. 'Very well. Show me.'

Cat comes sneaking up, jumps on to the desk and gets comfortable.

Minoo glances at it and it looks around the room. Minoo gets the feeling that it's trying to act disinterested. She takes out the key and hands it to Nicolaus, who turns it over in his hand as she tells him how she came by it.

'This unholy animal vomited up this artifact?' Nicolaus asks, almost proudly, as if Cat were his child, who had just done something amazing.

It lets out a meow and rubs against Nicolaus's hand. He pats its head distractedly, a little too roughly, Minoo thinks. But the animal looks content as it closes its one eye halfway and starts purring.

'I think I know what it opens,' she says. 'My parents have a safety deposit box where they keep their valuables. I checked their key, and this one is the same type. I thought of it because I saw Cat outside the bank on Storvall Square the day Rebecka died. I suspect it has a safety deposit box in your name, and this is the key to it.'

'Why in my name?'

'That's the only logical conclusion I could come up with. Cat turned up here first, didn't it?'

'Verily it did,' says Nicolaus, thoughtfully, 'and I have to admit that I've started to grow rather fond of the flea-ridden beast.'

Cat meows approvingly.

'You're right,' Nicolaus concludes. 'I ought to go over there and inquire.'

'Good,' says Minoo.

'I have just one question. What is a safety deposit box?'

Minoo bites her lip. 'I'll go with you,' she says.

'I won't allow it. We mustn't be seen together. The powers of darkness—'

'Okay, okay!' Minoo cuts in. 'But we don't know what's in the box. You shouldn't go alone.'

'That's precisely why I *must* go alone. I have no intention of exposing anyone else to danger,' Nicolaus says.

Minoo sighs. She can't let Nicolaus go off on his own. They still know nothing about the cat and what it's after.

She'll have to ask Vanessa for help, even though she has no desire to see any of the Chosen Ones after her embarrassing exit from the fairground.

When Minoo steps out of Nicolaus's room, the hallway is filling with students. She spots Linnéa talking to a girl with blue hair. Luckily she doesn't see Minoo when she gets her books out of her locker and hurries down the hall.

She is just about to walk up the stairs when she hears Gustaf call her name. She turns. There he is, in his thick down jacket, his cheeks rosy from the cold.

'Hi,' he says.

'Hi,' she answers.

She feels that people rushing past them on the stairs are looking at them. What does a guy like Gustaf Åhlander have to say to someone like Minoo? He's more popular than ever after Rebecka's death and the interview in the paper. Naturally, the school is teeming with girls eager to comfort him.

Gustaf pulls off his hat and shoves it into his jacket pocket. 'I just wanted to say thanks,' he says.

'For what?'

'For listening. At the church. And for telling me to speak to Rebecka's parents. I never would have dared otherwise. I felt like . . . well, if you could understand me, maybe they would, too.'

Minoo sees his eyes are wet. 'What did they say?' she asks.

'They were happy I came to the funeral and weren't angry with me. They understood. The newspapers had been after them, too. Rebecka's mother also regretted having spoken to Cissi. It was . . . nice. We sat there crying together.'

Now she understands what Rebecka saw in Gustaf. He has an incredible openness. Minoo wonders how he manages it in a town like this, where a guy's identified as gay for the least display of emotion. It means social death. 'Great,' she says. 'That everything went well, I mean.'

Gustaf nods and gives her a quick hug. Suddenly she wishes she knew him better. He lets her go and disappears down the hallway.

She is just about to go up the stairs when she sees Max on the landing above, holding a coffee cup. He smiles at her and continues up toward the classroom. Minoo remains where she is.

There hadn't been a trace of warmth in that smile or the slightest hint that they had a shared secret. It had been a teacher's smile to a student. Any student.

Anna-Karin gets off the bus and starts walking home. It's stopped snowing and the white blanket stretches across the countryside. She hadn't had the energy to stay at school

329

past lunch so for once it's still light when she arrives. That's the worst thing about this time of year for Anna-Karin: it's dark when she goes to school and dark when she gets home.

Grandpa is standing outside the barn talking to Jari's father, who's over today to fix the roof on Grandpa's cabin. It's hard to imagine that Jari and his father are related. His father is short and stocky, almost cube-shaped.

Anna-Karin stands to the side until he climbs into his car and drives off, and she's left alone with Grandpa.

'Hello,' Grandpa says, when he catches sight of her.

'Hi.' Anna-Karin walks up to him.

Grandpa looks up at the sky. 'If it were summer I'd say we were in for lightning,' he says.

Anna-Karin follows his gaze. The sky is an infinite mass of nothing. An even grayish-white without end. 'What do you mean?' she asks.

'Can't you feel that the air is full of electricity?' he says. 'Some kind of discharge is on the way, no doubt about it.' He looks straight at her. 'Can't you feel it?'

She shakes her head silently. Grandpa is like a living barometer. And he can read more than just the weather. He always knows exactly how the animals on the farm are feeling. It's as if they tell him in some mysterious way. And several times he's helped people in the area find water with his divining rod. He doesn't make a big deal out of these things. It's just something he does. But this time he seems confused by what Nature is telling him.

'I've never seen anything like it,' he mutters, and spits

into the snow. Then he attempts a smile. 'Maybe I'm going senile.'

'Stop it, Grandpa,' says Anna-Karin. She hates it when he talks like that.

His eyes are distant. 'I almost hope it's just the figment of an old man's imagination,' he says. 'I'm woken at night by whispering in the trees. And every morning when I look out of the window the forest seems to have closed in a little more tightly around us. It's as if it's preparing itself.'

'For what?' she asks.

He stares at her. It's as if they are standing on opposite shores of a sea, and Grandpa is trying to work out a way to cross to her side. 'Sweetheart . . .' he begins.

Everything unsaid stands between them. And that's so much. A whole sea of silence that has been there all Anna-Karin's life.

'I know I'm not always good at talking about . . . certain things,' Grandpa continues. 'We men didn't learn how to do it in my day. But I hope you know that I . . . that I love you.'

Anna-Karin is embarrassed. She wants to say she loves him, too, but she's unable to speak.

'And I would love you no matter what mistakes you made. Even if you did something wrong, I'd love you, and if someone wanted to hurt you, I'd defend you with the last drop of my blood.'

Anna-Karin feels her cheeks flush.

'I'm on your side, even if I don't know what it's about. And, God knows, there's a lot I don't understand right now. These are strange times.'

It's at this moment that she feels she could tell him everything. If you only knew how many people have wanted to harm me over the years, Anna-Karin wants to say. If you only knew what's going on in my life now.

It's my job to inform you that the Council has launched an investigation.

The principal's words echo in her head. She doesn't want to contemplate what form punishment by a witches' council might take.

A flock of jackdaws lifts from the forest across the other side of the pasture. They circle through the air, cawing frantically as if someone had frightened them. Anna-Karin can hear their hard wing beats from where she stands. They cluster beneath the white sky before heading off over the treetops.

Grandpa mumbles something in Finnish, his gaze fixed on the birds.

Anna-Karin looks at Grandpa. He looks at her. And they both know that the moment has passed. The sea still separates them, impossible to cross.

CHAPTER 35

Vanessa is standing in the lobby of the bank, leaning against a high table on which small cardboard stands of fliers ask whether she's considered getting a credit card, or if she'd like to borrow money for a new lawnmower and even her dream house.

She's promised Minoo to follow Nicolaus into the bank without his knowledge. Of course the stubborn old fool refused to accept the help he obviously needs, so she's been told to make herself invisible and keep an eye on him.

And he's supposed to be *our* guide, she thinks, glancing at him as he stands there, staring at his number slip. He's wearing a heavy, moth-eaten winter coat that looks as if he bought it at a flea market.

But she has to admit she's excited. She'll be the first to see whatever's in the mysterious safety deposit box. Furthermore, she likes going behind the principal's back. They had a class with her on Sunday, too, and it was no more fun than being in school. You might expect a course in magic to be thrilling, but they just sat there staring into the *Book of Patterns* with their mini spyglasses. All they'd gotten from it was headaches. It reminded Vanessa of the digitalized dot images in which you're supposed to be able to see 3D figures. She can never make them out.

Vanessa is watching the bank staff typing silently or speaking to customers in low, trust-inspiring voices. Everyone working here is neat and well dressed, and their footsteps whisper along the wall-to-wall carpeting. Vanessa tries to imagine what it would be like to work here and is instantly bored.

Her mother actually dated a guy who worked here. Tobias. He was as tedious as he was smug. When he met a rich girl from Gothenburg he'd dumped her without a second thought, and Vanessa had had to comfort her and hide the boxed wine.

Eventually, when her mother had been sitting at the dinner table, sniveling again, Vanessa had lost patience and told her off – maybe she should meet a guy who made her happy, she'd suggested. Her mother had just looked at her with bloodshot eyes and blubbered that Vanessa didn't understand. 'Love hurts,' she said. 'Or it isn't really love.'

Vanessa refuses to believe that. If it was true, there wouldn't be any point in being with someone. You might just as well screw around without ever having to wash someone else's dishes or whine about how he doesn't understand you.

That's probably why she doesn't want me to be with Wille, Vanessa thinks. She's jealous because we're happy together.

Vanessa's anger builds again. She and her mother still

haven't spoken. She hasn't even left a message on Vanessa's phone. Vanessa is sure that Nicke told her that it's better if she doesn't get in touch – she can just hear him saying that Vanessa has to 'learn that her actions have consequences'.

Vanessa has no intention of calling either. There's no way she'll let them win. Melvin's the only one she misses. Melvin, who was crying when she left.

A loud electronic yelp announces the new number on the screen. Nicolaus looks around, clearly confused. He's next, but he has no idea where to go – as if the blinking number above the only free teller didn't offer a clue. He examines his ticket as if he expects to find the answer there, and Vanessa sighs. She has to stop herself from going up to him and giving him a shove in the right direction.

A girl with long black hair is standing at the free counter. She's attractive and knows it. Unlike the other bank zombies, she's irritated, which, as far as Vanessa is concerned, is to her credit. She beckons to Nicolaus impatiently.

'It has the number one,' says Nicolaus, when he walks up to her.

'What?'

'The deposit box to which this key corresponds. It has the number one. That was the information I was given this morning when I telephoned.'

'You mean you have a safety deposit box?' she asks.

'That is what I have been told.'

She smiles professionally, but not one millimeter wider than necessary, while Nicolaus signs a few papers. 'This way.'

Nicolaus goes around the counter and Vanessa follows him. She hopes her shoes aren't leaving traces of melted snow on the carpet.

They walk along a hallway until they reach a pair of solid steel gates that the black-haired woman unlocks. 'It's just one flight down,' she says. 'I'm going to lock you in.'

Nicolaus looks horrified.

'Use the phone to call us when you've finished,' she says.

Nicolaus walks down the steps cautiously. Vanessa just has time to slip in behind him before the bank employee shuts the gate so hard that the metal bars ring.

The walls of the vault are covered with small rectangular numbered doors in dark-gray matte metal. Vanessa wonders about the money, jewelery and dirty secrets hidden in the boxes. Deeds revealing hitherto unknown siblings and illegitimate children. Illicit photos and love letters.

It's silent. There's a table and chair in the middle of the room.

Nicolaus scans the deposit boxes. At the very top corner there is a small door with '1' on it. He walks up to it determinedly and unlocks it.

Vanessa backs away when he pulls out the box, carries it to the table and sets it down. When she sees the shiny metal rectangle she is suddenly nervous. Nicolaus takes a step back and stares at it. It's obvious that he's also afraid of what the box might contain. In the world where Vanessa is now living, it might be a big black hole that sucks up the entire universe and turns it inside out. Or a miniature unicorn that spits concentrated acid.

Nicolaus reaches out to open the box, but stops short. He turns slowly and looks about the room. 'Vanessa?'

She holds her breath.

'I know you're there.'

Vanessa doesn't dare make herself visible since there must be surveillance cameras in the room. But she takes a step forward and touches Nicolaus's coat in confirmation. 'How did you know?' she murmurs.

'I didn't,' he answers. 'I guessed. There was something in Miss Minoo's behavior that put the idea into my head.'

'She was afraid there might be something dangerous in the box,' Vanessa whispers.

'And if there is, how are you going to help me?'

'At least then there are two of us. And I'm invisible.'

'Evil sees more than we think,' Nicolaus mumbles. 'You should go.'

'I can't get out – we're locked in. You might as well open the box and get it over with.'

'Then for God's sake take a few steps back!'

'I'm already standing a few steps back.'

Nicolaus takes a deep breath, as if he were going to dive under water. He reaches for the box, but stops short again.

'What is it?' Vanessa asks.

'I'm shuddering at the thought of what might be inside it,' he says.

'You're not the only one.'

'You don't understand. Ever since my awakening I've been wandering around in a fog. Now the moment has arrived when that fog might lift. I fear the answers I'm going to get. If I get any.'

All at once Vanessa feels an enormous empathy with Nicolaus. It must be difficult to fumble about constantly in the dark as he's doing. Yet he's stood faithfully by their side. He's always tried to help them find answers. Unlike the principal, who has the answers but won't share them.

'I can open it,' Vanessa says.

'No,' says Nicolaus, and takes another deep breath. 'This is my duty.'

'Suit yourself,' she says, and sneaks a little closer.

Nicolaus opens the box.

It contains a black book with two circles stamped into the cover. And next to it, a now familiar silver loupe.

'The *Book of Patterns*,' Vanessa says. 'And a Pattern Finder. It's like the ones the witches use.'

Nicolaus picks up the book. Lying underneath it is a white envelope with old-fashioned handwriting on the front:

Hand delivery to Nicolaus Elingius

He glances to the spot where he thinks Vanessa is standing. He's off by about three feet. Then he turns the envelope over. A red wax seal. Nicolaus carefully breaks it, opens the envelope and pulls out a thin sheet of paper. Vanessa reads over his shoulder.

At the time of my writing this, I have spent five weeks in Engelsfors. Five weeks of clarity. As soon as I returned, the veil was lifted from my eyes and I remembered my purpose and my goal. Still I am plagued by a feeling that this condition will not last.

My first intention was to write a complete account of my history and what lies in store in this Godforsaken place. Then it occurred to me that there is a risk of such a letter falling into the wrong hands, God forbid! This makes me choose my words carefully. I dare not disclose as much as I would like.

Even if the self that is reading this letter has likely once again sunk into the haze, at least I will have help on the way. If I read this in some unknown future it is because my faithful familiar has led me here.

Fear not, my lost self. Clarity will return. The cross of silver shall protect you and the Chosen One. In its vicinity you are as safe as you are at the sacred place.

As a final word of guidance, I give myself this maxim, the full meaning of which I have tried to embed in my memory:

MEMENTO MORI

Minoo reads the last lines again, then puts down the letter on Nicolaus's coffee table. The silver cross hanging on the wall opposite her must be the one to which the letter refers. A few minutes ago it was just a strange artifact. Now it has an aura of mystique.

Nicolaus is sitting with the *Book of Patterns* open in front of him and is twiddling the dials on the Pattern Finder. Cat is lying at his feet purring.

Of course, the cat is Nicolaus's familiar. Minoo can't believe she failed to make the connection when the principal told them about witches and their ability to connect with animals.

Witches.

Like Nicolaus.

She picks up the letter, reads it again and tries to understand.

Even Nicolaus is a witch. Everyone's a witch these days, except her.

Vanessa emerges from the kitchen and jumps out of the way when Cat tries to rub against her calf. 'Couldn't you have chosen a more hygienic familiar?' she asks.

'*Memento mori*,' Nicolaus mumbles. '"Remember that you are going to die."' If only I could remember what exactly I meant by that phrase.'

'Well, you remembered it when you wrote the letter,' Minoo says, trying to sound encouraging. 'So it'll come back to you. And your powers.'

'I hope to God you're right,' he says, and twiddles a little more with the Pattern Finder. 'How does this thing work again?'

'Like a radio,' Vanessa says. 'Sort of.'

'At least we've learned one important thing,' says Minoo, and points at the cross. 'Kärrgruvan isn't the only safe place for us to meet.'

'That's a relief,' Vanessa says, and pulls on her jacket which she'd tossed onto the floor. 'It's useless having a place without a bathroom. And we can meet here without Her Witchiness knowing about it.'

Vanessa zips up her jacket, and is clearly about to leave. It's all moving too fast for Minoo. Everything has changed now. They need to sit down and think about what it means. 'Don't you think we should tell the principal? This means that you're a witch, too, Nicolaus. She has to accept you now, doesn't she?'

'She may not be in league with demons,' says Nicolaus, 'but I've got a feeling we can't trust her and that so-called Council.'

'Suits me just fine,' Vanessa says, shrugging her shoulders.

'And the others?' Minoo asks.

'I'll tell Linnéa,' says Vanessa. 'You can tell Anna-Karin.'

'And what about Miss Ida?' Nicolaus asks.

Vanessa and Minoo exchange looks. It seems wrong to exclude Ida. It goes against everything that Rebecka was talking about, everything that Minoo has tried to hold on to: that they have to work together. But can they trust Ida?

'No,' says Minoo. 'We won't say anything to her.'

'I agree,' Vanessa says.

'She's also one of the Chosen Ones,' Nicolaus objects.

'As soon as we've found out a little more, we'll tell her,' Minoo says. 'We promise.'

Nicolaus looks at her doubtfully.

'We can't be sure she won't tell the principal,' she says.

It works. Nicolaus looks dubious, but he nods.

CHAPTER 36

The doors to the school cafeteria open in front of Anna-Karin. It's dark in there, so dark that she can only just make out the silhouettes of the people filling the space.

She doesn't want to be here. She never asked to be chosen. But she can no longer control the admiration of those around her. It's spread on to people she hasn't even *tried* to influence. They are simply affected by the fact that *other* people seem to adore her. And this is the result.

The Lucia crown on her head is heavy. A few drops of wax drip onto the head cloth protecting her hair.

'And one . . . two . . . one, two, three, four!'

The music and drama teacher, Kerstin Stålnacke, is counting enthusiastically. She's waving with such exuberance that her Santa-red tunic is billowing like a sheet on a clothes line. Her hennaed hair is sticking straight up on top of her head. On 'four' the Lucia procession starts singing behind Anna-Karin.

'*Natten går tunga fjät, runt gård och stuva . . .*'

Anna-Karin mimes the well-known but incomprehensible words as she marches slowly into the darkness.

The burning candles cast a warm glow around her as she

moves. Faces appear out of the darkness. There's Vanessa, breaking a heart-shaped gingerbread cookie into three pieces. And there's Minoo, watching Anna-Karin gravely. Kevin is rocking back on his chair and drumming his fingers on the table. Felicia and Julia smile like the fanatical members of the Anna-Karin cult they are. It was they who nominated her to be this year's Lucia. The song seems never-ending.

'Natten var stor och stum. Nu, hör, det svingar. I alla tysta rum, sus som av vingar.'

More drops of wax land on Anna-Karin's headcloth as she walks through the darkened cafeteria. The air smells of alcohol-free mulled wine and warm bodies, and when she approaches the back of the cafeteria, where they've cleared away the tables and chairs to make room for the Lucia procession, she catches a whiff of coffee from one of the teachers' tables.

When Anna-Karin takes her place at the front of the space, and the procession gathers in a half circle behind her, she sees the principal staring right through her. She starts to perspire with the heat of the candles, and a clammy sheen spreads across her face. The palms of her hands, in the traditional Lucia pose, are damp. Max is sitting next to the principal, smiling encouragingly at her. Petter Backman, known for putting his arm around his female students the first chance he gets, is on his other side and lets his eyes wander covetously over her.

Finally the song ends. Ida, who is a handmaiden and is standing to the right of Anna-Karin, belts out the final

'Luciaaa' so her voice carries above everyone else's. It's obvious that she wishes she could do a solo. Ida is used to being the school's Lucia, and Anna-Karin hopes that she'll resist the temptation to set fire to her hair with her candle. She is reassured to see the assistant principal, Tommy Ekberg, with a fire extinguisher at the ready.

One carol leads into the next, and Anna-Karin mimes through them. Kerstin Stålnacke flails her arms as if she has just stepped on a wasps' nest.

Anna-Karin catches sight of Jari, who is skirting one of the walls until he's standing just a few feet from her. He's alone. And he has eyes only for Anna-Karin. Her smile is suddenly genuine. And he smiles back, glowing and sparkling more brightly than any of the candles. It's nearly over.

'*Hej tomtegubbar slå i glasen och låt oss lustiga vara . . .*'
Anna-Karin holds Jari's gaze.

'*En liten tid, vi leva här, med mycket möda och stort besvär . . .*'

Anna-Karin hears Ida get ready to belt out the final verse.

'*Heeeeeeeeeeeeeeeeeeeee –*' The high note gives way to a piercing scream. '*. . . eeeeeeeeeeeeeeeeeeeeeeeeeeeee!*'

Everyone in the cafeteria falls deathly silent. The principal leans forward, about to stand up. There is a loud thud next to Anna-Karin and she whirls around so suddenly that the crown of candles slips off her head and hits the floor, some of the candles breaking loose. The singers in their long white gowns jump away to escape the flames, and out of the corner of her eye Anna-Karin sees Tommy Ekberg running toward her with the fire extinguisher.

Ida has dropped to her knees. Her eyelids are twitching and her eyeballs have turned so far into her skull that only the whites are visible. Her lips are moving and Anna-Karin thinks Ida is saying her name. She leans close to hear better.

Ida is as quick as a cobra. Her hand flies out and grabs Anna-Karin's wrist.

A white light flashes and Anna-Karin is blinded.

Anna-Karin sees a blue sky, and the edge of a roof. The roof of the school. She's lying there feeling so tired, so dreadfully tired. A hard wind is whipping her face. Her head is buzzing and throbbing and she's looking for Gustaf.

Gustaf. There's so much love inside her for him. It even breaks through the awful pain in her forehead.

Anna-Karin realizes she's no longer in her own body. She's inside Rebecka. As if she were a parasite looking at the world through Rebecka's eyes. She can't hear her thoughts, but each feeling and impression permeates her as if it were her own.

This gives way to longing for another person. Minoo. The only one who can help her. She fumbles for her cell phone and pulls it out.

She hears footsteps approaching from the open door behind her.

Rebecka and Anna-Karin turn together, in a single movement, a single body.

And there he is. Anna-Karin feels Rebecka's confusion.

'Hello,' she says. 'How did you know I was here?'

Gustaf doesn't answer. He approaches her but doesn't look her in the eyes.

Rebecka barely recognizes him. She doesn't understand. 'What is it?' she asks.

The next moment, Gustaf bends forward and helps her to her feet. But he doesn't let go of her. Instead he pulls her across the roof.

'Stop it, Gustaf . . . What are you doing? Let go of me . . .'

Her voice is weak. She has no strength left to scream and the pain that's throbbing in her head makes it even more impossible. Gustaf's face shows no emotion as he pulls her toward the edge – it's as if he just wants to get it over with. Rebecka tries to brace her feet against the roof, but they keep slipping.

'Gustaf, stop it! Please, stop!'

Gustaf turns her so that she's standing with her back to the playground below. The wind tugs at her clothes. Terror takes hold of Rebecka and paralyzes Anna-Karin.

Anna-Karin tries to shut her eyes, but she can't. Not while Rebecka is unable to take her eyes off her boyfriend. She still can't believe what's happening.

'Look at me,' Rebecka begs.

Gustaf meets her gaze. For a few silent seconds, Anna-Karin stares straight into those cold blue eyes. The sudden shove against her chest takes her by surprise and she falls. Her arms fly out, her fingers claw at the empty air and then—

Anna-Karin hears the excruciating thud as Rebecka's body hits the ground. But she feels nothing. Her head is lying so strangely, flat against the ground. She doesn't understand how she can still be alive. She tries to take a breath, but her lungs produce only a wet bubbling sound as her mouth fills with blood.

Suddenly something unknown intrudes into her consciousness. Rebecka recognizes the presence.

It's almost over, a strange voice says.

And then comes the pain, which can't be compared to anything Anna-Karin has ever known in her entire pain-filled existence. It's like a blinding radioactive light that incinerates every thought, every feeling, every memory that is Rebecka – anything she's ever been.

And then: ashes. Emptiness. A piece of blue sky way up there. A piece of blue sky that slowly gives way to darkness. Black ink slowly bleeds out and covers everything until the only thing left is that voice.

Forgive me.

Anna-Karin opens her eyes and looks straight into Ida's. She sees her own panic reflected back at her. She realizes they have just had the same experience. Ida lets go of Anna-Karin's hand and backs away from her.

Anna-Karin looks around. Hundreds of pairs of eyes are staring at her. One of the extinguished candles from her crown is still rolling across the floor. Tommy Ekberg is still on his way over with the fire extinguisher.

Here, in reality, no time has passed at all.

CHAPTER 37

The stars glisten in the black sky. The fir trees are weighed down with snow.

Everything looks peaceful, like a scene from a Christmas poem, Minoo thinks. If it weren't for the blue flame casting an eerie, flickering glow over their faces. If it weren't for what Anna-Karin and Ida have just told them.

Gustaf murdered Rebecka and therefore he must have murdered Elias. Gustaf is the evil they have to put a stop to.

'But I don't get it,' Vanessa says. 'How could you see all this?'

Anna-Karin, who has been sitting on the floor trying to pick clumps of candle wax from her hair, looks up at the principal at the same time as Ida. They are waiting for an answer. The bully and the bullying victim have been sitting next to each other ever since they got here.

'We often talk about past, present and future,' the principal says, 'but the notion of time as being linear, with a start and a finish, is false. The truth is that time is cyclical, a circle without beginning or end.'

Minoo glances at the others, strangely thrilled to be back.

Vanessa is listening with her mouth half open as the principal speaks.

'Sensitive witches with metal as their element can pick up on events from other points along the time circle, events that, according to the normal human understanding of time, have either taken place or haven't happened yet.'

'I don't care.' Ida glares at her. 'How do I stop it happening again? There's no way I want to have, like, another epileptic fit in front of the whole school.'

'There's nothing you can do to stop it,' the principal says, 'but you can learn to recognize the signs so that you know when you're about to have a vision. Try to find a calm, secluded place if your mouth starts to feel very dry, for example, or you get a powerful sense of unreality, dizziness or—'

'It won't happen again,' Ida says, mostly to herself. 'I'm not going to let it.'

'Your visions seem to be empathetic,' the principal says.

Linnéa snorts and Minoo has to suppress a smile. She never imagined that 'Ida' and 'empathetic' would ever be used in the same sentence, at least not without 'is not remotely' appearing in between.

'You see the visions through another person's eyes and feel what she or he feels,' the principal says, glaring reproachfully at Linnéa.

'But how could I experience everything, too, if Ida was the one having the vision?' Anna-Karin asks, plucking out a lump of wax. Several strands of hair come with it and she winces.

'You're connected together,' the principal says.

Minoo thinks she sounds like a lame self-help guru.

'I don't think it was Gustaf,' Ida says suddenly.

Everyone stares at her.

'What do you mean?' the principal asks.

'He wouldn't murder anyone. Why would he do such a terrible thing?'

'There could be all sorts of reasons—' the principal begins.

'You don't know G as well as I do,' Ida cuts in.

'You're not best friends just because you gave him a silly nickname,' Vanessa says.

'You seriously believe that G would kill Rebecka? His own girlfriend?' Ida exclaims.

'Men kill their girlfriends all the time,' Linnéa says coldly.

'I'm not so sure it was Gustaf either,' says Anna-Karin. 'It's hard to explain. It was him. And yet it wasn't.'

For Ida and Anna-Karin to be in agreement about anything is so shocking to the others that they're all silent for a long moment.

'I think we should get rid of him right away,' Linnéa says. The blue flame lights her pale face, making her eyes glitter darkly.

'What do you mean "get rid of him"?' Minoo asks.

Of course she knows, but she can't believe Linnéa's serious.

'What do you think I mean? What else are we supposed to do? Two of us are already dead.'

'You mean we should kill G?' Ida cries out. 'You're out of your mind!'

Minoo looks at the principal, but she's simply watching them. It's as if she wants to see what they make of this situation. As if it's some kind of test.

'We can't kill Gustaf,' Minoo says. 'I can't believe you'd even consider it.'

Linnéa looks at Minoo harshly. 'I suppose you and Rebecka weren't such good friends after all.'

Linnéa looks like a stranger. Her eyes are filled with hatred. And Minoo understands. She, too, has thought of revenge, fantasized about it, but now, when she sees the same feelings in Linnéa's face, she realizes how wrong it is to choose that path. How dangerous.

'I mean, you don't seem to care about punishing the person who did it,' Linnéa continues.

Anger flares in Minoo, like a rabid dog pulling at its leash, but she keeps it in check. 'We can't just murder him,' she says.

'He murdered Elias.'

'I don't think Elias would have wanted you to kill someone in revenge.'

For a moment she thinks Linnéa is going to hurl herself at her. But Linnéa stays where she is. 'First, you don't know a fucking thing about Elias. Second, Gustaf isn't "people". He's not even a human being. He's a demon!'

'He certainly isn't.'

Everyone turns to the principal. She's staring into the

blue flame. 'At least, I'd say that's highly unlikely. Demons seldom take on physical form in our world.'

'I don't give a shit about your statistics. Now that we know who the murderer is, we can stop him,' Linnéa says.

'*You* are not doing anything,' the principal answers harshly. 'Keep away from Gustaf. The Council will deal with this.'

'Because it's done such a fucking great job so far?' Linnéa shouts. Everyone stares at her. She stares back. 'How the hell can you just accept this? She refuses to tell us how we can defend ourselves!'

'I can't let you take action,' the principal says sternly. 'The Council has expressly forbidden me—'

'What exactly have they forbidden?' Minoo asks. 'That we defend ourselves? That we find out what we're fighting against?'

The principal meets her gaze. Minoo's heart is pounding: she isn't used to questioning authority, especially not the school's principal.

'You're right,' Adriana Lopez says finally. 'I'll tell you what we know about your enemies.'

'Did you say "enemies"?' Vanessa asks, 'Plural?'

'I'll explain *if you stop interrupting me*,' the principal says.

Vanessa rolls her eyes.

'As I said before, battles take place across dimensional boundaries,' the principal begins. 'That is what is about to take place here. The demons are trying to break into our world, and you are standing in the way.'

'And what is a demon? Some kind of devil, or what?' Vanessa says. 'Someone who possesses people? Could Gustaf be possessed?'

'Demons can influence people,' the principal says, 'but not against their will. They can, however, grant powers to those who agree to collaborate with them. Demons refer to it as "blessing" someone. Someone who has been blessed can do great damage. If Gustaf has been blessed, he's very danger-ous. He's in direct contact with demons. They're his power source. You mustn't go after him under any circumstances.'

'So you think that whoever killed Rebecka and Elias is a normal human being, who works for the demons?' Minoo asks.

'That's the Council's theory,' the principal says. 'They're working on your case night and day. But you have to help us. It's more important than ever that you study the *Book of Patterns*.'

'You still haven't answered my question,' Vanessa says. 'What's a demon?'

'Demons is the more correct term. They don't see themselves as individuals but as parts of a greater whole. They're a kind of borderline creature that lives between our world and the other. We don't know where they come from. We don't know very much about them at all.'

'What do they want?' Linnéa asks, and walks slowly toward the principal.

'It's all in the *Book of Patterns*,' she says, and takes what seems to be an unconscious step back. 'When the time is right, you'll find out.'

Linnéa stops so close to her that they're almost touching. At that moment the principal looks away. Linnéa gasps. 'You don't know. You and the Council – you don't know anything.'

Briefly, the principal's mask seems about to crack. But she quickly regains control of her features. 'That's not true,' she says.

'That's why you keep going on about the *Book of Patterns*,' Linnéa continues. 'You barely know how to use it yourselves. And you're hoping we'll be able to do it.'

'Your chances of being able to do it are much greater since you were born with your—'

'Exactly,' Linnéa interrupts. 'We're stronger than you are. You're afraid of us.'

'You've misunderstood everything,' the principal says, clearly trying to sound authoritative.

'No,' Linnéa says calmly. 'I've finally understood it.' She smiles triumphantly.

'The principal is not our enemy,' Minoo says.

'Oh, shut up,' Linnéa says. 'She wants us to stare at a book to find out what's going to kill us. Well, I intend to stop it instead.'

'You mean shoot first and ask questions later?' Minoo says.

'That's right,' Linnéa says. 'And I'm not going to let myself be stopped by someone who shouldn't even be here.'

Those words hit Minoo like a hard blow to the stomach. She can't look the others in the eye. She's afraid of seeing either pity or agreement.

'Stop that now,' Vanessa says.

'What the fuck's your problem?' Linnéa snaps.

'Well, let me see,' Vanessa says. 'Maybe I'm having a hard time forgetting what you said about killing Gustaf Åhlander. How are we going to do it? Stab him on the way home from soccer practice? Set fire to his house? Buy a gun from Jonte and shoot him?'

'They saw it was him!' Linnéa says, pointing at Anna-Karin and Ida.

'Yet they weren't convinced,' Vanessa says, 'so how can you be? You're just so desperate for someone to blame. And I get it.'

There's a warmth in Vanessa's voice that Minoo has never heard before. Linnéa looks at Vanessa and for a moment it seems that she's going to cry. Instead she grabs her jacket and walks away. Vanessa calls after her as she breaks through the shimmering capsule surrounding the dance pavilion. Linnéa stops and turns.

'We said we were going to stick together. We promised each other,' says Vanessa.

'That was when we thought it would make a difference,' Linnéa says. 'But it won't. We're all going to die anyway.' She points at the principal. 'And if you think she can protect you, you're mistaken. She was a good liar as long as she believed her own lies. But now she can't even lie to herself.'

'But the *Book of Patterns* . . .' Anna-Karin starts.

'Any one of you know how to read it?' Linnéa asks.

No one answers.

'Didn't think so,' Linnéa says.

Minoo feels a moment's shameful satisfaction: she's not the only one who can't decipher the mysterious symbols.

'It takes practice,' the principal insists.

'Don't ever talk to me again, okay?' Linnéa says.

To Minoo's great surprise the principal shuts up.

No one says anything until Linnéa has disappeared into the darkness.

'Well,' Vanessa says, 'does anyone have anything to add?'

Minoo has never heard such a telling silence.

'I don't know what you guys are going to do, but I'm going to get drunk,' Vanessa continues. 'Happy fucking Lucia, everybody.'

The others gather their things together and leave the pavilion in silence. Eventually Minoo and the principal are the only ones left. The blue fire is starting to dim. The light is just strong enough for Minoo to make out Adriana Lopez's features. She's looking straight at her gravely.

'I hope you don't believe what Linnéa said,' she says.

'Of course not,' Minoo answers. She may not altogether trust the principal, but the thought of her knowing less than them is too terrifying to even consider.

'Good,' the principal says, and her face softens into a smile. 'Minoo, you mustn't listen to the other stuff Linnéa said either. I'm sorry about how I expressed myself last time. I may have made it sound as if you don't belong here as much as the others. The Council and I are convinced that you have an important role to play. Your powers are simply more difficult to define.'

'Okay,' Minoo says. 'Thanks. I mean . . .' She falters.

'Minoo,' the principal says, 'perhaps I shouldn't say this, but I see a lot of myself in you. You take this seriously. And you don't show off for the sake of it, but are bright enough to listen to those who know more than you do. Those are valuable qualities. The truth is, I sometimes wish you were the only Chosen One.'

'Thanks,' Minoo mumbles, dizzy with all the praise.

'Would you like a ride home?' the principal asks.

'Thanks,' Minoo says again.

It's only when they drive out of the forest and see the lights at the center of Engelsfors that Minoo wonders how much of a compliment it is to hear you're good at taking orders blindly.

Chapter 38

When Minoo was little, she always felt that December dragged on forever in an endless wait for Christmas Eve, but now the days just fly by.

This semester Minoo has had a growing sense that she's falling behind at school. Not enough to affect her grades – but as if it may begin to. Now she's trying to catch up. She's been hard at her books and stays awake to cram with the help of coffee, sweets and Coca-Cola. She's started taking her Thermos mug to school so that she can excel during the first few lessons, rather than falling asleep with her cheek on the desk's smooth cool plastic surface.

They're performing a Christmas show on the last day of school. Ida's singing a solo – *'Gläns över sjö och strand'* – and is doing it with such a cheesy, fake R&B wail that the audience should be dying of embarrassment, but she receives thunderous applause. She lights up like the sun while the biology teacher, Ove Post, dabs discreetly at the corner of his eye.

The principal makes a short speech about how the coming new year will allow everyone to move on. Everyone understands that she's talking about Elias and Rebecka, that they should try to put what happened behind them. Automatically Minoo tries to catch Linnéa's eye, but she's not there. Minoo realizes she hasn't seen her since Lucia night. Maybe she hasn't been at school at all.

Afterward they gather in the classroom and Max hands out their report cards. When he passes Minoo her envelope he flashes the same impersonal smile he always bestows on her now.

The secret glance of mutual understanding they used to exchange is gone. Had it ever even been there? Maybe she'd imagined it.

But he kissed me.

She thinks about it for the millionth time – it's like a mantra she's repeated so often it's starting to lose its meaning. In dark moments she wonders if the evening at Max's house was just a figment of her imagination, a psychosis brought on by the pressures of getting good grades, supernatural death threats and far too many dreams of losing her virginity to her teacher . . .

Minoo glances at Anna-Karin, who is sitting diagonally behind her and has just opened her envelope. 'How'd it go?' she can't help asking.

Anna-Karin hesitates for a moment. Straight As. In every subject. Even PE.

How many did you deserve? Minoo wants to ask, but she bites her lip and smiles stiffly. 'Congratulations,' she says.

'Thanks,' Anna-Karin mumbles.

Her heart pounding, Minoo opens her own envelope, but

everything is as it should be. Only her PE grade falls short of Anna-Karin's.

Minoo is among the first to leave the classroom. She doesn't even say 'Merry Christmas' to Max. She can't handle another empty smile. When she steps out into the playground she sees her mother's car parked by the gate and is struck by an intense longing for home. As soon as she gets there she'll shut herself into her room, wrap Christmas presents and stuff herself with gingerbread cookies. . .

Gustaf is at the gates. He's standing stock still, staring straight at her.

Minoo looks for an escape route. Her mother beeps and Minoo waves. She has to pass Gustaf to get to the car.

He mustn't know that you know. Act like nothing's happened, she tells herself. He's just Gustaf. Good old Gustaf Åhlander.

Who has made a pact with demons.

Minoo forces herself to walk normally, quickly, but not too quickly, yet her heart is racing as if she had just run a marathon.

Gustaf looks so ordinary in his black down jacket and white woolen hat. Somehow that makes her even more scared of him. This is the guy Rebecka had trusted more than anyone else in the whole world. The one who had thrown her off the school roof. This is exactly how he'd looked.

'Hi,' Gustaf says, and smiles as she walks past him. 'Merry Christmas.'

'Merry Christmas,' Minoo croaks. She has to muster all

her self-discipline to stop herself running the rest of the way to the car.

They celebrate Christmas, just the three of them – mother, father and Minoo – and the holiday is characterized by the same safe routines as always. On Christmas Day they have a good long lazy morning. They play a Trivial Pursuit game from the 1990s, and as usual her father is annoyed by the badly formulated questions. Afterward Minoo goes up to her room and looks at her presents. The one she is most pleased with is a lavish book of Pre-Raphaelite paintings.

Exactly the one she'd wanted.

She sits at the head of the bed, semi-recumbent against the colorful pillows, and rests the book on her knees. She flips past the images of pale, serious women and men in clothes from bygone times and lingers on a painting of Ophelia from *Hamlet* – a girl in a white dress lying on her back in a stream, about to drown. The image makes her angry. Ophelia is filled with bliss and there's something almost erotic about the painting – as if it was somehow delightful or sexy that Hamlet's girlfriend had drowned herself when everyone she'd trusted had let her down or died.

Minoo keeps flipping the pages, and when she comes to Rossetti's painting of Persephone, she is mesmerized.

So this is how she looked. The girl Max loved. The one who had killed herself. Minoo knows that the human psyche is complicated, that there are no simple answers or solutions, but part of her cannot understand how someone loved by Max could be so unhappy.

She puts down the book and closes her eyes. Once again she revisits the events of that evening at Max's house, but she lets them take another turn. Max doesn't break off the kiss, but continues, lets his hand slip underneath her shirt and over her breasts ...

But it's hard to relax and lose herself in the fantasy. She feels watched, as if someone is peering into her mind and can see the adult film being screened there.

Minoo listens. Her mother is clattering in the kitchen. She's in a bad mood again – you can hear it in the way she's emptying the dishwasher. Her parents have had a fight about how they think the other is working too hard again. Her father has gone back to the newspaper to check the material that'll be printed after the holiday.

Minoo gets up and goes into the bathroom. She looks at the old map of Engelsfors where Kärrgruvan has been blotted out since the night of the blood-red moon. She puts up her hair in a ponytail before bending over the sink and lathering her face. She rinses it with ice-cold water and examines herself in the mirror.

A black shadow moves silently through the air behind her and disappears through the bathroom door. It had had no form. It might have been a cloud of black smoke, or those spots you see when you've rubbed your eyes too hard.

She opens the door and looks out at the dark landing. Nothing. Just her imagination, she tells herself.

Part Three

'Merry Christmas, bitches!' Vanessa shouts. She turns up the volume on the amp connected to the computer and climbs onto the table. Then she helps Evelina and Michelle up. They almost bump into each other as they dance. Vanessa steadies herself with the palm of her hand against the ceiling. Her top rises above her belly button as she rocks to the music. Her heels dig into the soft, cheap pine of Jonte's kitchen table.

She and Evelina are dancing close to each other and Michelle sinks to her haunches, shakes her butt and rises again. The boys watch with a horny glint in their eyes, but Vanessa ignores them. She looks at her friends, her two best friends in the world. An old song by Beyoncé and Jay-Z has started to play, and all three squeal with delight. They used to dance to it in Vanessa's living room when they were little – at her house they could play music at full blast – and her mother had liked it so much that she used to come in and dance with them. Evelina and Michelle thought Vanessa's mom was the coolest in the whole world, and back then so did Vanessa. Of course that was BN: Before Nicke.

The happy feeling dies a little when she thinks of her mother. This is the first Christmas they haven't celebrated together.

'Nessa!' Evelina shouts over the music. 'How are you feeling?'

Vanessa meets her drunken gaze. If anyone would understand it's Evelina. Since her parents were divorced, her mother has dated every asshole there is in Engelsfors. For a few months in seventh grade, Evelina had virtually lived at Vanessa's house. That was when her mom's latest flame had offered to help Evelina wash certain difficult-to-reach places in the shower, a level of degeneracy to which Nicke had never come close.

Yeah, Evelina would understand. Michelle too, for that matter. But who wants to talk about that shit?

'Fucking awesome!' Vanessa screams back, and flashes a blinding smile.

She's going to forget all this crap and party like there's no tomorrow. After all, there might not be. May as well take advantage of it. When Michelle hands her a can of beer, she chugs it and then hurls it across the room, hitting Lucky in the back.

Her engagement ring catches her eye.

Everything's going to be fine, she thinks. Everything's going to work out.

Wille breaks free from the throngs of partiers and stands below her. His eyelids are heavy and he's got a silly smile on his face. Vanessa squats, wobbles unsteadily, takes his face in her hands and kisses him hard. He tastes of smoke and alcohol, and his tongue is warm and wet in her mouth. She sits on the edge of the table, wraps her legs around Wille's waist and pulls him closer to her. Then she puts her arms around his neck. A slow song she has never heard before filters out of the speakers.

'You're so fucking sexy,' he whispers.

His warm breath against her ear radiates through her body. She sucks his lower lip and bites it. He laughs.

'Watch it,' he whispers, and lets his hands slide down to her butt.

'Do you want to go somewhere else?' she says.

Wille doesn't answer. He lifts her down from the table. They hug each other. The song builds, filling the room, as they hold each other. The music is like a bubble that encapsulates her and Wille, while everyone else fades into the background. The only thing in the world that means anything is right here right now, in the warmth of their bodies pressed together.

'We should go away,' Wille whispers, into her ear. 'Fuck school. Let's go to Thailand. You hardly need any money there. Just lie on the beach all day long. Fuck and smoke all night. Just you and me. That's all we need.'

She's never been to Thailand, but she can see it so clearly: white beaches, sparkling blue sea, Wille's suntanned body, never having to feel cold again. To run away from everything, from her mother, from fear, from magic books and heavy responsibilities. Why not?

The song cuts off abruptly and changes back to hip-hop.

'Come on,' Vanessa whispers. She takes Wille's hand and leads him to the stairs. When she glances over her shoulder she sees that Evelina and Michelle are still standing on the table. They're boogying drunkenly, but still managing to look sexy. Lucky is kissing a blue-haired girl, one of Linnéa's friends. But Linnéa is nowhere to be seen.

'I love you,' Wille says, as they sink on to Jonte's bed.

She rips off her sweaty top while he unbuttons her jeans, pulls them down over her thighs and calves, then struggles to get her feet out. He takes off his T-shirt and lies down next to her.

'You mean it?' Vanessa murmurs.

'That I love you?'

'That you'd like to go away with me. Just like that.'

'Let's leave tomorrow,' Wille whispers, slurring a little. 'We don't even have to pack. We don't need any clothes.'

He tries to wriggle out of his jeans and falls off the bed. Vanessa laughs and helps him up. She kisses him and lets her hand caress him outside his boxers. Wille groans and coaxes off her pants, kisses her breasts, stomach and continues downward.

Vanessa doesn't care about what's happened, doesn't care about the future. Only Wille means anything to her, and how he can make her forget everything.

Afterward, Wille goes to look for a beer. She pulls on her clothes and notices that her top smells like smoke. She heads into the bathroom to pee and touches up her makeup. She finds a half-full bottle of wine under the sink and has a few swigs as she gets ready. She blows exaggerated kisses at the mirror, poses, flashes her breasts at herself and giggles. She's nearly hammered.

When she opens the door, Linnéa is standing outside, leaning against the wall, smoking a cigarette. She's wearing a short black dress with a corset top, fishnet stockings and black boots. Her eyes are heavily made-up underneath her long black bangs. They gaze at each other.

'You look pretty wasted,' Linnéa says finally, with a smirk.

'How kind of you to say so,' Vanessa says, and grins back.

She's unexpectedly happy to see Linnéa. Tonight seems like one long love trip. She wonders vaguely if someone put ecstasy in the wine she just drank.

'Wasted, but hot,' Linnéa adds.

'You look hot, too,' Vanessa says. 'But not wasted.'

'Only on the inside.' Linnéa smiles.

Vanessa wonders if Linnéa's drunk. She's probably the sort of person who never really shows it.

'Things got pretty . . . intense last time,' Linnéa says, and Vanessa wonders if that's her way of saying, 'Sorry I acted like a bloodthirsty maniac.'

Linnéa laughs, showing off her perfect teeth.

Shit, she really *is* hot, Vanessa thinks.

'But I meant it,' Linnéa continues. 'We can't trust the principal. She really can't protect us.'

Vanessa lays her hand on Linnéa's arm and stares into her dark eyes. She's feeling a bit dizzy. Crap, she shouldn't have drunk that wine. But she can't let Linnéa see how drunk she is because then Linnéa will never take her seriously, and what she's going to say now is important. 'Even if that's true it doesn't make any difference. We have to stick together. We promised each other.'

Linnéa's arm is cool, and suddenly Vanessa is worried that her hand is sweaty. She removes it and almost loses her balance.

'Speaking of which,' Linnéa says, 'we're not the only ones here tonight.'

Vanessa doesn't understand what she means.

'There's another witch in the house,' Linnéa whispers theatrically. Then she adds, more seriously, 'And we should probably go and see what she's up to.'

CHAPTER 39

Jari opens a can of beer with a frothy hiss and hands it to Anna-Karin. Carefully, she licks away the foam that has flowed over the edge and takes a big gulp. It doesn't taste very nice, but it's not disgusting either. It's bitter and a little metallic. She has a few more gulps and suppresses a burp.

Most of the people here are older. They've never been affected by Anna-Karin's powers, and it's hard to control them, now they're filling the house with their clumsy movements. They're swaying back and forth in small groups everywhere, falling into each other, talking far too loudly. Anna-Karin can't get a proper hold on the minds of people under the influence of alcohol and, she suspects, other substances.

The music is deafening. She finishes the beer and crumples the can. Jari takes it and immediately hands her another one. She smiles gratefully.

'Cheers,' he says.

'Cheers.'

The beer cans meet in the air and she tips her head back to let the drink run down her throat. It's surprisingly easy to get used to the taste.

Anna-Karin is starting to relax. She lets go of her control a little. It doesn't really matter what anyone here thinks of her, as long as Jari looks at her like that.

She feels quite attractive tonight. She's wearing a short bright pink dress with silver glitter. It has a low neckline and fits tightly around her breasts while concealing her stomach. Julia and Felicia thought she should choose something that was tight all the way down, but Anna-Karin wasn't up for that.

Some drunken guy yells, 'Looks like a pig's escaped the Christmas slaughter!' He points at her, and his friends laugh. Anna-Karin feels a familiar stab in her gut. It's been a long time since anyone has said anything like that to her – she had almost forgotten how much it hurt.

She empties the beer can in silence and wonders about a suitable act of revenge. Jari is still gazing at her with rapt adoration.

Come here. Show them.

Jari throws himself at her. It's as if he's been longing for her for a hundred years and can't contain himself for another second. His lips press against hers. Then she feels the tip of his tongue in her mouth and opening it.

'Jari, what the fuck, man? Are you serious?' his friend says.

But Jari doesn't answer. He grabs Anna-Karin's neck and pushes himself even harder against her. Her head is spinning while his tongue explores her mouth. She can barely keep up. It's her first kiss and she feels as if she's being eaten alive. But at least that guy and his friends have shut up. Now she has to breathe. She pulls away. 'Could you get me another beer?' she asks.

Jari opens his eyes and smiles. Gratefully, as if he lives to fetch and carry for Anna-Karin, he trots away to fetch the beer, chilling in the snow outside.

'Come on,' someone hisses brusquely, pulling at her elbow.

Vanessa.

Anna-Karin allows herself to be led away. They pass Linnéa, and she follows them into a room where a few guys are sprawled on the floor playing video games. It's comparatively quiet. They squeeze themselves into a corner of the room, as far from the boys as possible.

'What the hell are you doing?' Linnéa asks.

'We saw your little show in there with Jari. What's wrong with you?' Vanessa snaps.

They're bullying her, forcing her into a corner and yelling accusations at her. Just because she doesn't do exactly as they want. Do they expect her to go back to being the old Anna-Karin, the one who never dared look anyone in the eye, the one who was always alone?

The throbbing bass line from the music vibrates through the walls of the room. The boys on the floor shout in unison when something explodes on the TV screen.

Vanessa and Linnéa are standing way too close. Anna-Karin doesn't know if two beers is a lot, she just knows she wants another. Now. 'Leave me alone,' she says. 'I know what I'm doing.'

'Do you really?' Linnéa says.

'I've got it under control.'

'I don't think you do,' Linnéa says. 'You're getting addicted. And this whole thing with Jari, it's—'

'What business is it of yours if I have a boyfriend?!'

'None,' Vanessa says. 'You can have as many boyfriends as you like. Only Jari isn't your boyfriend. You've used your power on him.'

'Don't think we don't understand, Anna-Karin,' says Linnéa. 'I know what it is to be an outcast. I know what it's like to want something you can never have.'

Linnéa's eyes are oozing syrupy pity. Anna-Karin can almost read her thoughts: *Poor Anna-Karin. She's so ugly and desperate that she has to use magic to get someone to want her. There's nothing about her that anyone could like. And she might be able to fool everyone else, but we'll always see her as she really is. The stupid, fat, disgusting, sweaty, flabby, awkward, useless, loser hick she's always been. She puts on a new dress and thinks she's as good as anyone else. How fucking sad.*

'Go to hell,' Anna-Karin says slowly.

Her rage is so intense that it scares her. She jostles Vanessa as she pushes past her and throws open the door.

The place is packed with people. Anna-Karin forces her way through the crowd, searching for Jari. The warm bodies form an impenetrable mass of flesh. It's like one of those nightmares when you're trying to run but can't get anywhere. She ducks to avoid glowing cigarettes, jumps out of the way of beer spilling and searches for an opening in the throng. Eventually she can't take it any more.

Get out of my way, she commands.

It's like when Moses parted the Red Sea. Everyone takes a few steps to the side so that Anna-Karin has free passage. She breathes a sigh of relief. Now she can walk calmly through the building at her leisure while the others are crammed together like sardines, forming a heaving, living wall along her path.

She searches for him everywhere but can't find him. Eventually she crosses the hallway and opens what must be a door to the basement. She slips inside and closes the door behind her. A naked bulb lights the rough, unpainted pine planking that lines a staircase. Anna-Karin heads down it to another door, which she opens. Much of the little basement is occupied by a boiler and a huge freezer, each trying to drown the other's loud humming. When she shuts the door, the music and loud voices dampen to a muffled drone.

An old grandfather clock is propped against one wall, with a broken guitar and two sleds. The junk of everyday life. It smells of stone, damp and earth. On the other side of the room, a green metal door stands ajar. Anna-Karin knows instinctively that she shouldn't go through it. Perhaps that's why she can't resist.

The light nearly blinds her. The room is big and the walls are white. UV lamps hang from the ceiling above neat rows of green plants. It's warm and damp, and she hears a monotonous whirring as if from electric fans.

How strange, she thinks, that someone would grow vegetables in their basement. Then she understands. How naïve she is. The green plants growing beneath the lamps are cannabis. Or marijuana. Or is it the same thing? She has no idea.

She looks at the table, which is cluttered with tools and a pile of well-thumbed instruction manuals. And, next to the manuals, a gun.

Anna-Karin moves closer. The gun is black with a brown handle. It looks as if it's been used.

Just then she hears footsteps on the stairs and a door opening. Her eyes dart around nervously. The footsteps are coming closer. There's nowhere to hide.

A tall, lanky guy enters the room. He's wearing a gray hat pulled down over his eyebrows. He has a dull yet intense look in his eyes. Anna-Karin knows instantly who it is. Jonte.

'This door's supposed to be locked,' he says.

'It was open,' Anna-Karin says. 'I didn't know . . .'

Jonte's eyes narrow. He comes closer and Anna-Karin backs away until she hits the table.

'What the hell are you doing here?'

Anna-Karin directs her power at him, tries to envelop him in a soft, pleasant feeling. Jonte stops short and cocks his head to one side, a bit like an animal listening for danger. Then his face relaxes, but he doesn't quite let down his guard. Anna-Karin can't get a hold of him. The beer, of course.

'Anna-Karin?' Jari's voice calls out.

'I'm here!' Anna-Karin shouts back, a little louder than necessary.

She feels an enormous sense of relief when Jari comes in the room. 'Hey, babe,' he says, and smiles.

'Who is she?' Jonte asks, his voice still full of suspicion.

'It's cool. She's with me,' Jari says. 'Anna-Karin, this is Jonte, who's throwing this party.' He holds up a clear bottle of brown liquid and grins at her.

'Better than beer,' he says triumphantly.

'Get this skanky-ass bitch and that skunky-ass homebrew the fuck out of here,' says Jonte with contempt.

'Don't you fucking—' Jari says threateningly, and takes a step toward him.

'It's okay,' Anna-Karin says quickly. 'Come on, Jari.'

The noise from the party grows in intensity as they go up the stairs. 'Jonte's weird sometimes,' Jari says. 'His brain is, like, fried. Know what I mean?'

He laughs hoarsely and holds out the bottle. Anna-Karin pauses to take it. Vanessa and Linnéa are most probably still up there. She swigs and nearly retches. Her mouth seems to be filled with napalm, but she forces herself to swallow. The liquid burns all the way down her throat. She gags a few times as if she's going to puke and hopes Jari doesn't notice.

'Good shit, huh?' Jari says.

'M-hm.' She has another swig. This time it goes down more easily, as if the first gulp had numbed her mouth and throat. She tips the bottle back again, lets more of the liquid run down her throat.

'Take it easy.' Jari laughs.

Just for that Anna-Karin, of course, has to take an extra gulp before she hands it back to him.

As she opens the basement door, they're hit by a full-frontal assault from a wailing hard-rock guitar.

Minoo is dreaming of Ophelia. Ophelia who is Rebecka. She's drowning and Minoo is trying to save her. She wades into the stream. It's surprisingly deep and she has to struggle against the current to stay upright. She tries to grab the white nightgown that is billowing around her friend in the water. But it keeps slipping through her fingers. Rebecka looks at her with doleful eyes, as if she's sad for Minoo.

Minoo . . . Minoo, you have to wake up now.

Minoo objects, still half asleep. She hasn't finished her dream. She has to grab Rebecka.

Wake up.

She opens her eyes and looks around in a daze, adjusting slowly to the darkness. The familiar contours of the room come into view. She tries to remember what woke her, but she has difficulty concentrating.

Minoo . . .

Her heart skips a beat. It's a voice that isn't a voice. It's inside her head, disguised as one of her own thoughts. It's warm and comforting, and it terrifies her.

Minoo sits up in bed. She fumbles for the lamp at her bedside and presses the switch.

She looks around, her heart pounding. The fear is so intense that she feels like a hunted animal, driven by instinct. She doesn't dare breathe. The awful presence will find her if she makes the slightest sound.

The bedside lamp flickers.

Get up.

Minoo's body obeys: she gets out of bed and walks toward the door.

And she realizes that the awful presence is inside her.

When she steps out into the hallway, the bathroom door is wide open. The sound of running water reaches her ears. The bathtub is filling. Step by step she approaches the open door.

No pain, the voice whispers. *No pain, I promise.*

Minoo walks quietly into the bathroom and the door swings shut behind her.

CHAPTER 40

Jari leads Anna-Karin into one of the smaller rooms upstairs. Cushions are scattered about the floor and there's a ping-pong table. Two girls are plucking ice cubes from each other's glasses, then passing them between their mouths with kisses. It's clear that they're putting on a show for the guys who are sitting on the cushions.

Anna-Karin props her elbows on the ping-pong table. The whole world is heaving, as if she were at sea. She doesn't feel quite so sick if she focuses straight ahead.

'Are you all right?' Jari asks.

Sweet, considerate Jari. With his sweet, beautiful eyes. It can't just be Anna-Karin's magic that makes him look at her like that. He must really like her.

'I feel so *fuuucking goood*,' she says. Her tongue is sort of numb. Slack and numb, can't quite keep up. And her head feels so heavy it's hard to keep it upright. But what she says is true. She feels so fucking good. She's with Jari. The boy of her dreams.

'It's not just because I've been fat and ugly all my life that I've become like this. It's my mother's fault. I fucking believe that. She's made me totally anti-men. She's never . . .'

Here Anna-Karin has to swallow back the puke that bubbles up her esophagus before she can continue. She clears her throat and looks around the room to include the guys sitting on the floor cushions. 'She's never said anything good about you. I mean, not, like, *you* guys, but like *guys*. You know?' Anna-Karin isn't sure if she's about to laugh or cry. Everything's so much fun and so terribly sad at the same time. And so unsteady. 'But you're so fucking nice. I'm so fucking happy you exist. Guys are fucking nice. Guys, guys, guys. More guys!'

She can hear how idiotic she's being. She's always thought that drunk people have no idea how stupid they sound. Now she knows that when you're drunk *you just don't care* that you sound ridiculous. She doesn't give a flying fuck. About anything. It's like a thousand pounds have been lifted off her chest.

'Maybe you should give her some water,' she hears someone tell Jari.

Why are they talking about her as if she isn't there?

Anna-Karin staggers along the edge of the ping-pong table to Jari. She's using all her power to keep her hold on him. The other people in the room probably don't like her. But who cares? Jari is the only one who matters.

'Who do you love?' Anna-Karin asks, looking at him.

'You, of course,' Jari answers, without blinking.

Anna-Karin takes a few steps toward him, trips and falls into his arms. Her forehead smacks against his eyebrows, but she barely feels it. She throws her arms around his neck and opens her mouth.

At first he kisses her gently. She tries to lean against him to keep her balance while she thinks about how many words rhyme with what they're doing – nuzzling, guzzling . . . puzzling? Rustling? And then she stops thinking. The only things that exist are their mouths. Her tongue in his mouth, his tongue in hers. She licks his lower lip and he moans. Their teeth knock together a few times. Anna-Karin becomes increasingly bold. She sucks his tongue – she can hardly believe she has the courage to do it. She lets her hands roam over his shirt, then slips them underneath it. He's thin. She feels the hard squares of his stomach. His skin is warm. The soft fuzz below his belly button. Her fingers fondle his jeans. He groans.

'Jesus Christ!' a girl cries out. 'Can't you go and fuck somewhere else?'

Anna-Karin and Jari open their eyes and look around, bleary-eyed. Without taking his eyes or hands off her Jari says, 'I don't know what this chick does to me.'

Anna-Karin licks her lips in the way she's seen girls do in the porno films she's watched in secret. She realizes she's licking off Jari's saliva – it's all over her mouth – but for some reason the idea doesn't disgust her. In fact, it turns her on.

Anna-Karin leans toward Jaris's ear and whispers: 'Let's find somewhere we can do it. I want to do it with you right now.'

Jari nods and gives her a feather-light kiss on the lips. It sends electric shockwaves surging through her. She wants more. Now.

They return to the throbbing heart of the party. Seeing

all these people again is a shock. Anna-Karin tries to get them to move out of the way, tries to focus on their bodies, but she can barely stand.

She lets Jari go first, beat a path for them.

'Upstairs?' he calls, over his shoulder.

Anna-Karin nods, but then she sees Vanessa and Linnéa. They're coming toward her, looking pissed off. What a joke. She lets go of Jari's hand. 'You go and see if any rooms are free. I'll follow you in a minute.' She crosses her arms and waits for them. This time she's not going to run.

The water is gushing from the bathtub faucet. Minoo can only watch as the water level rises. The steam has fogged the mirror and is making her pajamas stick to her.

Minoo is somewhere inside herself, trying to get out. She's a prisoner inside her body, locked behind her face. Behind her she hears the door latch turning, then locking with a click. She tries to scream, but the sound never reaches her vocal cords.

Every detail in the bathroom is crystal clear. She can see every thread in the fluffy bathroom carpet she's standing on. Every drop of water gushing from the tap. The dark gray seam between the white tiles.

Leave me alone! she screams inside her head. *Let go of me!*

I can't.

The most frightening thing is that the voice is so warm and friendly, so pleasant.

The faucet turns off. She looks at the water, at the little

specks of dust floating on the surface. A few last drops dribble from the tap.

There's a knock at the door.

'Minoo?' her mother says. Her voice is heavy with sleep.

Minoo can see her in her mind's eye, standing on the other side of the door, only a few feet away, wrapped in her washed-out dark red bathrobe.

Mom! Minoo thinks. *Mom, help me!*

'I woke up and couldn't sleep so I thought I'd take a bath. Sorry if I woke you,' Minoo hears herself say.

'Okay. Just be careful you don't fall asleep in the water,' her mother says, and leaves her.

Minoo takes a few steps forward. The heat rises toward her face.

It's almost over. You don't want to stay here. You have no idea what awaits you in this world. It's only going to get worse. Much, much worse. And all for nothing. There's no point in fighting against it. You appreciate logic and you've already worked that out, haven't you? You can't win.

She puts one foot into the bath. The water is hot, but not enough to scald her. She puts in her other foot. The legs of her pajamas stick to her calves. She pleads with the intruding presence to let her go. Begs.

All of your suffering, Minoo, it's just the beginning. Trust me. This is so much easier.

Minoo's body is engulfed in water as she eases herself into the bath. Her pajama top is full of air and swells like a balloon as she struggles to keep her head above the water.

For a moment she can see what is holding her – a haze of

black smoke surrounds her. She concentrates all her willpower on dispersing it. The smoke dissipates slightly.

Minoo regains control of her hands. She grabs the rim of the bathtub, clings desperately to it. Her arms are shaking with the strain.

Let go, Minoo.

The strength drains from her fingertips as they are pried away from the bathtub. She sinks. The warm water closes above her face.

There's no point in resisting.

If her mother has gone back to sleep, she or her father might not try the bathroom door again until tomorrow morning. Will it be unlocked by then? Or will they have to break it down? Will Minoo's eyes be open under the water, staring blindly?

The black cloud drags her down into the water until her head hits the bottom of the tub.

Forgive me.

'Come on. We'll take you home,' Linnéa says.

'Forget it,' Anna-Karin tells her.

The cigarette smoke hangs in the air like a bank of fog, mixed with other, sweeter smoke. Anna-Karin decides that a glass of water wouldn't be a bad idea after all.

An elbow comes against her from behind, and she lurches unsteadily. For a moment she thinks she's going to lose her balance and fall, but she flails her arms and manages to stay on her feet.

'Shit! She can't even stand,' says Vanessa.

'Somebody pushed me!' Anna-Karin says. Anger flares and clears her head. She understands now. It must be tough for Vanessa not to be the center of attention anymore, that Jari wants Anna-Karin now, not her. 'I'm not going anywhere,' she says. 'You can go home if you want to.'

'You've had enough of an adventure for one night,' Linnéa says.

'I'm staying here all night,' Anna-Karin says, 'and Jari's going to pop my cherry.'

Vanessa's jaw literally drops. Anna-Karin has never actually seen that happen before.

'You mean you're going to rape him,' Linnéa says.

'You wish,' Anna-Karin says.

'If you have sex with him against his will it's rape.'

'You and I both know he'd never do it voluntarily,' Vanessa adds.

'Getting laid is all men ever want to do!' Anna-Karin snaps. 'Which guy would say no? Huh?'

'Anna-Karin,' Vanessa says firmly, 'that's not how it works. Jari is a human being, not someone you can just use. Would you think it was okay if a guy did that to a girl?'

'It's not the same thing. Anyway, Jari wants me for real, no matter what you think.'

'You're going too far now,' Linnéa says.

'Hypocrites!' Anna-Karin shouts. 'Everyone knows that Vanessa is a slut. And you're a fucking junkie, the daughter of a drunk—'

A hard smack. Anna-Karin's cheek stings. Linnéa has slapped her across the face and everyone turns. It's noticeably quiet suddenly, apart from the music, which is hammering away throughout the house. Anna-Karin does all she can to hold back the tears that are stinging her eyes.

She sees Jari coming down the stairs and goes to meet him.

'Is anything wrong?' he asks anxiously.

'I want to go home with you,' she says.

The last few air bubbles escape from the corner of Minoo's mouth and rise toward the surface of the water. Her chest cramps. She struggles against the black cloud, which wants to open her mouth and let her lungs draw in water.

There's a buzzing in her ears, which rises and falls with her heartbeat. Water is trickling into her nose and down into her throat.

No!

Suddenly the iron grip on her body relaxes.

I can't do it . . .

And the black cloud, which has been swirling around her, is gone.

I won't do it. I won't listen to you.

Minoo's arms fly out of the water into the air. Adrenaline is surging through her, giving her the strength she needs. Her arms fling themselves over the edge of the bathtub and she heaves herself into a sitting position.

Water pours over the sides of the tub, spilling loudly onto the floor. She splutters and coughs until she gags, and then, at long last, she can draw air into her lungs. A little water comes with it and she coughs, again violently. This time she's close to vomiting.

Minoo stands up on shaky legs and almost falls in the bath. Supporting herself on the sink, she climbs out and has to sit on the toilet. Water runs from her hair and from her pajamas. She breathes heavily and a big pool of water forms on the tiles at her feet. She doesn't dare believe it's over.

She jumps at a sudden pounding on the door. Someone pulls at the handle. 'Minoo!' her mother cries.

The relief is so powerful that she starts to cry. She wants to unlock the door and throw herself into her mother's arms. But how would she explain her drenched pajamas?

'What's going on in there?' her mother calls, and beats on the door again.

Minoo takes a few deep breaths. 'It's all right. I fell asleep in the bath,' she calls back. Her voice is hoarse and cracked. She barely recognizes it when it echoes from the tiles.

'Good Lord, Minoo! I told you, didn't I!'

Minoo rests her forehead in her hands. Her whole body is shaking.

'I'm sorry,' her mother says, in a softer voice. 'I just got so frightened. Would you like me to come in?'

Minoo forces a smile in the hope that it'll make her sound normal. 'It's okay. I'm just going to clean up in here,' she says.

She takes off her pajamas, which land heavily on the floor with a smack. She hesitates before she dares to put her hand into the water and pull out the plug.

◎

Anna-Karin sits down on the unmade bed. She's still wearing her bright pink dress. Her hair flows out over the pillow when she lies down. She closes her eyes to stop the room spinning, but feels worse.

She's sobered up a little during the long walk through the forest and now she's very nervous. 'What if your parents wake up?' she whispers.

'They won't. Their room is on the other side of the house.'

Jari pulls off his shirt. He's not wearing an undershirt underneath. His skin is pale, smooth and taut over his muscles. Anna-Karin hardly dares look but can't stop herself. He unzips his jeans and bends down to pull them off, his face hidden beneath his long dark hair.

Then he's in a pair of black boxer shorts that are so tight she can see the contours of what lies underneath. He moves toward the bed, still wearing his socks. For some reason she focuses her panic on them.

Take them off! Take them off!

He stops short and yanks off his socks as if they're on fire. Then he smiles apologetically at her and crawls into bed. They lie beside each other for a moment as he plays with a wisp of her hair. His knee slides up her legs as he moves closer. He kisses her probingly as he reaches for the hem of her dress and pulls it up toward her hips.

You and I both know he'd never do it voluntarily.

Anna-Karin stops him. She lays a hand on his cheek, and looks deep into his eyes, trying to read his lustful, slightly glazed expression. Does he really want to be here? Does he really want to do this?

She takes a deep breath and holds his eyes. Then she switches off, cuts the power flowing out of her.

At first nothing happens. He looks at her with a patient but confused smile.

Then something changes in his eyes. It's as if a film is lifted. A spark is suddenly reignited.

Jari looks away, scratches his arm distractedly. Looks at her again. And really *sees* her.

She knows that look. She's seen it before.

'What the fuck are you doing here?'

The room starts to spin again, as if she's falling backward in endless slow motion. A powerful twinge of nausea surges through her, like a convulsion. It can't be ignored.

She leaps out of bed and tears open the door. The force of the bile builds in the pit of her stomach. Anna-Karin looks around the darkened hallway in panic. Lots of doors.

And here it comes, erupting into her mouth with the speed of a cannonball. She bolts into the hall, keeps everything inside her mouth by clenching her teeth. Some shoots up her nose and that alone is so disgusting that she's certain more will come at any moment. Her stomach groans, and she sees the little heart nailed on one of the doors. She yanks desperately at the handle. But the bathroom door is locked.

Someone's in there.

Anna-Karin drops to her knees. Vomit spurts from her mouth, dripping out of her nose. Her whole body shudders, as her stomach sends fresh streams splashing over the floor and walls. It sounds like someone emptying a bucket of water.

It's over in a few seconds. She wipes her mouth with the back of her hand, can't bear to look at what she's left behind.

'Jari?' a woman calls, from inside the bathroom.

Anna-Karin's head feels so heavy that she just wants to lie down and close her eyes, but she stands up and runs back to Jari's room. They almost crash into each other in the doorway.

'What the fuck's going on?' he asks.

At the other end of the hall, someone, undoubtedly Jari's mother, flushes the toilet. Anna-Karin looks at Jari one last time. His eyes reflect disgust and disbelief.

She runs.

She runs toward the front door that she and Jari snuck through just fifteen minutes ago. Her sweaty fingertips can barely get a grip on the knob, but then the door flies open. She's hit by a blast of cold air and remembers her jacket, grabbing it from the coat rack on her way out.

Behind her she hears the female voice curse with revulsion, and realizes that the woman has probably just stepped into her pool of vomit.

Anna-Karin might have been able to put everything right, control Jari and his mother and make them forget everything, but she hates herself too much. Disgusting, stupid Anna-Karin – see what happens when you try to get things you don't deserve.

Anna-Karin runs like she's never run before. She becomes one with the wind. She shoots across the front garden, into the forest. Her head throbs and her stomach aches, but still she runs on, and on, and on.

CHAPTER 41

It's cold in the principal's car. Minoo had texted her as soon as she'd got back into her room and they'd agreed to meet here, on a dirt track in the forest a few miles from Minoo's home.

'Take it from the beginning,' Adriana Lopez says.

A milky-white layer of condensation forms on the inside of the windows as Minoo recounts what happened in as much detail as she can. But, for some reason she can't explain, she leaves out the black smoke. Somehow she can't make herself mention it, almost as if there's something forbidden or shameful about it.

When she's finished, the principal takes out a blue Thermos and two plastic mugs from the glove compartment. She pours hot liquid into the mugs. 'Drink some of this,' she says, and hands one to Minoo.

'Is it . . . magical?'

Adriana smiles. 'It's Earl Grey.'

She sips cautiously and Minoo follows suit. The honey-sweetened tea burns the tip of her tongue.

'I really don't like these forests,' the principal says thoughtfully. She leans over the steering wheel and peers out of the windshield. 'Tell me again what the voice said just before it let you go. Try to remember exactly.'

Minoo does her best, but the night's events are already melting together into a single mass. It's hard to pin down facts when the thing she remembers most vividly is panic.

'It said, "No", all of a sudden. Then it said, "I can't do it, I won't do it. I won't listen to you."'

Adriana nods. It's snowing. Big fluffy flakes land gently on the windshield, sticking together. 'Do you think the voice was saying that to you or to someone else?'

'What do you mean?'

'"I won't listen to you." Doesn't it seem strange that the voice would be saying that to *you*?'

Minoo tries to collect her thoughts. 'You mean that maybe there were two of them? That they were talking to each other?'

'Two or more,' Adriana says grimly.

Minoo's stomach roils. Could several wills have fought over her tonight? What if the other wins next time?

'Are you sure you've told me everything now? Every detail may be important.'

Minoo concentrates on the snowflakes. 'Yes,' she says.

'How are you feeling?'

'I don't know. All I can think about is Rebecka. And Elias. Now I know how scared they must have been and how they must have struggled. And the voice that felt it had the right to decide whether we lived or not, that said everything was meaningless . . . It makes me so angry now.'

The principal nods gravely. 'If something had happened

to you tonight, I would never have been able to forgive myself. I know you're all disappointed in me, but I'm just following the Council's orders.'

Minoo realizes that was almost an apology. 'You mean the Council's wrong?'

'No,' the principal responds emphatically. 'Absolutely not. I just wish I could do more for you. I know you think I'm some kind of ice queen . . .' she pauses '. . . but I care about all of you. I care about you, Minoo. The last thing I want is for anything to happen to you. What happened to Elias and Rebecka torments me more than I can say.'

So there *is* a human being beneath the principal's cool exterior.

'You have to promise me to be careful and not take any action on your own,' she continues. 'I know it's difficult, but we have to trust the Council's judgement. And study the *Book of Patterns.*'

It's the first time the principal has said 'we' without meaning herself and the Council.

'I promise,' Minoo says, and empties her mug before setting it in one of the cup holders between the seats. 'I should go home now.'

'Shall I drive you?'

Minoo shakes her head. 'It's okay,' she says, and climbs out of the car.

'Remember what I said,' Adriana urges, before Minoo shuts the door.

Minoo nods obediently to her through the side window and waves.

Once the principal's car has disappeared around the corner, Minoo takes out her phone and calls Nicolaus. After a few minutes they decide what has to be done. Everything that the principal said has confirmed what they already suspected. They can't wait for her and the Council any more. They have to take charge of their own lives. While they still have them.

CHAPTER 42

R ubber soles squeaking on the floor, angry shouts and cheers, muffled thuds when a shoe connects with a ball. The school's gym feels completely different when Engelsfors Soccer Club practices there. It's filled with another kind of energy, more focused, but the smells are the same. Sweat, rubber and stale air.

Vanessa is sitting invisibly in the stands, trying to take an interest in the practice game to make the time pass more quickly. She's not succeeding. She's never understood how anyone can be bothered to do something so meaningless as chase after a ball, much less watch other people doing it. There's at least a billion things she'd rather do than follow Gustaf.

If Gustaf is a serial killer in league with demons, he's doing a very good job of hiding it. Vanessa wonders if she's thrown away half her Christmas break for nothing.

Kevin Månsson's burly father is the coach, and now he blows the whistle. Vanessa looks at the big clock hanging above the wall bars. At last. The guys on the floor gather in a group, exchange the obligatory backslaps, drink water from plastic bottles, pretend-wrestle and howl. Vanessa sighs impatiently. It's at moments like these that she remembers why she could never be with a guy her own age.

She tiptoes down from the stands and attaches herself to the boisterous band. She's learned not to wear perfume or wash her hair before she tails Gustaf. She made that mistake the first time she attended a practice game. Kevin Månsson had started shouting that someone smelled like a fag and began sniffing around, like a bloodhound on speed, to find the culprit.

She follows them into the changing room, where they untie their laces and pull off their sweaty shirts. They root around in their bags for towels and shower gel.

It's like entering a secret parallel universe. She's seen some of the cutest guys in the school lathering themselves in the shower. On the other hand she's also seen Kevin, alone, discover a big zit on his upper arm, suck out its contents and spit into the trash. Some things you just don't want to know about other people. Some images you simply can't forget, no matter how much you'd like to.

Gustaf isn't like the others. More low key. As if he doesn't have a lot to prove. That's probably why girls have always fallen in love with him.

He's sitting in the sauna now. His skin is gleaming with sweat. He's surrounded by the others, and yet isn't really with them. Vanessa can see that he's pretending to laugh at their jokes. No one picks up on it, and she wonders if he was like this even before Rebecka died.

Before he killed her.

If it was him. Could it really have been Gustaf?

Part Three

◎

Early this morning everyone except Ida met at Nicolaus's house. They've been there every morning since the attack on Minoo to practice resisting magic.

The sessions usually consist of Anna-Karin trying to get them to do something, one by one, while they try to block her. She was surprisingly reluctant but eventually let herself be talked into it. 'But I'm only going to do harmless things,' she said.

Then she directed her power at Minoo, who was seized by an irresistible urge to sing a cheesy song from a musical. She had belted out an entire verse and chorus before she'd managed to block the rest. 'That was *not* harmless,' Minoo said, bright red in the face.

Since then they've been keeping the exercises simple. Anna-Karin might order them to pick up a pen from the floor while they resist doing it.

So that Anna-Karin also had a chance to practice resisting, Nicolaus has suggested this morning that Vanessa make herself invisible and Anna-Karin try to see her. Eventually she succeeded, covered with sweat from the effort. Vanessa was noticeably shaken. 'That makes me feel *so* secure when I'm supposed to be secretly following a guy who's in league with demons,' she said, as she was leaving to do just that.

Minoo and Anna-Karin went straight from Nicolaus's apartment to the fairground for a reunion with the principal.

Now Minoo's head is throbbing. She just wants to lie down and sleep in the middle of the dance floor. The

397

principal drones on about the *Book of Patterns*, while Minoo, Anna-Karin and Ida twiddle their Pattern Finders and flip through the infuriating book.

'Minoo?'

For a moment Minoo is unsure whether she'd dozed off. She looks up and meets the principal's eye.

'How are you coming along? Do you see anything?'

Her enthusiasm never wanes. Minoo twists the Pattern Finder and shakes her head.

'It's incredibly important that you make an effort,' Adriana says. 'I wish I understood why Vanessa and Linnéa aren't taking this seriously. Do you know why they haven't been coming?'

'No,' says Minoo.

She shouldn't have to explain why Linnéa isn't coming – the principal herself is the reason – but she comes close to launching into a hysterical spiel about how Vanessa seemed sick the last time she saw her, really sick, and besides, she usually goes to stay with relatives in the south over Christmas – um, Spain, I think it was.

Once she had seen a TV program about how to catch someone in a lie: their explanations are always too involved and they're a little too interested in explaining every detail. Now Minoo tries to swallow the words that are trying to get out of her mouth.

Luckily she's cut off.

'I think I see something,' she hears someone say.

Ida is sitting on the floor cross-legged, peering through the Pattern Finder at the open book in her lap. 'At first they were just a collection of symbols and then . . . I get it now.'

'What can you see?' Minoo asks. 'I mean, is it an image or words?'

But no one's listening to her. Instead the principal moves next to Ida in what seems like a single stride and slams the book shut.

'What are you doing?' Ida shouts.

'Open it again,' the principal says. 'Open it and concentrate on what you're looking for. Once you've seen something in the *Book of Patterns*, you'll be able to find it again.'

Ida pouts but does as she's told. She furrows her brow in caricatured concentration and flips through the book with the Pattern Finder pressed to one eye. She twiddles it and flips through the pages, twiddles and flips.

'There!' she cries.

The principal looks at her with almost reverent attention, which makes Minoo envious to the depths of her soul.

'But it's still just symbols. It doesn't appear as text I can read, but I can still, like, understand somehow what it says,' Ida says.

'That's usually how it works,' the principal says patiently. 'What does it tell you?'

Minoo pulls out her notepad and listens intently.

'Okay. Here's sort of what it says. That it's, like, built for one. Then it works just great. But if more people try to get in, someone is always left out. And if the one who's outside disappears, the next one ends up outside. And then the next. And the next. And the next. Until everyone's gone.'

Minoo lowers her pen. It had made no sense to her at all.

'What exactly is *it*?' Anna-Karin asks.

'It's, like . . . this *thing*. It's something to do with us.'

'But what sort of thing?' Minoo asks, irritated.

'It's like a . . . I can't explain! Some kind of atmosphere or something.'

Minoo is about to explode with frustration. 'Atmosphere? Come on, Ida, you must be able to explain it better than that.'

'Well, read it yourself, then!' Ida says, and adds, with her trademark venomous smile, 'Oh, I'm sorry, I forgot. You don't know how.'

Minoo grits her teeth and raises her Pattern Finder.

The book is both a transmitter and a receiver.

Maybe it's ready to transmit to her too.

Minoo opens her book again, heart pounding, and sees Anna-Karin do the same.

She stares at the small symbols, then twiddles and flips. But nothing happens.

'I don't see anything,' Anna-Karin says.

The principal looks at Ida with delight, as if she were a child prodigy. Not only does Minoo find it incredibly unfair but she wonders how reliable the book can be if it has chosen to communicate with Ida of all people.

The black winter sky sits like a dome over the cemetery. It's so cold that your nose hairs stick together when you breathe in. On days like this Vanessa can hardly believe she'll ever see the sun again. It feels unreal to imagine that it's still out there somewhere in space.

They enter the newer part of the cemetery. Here, most of the graves are marked with discreet stone slabs that lie flat on the ground. It's as if they don't want to attract too much attention, unlike the ostentatious blocks used for the older graves.

Gustaf's sports bag is slung over his shoulder and is swinging in sync with his footsteps. He's walking quickly, as if he's in a hurry, and Vanessa almost has to run to keep up with him.

He turns off onto a snow-covered path. Some of the graves are cared for by family while others lie hidden under a white blanket. Vanessa starts to worry that Gustaf will hear her footsteps crunching, turn and see her tracks, so she tries to step in his and walk as quietly as she can.

Gustaf puts down his sports bag. Then he walks the last few steps up to the square marble headstone that bears Rebecka's name, and squats in front of it. Next to it stands another with the name 'Elias Malmgren'. Vanessa shivers, but it has nothing to do with the cold. Gustaf takes off a glove and runs his finger over Rebecka's name, which has been carved into the stone and filled with gold leaf. 'Hello,' he whispers.

Then he falls silent. Vanessa stands stock still and shoves her hands deep into her pockets to keep them warm.

'Sorry I haven't been out to see you before now,' Gustaf says. 'I've sort of felt like you're not buried here . . . I mean that this isn't where you are. But I can't find you anywhere else. So now here I am. And I don't know if you can hear me, but I hope you can sense somehow that I'm here, and know that I think about you every day. I miss you. I talk to you every night before I fall asleep.'

His voice is tense, and his breathing uneven. A few tears run down his cheeks.

'I don't know what I'm going to do without you,' he continues. 'I don't know which way is up or down. I miss you so much it feels like I'm going to be sick. And I don't know if you can ever forgive me. Please, you've got to forgive me.'

Gustaf bends forward so she can no longer see his face. His words crumble into inconsolable sobs. It's unbearable. It's far too private. But she daren't sneak away in the squeaking snow.

'You've got to forgive me, you've got to . . .'

Gustaf repeats the words in a drawn-out wail.

Vanessa lowers her eyes and tears run down her own cheeks. When she looks up again, Gustaf is standing. He lays something on the gravestone before he walks away. She watches him until he's some distance away. Then she goes up to the grave. Lying on the black marble is a necklace set with little blood-red stones.

It's actually *really good* for *everyone* that Ida found a pattern in the book, Minoo tells herself. And of course I must have a power, too. After all, Linnéa's got an element without having any powers. That must feel *even worse* to her.

Part Three

It's so dark that it could be the middle of the night. She tries to avoid slippery patches of ice as she walks. The ground is still strewn with the remains of spent fireworks from New Year's Eve. Electric candlesticks and Christmas stars glow from windows she passes.

She hasn't met anyone since she left the fairground. In this town it's easy to gain the impression that you're the last person on earth.

She stops and listens. It's deathly silent. Nothing but darkness, snow, and drab, featureless houses.

Despite that, she doesn't feel entirely alone.

She turns and thinks she can discern a figure, black against black, further down the street.

She walks faster. Tries to make it look natural. Doesn't want to show she's afraid.

When she passes under the overpass by the railroad station, she hears footsteps that aren't hers echoing off the stone walls of the tunnel.

A lone car drives past. When it disappears the world feels even more desolate. No one lives on the other side of the overpass. There's just a string of closed-down gas stations that Minoo can barely make out in the darkness. The streetlamps are spaced wide apart here and she thinks of the black smoke, how it could float toward her unseen, suspended in the darkness.

She is walking even faster now, almost running.

The other footsteps draw closer.

And closer.

'Minoo, wait!'

It's Gustaf. She stops and turns.

'Sorry, did I scare you?' he says.

There's no point in trying to run. Minoo forces a smile as if it were a nice surprise to see him there. She feels like she ought to say something, but when she tries, all that comes out is a choking sound. 'No,' she finally croaks, when he's just a few feet away.

It's Gustaf. And yet not Gustaf. There's something about the way he's looking at her – as if he finds her fascinating.

'What are you doing here?' she asks, and tries to make it sound like an innocent question, as if she isn't suspicious in the least.

She has the feeling it didn't work.

'I was out for a walk,' Gustaf says. He continues to look at her intently. She feels like a lamb with a hungry wolf.

'I've been thinking about you,' he says. 'When we spoke on the steps . . . it was as if all the pieces fell into place.'

'What do you mean?'

It's like being in a strange dream, one in which everything is familiar, yet feels totally wrong. Gustaf moves closer until their puffy jackets brush.

'I think about you all the time,' he says. 'At first I thought it was because you remind me so much of her. But now I finally understand. I understand.'

This can't be happening. She's more convinced of that with every passing second. She's ended up in one of those parallel worlds that the principal was talking about.

'I like you,' he continues. 'A lot.'

When he bends forward and kisses her, she doesn't realize

he's doing it at first. She has time to notice that his lips feel soft and warm and sort of melt into hers. That even though his mouth is new to her, it doesn't feel strange. And a tiny part of her misses it when she shoves him away. 'What are you doing?'

He shushes her and grabs her jacket to pull her to him.

Minoo breaks free and Gustaf loses his balance, slips on the icy pavement and drops to his knees. He looks at her with an expression of desperation. 'Can't you get it into your head that Rebecka is dead? We have to move on!'

She's disgusted by what he's said. It rouses her from her dreamlike state and makes her wipe her mouth. She wants to remove any trace of that kiss.

'I'm sorry,' he says. 'I can't believe I said that.'

'Neither can I,' she says, and backs away.

'Minoo . . .'

'Leave me alone.' She walks away, more scared than ever of slipping on the ice.

She wants to scrub her mouth with steel wool and rinse it with bleach. She hears him call her again.

Fucking creep, fucking creep, fucking creep.

She's not sure whether she's referring to Gustaf or herself.

Then she remembers Vanessa. Gustaf's invisible tail.

She must have seen the whole thing.

Vanessa has almost reached the cemetery gates when Cat pops up. It scowls at her with its one green eye. Apparently both dogs and cats can see her when she's invisible. They don't even need two eyes to do it.

'What do you want?' Vanessa asks in irritation.

It meows and turns down a very narrow, virtually snowed-over path that disappears between the old grave-stones. It turns to look at her, as if to make sure she's following.

Vanessa looks at Gustaf, who is waiting for the bus some distance down the road. She deliberates with herself as to what she should do.

The moment in front of Rebecka's grave has made her feel uncomfortable. Gustaf isn't guilty. She's sure of that. Enough of this crap. She wants to go home and forget the whole thing. Warm her frozen body in a hot bath, read Sirpa's Harlequin novels, and eat sweets left over from Christmas Eve, even though only the disgusting ones are left.

The cat is meowing loudly and persistently. Just then Vanessa's phone vibrates in her pocket. She struggles to pull it out and hits Answer with her thick-gloved finger.

'Hello?'

'I just wanted you to know that it's not what you think.'

It's Minoo. She sounds out of breath and worked up.

'What do you mean?'

'With Gustaf.'

'I know,' says Vanessa. 'Or – what are you talking about?'

Minoo falls silent. Eventually she says, 'What are *you* talking about?'

'I followed him to the cemetery.'

'When?'

'Just now. A few minutes ago.'

Minoo is silent. Then she says, 'That's impossible.'

'Are you saying I'm lying?'

'I saw Gustaf. Just now. By the overpass.'

It takes Vanessa a while to understand what she means. It's as if her brain has frozen. She looks down the road to where Gustaf is climbing on to the bus. 'But that's on the other side of town,' Vanessa says flatly. 'Are you sure it was him?'

'Believe me, it was him.'

'But that *is* impossible,' Vanessa says, as if that wasn't already obvious.

CHAPTER 43

It's hot in the barn. Anna-Karin has just helped Grandpa with the morning milking. He's gone back into the house, but she's stayed behind. She's moving from stall to stall, looking at the cows, hoping their calm will rub off on her.

Her phone vibrates in her pocket, but she ignores it. She knows it's Julia and Felicia. They won't leave her alone, even though Anna-Karin has told them she's ill.

It's the last day of the Christmas break and, for the first time since she left preschool, she doesn't know what awaits her at school.

Before, at least, she had known who she was. There was a certain purity about that. She'd known the deal. There was security in having nothing to lose – things could only get better; she could dream of being freed one day from the role assigned to her in this loathsome town. Now she's more frightened than ever, afraid of reverting to the person she'd been before, afraid of continuing to be the one she's become.

She had stopped using her power after Jonte's party, and the change had been immediately apparent. Her mother might start baking in the middle of the night, then not have the energy to take the trays out. She'd just sit smoking at the kitchen table while the cinnamon buns burned to a crisp. One moment she was hugging Anna-Karin so hard it hurt, and at the next she was saying she wished Anna-Karin had never been born. She switches back and forth between new and old mother – and both have become *much worse*.

Anna-Karin can't imagine what's going to happen with all the hundreds of people she's been influencing at school. Will Julia and Felicia alternate between kissing her feet and pushing her head down the toilet?

She hears a car pull up in front of the house. The doors slam and Grandpa shouts his usual cheerful greeting. Anna-Karin walks up to a grimy window and peers out.

It's Jari's father. He's talking to Grandpa, who hands him an electric drill.

Jari is sitting in the car.

Anna-Karin doesn't have time to duck. He's already seen her. And his eyes are wide with fear. As if he's terrified of her.

She walks away from the window.

If she wasn't sure before, she is now. She made the right decision. She'll never again use her magic to change her life. Controlling her power is no longer the issue. She's terrified of being unable to control herself.

Minoo climbs down the embankment and trudges on through the deep snow. The sun, which has barely mustered the energy to rise, shines low in the sky, forcing her to squint. Soon it'll disappear behind the firs.

Her breath billows out of her mouth in great plumes as she steps onto the dirt path and walks along it. It's the last day of the Christmas break. At the start of each semester. Minoo usually feels a mixture of fear and expectation. Now the stakes are much higher. Now their lives are on the line. If she survives, her heart is sure to be torn apart. Just a few weeks ago Minoo had never been kissed. Now she's kissed her teacher *and* her dead friend's boyfriend, who might have murdered her but definitely has a doppelganger and is probably in league with demons.

Barely twenty-four hours have passed since Gustaf kissed her, and she hasn't told anyone. She's so ashamed that she can't bear to think about it. How could she ever explain something like that? As soon as she even considers telling the others, she sees Linnéa's look of contempt.

I suppose you and Rebecka weren't such good friends after all.

To top it all off, Nicolaus gave her a talking to this morning. He's refusing to let them use his apartment unless they invite Ida to their training sessions.

'She deserves the same chances as you. A chain is only as strong as its weakest link. If you don't tell her soon, I will.'

I'll tell her. I'll tell her today, she thinks. No matter what the others say.

She reaches the frozen stream when she catches sight of something black moving along the ground. She knows who it is before she looks down.

Cat meows glumly and Minoo looks at it with a warmth

that takes her by surprise. Nicolaus didn't want to come, but his familiar is here. A part of him.

'Let's go,' Minoo says.

They're such a motley crew, Minoo thinks, as she walks through the fairground gates.

Vanessa, who looks as if she's freezing in her far-too-thin jacket; Anna-Karin, like an overgrown child, with her brightly colored woolen hat pulled low over her forehead; Linnéa, hidden inside a leopard-print fake-fur coat; and Ida in her white down jacket.

Minoo puts her backpack on the stage and pulls out some sheets of paper she's printed from the Internet. She's nervous. But when she catches sight of Cat, who jumps up and lies down next to her – she feels a little stronger. She meets Ida's gaze.

'Ida,' she asks, 'have you found anything in the book?'

Ida shakes her head and smacks loudly on a piece of gum – Minoo gets a whiff of synthetic watermelon. 'Nothing about G and a mysterious twin anyway,' she says, with a secretive smile that's intended to hint she's found other things – things she has no intention of telling Minoo.

Minoo swallows her irritation and looks down at her papers. 'I may have found something,' she says.

The others wait. It's quiet, except for the wet smacking from Ida's mouth.

'So, the question is how could Gustaf be in two places at the same time?' Minoo begins.

The smacking stops.

'No,' Ida says. 'The question is why we don't go to the principal.'

'You know the answer to that,' Linnéa says. 'Because she won't do anything, except stop us.'

'Maybe she can help us if we just as—'

'We have to help ourselves,' Linnéa says.

She gives Ida such a look of contempt that Minoo can't help but be impressed. But Ida just scoffs and starts chewing her gum again. 'Can you imagine what the principal would do if she found out about this?' she says.

'But she's not going to,' Linnéa says. 'Is she?'

Ida doesn't answer, just goes on chewing.

'*Is* she?' Linnéa repeats.

Ida shrugs her shoulders. 'I guess we'll have to see about that.'

Minoo fingers her papers. She's already lost control of the situation. She clears her throat. 'Ida,' she says. 'We have to know we can trust you.' Even though we lie to you, she thinks, and feels sick.

'I have no reason to feel any loyalty toward any of you.'

'We promised each other we'd work together and look out for each other.'

'I'm here, aren't I?' Ida says, throwing out her hands. 'But I'm going soon if you don't get started.'

'God, we'd really miss you,' Linnéa mumbles.

'As I was saying,' Minoo breaks in, before they start squabbling again, 'I've tried to find an explanation for how Vanessa and I could have seen Gustaf at the same time. I started searching under "doppelganger" online and it turned out you can find them in pretty much all mythologies.' She looks up, as if to make sure that the others are paying attention.

'I thought the principal's Soviet-style censorship machine had removed all truth from the Internet,' Linnéa says.

'But she also said that traces remain,' Anna-Karin counters.

Minoo looks at her in surprise.

'Well, that's what she said,' Anna-Karin mumbles.

'Exactly,' says Minoo, feeling like a teacher giving praise. '*Doppelgänger* is German, meaning literally 'double-walker'. The old Irish myths mention a creature known as a *fetch*. There are Norse myths about *vardøgern*, a kind of ghost-like premonitory apparition of a person who hasn't been there yet. In the far north of Finland it's called an *etiäinen*. All the mythologies agree that the appearance of a doppelganger is a bad omen. If you see your own doppelganger it's usually a sign that you're going to die.'

Minoo flips through her pile of papers.

'But I'm not sure that's what we're looking for. I stumbled on some references to a kind of sister phenomenon known as *bilocation*. It appears throughout the world. There are references to it in early Greek philosophy, Hinduism, Buddhism, shamanism, Jewish mysticism—'

'So what is it?' Vanessa asks impatiently.

'It's the ability to be in two places at the same time,' Minoo says. 'You create a double that can gather information while you're somewhere else. I haven't really understood if the double has a will and intelligence of its own, or whether it's sort of on remote control. But that's the best explanation I've been able to find.'

'So only one of the Gustafs we saw was the real Gustaf,' Vanessa says. 'What was your Gustaf like?'

'There was definitely something wrong with him,' Minoo says. 'You must have been following the original.'

'It must have been the double that killed Rebecka,' Anna-Karin says. 'Because it sort of wasn't him.'

The urge returns to rinse her mouth out with bleach. There's no doubt any more. The Gustaf Minoo saw, the one who kissed her, was the same Gustaf who had killed Rebecka.

'That makes sense,' Linnéa says, deep in thought. 'If Gustaf is such a thoroughly nice guy, like you say, he'd never be able to murder someone. Why not create a double to do your dirty work for you?'

Minoo feels her ears heat. Why did Gustaf kiss her?

'Minoo,' Linnéa says, 'you heard two voices when he was trying to kill you. Could Gustaf and his double have been talking to each other?'

'One wanted to kill you and the other didn't,' says Anna-Karin, thoughtfully.

'That would mean the double has a will of its own,' Vanessa points out.

Everyone falls silent for a moment.

'So Gustaf isn't dangerous. His double is,' Anna-Karin says.

'The double *that he created*,' Linnéa says. 'So he's definitely not innocent.'

'How do we know he created it?' Anna-Karin asks. 'I mean, maybe it came into existence on its own.'

'The only one of us who can find out any more about how this works is Ida,' Minoo says, and hears resentment in her voice.

'All right, I'll give it another try,' Ida says. 'But what do you think the principal would say about Vanessa stalking G all day?'

'You can ask her,' a familiar voice responds.

In a perfectly synchronized movement, everyone turns to see her walking toward the dance pavilion, her long black coat sweeping across the snow.

Cat hisses viciously at her raven, which caws as it glides through the air and alights on the railing of the dance floor.

'I tried to tell them!' Ida shouts. 'You heard that, didn't you?'

'I'm disappointed in you,' the principal says, ignoring Ida. She glares accusingly at Minoo. 'Especially you. Didn't I expressly tell you not to do anything on your own?'

Minoo is at a loss for words.

'And Vanessa,' the principal adds, 'do you realize how much danger you're putting yourself into by following Gustaf? The Council regards him as a particularly potent threat and has appointed . . .'

She is interrupted by a low laugh. Minoo has never heard it before, and it takes her a moment to realize it's coming from Linnéa. She's laughing so much she can hardly breathe.

Everyone stares at her.

'Sorry . . .' Linnéa whimpers. 'But . . . it's just so . . . fucking . . . tragic.'

Adriana crosses her arms. 'Perhaps you'd care to share your little joke with the rest of us.'

Linnéa's laughter peters out and her face hardens. 'How long do you intend to carry on this charade?'

'I don't know what you're talking about,' Adriana says. 'Now, you must tell me everything you've found out about Gustaf—'

'No,' Linnéa says, without releasing the principal from her gaze. 'It's time for you to tell us what you and the Council are actually doing. You pretend to be as powerful as gods, but all you can do is light little fires. The only way you can control us is by tricking us into believing we need you. But when it comes down to it, you don't actually know anything. You *can't* protect us, even if you want to.'

'That's not true,' the principal says.

'Have you forgotten about the circles we saw at her house?' Minoo says impatiently to Linnéa. 'They could teleport her from Stockholm to here – powerful magic.'

But Linnéa ignores her. She's focused on Adriana, like a laser beam. 'You already have two lives on your conscience, but maybe you want us all to die. Perhaps that's your purpose.'

'No!'

Her voice reminds Minoo of a bird's shriek. The principal presses her lips together. Minoo can see that she's trying to keep composed. But it's too late. Her mask has cracked. She can no longer hide her fear.

She takes a deep breath and lets out the world's longest sigh. 'I don't even know where to begin.'

'Start with the circles in your house,' Linnéa suggests. 'Explain to Minoo why they weren't so impressive, after all.'

Linnéa is looking triumphantly at the principal, but Minoo is terrified: she doesn't want to hear what's about to be said. If the principal and the Council aren't as all-knowing and powerful as they've claimed, she'd prefer to live with the lie. The principal has been the only authority they've had – the only one with any answers. The notion that they might be completely alone, without any guidance, is simply too horrifying.

'The circles . . .' the principal starts, then pauses. 'It took six months and five witches to perform the incantation. It was the equivalent of the world's most expensive alarm system, the only difference being that when the circles have been used once the whole procedure has to be performed again. Linnéa is right. The fire magic you've seen me do is the only thing I can manage without difficulty. Anything else requires days, often weeks, of preparation and almost always the help of other witches.'

She pauses again, as if to catch her breath. It looks as if every word she utters is painful, but out they come – one after the other.

'Unlike you, I wasn't born with powers. I grew up in a family of trained witches, raised in the belief that the Council always does the right thing.' She pauses a third time. 'I feel enormous guilt for what happened to Elias and Rebecka. We should have done more to prevent . . . We should have been more open with you from the start.'

She falls silent and looks at the ground. The raven flaps through the air and lands on her shoulder. It tucks its head under one wing.

'And the all-powerful Council?' Linnéa asks, with a smile that borders on smug. She's behaving like a sadistic interrogator, Minoo thinks.

'They're afraid of you,' the principal says. 'If they knew I was being so open with you now, I'd be punished. They want me to control you, get you to find the answers in the *Book of Patterns* that they can't see, and use that knowledge to strengthen the Council.'

'So the Council is as useless as you are?' Linnéa asks.

'You don't have to kick her when she's down,' Minoo says. 'You exposed her. That's enough.'

'I understand you're disappointed, Minoo. No teacher to suck up to any more,' Linnéa says.

'It's not true that the Council is powerless,' the principal interrupts shrilly. 'You mustn't dismiss it. The Council is well organized and many across the world submit to its authority. Together they can perform powerful magic. They could take drastic action to bring you to heel.' She glances at Anna-Karin.

'Drastic action?' Linnéa says scornfully. 'I don't think they've shown any stomach for that.'

The principal hesitates. Then she unbuttons her long winter coat, revealing one of her typically well-tailored suits with a white blouse. She undoes the three top buttons.

Minoo has to look away.

The fire symbol is branded just below the principal's left collarbone in a web-like patch of scorched skin.

'I planned to leave the Council once,' the principal says, with a mirthless smile. 'There was a man. You may think this looks bad . . .' She meets Linnéa's gaze and holds it. '. . . but it's nothing compared to what they did to him.'

Linnéa's face is tense and her mouth half open. She takes a few staggering steps backward.

The principal buttons her blouse and refastens her coat. 'I suggest you all go home. School starts tomorrow. Ida can search in the book,' she says. 'But that's all you should do.'

She turns and looks at Minoo. For just half a second too long. There's something knowing in her eyes. Something enigmatic that Minoo can't interpret.

'Absolutely nothing else,' the principal says.

'Ida!' Minoo shouts. 'Wait!'

Ida stops but doesn't turn.

'I need to talk to you,' Minoo says, when she comes up.

Ida looks at her reluctantly. Her eyes seem almost unnaturally blue against her white jacket and the snow. She's as cute as a doll – an evil doll, but still . . .

No, she mustn't think like that. It's time to turn the page.

'I know what you're thinking,' Ida says. 'You've been meeting in secret. At Nicolaus's house. We're safe at his place, because he's got a magic silver cross on his wall. It said so in a letter in a safety deposit box that Cat showed you. Cat is Nicolaus's familiar. Nicolaus is also a witch. His element is wood, but you didn't know that.'

Minoo stares at Ida as she tries frantically to think of an explanation. Who told her?

'The book showed me,' Ida says triumphantly. 'It said you've been practicing your magic without me.' She wipes the tip of her nose. 'You're bullying me.'

'No . . .'

'Really?' Ida says. 'So you didn't say you thought the world would be a better place if I were dead?'

'I'm sorry,' Minoo says. 'Very sorry. And it was wrong of us to keep our meetings secret from you. But I was going to tell you about it now.'

'Because I'm the only one who can read the book. You need me.'

'Yes. We need you.' Her words catch in Minoo's throat as she speaks them. 'Are you going to help us? Without telling Adriana?'

Ida snorts. Then she looks away. 'The book says I have to help you. Otherwise it won't show me any more.'

The situation with the snitching book becomes more and more bizarre.

'Can you look for something to help us find out the truth?' Minoo asks.

'I guess so. But I'm doing it for G, not you.'

CHAPTER 44

Vanessa wakes up because she's cold. She's wedged in the gap between the bed and the wall. Her head is full of nightmare images. The principal's burn. Gustaf at Rebecka's grave, digging up Rebecka's coffin. Cat's staring green eye.

Vanessa turns over to look at her slumbering boyfriend. Wille has taken all the covers again and wrapped himself up in them like a Wille burrito. Only his hair is sticking out. Vanessa kicks him angrily, but he just snuffles and turns over.

She glances at the Batman alarm clock, a relic from Wille's childhood. She has to get up in five minutes anyway. She clambers over him and almost loses her balance as she slides out of bed.

Wille's room has always looked like an archaeological dig with layers of artifacts from different eras. Since Vanessa moved in it's twice as bad. Neither of them can keep the place tidy and, for better or worse, Sirpa ignores everything that goes on, declaring it 'their space'.

Vanessa feels something soft and sticky under her foot. She's stepped on a bologna sandwich.

Her anger explodes like a geyser. She picks up one of

Wille's slippers and throws it at the bed. It bounces off the headboard and lands on his face. The burrito wakes up.

'What the fuck is your problem?' he says groggily.

'What the fuck is your problem?' Vanessa mimics. 'I'll tell you what the fuck my problem is. I've just stepped on the disgusting old sandwich you tossed onto your disgusting fucking floor!'

Wille sits up, still wrapped in the blanket. 'It's not my freaking sandwich,' he says.

'I. Don't. Eat. Bologna,' Vanessa enunciates, as if Wille were old and deaf. 'Just look at this place!'

'You live here too.'

'I'm at school all day! You don't do anything! Can't you at least clean it up?'

'You've just had, like, the longest frigging Christmas break ever. You clean up your shit and I'll clean up mine,' he says, and pulls one of her bras from under his pillow. He flings it at her, and it lands at her feet.

Vanessa wants to scream at him, but the thought of Sirpa in the next room stops her. Instead she grabs the bra and throws it back at Wille. It lands on his head with one cup hanging over his face.

'Give me a fucking *break*,' Wille whines, but he's smiling.

Vanessa picks up a car magazine from the floor and hurls it at him.

'Stop it,' Wille says, and is hit by a disgusting-looking sock. 'That does it!' he says. He jumps out of bed, grabs Vanessa and carries her back to the bed.

'Let go! I've got bologna on my foot!'

'I don't give a shit.'

'I have to go to school!'

'No, you don't.'

'I do! The holidays are over!'

'The first day of the spring semester is always field day,' says Wille, and lays her on the mattress.

Vanessa smiles. She'd forgotten that. She grabs the covers and wraps them around her. Field day is a free day. Everyone knows that.

'Then I'm going back to sleep,' she says. 'And you're going to throw away that revolting sandwich. And wipe my heel,' she adds, waving her foot.

Wille leaves the room and Vanessa shuts her eyes. She falls asleep surprisingly quickly, waking up briefly as Wille wields a tissue on her foot, bowing sarcastically when he's done.

The pain is so sharp and so sudden that for a few seconds Minoo forgets how to breathe. She's sure she's broken her tail bone and the ice underneath her.

She hears catcalls and mittened applause and tries to laugh – *No problem, I'm fine. Doesn't hurt a bit* – even though the tears are stinging the corners of her eyes.

She had chosen to spend the day on skates because Max is supervising the activities at the Engelsfors sports field. Of course he's barely looking in her direction.

Minoo tries to stand up. The skates slip from under her so her legs splay in impossible directions. She puts her hands against the smoothly polished ice and tries again. This time she lands hard on her knees. Fresh pain shoots up her thighs.

She hears someone come toward her across the ice. She looks up just as Max brakes perfectly, showering her with a thin mist of ice crystals. He holds out his hand and helps her up, but she almost falls over again and is in danger of pulling him down with her. Max wobbles. They support each other for a moment in what looks almost like an embrace. She gets the giddy feeling that he's about to kiss her again.

'Are you all right?' he asks, and gently lets go of her.

No, I'm freaking not, Minoo wants to say – actually, there's a lot she'd like to say. Instead she says, 'No. My right knee really hurts. I don't think I can skate any more.'

'Then go home and rest,' Max says.

He's completely impersonal again. It's painful for her to be so close to him and unable to touch him. She feels as if he's ripped her heart out, thrown it on to the ice, set fire to it, stomped on it, stuffed it back into her chest, sewn it up, and started all over again.

'I've handed in my notice. I'll be leaving at the end of the spring semester.'

He doesn't bat an eyelid when he says it. His gaze is fixed on Julia and Felicia, who are making failed attempts at pirouettes.

'But that doesn't mean I don't like you,' he continues, in a low voice. 'Quite the opposite.'

Finally he looks her in the eyes.

'I like you far too much.'

Then he skates off. A few quick strides and he's gone.

Minoo is left alone, looking after him and trying to understand what she has just heard. The pain has subsided. Instead she is filled with a new and dangerous sensation.

Hope.

Anna-Karin shuts her eyes and glides down the hill. She's skied here a thousand times before and knows every curve. The rush of air hits her face. The snow is whispering beneath her skis. She feels light and free. She opens her eyes and blinks at the sun as she coasts into the next curve.

Anna-Karin used to go cross-country skiing with Grandpa on these trails in winter, and it's always been the obvious choice for her during school field days. It's the only sport she's reasonably good at, and she loves shooting through the forest among the fir trees. She's never had to worry about meeting any of her bullies on these tracks: cross-country skiing is not the sport of choice for the in-crowd.

Anna-Karin relishes being alone. She has to steel herself for the new semester and the difficult task she's set for herself.

If only she didn't have such a vivid image in her mind of the principal's scarred skin.

It's nothing compared to what they did to him.

What will the Council do to Anna-Karin?

There's a rest stop a short distance ahead. She sets her sights on the dark brown wooden roof, the solid table with its two long benches, and picks up speed.

When she reaches it, she sticks her poles into a snowdrift, takes off her skis and stands them alongside. She opens her jacket to let in the cold air and tosses her backpack onto the table. She has just started to take out her packed lunch when she hears a skier swishing toward her.

The figure catches sight of her, stops, looks around, then skis in closer. Anna-Karin sees her blonde hair and puts down her drink.

It's Ida.

'What do you want?' Anna-Karin asks, as she comes up.

'Just to say hi.'

Anna-Karin glances around automatically. Are Robin, Kevin and Erik hiding in the forest? Or any of the others that Ida has tormented her with over the years? Can they already be out to get her?

'Now you've said it,' says Anna-Karin. 'So leave me alone.'

'It's a free country.'

'What – are you still in elementary school?'

'I just want you to know one thing,' Ida says, taking off her skis. She looks almost unnaturally healthy, as if she lives on vitamins, organic vegetables and outdoor activities in clean alpine air. 'This term's going to be different. You took away everything that was mine, and now I'm taking it back. You can't stop me. You're going to regret ruining my life.'

So says Ida. The Ida who had made Anna-Karin's life miserable for nine excruciating years.

It's as if something bursts inside her, something she hasn't been completely aware of. It's like the thin membrane inside an eggshell, a protective layer that has somehow held together the roiling mass of angst, fear and rage. Now it breaks, and all the ugliness and venom pour out, spreading through her: a dark, seething sludge of pure hatred.

'Everybody hates you, Ida,' Anna-Karin says. 'Don't you know that?'

'Thanks to you, yeah. But don't go thinking—'

'No,' Anna-Karin carries on relentlessly. 'Everybody has always hated you. They just pretended to like you because they were afraid of being your next victim. It makes no difference what you do to me. It won't change what they think of you.'

For a moment Ida looks as if she's about to cry – the tears are just beneath the surface. 'Nobody's friends with you because they want to be either,' she says.

Anna-Karin moves a step closer and Ida backs away. 'Maybe, but I never hurt anyone. You did, all the time. What I did is nothing compared to what you've been doing.'

'You're such a fucking *freak*!'

'You ruined my *entire* life,' Anna-Karin says. She walks forward a few more steps. Ida's heels are pressed against a snowdrift.

'It wasn't just me,' Ida says defiantly.

'No. But you were one of the ones who started it. I never understood why you picked on me. I used to lie awake at night trying to figure out what was wrong with me so I could change. I discovered loads of things to hate about myself. I tried everything. But it was never enough. Not even when I gave up, when I did everything not to draw attention to myself.'

Anna-Karin glimpses a momentary hesitation in her.

'No, it wasn't enough,' Ida says slowly, as if she really wants Anna-Karin to hear every word. 'You should have killed yourself.'

The dark wave that has built inside Anna-Karin washes over her. She allows herself be swept along by it.

She throws herself forward. She's heavier than Ida and adrenaline makes her strong. Ida topples to the ground. Anna-Karin pins her shoulders to the snowdrift and straddles her waist. Ida struggles, twists and strains, but to no avail.

'Let go! I can't breathe!'

It's as if the power inside Anna-Karin has a life of its own. A living entity that has been lying in wait, biding its time for this very moment.

Go *away, leave this town and never show your face here again.*

Ida's pupils widen. Anna-Karin sees her struggle to resist, her face turning redder and redder.

Be gone . . .

There is an invisible wall between her and Ida.

Anna-Karin recognizes it from the practice exercises. Ida resists.

Anna-Karin pushes harder, puts all her will and concentration behind her power to break through the wall between them. It buckles but doesn't break. Finally Anna-Karin realizes she has nothing left to draw from.

Exhaustion overcomes her. She tumbles to the side, into the snowdrift. Ida gets up, staggering, but triumph shines in her eyes. And Anna-Karin realizes she fell into Ida's trap. She allowed herself to be provoked. Just as Ida had wanted.

'I'm not afraid of you any more,' Ida says. 'The book taught me how to do it. It's on my side.' She stumbles toward her skis and puts them on. Anna-Karin is unable to speak.

'You should follow your own advice,' Ida says. 'You should leave. Tomorrow school starts for real, and then everything will be just as it should be.'

She glides down the track. Anna-Karin shuts her eyes. If she lies here long enough she'll freeze to death. It wouldn't matter much. 'I can't take it any more,' she whispers. 'I can't take it any more.'

CHAPTER 45

Number seventeen. Number nineteen.

What am I doing? Minoo thinks as she walks along Uggelbovägen Street.

Number twenty-one. Twenty-three.

The orange streetlamps cast their eerie glow over the freshly cleared road. The banks of snow are marked here and there with random squirts of dog pee. She passes numbers twenty-five, twenty-seven and twenty-nine.

This is something Vanessa might do. Or Linnéa.

Thirty-one and thirty-three.

Definitely not Minoo Falk Karimi.

She stops at number thirty-five and looks toward house number thirty-seven. The light is on in Max's window. She can still turn around and go home. It's still possible. She can still pull out.

But if she leaves now, she'll never know.

She walks up to Max's door and reaches out to ring his doorbell. She stops when she hears voices inside the house. Is the TV or radio on? Or does he have a friend a friend with him? *A woman?*

It's never occurred to her that Max might have a private

life. In her mind he's always existed in a vacuum when he hasn't been at school.

What if he has friends with him for dinner? What will they think? That Max is some kind of semi-pedophile who takes advantage of his students? And that she's a stupid little airhead with a penchant for older men?

Perhaps Max's friends would think it quite normal for him to be with a girl who's barely started tenth grade, and he probably wouldn't be embarrassed in the slightest.

'How did you two meet?'

'Well, Minoo is a real whiz at quadratic equations, and we really hit it off!'

Suddenly she can imagine how repellent it would look to other people.

Does Max have brothers and sisters, parents? What fun family gatherings they'd have. She'd have to sit at the kids' table while the grown-ups talked. And what about her own parents? Her father would wonder if he had brought on a father fixation by working too much during her childhood. Her mother would find a less than flattering diagnosis for Max, and dispatch Minoo to a psychiatric ward for adolescents.

Even if they were to try to keep their relationship secret, it would get out. Secret love affairs never remain secret for long in Engelsfors. Then the school would report Max to the police. He'd never be able to work again as a teacher.

She lowers her hand.

Suddenly a new dimension has been added to her

relationship with Max: reality. She had avoided it until now. But Max had seen it all along.

When you're older you'll realize how young you actually were.

She had sat on his sofa, trying to convince him of how mature she was, when all she'd really done was prove the opposite.

The voices inside are suddenly silenced and Minoo realizes it must have been the TV. She hears footsteps. Max is walking around. He goes from the living room to the kitchen, fills the sink with water, starts clattering dishes.

She had come here to convince Max that they have to be together, that they shouldn't care what other people think. But now that she can see everything so clearly, she can't pretend not to.

There's only one thing she can do. And one thing she has to know.

The doorbell is surprisingly soft and melodic.

The clattering in the kitchen stops. Footsteps approach. Minoo stands her ground, trying to breathe calmly even though her heart is pounding with a blistering techno beat.

The latch turns. The door opens.

Max appears, lit from behind. He's wearing a white T-shirt and black jeans. His hair is ruffled and he is pale, with dark circles under his eyes. Somehow that makes him even better-looking. He's like a tragic young poet – a Keats or a Byron. He's drying his hands on a dish towel.

'Hi,' she says. 'I'm sorry to disturb you like this.'

'Minoo—'

'Please, just listen to me. I've been thinking about what you said. And I know you're right. We can't be together.'

It's painful for her to say it. The logical part of her brain sees things clearly but that doesn't change the fact that she loves him. Perhaps more than ever.

'I'm not going to come here again like this. I'm not going to tell anyone about us so you don't need to worry. There's just one thing I want to know . . .' She falls silent. The question had seemed so simple and straightforward. Now it seems too momentous to ask. She looks at his hands, which are playing with the towel.

'What do you want to know?' Max asks softly. 'If I meant what I said? Because I do. I love you, Minoo. I've loved you since the first day I set eyes on you.'

'I love you, too,' she says, and it feels so natural. 'But I know now that it's not possible. What I have to know is . . . can you bear to wait for me?'

She can't look him in the eyes. 'I'll be eighteen in a little over a year. And then you won't be my teacher.'

She looks up and can tell he's hesitating. A year is a lot to ask. An eternity. 'I understand if you can't make any promises,' she mumbles.

He's quiet for a long moment. Then he says, 'A year is nothing. I'll wait for as long as it takes.' He reaches out and strokes her cheek. A gentle caress that almost shatters her logic.

Just one night, she wants to say. Just one night together. That can't make any difference, can it? And she sees in his eyes that he wants it as much as she does.

She pulls away from his hand. 'I have to go,' she says.

She turns and starts walking. Thirty-five, thirty-three, thirty-one, twenty-nine. Only now does she hear him shut his front door. She speeds up. Twenty-seven, twenty-five, twenty-three, twenty-one, nineteen, seventeen. She stops. Turns.

The street looks just as it did before. Yet everything has changed.

Anna-Karin can't sleep. She's lying on her side, staring into the room. The blinds aren't pulled down and she can see the stars through the window. Tonight they seem more distant than ever.

Tomorrow it begins, she thinks. Tomorrow I have to go to school and be Anna-Karin Nieminen without magic. The girl everyone hates or, if she's lucky, doesn't notice.

That must be my true self, she thinks. That must be my lot in life. Why else would it have gone so wrong when I tried to change it?

Deep down she had known all along that what she was doing was wrong. It was just that she'd felt it was worth it so she had ignored the warnings, turned a blind eye to the signs. But what good had it done her? Is she happier? No.

Anna-Karin closes her eyes, but her brain keeps whirring, like a crashing computer. She opens her eyes again. There's no point.

Anna-Karin.

She recognizes the voice from the vision on Lucia night. It belongs to Rebecka and Elias's murderer.

Life isn't worth living. You're going to suffer. Every day you're going to suffer.

A great calm spreads through Anna-Karin. She feels her body go numb as it climbs out of bed. Her feet walk on to the landing. One step down the stairs, then another.

Anna-Karin allows herself to be guided into the kitchen. She doesn't resist. What the voice is saying is true. If anyone knows that life is suffering, it's Anna-Karin. The B.O. Ho. The fat kid. The country bumpkin. The girl who had to use magic to make her own mother care about her.

She feels relieved. She doesn't need to be afraid any more. Soon it will all be over.

The voice says no more. It knows that Anna-Karin doesn't need convincing.

There's a faint smell of cigarette smoke in the kitchen. The wall clock is ticking away the seconds. Her feet move across the floor to the knife stand next to the stove. Her hand reaches out and takes a firm grip on the biggest knife. It feels strange to see her hand like that, see it grab something even though she can't feel it. As if it belongs to someone else.

Don't worry. You won't feel any pain.

Her hand angles, turning the blade toward her throat.

She catches sight of Grandpa's house outside the window. Grandpa loves her.

And if Grandpa loves her, she can't be completely worthless. She doesn't deserve this.

Nobody does.

Suddenly Anna-Karin is afraid. That can mean only one thing. She wants to live. She doesn't want to die.

The edge of the blade brushes against the soft skin of her throat.

Anna-Karin starts to resist. The other tries to press the knife into her neck. She can feel her carotid artery beating against the blade. Her skin is so thin there. All it will take is a little slit and her blood will spurt all over the kitchen. It's as if an iron hand is clenched around her wrist. Her arms are shaking from the strain as she struggles to resist. The line separating life and death is so fine.

You're alone, Anna-Karin. Alone. Why should you go on living? You're worth more. Maybe you'll get another chance after death.

But she's not listening now. She can't leave Grandpa. And she can't abandon the other Chosen Ones in the battle against evil.

She isn't weak any more. She's no victim. She controlled the entire school. This is nothing. She's got more power than this cowardly bastard who doesn't even have the guts to show himself to the one he's killing.

Let go!

Her power surges through her body and the knife falls to the floor. Anna-Karin slumps down and stares at it. She's breathing heavily.

A familiar squeaking sound comes from outside.

Anna-Karin gets up, sweat pouring off her. She goes to the window. The barn door is wide open, like a gaping mouth in the red-painted wall. She has the feeling that whatever had tried to take control of her body is playing with her.

She goes out into the hall, pulls on a pair of fur-lined

shoes and her thickest winter jacket, then opens the door.

It's strangely quiet outside and there's no wind. All the windows are dark in Grandpa's house. She knows she should call the other Chosen Ones. She knows she shouldn't do this alone. She knows it could be a trap – it's likely that it is. But she's tired of running away, tired of being afraid.

She feels as if she could face down anyone. She'll bring the killer to his knees and force the truth out of him. And then she'll call the others. After the threat has been neutralized. Then perhaps she'll have atoned her crimes. Even in the eyes of the Council.

She stops at the barn door. A familiar smell wafts toward her. She can hear the cows moving in their stalls.

'Show yourself,' Anna-Karin says.

A cow moos softly. Another snorts. Anna-Karin takes a step inside and switches on the light.

All she sees are rows of cows looking at her with their big brown eyes. Anna-Karin walks further inside.

The crash comes so suddenly that she screams. She spins around. The barn door is closed. As if it had blown shut. On a windless night.

She goes to the door and pulls at it. It's locked. Bolted from the outside. And that's when she smells the smoke.

'No!' she shouts. 'No! Let me out!'

The cows moo and kick in their stalls. They've also smelled the smoke and know what it means.

The smoke grows thicker with every second. A loud crackling rises quickly to a deafening roar.

Fire.

Anna-Karin looks for something to smash down the door. The smoke stings her eyes. She realizes the fire is spreading faster than should be possible. It's coming from every direction. It becomes unbearably hot.

'Anna-Karin!'

Grandpa has managed to get in and is rushing forward as fast as his old legs can carry him. When he reaches her he shoves her toward the door.

'Run!' he shouts.

But she can't leave him. He hurries along the row of stalls, opening them. The cows race out in a wild panic, pushing and bunching together, mooing loudly in their desperate flight. A few jostle past Anna-Karin and she falls headlong on to the concrete floor. Her ankle twists beneath her. All around her the heavy bodies gallop past in a frenzy and she shields her head with her arms.

But she doesn't have time to call for help before Grandpa is at her side. He's there with his rough, powerful hands and helps her up, letting her lean on him. They're only a few feet from the door now, a few steps from safety. Anna-Karin doesn't see the falling beam until it hits him. He crumples to the floor.

'Grandpa!'

She doesn't feel her own pain now. She has to get Grandpa out. She pulls and drags at him and suddenly they're in the snow, but Anna-Karin keeps going, moving away from the barn until she can go no further.

The fire engulfs the old wooden building with a roar. She hears her mother scream inside their house. But Anna-Karin has eyes only for Grandpa. He looks at her. Grandpa, dear, sweet Grandpa.

'Anna-Karin . . .' he says faintly. 'I should . . .'

And then his words give out.

Part 4
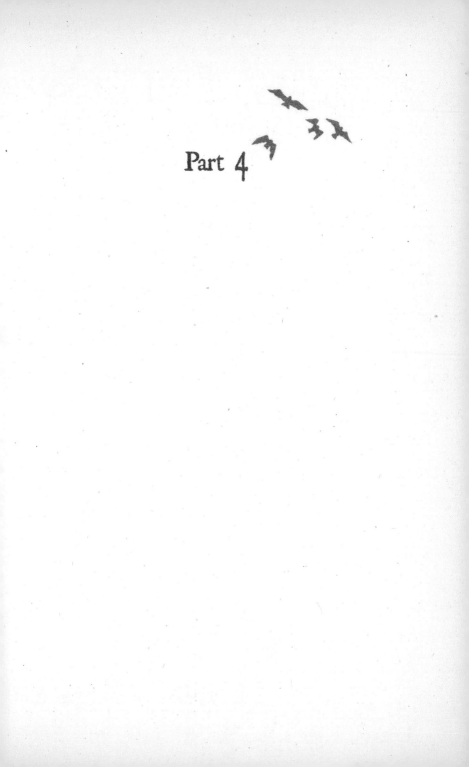

CHAPTER 46

The Crystal Cave's sign is midnight blue set with gold curlicue lettering and a sprinkling of little stars and half-moons. Vanessa had hoped that Mona Moonbeam's shop would be closed. Yet another forgotten victim of the City Mall, a.k.a. the final resting place of failed businesses. But she had caught a whiff of cigarettes and incense as soon as she'd opened the door to the mall. And now she can see through the shop window that three people are waiting to be served in the Crystal Cave. Mona is wearing the same denim outfit as last time, and is receiving a wad of banknotes from an old man who looks to be somewhere between eighty and death.

Vanessa spits out her chewing gum so violently that it bounces against the floor.

Why was she so stupid as to bring up the Crystal Cave? Why had she let herself be talked into coming here?

She knows the answer, of course. They're desperate.

The *Book of Patterns* has shown them they need ectoplasm but, of course, refused to tell them how to get it.

Vanessa has started to hate that book. It behaves like a grumpy old hag. She's shaken her own copy viciously, threatened to rip out every single page if it doesn't show her how to solve the mystery of Gustaf and his doppelganger. But nothing appears to her through the Pattern Finder.

Ida is still the only one who can read the *Book of Patterns*. But in front of the principal, whom they still see on Saturdays, she pretends it's not showing her anything. What Ida finds in the book they discuss at Nicolaus's house.

When the book wanted them to practice detecting each other's energies, it had taken Ida a quarter of an hour to explain what they should do. But it had offered no insight as to the point of the exercise.

'Don't blame me,' Ida said. 'I'm just reading what it says.'

Minoo had tried to put a positive spin on things. She said that the *Book of Patterns* probably knew what they needed, that there must be a really important reason why they had to learn this.

They had no alternative than to put their trust in the grumpy old hag of a book and try the exercises it recommended, no matter how meaningless they seemed. They took turns sitting blindfolded on a chair in Nicolaus's living room and concentrating on where the others were standing.

Minoo was the first to sit in the chair but she couldn't find anyone. When she took off the blindfold, she looked devastated. 'Put through a meat grinder,' as Vanessa's mother sometimes said. Vanessa felt sorry for her.

Ida had pulled it off perfectly on the first try and was almost bursting with smugness. She would have loved to give herself a round of wild applause and do cartwheels across the room.

Linnéa had done pretty well, too. When it was Vanessa's turn to sit in the chair, she'd been more nervous than expected. The soft blindfold – actually one of Nicolaus's old, musty scarves – was fastened behind her head. It was unpleasant knowing that everyone was looking at her yet she couldn't see them.

Her senses had played tricks on her the whole time. At one moment she thought she'd heard someone giggle, at the next it was so quiet she was sure everyone had left.

It was only after Nicolaus had urged her to relax that it started to work.

Then she could feel the others, faintly at first, but the more she trusted the feeling, the stronger it became. Eventually there was no hesitation: she could point out where they were standing, one by one, in quick succession.

Vanessa would never be able to explain how she did it. It was as if she could detect the other Chosen Ones using a sense she hadn't been aware she possessed. Not smell or taste, not hearing, touch or sight. It was something else altogether.

The book also taught them a magical version of hide-and-seek, or 'pendulation' – that was the word Ida had used when she'd tried to explain the procedure. A Chosen One would stand in Nicolaus's living room while the others would go into the kitchen, shut the door between the two rooms and sit at the kitchen table. Then they would spread a diagram of the apartment on the table. The one doing the exercise would take Ida's silver necklace and let it hang like a pendulum above the diagram.

Vanessa was the first to try. She took Ida's necklace while Linnéa waited in the living room. At first the little silver heart just hung there without anything happening. But when she started moving it back and forth over the diagram and concentrated on Linnéa, it swung faster and faster in a clockwise motion over a certain point.

'Linnéa is standing to the left of the coffee table,' Vanessa said.

Nicolaus opened the door, looked into the living room and reported that Vanessa was right. 'Pendulation' doesn't always work for Vanessa, but she manages to find Linnéa each time.

It was strange in the beginning, but the novelty soon wore off. The book insisted they should practice this over and over again, but never provided them with anything new. Minoo's constant babble about how the book was both a transmitter and a receiver, and that whatever it showed them had to be important, was sounding more and more hollow with every passing week.

But now, after two months, the transmitter finally changed frequencies. They've finally learned something that could help them find out the truth about Gustaf and his doppelganger.

A bell jangles when Vanessa opens the door to the Crystal Cave. The plucked harp strings, burbling water and birdsong are filtering out of the speakers. Vanessa feels as if someone is plucking directly at her nerves.

She almost bumps into Monika of Café Monique, who smiles so widely that her eyes almost disappear behind her cheeks. It's the first time Vanessa has ever seen her smile. She's carrying a big, rustling plastic bag in her arms with 'Crystal Cave' written on the side in the same curlicue lettering as the sign outside.

'Vanessa! How nice to see you!' she says, and adds, in a conspiratorial whisper, 'Isn't she amazing?'

It takes Vanessa a second to realize she's talking about Mona Moonbeam.

'Absolutely,' she answers. 'Totally amazing.'

'Good luck,' Monika says, and gives her a gentle nudge before she leaves.

Vanessa notices that the shelves are full of new products. Most striking among them are a couple of large crystal fountains with dolphins suspended above the water's surface, frozen in their frolic. The copper dragon that was standing by the red curtain is gone. Not only is the Crystal Cave still there, but business seems to be booming.

Vanessa waits until she's alone with Mona. She stops at the shelf of porcelain cherubs and fingers the price tag stuck to the biggest. The one Linnéa had liked.

The doorbell jingles again as the last customer leaves. Mona is still behind the counter, lighting a cigarette. 'I assume you're not here to buy a dream-catcher,' she says.

'How do you know?'

'That kind of knick-knack is the last thing a real witch would be interested in,' Mona says.

Vanessa's shock must have registered clearly on her face

447

because Mona is grinning with such satisfaction that both rows of yellowed teeth are showing. She goes to the door, locks it and flips the 'Open' sign to 'Closed'.

'How did you know I was a witch?' Vanessa asks.

'I saw it in your hands. And in the teeth. Not that I needed the Ogham characters. It's just fun to take out that pouch in front of smart-ass little girls.'

'Why didn't you say anything when you read my fortune?'

'You didn't know it yourself then, and it wasn't my responsibility to tell you. That job was already taken.'

'If you could see that I'm a witch, does that mean you're also—'

'What a silly question. Of course I am.'

When Vanessa had suggested the Crystal Cave to the others, it had been a gamble. She'd thought that Mona was just your typical crystal-rubbing ex-hippie. A bit nutty, but harmless. Or, rather, Vanessa hoped she was, considering the fortune she'd received. If it's true, then goodbye Wille, hello, death. Vanessa looks at Mona, sizing her up. Tries to decide what to do. If Mona is a witch . . . what sort of witch is she? Does she know the principal? Does she report to the Council?

Vanessa looks around the shop. She looks at the crystal fountains. Thinks about Monika's smile. Monika who *never* smiles. Looks toward the red curtain. Looks at Mona Moonbeam as she stands there, puffing away, in her denim outfit with butterflies on it. Suddenly she understands how everything is connected.

'You're tricking them,' Vanessa says.

Mona raises an eyebrow, but doesn't say anything.

'When you read my fortune, you first tried to pull some kind of hocus-pocus crap on me to make me believe all your clichés. I felt there was something . . . and I wouldn't fall for it. That was when you got annoyed, wasn't it? And then you told my fortune for real.'

'I was annoyed as soon as I laid eyes on you,' Mona says. 'And as for your fortune, I remember you weren't especially pleased to hear the truth.'

She moves closer to Vanessa and blows a huge cloud of smoke in her face. 'Can you honestly believe people want to hear their actual fortunes?' she asks. 'They want to feel happy when they walk out of here. Have a little hope for their future. And I'd say they need it in this backwater.'

'So is this some act of charity for you?' Vanessa says sarcastically.

'Of course not,' Mona snaps. 'It's business. A happy customer is a regular customer. What I do doesn't harm anyone.'

For once Vanessa is grateful to the principal for constantly droning on about the Council.

You're not allowed to practice magic without the Council's express permission.

You're not allowed to use magic to break non-magical laws.

And you're not allowed to reveal yourselves as witches to the non-magic public.

'I wonder if the Council would see it that way,' she says.

'You dupe people. And you're the first successful business in the City Mall since it was built. Not especially discreet.'

Mona is about to take a drag, but her hand stops before it reaches her mouth. 'What do you want?'

'I want to know how we can help each other,' Vanessa answers. 'I'll keep quiet about your activities if you keep quiet about mine.'

Mona stares at her, as if she's trying to decide whether Vanessa's threat is serious. Vanessa stares back at her. Doesn't even blink. Mona is the type who would never respect her if she looked away. Finally Mona snorts, but Vanessa spots a glint of appreciation beneath those turquoise-daubed eyelids.

'You've got some nerve, I'll give you that. Mona Moonbeam is no snitch, that much I can promise you, but she's not someone you can push around either. Don't you forget that.'

'I won't,' Vanessa says. She hesitates. 'There's something I need to get hold of. Do you have things in stock that aren't on display in the shop?'

Mona lights a new cigarette from the old one and smiles wanly. 'Tell me straight out what you're looking for.'

'Ectoplasm,' Vanessa says.

Mona smirks and nods, then ducks behind the curtain.

Vanessa takes the opportunity to text Minoo. 'Got the ectoplasm.'

Now all that's left is the problem with Anna-Karin.

Mona's bracelet rattles at the other side of the curtain. When she comes out she's holding a brown glass jar filled with a light-colored cream. 'Extra virgin,' Mona says, and holds out the jar.

It's warm – warmer than it could have become from Mona's hand. Vanessa tips the jar to the side. The ectoplasm barely moves. It looks like partially congealed meringue. She unscrews the lid and sniffs. It is odorless, the olfactory equivalent of deafening silence. 'What exactly is this stuff?'

'Soul matter,' Mona answers.

'Never heard of it. How do you make it?'

'You don't. It's excreted by witches when they act as mediums for the dead.'

Vanessa recalls the white substance oozing out of the corner of Ida's mouth when she hovered in the fairground that first night. She puts the lid back on and screws it tight. The warm contents jiggle inside the jar.

'Looks to me like you're scared of your first ritual,' Mona says.

'Who says it's my first?'

Mona doesn't answer. She just rattles out her irritating chuckle and lights another cigarette. If chain smoking were a sporting event, she'd be world champion several times over. Vanessa looks at the jar again. She doesn't like asking Mona questions, but no one else can answer them.

'Do you have to use this . . . drool?'

'I don't know if you *have* to exactly,' Mona says. 'If you're just doing some light magic you can use chalk or graphite to draw the circles. If you're in a round room you can use the walls as the outer circle. But proper ecto binds the energy better than anything else. If you try to perform heavy-duty magic with chalk circles the whole thing'll go *poof.'*

'Poof?'

'That cute little head of yours will go up in smoke.'

Vanessa is suddenly very thankful that the Crystal Cave exists. They had discussed trying something else if they couldn't get their hands on ectoplasm.

'How much is it?' Vanessa asks.

'Five grand.'

'*Five thousand?*' That's exactly how much money Vanessa has in her bag. Hardly a coincidence, she thinks. It's no easy job negotiating with a clairvoyant.

'Were you expecting a student discount? It's not like you just spit out all this stuff in a single session. It takes a long time to collect enough for a jar.'

'But five thousand? Seriously?' Vanessa says quickly, so that she doesn't have to listen to a lengthy description of the finer points of spittle harvesting.

'If you want to blame someone, blame the Council,' Mona says. 'They control all official trade in ectoplasm. That means the rest of us have to add a surcharge for the risks we take. I'm sure you understand how it works, considering what your boyfriend does for a living. Have you dumped him yet, by the way?'

Vanessa doesn't answer. She digs out a handful of hundred-dollar bills from her bag. They're crumpled. Nicolaus literally had them hidden under his mattress.

Five thousand crowns is more money than Vanessa has ever held. Mona takes it without blinking. It's obvious she's used to dealing with such sums. She puts the jar of ectoplasm into one of her crackly plastic bags and hands it to Vanessa across the counter.

'Do come again, won't you?' she says. 'You should all shop here more often because I've stocked up. With the biggest trans-dimensional war about to start, business should be brisk.'

'Do you sell to those collaborating with demons, too?' Vanessa asks.

Mona just smiles and releases a cloud of smoke from her nostrils. She looks like an old dragon in its lair.

'Sorry, I forgot,' Vanessa says contemptuously. ' "Mona Moonbeam is no snitch." The only thing that matters to you is business, yes? All customers are good customers.'

'Well well well, I see you're not as blonde as you look.' Mona smirks.

Vanessa makes for the exit without a word.

'You've still got *nGéadal* hanging over you. Don't forget that,' Mona calls after her.

It is only once Vanessa has made it out of the desolate City Mall that she realizes exactly what Mona said. *You should all shop here more often*. She knows they're more than one. Vanessa isn't even surprised.

'Nessa!'

It's a voice she hasn't heard for three months. Vanessa turns and sees her mother outside the Crystal Cave.

'Hello,' her mother says.

Her hair is bleached a few shades lighter. She's wearing a jacket Vanessa doesn't recognize. Signs that her life has continued without her daughter. 'Hi,' Vanessa answers.

An awkward silence settles between them. There are a thousand things to say, a thousand reasons to stay silent.

'I've got to go,' Vanessa says.

Her mother nods. 'See you around,' she says, as if they were casual acquaintances who had bumped into each other on the street. She opens the door to the Crystal Cave. A puff of incense and she's gone.

Vanessa looks after her. What had she expected?

I miss you.

Sorry.

Come home.

CHAPTER 47

Anna-Karin hears a laugh echo behind her and stops in the hallway leading to the school library. She stares at the floor until the girl gang has walked past. It's an old habit that's come back. Of course they weren't laughing at her. No one does any more.

The first week after the fire she had refused to go to school or leave the farm. She had spent her days in front of the TV.

'I would have thought you cared enough about your grandpa to visit him at least once,' her mother snapped. The mood swings are gone. Her mother is back to her permanently disgruntled self.

On Sunday the doorbell had rung. Anna-Karin was sitting there with her bandaged foot propped up, a bowl of chips in her lap and no intention of going to see who it was. But the person outside didn't give up and eventually let themselves in through the unlocked door.

Adriana Lopez's elegant appearance made the living room look shabby. Anna-Karin was happy that her mother wasn't home.

'How are you?' Adriana asked, and sat down in Grandpa's armchair.

Anna-Karin said nothing. She wouldn't answer any of the principal's questions. She had decided never to tell anyone what had happened that night. How recklessly she had behaved. That the 'accident' hadn't been an accident. And that she had very nearly caused Grandpa's death. He will never be the same again, according to her mother.

Eventually the principal got tired of Anna-Karin's silence, stood up and said that she expected to see her at school the following day.

Only when she was on her way out the door did Anna-Karin say, 'I've stopped using my powers. And I'll never use them again. Ever. You can tell that to the Council and the others. I'm going to stay away from all of you. It's best for everyone.'

'But you have been Chosen.'

Anna-Karin didn't respond to that either.

When she went back to school for the first time after the Christmas break, she lingered at the gates for a long time on her crutches. Would they hate her more than ever? Would they have figured out that the fat B.O. Ho, the manure-stinking hick, had been tricking them all along?

But then Julia and Felicia were walking toward her with Ida. Julia and Felicia didn't even look in her direction. It wasn't that they ignored her. They weren't treating her like air. She was air. Not the slightest hint of recognition.

But Ida saw Anna-Karin and let her gaze linger on her for a few seconds. Then she pretended to laugh at something Felicia had said, and they disappeared in a cloud of blonde hair and a fresh blossom scent.

Two months have gone by since then and Anna-Karin has become the ghost of Engelsfors School. It's as if all memory of her has been expunged. For better and for worse. Even her teachers forget about her sometimes, fail to see her raised hand or hesitate before reading out her name from the roster.

Anna-Karin hurries into the library and looks around furtively. The librarian doesn't look up when the ghost girl mumbles, 'Hello.'

She slips into the little niche where she usually sits. It's hidden behind a bookshelf and most people don't realize it's there. She holes up there with a physics book in a well-worn black armchair. The last few weeks she's spent every free moment filling her head with facts to stop herself from thinking.

'Hi,' she hears Linnéa say.

Anna-Karin doesn't look up. Instead she lowers her head and hides behind her hair. She's already said she doesn't want to speak to them. At least a hundred times.

'I'm not leaving here until you speak to me,' Linnéa says.

Then you'll have a long wait, Anna-Karin thinks. I've practiced being silent for nine years.

'What's the matter with you? You can't do this. We need you. And I think you need us, too.'

Anna-Karin remains stubbornly silent. But she's surprised. Linnéa doesn't sound like she usually does. She actually sounds as if she cares. She's usually so impatient, as if she's pissed off with the whole world.

'Okay.' Linnéa sighs. 'But something's happened.

Something good.'

'What?' Anna-Karin mumbles, with reluctant curiosity.

Linnéa leans forward and lowers her voice.

'The book has shown us how to make a truth serum that we'll give to Gustaf. Then we'll get him to tell us about his doppelganger. But to make the serum we have to perform a ritual. It's a much more powerful kind of magic than we've ever done before. And you have to be there. It's all up to you and me. Earth and water.'

She might have known, Anna-Karin thinks. Linnéa wants something, which was why she pretended to care about her.

'No,' she answers. 'You'll have to do it without me.'

'Anna-Karin . . .'

'There's no point in pestering me. Go away.'

Linnéa is rummaging in her bag. 'Not until you've helped us.' She takes out a needle and a lighter.

Anna-Karin shrinks in her chair. Linnéa holds the needle in the lighter's flame. Then takes out a Kleenex and a little test tube. 'If you're not going to help us, then we need your blood. According to the book, the ritual is a lot more dangerous if you're not there when we lay down the circles, but if we put some of your blood into the power symbol, it'll make it a little easier for me to control the energy. "Little" being the operative word here.'

Anna-Karin understands only about half of what Linnéa just said. The others must have made huge strides without her.

'I only need a few drops,' Linnéa says.

'Okay,' Anna-Karin says. 'Just so long as you leave afterward.' She holds out her left hand. It doesn't hurt when Linnéa pushes the point of the needle into her index finger. But it does when she squeezes out a few drops of blood and lets them drip into the test tube. Anna-Karin has to look away. Linnéa squeezes harder, pressing out more drops.

Eventually she wipes Anna-Karin's finger. She throws the needle and the bloody Kleenex into a wastepaper basket, presses the stopper into the test tube, and puts it into her bag with the lighter.

'I know the accident must have been very difficult for you,' she says, handing Anna-Karin a Band-Aid, 'but you really can't just think about yourself.'

'You don't understand anything.'

'You're right. What do I know about having a hard time?' Linnéa says, her voice dripping with sarcasm. 'Thanks for your help.'

She disappears behind the bookshelves. Anna-Karin's finger is throbbing gently as she puts on the Band-Aid. She opens her physics book again and tries to read, but she can't absorb a single line. She gives up and curses Linnéa. Now she has to find another hiding place.

'Anna-Karin is really starting to piss me off,' Vanessa says.

Minoo is sitting at Nicolaus's kitchen table. He and Cat have left them alone in the apartment. Minoo feels a little sorry for him, having to spend the whole evening at Sture & Co. waiting for them to finish. The *Book of Patterns* was very clear that only the Chosen Ones could be present during the ritual.

Minoo is stirring a plastic bowl with a wooden spoon, watching as Anna-Karin's blood dissolves into the gloop they're going to use for the power symbol in the inner circle. She's been mixing it for fifteen minutes and now she's getting a cramp in her arm.

'Stir into a smooth paste,' Ida reads from the book, as if it were a cake recipe.

In addition to Anna-Karin's and Linnéa's blood, the mixture consists of ectoplasm, earth from Elias and Rebecka's graves, milk left to curdle in the moonlight, and spit from Minoo and Vanessa. Now all that's missing is a dollop of Ida's saliva.

'First she spends the entire autumn acting like a diva at school and fucking things up for us,' Vanessa continues, 'and now she doesn't want anything to do with us, and she's fucking us over again. It's not as if any of the rest of us volunteered for this.'

'I know,' Minoo says. 'But I think things have been pretty hard for Anna-Karin with everything that's happened. They'll have to sell the farm, I heard.'

The fire has attracted a lot of attention. Rumors are rife that Anna-Karin's mother set fire to the barn to cash in on the insurance.

'But why is she avoiding us?' Vanessa asks. 'All we've done is tried to support her.'

Minoo has wondered the same thing. Anna-Karin has ignored all her attempts to get in touch. In the beginning she didn't think it strange. Anna-Karin had to be in shock. But she's become increasingly convinced that Anna-Karin is hiding something.

'I think there's something fishy about that accident,' Linnéa says, as she enters the kitchen.

'Why?' Minoo asks.

'I just feel like she's hiding something.' Linnéa goes up to the table and glances into the mixing bowl. 'Ugh, gross,' she says.

'Looking forward to doing some finger painting?' Vanessa asks Linnéa.

'One of you can take over now. My arm's about to fall off,' Minoo says.

Linnéa takes the bowl and spoon out of Minoo's hands and starts stirring. Minoo leans back in her chair and watches her.

This is the first ritual they'll perform, and since Anna-Karin refuses to take part, their chances of success have plummeted. Now it's up to Linnéa.

The front door opens and slams shut.

'And here comes Ida,' Linnéa says, not with hostility but far from enthusiastically.

Ida has dark circles under her eyes and is sniffling. She's got the flu that's been going around at school and should be at home.

Linnéa hands the bowl to her without a word. Ida coughs and spits into it. Linnéa grimaces and gives it another stir with the spoon.

'Shit,' she says.

Minoo looks into the bowl. What had been a grainy gloop just a moment ago has turned into a smooth reddish-brown paste.

'Well, we'd better get the show on the road,' Linnéa says.

The few pieces of furniture in Nicolaus's living room are lined up against the walls. The blinds are drawn. All the lights are switched off. Ida has lit stocky white candles and placed them around the room, four in each corner. For some reason, the ritual cannot be performed either in daylight or with electric lighting.

It looks like something out of a B-movie in which the protagonists are about to engage in either satanic worship or a sex orgy or both, Vanessa thinks.

'Now remember,' Ida says, 'once the ritual has begun, no one is allowed to leave the room or cross the outer circle. If that happens the whole thing's ruined. If you need to go to the bathroom, do it now. I've got to take a painkiller.'

She disappears into the kitchen.

Linnéa is standing in the middle of the room. She's put her hair into a ponytail and pushed aside her long bangs. Vanessa can see that she's afraid.

The light from the flickering candles dances across the walls and their faces. The gravity of the moment starts to sink in.

'Okay.' Ida coughs as she comes back into the room. 'Are you ready, Linnéa?'

'Yes,' she answers quietly.

Vanessa unscrews the lid of the jar with the rest of the ectoplasm and hands it to Linnéa. She takes it, then grabs Vanessa's hand. 'If anything goes wrong . . .' she mumbles.

'It won't,' Vanessa answers. 'You can do this. And we'll be here all the time.'

Linnéa nods and lets go.

Minoo steps forward and places the mixing bowl with a small empty glass jar on the floor at Linnéa's feet. If they succeed, the jar should be full of truth serum when the ritual is over. 'Good luck,' she says.

'Thanks.'

'Good luck,' Ida mumbles.

Linnéa casts her a glance. 'Thanks,' she answers briefly. 'Here goes.'

Vanessa stands by the wall with Ida and Minoo. Fucking Anna-Karin. She should be here, too. She shouldn't have let Linnéa do this on her own. For the two of them the burden – and the risk – would have been much less.

'The circle that binds,' Ida says.

It has begun.

Linnéa takes a long, deep breath. Then she dips the three middle fingers of her left hand into the jar of pure ectoplasm and sinks to her knees. Slowly she starts to draw the outer circle.

Her fingers leave an unnaturally even trail of ectoplasm on the light parquet floor. It's as if the meringue-like paste has a will of its own and adjusts itself correctly of its own accord. Vanessa knows that it's impossible to draw a perfectly round circle just by touch, yet that's exactly what Linnéa is doing.

When the circle closes around Linnéa, Vanessa feels a tingling sensation run through her body. The silence in the room becomes more compact. All they can hear is Linnéa's breathing. She stands up and wipes the sweat from her brow. She doesn't see them any longer. She's withdrawn into herself.

'The circle that gives power,' Ida says.

Linnéa goes to the middle. She dips her hand into the ectoplasm again and starts drawing the inner circle in the same manner. Her white camisole is damp. Sweat is trickling down her neck, between her shoulder blades, and dripping from her hairline. The drops appear to evaporate as soon as they hit the floor.

When the inner circle is closed, Vanessa feels the same tingling, but more intensely now. It vibrates through her whole skeleton to her teeth. Linnéa straightens and teeters.

'The power sign,' Ida whispers.

Linnéa takes the mixing bowl, dips her hand into the reddish-brown paste and draws the symbols of the water and earth elements so that they form a single unit.

Vanessa gets goose bumps all over her body. A low drone, almost beyond what is audible to the human ear, fills the room. Her eardrums are aching. And there's something wrong with the shadows. There are more.

Vanessa's hands seek Minoo's and Ida's. Or is it their hands that seek out hers? She isn't sure. But somehow she knows it's helping Linnéa.

Linnéa places the empty jar on the power symbol and presses her hand over the opening. Her rapid breathing can be heard above the drone. The muscles in her arm tense and her back arches, like a cat's. The drone vibrates in Vanessa's blood, rising and falling as the shadows pulse across the walls. Voices whisper ancient forgotten languages. The air tastes of salt. Linnéa's chest heaves faster and faster and faster.

Suddenly Linnéa pulls away her hand from the jar and collapses in a heap.

The candle flames flicker and nearly go out. Once they're burning steadily again, the strange shadows are gone. The low drone is gone, too, and the sounds from outside seep back into the room. Vanessa can hear the TV in the apartment above, a child running around. She lets go of the others' hands.

'Linnéa?'

Linnéa doesn't answer. Doesn't move.

'Is it over?' Minoo asks.

'Wait a minute,' Ida says.

Vanessa tries to see if Linnéa's breathing. It's impossible to tell. She starts to panic.

'Don't break the circle!' Ida shouts.

But it's too late. Vanessa is already beside Linnéa. She drops to her knees and bends forward, lays her face next to Linnéa's. Relief washes over her when she sees Linnéa's lips move, as if she's trying to say something.

'I'm here,' Vanessa whispers, and takes Linnéa's sticky hand.

'Shit,' she hears Ida say. 'We've been at it for two hours.'

'Did it work?' Linnéa asks faintly.

Vanessa looks at the glass jar Minoo lifts. There is an inch of murky liquid at the bottom. It doesn't look at all like Vanessa imagined a magic potion to be. On the other hand, she doesn't know what she imagined. Something that glows in the dark, perhaps. Swirling wisps of smoke rising off it. Mysterious glitter. This looks as if someone dived into the muddy depths of Dammsjön Lake and brought back a water sample.

'There's only one way to find out,' Minoo says.

Linnéa is sitting at Nicolaus's kitchen table, guzzling orange juice between mouthfuls of macaroni wolfed straight from the pot. She looks incredibly tired, but at least she's no longer half-dead. Vanessa is relieved. The ritual is over and Linnéa is fine. Whether the potion works or not seems far less important.

'I'm not going to do this,' Ida says, and pops another painkiller. 'I'm sick. And I've been taking paracetamol. I might get side effects.'

'Come on,' Linnéa says, through another spoonful of macaroni. 'We have to test it before we can use it on Gustaf.'

'Easy for you to say when you don't have to—'

'Excuse me, but don't you think I've done enough for one night?' Linnéa asks.

Ida shuts up.

Three small coffee cups full of juice stand on the table. Linnéa has poured a drop of the truth serum into one.

'Let's all drink them at the same time,' Minoo says, looking terrified. 'Linnéa, have you thought of a question? Nothing too personal.'

'No, of course not,' Linnéa says, with a smile that makes Vanessa nervous.

She doesn't have any secrets. Or does she? What if she's the one who gets the cup that will leave her mind wide open for Linnéa to rummage around in? What if Linnéa asks something that Vanessa doesn't even know she wants to keep secret?

Vanessa reaches for the middle cup, but Ida beats her to it. Vanessa takes the left one and Minoo takes the right.

'I can't believe I'm going along with this,' Ida mutters.

'Okay,' Linnéa says. 'One. Two. Drink!'

Vanessa empties hers in one go and puts the cup back on the table. She runs her tongue around her mouth, checking for any weird aftertaste. Ida burps.

'Minoo,' Linnéa says, smiling widely. 'What are you most afraid I'll ask you right now?'

Minoo smiles back. She looks relieved. 'I'm not telling you,' she says.

Linnéa's dark eyes bore into Vanessa's. 'And you, Vanessa? What are you most afraid that you'll be forced to reveal?'

'I'm not afraid of anything.' It's only when she hears herself lie with such conviction that she's sure she's made it.

They all look at Ida. It's the moment of truth. If it doesn't work on Ida it doesn't work at all.

'And you, Ida?'

'What the fuck?' Ida says. 'I can't believe this is happening to me for the second time. I think it's *sooo* unfair that I'm the one who ended up drinking the truth serum – Anna-Karin forced me to tell the truth that time at the fairground, and I really don't want to tell you all that I've had, like this, enormous crush on G since fourth grade.'

She claps a hand over her mouth, her eyes widening in horror.

'Looks like the serum works,' Minoo says.

'What did I say?' Ida asks.

'That explains a lot,' Vanessa says, and starts laughing.

'What? Tell me!'

'The serum's made you forget straight away. It's better like that, don't you think?' Linnéa asks, with a grin.

Ida gets up and wraps her cardigan tightly around her. She gives an exaggerated sniff, as if to remind them that she's sick and that they should be nice to her. 'Whatever I may have said, I can stand by it,' she says. 'And now I'm going home to bed.'

'Get better soon,' Minoo says.

Ida sniffles again and twiddles her necklace. 'If any of this gets out at school you'll all be in big trouble,' she says.

'Don't worry,' Linnéa says. 'We won't let anyone know that you actually have feelings.'

When Anna-Karin steps into the hall she's met by a barrage of laughter from the TV. She doesn't have to look into the living room to know that her mother is lying on the sofa.

Maybe she's fallen asleep with a cigarette in her hand again, but Anna-Karin can't be bothered to check.

She goes into the kitchen, takes out a box of chocolate balls from the fridge and a bag of white buns from the bread box. She eats her chocolate-ball sandwiches standing up, washing them down with a glass of milk. But they don't give her the nice dozy feeling they usually do. They just make her feel sick.

She looks through at the window at Grandpa's cabin. As if he might suddenly be sitting in his usual spot, beckoning her over.

She wonders if he's noticed that she hasn't been to see him in the hospital.

Suddenly she feels something warm and soft pressing against her calf. She bends down and meets Pepper's green gaze. 'Hello, sweetie,' she whispers. She sinks down on to the kitchen floor and lifts the cat up in her arms, massaging its soft fur.

Pepper purrs. The people on the TV laugh.

'At least you like me again,' she murmurs.

But despite Pepper's best efforts she feels more alone than ever. Linnéa's words chafe at her. She's told herself that she withdrew for everyone else's sake. She's dangerous. She can cause injury. But is Linnéa right? Is she just being selfish and cowardly?

CHAPTER 48

Minoo is staring at the numbers in front of her. A quadratic equation that ought to be a cinch. But she can't get anything to add up.

The lunch bell rings, setting off a cacophony of chairs scraping, books slamming, zippers opening and closing. Minoo glances at Max, who gives her a little smile. He hides it behind his coffee mug. Her heart leaps. The secret understanding between them is back.

She'll soon turn seventeen. In a year she'll be of age. An adult in the eyes of society. A year is nothing, he'd said. He's prepared to wait.

It's almost unbearable to have to see him every day now that she knows he loves her, too. One fine day she won't be able to stop herself running up to his desk and kissing him in front of everyone. It's just as well he's leaving by the summer.

Minoo follows the flow of students out into the stairwell. She's checked Gustaf's schedule. They have lunch at the same time. Should she speak to him when she sees him in the cafeteria? Or should she wait until after school?

She's managed to avoid him ever since that afternoon by

the overpass. He's tried to approach her a few times at school, but she's always slipped away. Now she's been racking her brains for what she should say to him, but she decides it's impossible to plan a conversation. She'll have to improvize.

When she reaches the ground floor and turns down the hall leading to the cafeteria, she spots Linnéa.

She's standing with her back to a row of lockers. Erik Forslund and Robin Zetterqvist are in front of her. When Linnéa tries to leave, Erik's hand flies out and hits the locker next to her with a bang. She's trapped.

The other students pretend not to notice as they walk past. No one seems to remember any more Erik wetting himself in the playground or Robin begging for crumbs from Anna-Karin's table. They're back on top.

Minoo adjusts her backpack and moves closer.

'How much do you want, then?' she hears Erik ask.

'Get out of my way,' Linnéa says, and tries to shove him aside.

'Or maybe you've started doing it for free now.'

Suddenly Minoo is afraid. Everyone else has disappeared into the cafeteria. She moves closer, tries to get her footsteps to sound resolute.

'Answer me!' Robin says.

'Leave her alone!' Minoo shouts.

The words echo in the deserted hallway. Erik turns and looks at Minoo in disdain.

'I didn't know you had a girlfriend,' Robin says to Linnéa.

'What – are you jealous?' Linnéa says. 'You know you'll

never get to see pussy in real life.' She smiles at him.

For a moment Minoo thinks Robin's going to hit her. It's obvious he's dying to wipe the smile off her face with his fist. Instead he grabs Linnéa's bag and dumps the contents on the floor. Makeup, cigarettes, cell phone, pens, school books and Linnéa's black notepad scatter everywhere.

Linnéa tries to throw herself over her things, but Erik holds her fast while Robin kicks them around. He stomps on her phone so the screen cracks.

'Let her go,' Minoo says.

Robin picks up the black notepad and flips through it. Minoo glimpses densely written pages, red, blue, green and black ink. Drawings and patterns.

'What's this?' Robin asks. 'Your diary?'

Linnéa tries to break free of Erik's grasp, and when she doesn't succeed, she throws her head back in a failed attempt to headbutt him. That pisses Robin off even more.

'Now let's see . . .' he begins.

Minoo goes up to Robin and tries to snatch the book, but he laughs and easily holds her at a distance with one outstretched arm while he flips through it with his other hand and starts to read: 'All the others were sitting with their eyes twinkling, like perfect little children on Christmas Eve and AL was Santa Claus. I can't take it much longer. M is the worst, always so fucking eager to be the best in the class. She gives me a headache.'

Minoo has no doubt who 'M' is. It stings, but the most important thing is to get hold of that book before it exposes them all. She makes another lunge at Robin and manages to touch it. A page is almost ripped out under her outstretched fingers, but Robin shoves her away.

'Doesn't it say anything about how she fucks for heroin?' Erik asks.

'Wait a minute, wait a minute . . .' Robin says, and continues flipping through the notebook.

Linnéa twists, jerks and pulls at Erik's arms in a wild attempt to dislodge him. He just laughs and holds her closer.

'You like this, don't you?' he pants in her ear.

'Let go of me,' Linnéa barks.

Robin carries on flipping. '"I have to tell the others,"' he reads. '"Everything's so fucking complicated."'

He looks at Linnéa and smirks mockingly. 'Oh, I think I'm gonna cry soon,' he says, and returns to the book. '"I should have said something from the beginning. Now it would just ruin everything. They'd hate me if they knew."'

Linnéa lets out a loud, maniacal scream. It echoes down the hall. Everything comes to an abrupt stop. That's enough. Linnéa kicks Robin between his legs with her steel-toed boot. Hard connects with soft. Robin howls and drops to all fours. The book falls out of his hand and slides across the floor.

Minoo bends down and catches it.

'FuckingcuntI'mgonnakillyou,' Erik hisses, as if it were one word, and twists Linnéa's arm behind her back.

Minoo has never been in a fight, not even as a child. She has no brothers or sisters to fight with, and in preschool she was always a good girl. Now she wriggles out of her backpack.

It's heavy. Full of books.

Linnéa cries out when Erik twists her arm even harder. Minoo shuts off her brain and lets her instincts take over.

She swings her bag in a wide arc. It hits Erik's head so hard that he stumbles backward into the lockers.

Linnéa breaks free of him. She throws herself to the ground and gathers up her things. Her jar of face powder breaks, sending up a cloud of white dust.

'The book!' she shouts to Minoo.

The adrenaline starts pumping through Minoo's body when she sees Erik climbing to his feet behind Linnéa. She almost doesn't register what Linnéa says.

Linnéa gets to her feet with her bag in her hand. She grabs the book from Minoo and runs.

Minoo is running, too, but Linnéa is a lot faster and has soon disappeared through the front doors. Minoo dashes down the steps to the cafeteria.

'Fucking dykes!' Erik shouts, somewhere down the hallway behind her.

Vanessa is sitting in Wille's car looking at the Lingonberry Preschool playground with its monkey bars and snow-covered sandbox. Five lumpy snowmen are standing to attention in front of the familiar building.

Vanessa looks at the clock on the dashboard. She should have just enough time. As long as Nicke or her mother hasn't decided to pick him up early today . . .

'I'm so nervous,' she says.

Wille leans across the seat and kisses her cheek. 'Should I

wait for you?'

'No, it's okay.'

'Are you sure?'

'Yes. It'll only stress me out knowing you're sitting out here.'

That's only half the truth. The other half is that she wants to be alone afterward.

'Okay. I'm going to Jonte's place,' he says. 'I'll see you tonight.'

Vanessa swallows a comment about there being a thousand things Wille should do instead of going to Jonte's place. But she's sick of hearing her nagging voice.

She feels like an adult in the worst way whenever she's with Wille, these days. She's never sighed so much in her whole life as she has since they started living together. It's as if she's turned into her mother.

Wille still hasn't mentioned the email she sent him the day before yesterday, with links to the few job listings on the homepage of the Engelsfors employment office. She can understand that it wouldn't be much fun to work at the saw mill, or clean offices overnight at the town hall, but it would be temporary. As soon as she's left school they can do whatever they want. Together.

She climbs out of the car, and he waves to her through the windshield after she's slammed the door. She loves him. But she doesn't know if that's enough any more.

'Vanessa! We haven't seen you for ages! Are you picking up Melvin today?'

Amira had been working there when Vanessa was in

preschool, and she was Vanessa's favorite teacher. She still wears the same suspender-skirts now as she did then, and every time Vanessa sees her she gets flashbacks of story time and rosehip soup, and of when Amira caught her and Kevin in the playhouse.

'I'm just here to say hi to him,' Vanessa says. 'Is it okay if I give him a present? Maybe you have rules or something . . .'

Amira looks at the bag she's holding. Vanessa wonders if Amira knows she isn't living at home now.

'Okay,' she says. 'We can make an exception for you. But do it away from the other kids so they don't see. There'll be such a fuss otherwise.'

'Thanks,' Vanessa says.

'Go on into the lunch room and I'll bring him to you.'

The low table where the children eat has been cleared. The dark blue blinds decorated with circus animals in bright colors are pulled down halfway, and the room is gloomy. It smells of plastic and cleaning fluid. Everything has been adapted for little kids, and it's hard for her to imagine she herself was once that small.

'Come on, Melvin. Vanessa's in here,' she hears Amira say and turns around.

Melvin is standing in the doorway looking at her guardedly. He's wearing a blue-striped shirt, jeans with an elastic waistband, and slipper socks. His hair is longer and curly at the temples. Vanessa puts down her bag and manages to refrain from crying out, 'Gosh, you've grown!' like some elderly relative. 'Happy birthday!' she says

476

instead, goes down on her knees and holds out her arms.

Melvin looks at her. Then he hides his face against Amira's leg.

It's as if someone's giving her a Chinese burn on her heart. Because that's what Melvin does with people he doesn't know. Vanessa lowers her arms.

'Are you shy, Melvin?' Amira says in her sweet voice.

'We haven't seen each other for a bit. I don't know if he . . .' Her voice chokes. She's on the verge of tears. She can't let it happen. She can't start sobbing on her little brother's birthday and traumatize him for life.

You already have, a voice says inside her. Just by walking out the door and disappearing. Of course he doesn't trust you. Maybe he doesn't even remember you.

She draws a deep breath and tries to swallow the lump in her throat. 'I brought you a present,' she says, and pulls a package out of the plastic bag. She sets it down on the floor between them. 'A birthday present,' she says.

Melvin looks at her a little skeptically. Then he takes a few cautious steps. Stops. 'Two,' he says, and holds out his hand with two fingers raised.

'Yes, you're two years old today,' Vanessa says, and blinks away a few tears. 'What a smart boy you are.'

Melvin flashes a little smile. She nudges the package closer to him. Slowly he touches the paper with his chubby fingers. He rips and tears at it a little haphazardly while Vanessa secretly unfastens the tape.

Eventually he pulls out a soft toy penguin with big eyes.

As soon as Vanessa had seen it she'd known she had to get it for Melvin. Now she's suddenly uncertain about her choice.

'Wow, what a nice penguin!' Amira says.

Melvin holds it in front of him. If Melvin hates her present, Vanessa thinks, she'll lie down on the floor and bawl her eyes out until Amira comes over and picks her up.

'Do you like your penguin?' Vanessa asks.

'Pingu,' Melvin says, and shakes it ecstatically.

She is pathetically happy and close to crying again.

'Can I have a hug now?' she asks.

She can't hold back any longer. She so wants to take him in her arms, feel his warm little body against hers.

Melvin looks terrified. 'No,' he says. Then he takes the penguin by its wing and toddles out of the room.

Amira is full of sympathy. 'He's just a bit shy because he hasn't seen you lately,' Amira says.

Of course her mother couldn't have kept quiet. And Nicke had probably described it as Jannike's pain-in-the-ass daughter going off the rails and moving in with the town drug dealer. Vanessa wants to explain everything to Amira, win her over, but she has to leave before she starts sobbing for real.

She says goodbye and hurries out into the street.

The preschool is at the top of a hill from which she can see virtually all of Engelsfors. That disgusting little shithole full of people who think they live in the most important place on earth. God, how she hates them. God, how she wants to get away.

Now, when she's free to cry, it's as if her tears have evaporated.

There's nowhere she wants to go. Not to Wille and Sirpa's house. Not to her mother and Nicke's. She doesn't feel at home anywhere.

Minoo is standing outside the library trying to look relaxed when the bell rings after the last period. She looks at the door to Gustaf's classroom. It remains closed. Maybe Ove Post has let a dissection run too long again.

The principal is coming toward her. She walks straight up to Minoo. 'What are you doing here?' she asks, as if there's something suspicious about her standing outside the library. She glances at Gustaf's classroom.

'Waiting for a friend.'

The principal eyes her lingeringly. Then she nods and walks off.

Finally Gustaf's classmates are filing out into the hallway. Nervously Minoo switches on her phone and hopes she appears to be writing an important text message.

She doesn't see Gustaf until he's next to her.

'Hi,' he says.

'Hi! I was waiting for you,' she says, in as normal a tone as she can muster.

Gustaf looks happy. 'You were?'

Minoo tries to focus on the bridge of his nose between his eyebrows so that he'll think she's looking him in the eyes, like a normal human being with nothing to hide. 'I thought maybe we could do something this weekend,' she says, hoping he won't interpret this as a invitation to go out on a date with her. Her ears are so hot that they might shrivel, like two sun-dried tomatoes.

'I'd love to! What do you want to do?' he asks.

'Just hang out. We've got relatives visiting,' she lies, 'so maybe we could go to your place.' Yeah, that had sounded totally spontaneous.

'Okay. I've got soocer practice, but you could come over around four.'

'Are you going to be alone?' She hears immediately how that sounded and the tomato color spreads across her entire face. 'I just mean if we want to be undisturbed . . . to talk about Rebecka or something. Not that we have to talk about her. But you know . . .'

'I know.'

'I'll see you tomorrow,' Minoo says.

Gustaf lunges forward and gives her a hug. She has to stop herself from recoiling. She remembers how he pulled her to him in the darkness by the overpass. This feels completely different.

'I'm so happy you want to meet up,' he says, and lets her go. 'I thought you were avoiding me.'

Minoo focuses on the bridge of his nose again. 'Not at all!' she says. 'Why would I do that?'

Chapter 49

The rough walls of the waiting room are a depressing mint green. Someone has painted a waist-high border of happy ducks pecking at the ground. Somehow they make the atmosphere a thousand times worse.

Anna-Karin is sitting on the sofa staring vacantly ahead. Outside the room, hospital staff are running to and fro. A few are talking far too loudly to each other, as if this is any old job, not one where people are sick and dying. Alarm signals buzz and beep.

Anna-Karin looks at the ducks again. They're smiling at each other with their blunt bills, apparently moving along in time with a gay little melody. She realizes why she finds them so awful: no one wants to be in this room. You're only here if your worst nightmares have come true. But someone had thought that the ducks' perkiness would rub off on whoever was sitting here.

A male nurse with tribal tattoos down both arms pops into the room and asks Anna-Karin to come with him. They've finished today's tests on Grandpa.

Anna-Karin feels as if everyone is looking at her askance as she follows him down the hallway. *There goes that girl who hasn't even been once to see her poor grandfather. She ought to be ashamed of herself.*

The nurse stands outside Grandpa's room and gestures for Anna-Karin to go inside.

She looks at the open door. More than anything she'd like to bolt down the long hallway and escape into the fresh air, away from the smell of hospital and sick bodies. Away from Grandpa.

Grandpa.

She walks past the nurse. Washes her hands thoroughly at the little sink inside the door, then rubs them with sanitizer from the pump bottle attached to the wall.

The room is ghostly in the dim afternoon light. An old man lies in the nearest bed, with fingers as crooked as claws. His eyes are squeezed shut and his toothless mouth gasps air. Anna-Karin's insides go cold before she realizes that he isn't Grandpa. She hurries past him.

A light-gray curtain is drawn halfway around the other bed.

At first she sees only his legs delineated beneath the light blue hospital blanket. When she's closer she can see his arms resting outside the blanket. Needles attached to long tubes have been inserted into the back of his hands and secured there with papery tape. Another tube feeds out from beneath the blanket. Anna-Karin follows it with her eyes to a bag of urine hanging from the bed near the floor.

She takes a few more steps and there is Grandpa's face. It's almost transparent in the pale light from the window. Yet another tube feeds into his nose. An IV stand has been placed next to the bed. A beeping sound comes from a machine with wires that disappear under the collar of his nightshirt. He's like a machine into which fluids are pumped in and out.

Anna-Karin takes her last steps to the edge of his bed. 'Grandpa,' she says.

He turns toward her. His features have sort of collapsed. The skin looks smoother. It's Grandpa lying there, yet not. All the qualities she identifies with him, the strength, the alertness, the vitality and intelligence, are all missing.

She wants to hug him, but doesn't dare. She's afraid of hurting him. Afraid he won't want her hug.

'Grandpa . . . It's me. Anna-Karin.'

Grandpa looks at her silently. It's impossible to tell whether or not he recognizes her.

Only now does she realize she's crying for the first time since elementary school. 'I'm sorry. It's all my fault,' she whispers, and sniffles. 'I'm sorry.'

Grandpa blinks a few times. He seems to be trying to focus. Her mother had said he was so heavily medicated he was completely out of it.

'They told me it was dangerous,' she continues, 'but I never thought it could be dangerous for anyone but myself. Least of all you. But I've stopped now.'

She takes his hand, careful not to disturb the needles.

'I should never have started in the first place. I should have listened to the others. I know that now, but it's too late. I've ruined everything. Grandpa, you've got to get better. Please. *Please.*'

Grandpa blinks again. He opens his mouth and manages to say a few words. She can barely make them out, but he's speaking Finnish. She's heard the language now and then throughout her childhood, but never learned it.

'Can you say it in Swedish, Grandpa?'

'They said on the radio that war was coming,' Grandpa says slowly. 'Everyone has to choose which side they're on.'

'Everything's going to be fine,' Anna-Karin says. 'You mustn't worry, just get better.'

Grandpa shuts his eyes and nods weakly. 'My father said, "If we don't do something now, we'll have to live with the shame for the rest of our lives."'

Anna-Karin strokes his head as he drifts off to sleep. His hair is thin and silky. His forehead is cool, almost cold.

'He's your grandfather, isn't he?' a nurse says, as she enters the room.

Anna-Karin nods and wipes away her tears with the back of her hand.

'I know he looks awful . . .' The nurse explains what all the wires, pumps and needles are for. Anna-Karin feels a little better when she understands what they're doing for him. These people have a plan for how they're going to keep him alive, make him better.

'He's improving,' the nurse says. 'It may not look like it, but he is.'

Anna-Karin meets her gaze for the first time. Even if she hadn't seen her picture in the paper, she would have recognized her. Rebecka's mother is an older copy of her daughter. She smiles at Anna-Karin, a smile that is also Rebecka's. She's lost her daughter yet she's trying to comfort Anna-Karin. What if she knew that Anna-Karin is among those who could find Rebecka's murderer but has decided to do nothing? *If we don't do something now, we'll have to live with the shame for the rest of our lives.*

Minoo has almost fallen asleep when she hears a mysterious sound in her room, a rhythmic buzzing. She can't tell where it's coming from.

The old fear rouses her and she sits up wide awake, sure she's going to see black smoke coiling along the walls and across the floor toward her bed . . .

But the room looks normal. And now she realizes where the sound is coming from. Her phone is vibrating on the bedside table.

'Hi,' Linnéa says, when she answers.

Minoo switches on her little green bedside lamp. 'Hi.'

'Thanks for helping me today,' Linnéa says.

'No problem.'

'Robin and Erik are such fucking assholes. That was one good thing about Anna-Karin exerting her power over the school – that everyone hated them. I'm sorry they read out that part from my diary. It wasn't about you. Well, it was, but I was having a bad day.'

Linnéa speaks quickly, as if she feels she has to apologize but wants to get it over with. Is it even an apology? Minoo feels a painful twinge when she remembers what it said about 'M': *She gives me a headache.*

'Let's forget about it,' she says, and wishes it was that simple.

'Okay. I'm calling because I have to tell you something,' Linnéa says. 'I can read the *Book of Patterns* now, too.'

'Since when?'

'Just a minute ago. And I've found something. I'm sitting here now, looking at it through the Pattern Finder. And now that I've found it, I can't understand why I didn't see it all along.'

Great, Minoo thinks. Pretty soon that damn book will be transmitting to everybody except me. 'What's it say?'

'It's hard to explain. I'm not sure I understand it. That's why I wanted to talk to you. You're probably the only one who can work out what it means.'

'I can try.'

'Okay . . . It's about . . . this thing. I can't explain it. This thing, whatever it is, is meant for one person. If it's shared, it won't work properly.'

Minoo feels the tingling she experiences when she's close to solving a difficult math problem. What Linnéa is saying sounds familiar.

'Go on,' she says, as she opens the drawer of her bedside table and takes out her notebook.

Linnéa sighs. 'The problem is that one person will always end up outside this thing. And if that person dies, another person ends up outside it. And then the next. And the next . . .'

'Wait,' Minoo says. She fumbles as she flips back and forth through her notebook.

486

'What is it?' Linnéa asks.

'Ida talked about the same thing when she discovered she could read the *Book of Patterns*,' she says, and finally finds the right page. 'This is what she said: "That it's, like, built for one. Then it works just great. But if more people try to get in there, someone always gets left out. And if the one who's outside disappears, then the next ends up outside. And then the next. And the next. And the next. Until everyone's gone." She said it was like some kind of atmosphere.'

All the pieces fall into place. There's the answer. Beautiful. Crystal clear. Minoo doesn't need the answer to know it's correct. 'I know what the book is trying to tell us,' she says. 'It's about the magic protection. What Adriana was talking about in the beginning. The thing that she and the Council thought was protecting us. Now you know that, try looking in the book again. Maybe it'll change what you see in the patterns.'

'Hang on,' Linnéa says.

She's silent for a long moment. Meanwhile Minoo hears her mother come up the steps and go into the bathroom. She must just have come home from the hospital. Water starts gushing from a tap.

'Okay,' Linnéa says. 'It's definitely talking about the protective magic. It was created for a single Chosen One. The book is trying to explain what the side effects are when it's been expanded to cover seven people. It can't protect everyone at once. One of us will always be left out. It's like a kind of safety valve. This magic can't contain multiple psyches, emotions, wills and thoughts. Like, it

487

would implode if it tried to keep a tight defense around all of us.'

'So someone always ends up outside its protection,' Minoo says. 'And as long as that person is alive, the rest of us are hidden. But if that person dies . . .'

'. . . then someone else becomes exposed,' Linnéa concludes.

Minoo gropes for the next logical link in her chain of thought.

'Elias must have been the first who was unprotected,' she says, 'and when he died, it was Rebecka's turn. Then mine. I'm the one who's unprotected now.'

They fall silent.

'But why did the attack on you fail?' Linnéa asks eventually. 'We don't know what powers Elias may have had, but Rebecka could throw heavy shit around just using her mind. Is there something you can do that they couldn't?'

'I don't know,' Minoo says.

But she thinks about the black smoke. How she was able to make it disperse, at least for a moment. She wishes she could tell Linnéa about it, but she still feels ashamed to talk about it.

'I suppose we'll get all the answers tomorrow,' Linnéa says, 'when you speak to Gustaf.'

'Let's hope so.'

'Are you scared?'

Linnéa is probably the only person in the world who would have to ask that.

'Oh, no, I'm really looking forward to it,' Minoo answers.

Linnéa laughs. Then she says gravely. 'Good luck.'

They hang up and Minoo lies down on the bed. She shuts her eyes. Her thoughts hurtle through her mind until she feels as if she'll suffocate under their weight.

Why did Elias and Rebecka die while she got to live?

Elias died at school. So did Rebecka.

The school is a place of evil.

Is the evil that's after them weak outside the school?

She thinks about the crack in the playground.

She thinks about the blood-red moon that hung heavily over Engelsfors's whispering forests.

She thinks about Cat, about the letter Nicolaus wrote to himself. The last words. *Memento mori.*

Remember that you are going to die.

She thinks about the list of questions she prepared for Gustaf this evening. She thinks about Gustaf outside the library and Gustaf in the darkness by the overpass. Gustaf who was loved by Rebecka. Gustaf who may have killed her.

I can't do it. I won't do it. I won't listen to you.

Those words follow Minoo into her sleep.

CHAPTER 50

The sun is filtering through the half-open blinds in Nicolaus's living room. Anna-Karin is sitting on one of the chairs, hunched forward, staring at her feet. She's wearing red socks. Her left big toe is peeping out.

Now she's told him everything, without looking him in the eye. She's told him about her mother. About the boiling water. About Jari. About the 'accident'. That it was really an attack against her. That she'd tried to play the heroine and it ended in disaster. She's just finished telling him about Grandpa and now there's nothing more to say. She's told him everything and Nicolaus still hasn't said a word.

Anna-Karin runs her foot across the floor and something sticky attaches itself to her sock. She bends down and plucks at something white, like chewing gum.

'Ectoplasm,' Nicolaus says. 'They performed a ritual here the other day. You were indirectly involved, from what I understand.'

Anna-Karin looks up. His expression is warm. She's been expecting a scolding. Now she has to fight to hold back the tears. She's been having regular crying fits ever since she visited Grandpa yesterday. It's as if all those years of pent-up sadness are coming out.

'Do you hate me?' she asks.

'Of course not.'

'But the others do, don't they? They've got to.'

'Nobody hates you, Anna-Karin,' Nicolaus says calmly. 'But you should have told us earlier.'

Anna-Karin nods. 'I was ashamed.'

'We all do things we're ashamed of,' Nicolaus says.

'But I've done so many.'

Nicolaus cocks his head to one side in a way that reminds her a little of Grandpa. 'Consider my fate for a moment, if you will. I have but one single task: to guide the seven of you. And already two of you are lost. If anyone should feel shame, it's me.'

'Do you?'

'I did,' he says. 'But I realized that self-pity had become a place where I hid from the world. A kind of poisoned refuge.'

Anna-Karin says nothing. She picks at the white clump. It feels warm.

'You've made many mistakes. But just as you must learn to forgive your fellow human beings, you must also learn to forgive yourself. Forgiveness is always at hand, Anna-Karin, if you have the courage to accept it.'

Anna-Karin lets Nicolaus's words sink in. She thinks of Grandpa again.

And I would love you no matter what mistakes you made. Even if you did something wrong, I'd love you, and if someone wanted to hurt you I'd defend you till my last drop of blood.

'I'm afraid of what the others will say,' she almost whispers. 'It'd feel easier if I could tell them one by one . . . Or, at least, not all at the same time.'

'Start with the one you feel most comfortable with. Then we'll call the others together.'

'I was thinking about something from that night,' Anna-Karin says. 'The person who attacked me . . . Gustaf or his double or whoever it was. He must be like me.'

'How do you mean?'

'The voice in my head and how it controlled me. It's almost like what I can do to others. The one who's trying to kill us must be an earth witch.'

Gustaf's family lives on the outskirts of town. The afternoon sun makes the blanket of snow sparkle. The naked birch branches are covered with a thin layer of ice – they look as though they've been crafted from delicate glass. Beyond the field, the black water of the canal swirls slowly past. Minoo wonders how many times Rebecka walked along here with Gustaf.

Footprints appear in the snow next to her as she walks. She and Vanessa have claimed to have caught the flu to escape today's practice session at the fairground. The principal swallowed their lie without comment. Minoo doesn't doubt the woman's intelligence, but it's surprisingly easy to lie to her.

They turn down the last street before the edge of the forest. The town houses have two floors, with the same dark red wooden paneled façades and black window frames.

They stop in front of Gustaf's door.

Minoo almost wishes she could have carried out this task on her own. What will Gustaf say when he thinks they're alone? Will he expose her as someone who goes around locking lips with her dead friend's murderer? What should she say if he does? How will Vanessa react?

Minoo rings the doorbell. She takes a deep breath and Vanessa gives her hand a squeeze. She doesn't know if it was meant to say, 'Let's do this', 'You'll be fine' or 'Pull yourself together, for Christ's sake. You look like you're about to shit your pants.'

Gustaf opens the door. His hair is still wet from his shower. It's a few shades darker and frames his face, making his eyes light up even more clearly. 'Hi!' he says. 'Come in!'

She takes off her shoes and places them on a newspaper that's spread on the floor.

'I'm just making us something to eat,' Gustaf says, and disappears into the kitchen. 'Do you like tuna?'

Minoo hates tuna. It's cat food. Hopefully, she won't have to eat all that much. 'Yeah, of course!' she shouts back.

She glances at the closed door. Somewhere over there Vanessa is removing her shoes and putting them in a plastic bag. Suddenly one falls onto the floor and becomes visible.

'Everything all right?'

Minoo turns. Gustaf is standing in the doorway.

'I dropped my shoe,' Minoo answers, and probes his face for any sign of suspicion. She doesn't detect any. 'I'll be right with you,' she says, and he disappears back into the kitchen.

Minoo turns in time to see the shoe vanish into thin air. She raises an admonishing eyebrow in Vanessa's direction, then heads into the kitchen.

Gustaf is setting the table. His father is folding away his newspaper and getting up from the table when Minoo enters.

Minoo curses inwardly. It would have been much easier if Gustaf had been alone at home. But she smiles at Gustaf's father, holds out her hand and introduces herself.

'I'm Lage,' he says.

Lage is quite old, but she can see he was every bit as good-looking as Gustaf when he was young. He is tall and erect, and has a fine head of silvery hair. His handshake is firm and warm. 'I've heard a lot about you,' he says and it feels as if his right hand swallows up Minoo's when they greet each other.

Minoo fumbles for an answer, but fear leaves her at a loss for words. She just smiles and hopes she'll come across as shy rather than rude. Lage smoothes out a few crinkles in his folded newspaper – a copy of today's *Engelsfors Herald* – and raises it to his forehead in mock salute. 'I'll leave you two in peace,' he says. 'I'll be in the basement working on the new track if you need me.'

'"The new track"?' Minoo asks, once he's disappeared.

'He's got a model railroad,' Gustaf says, and puts out two glasses. 'It's pretty cool. He's built a model of old Engelsfors and laid the tracks along the same route as the actual ones. There are lots of stretches of track around here that haven't been used since the mine and steel works closed down.'

494

'That sounds . . . cool,' Minoo says.

Gustaf laughs and pours cola for them. 'Okay, maybe that was the wrong word,' he says. 'Sit down.'

She sinks on to a chair and Gustaf is immediately wolfing down his food. Minoo picks cautiously at her tuna. She wonders where Vanessa has positioned herself in the kitchen. Has she already poured the serum over Gustaf's food? Will he be able to taste it? How will it affect him? Is there a non-human part of him that will realize and react? Does he already know what they're planning?

Minoo aims at a lettuce leaf. She folds it laboriously with her knife and fork, then stabs the fork through the little green package. She raises it to her mouth, opens and then, as she'd known it would, the lettuce leaf unravels and vinaigrette dribbles down her chin.

She's sure she hears Vanessa stifle a giggle, and Gustaf grins at her. 'I always do that,' Minoo says.

'I'm the same,' Gustaf says. 'You should see me eating tacos.'

She wonders if he's lying to make her feel better. She's never seen Gustaf do anything clumsy. 'But tacos don't count,' she says. 'That's a dish with built-in humiliation.'

Gustaf laughs. 'Rebecka said you were funny.'

And then she sees an ever-so-faint ripple appear on Gustaf's cola. Vanessa has poured in the serum.

'I was so happy when you said you wanted to meet,' Gustaf says. 'You and I knew Rebecka better than anyone. It somehow feels important that we keep in touch. You know what I mean?'

'Yes,' Minoo answers. She has to force herself not to stare at Gustaf's glass.

'She often talked about you,' he says.

He raises his glass to his mouth and takes a few sips. Minoo forces herself to drink a little from her own. Don't stare, she thinks. Don't give yourself away by staring.

'Do you think the cola tastes strange?' Gustaf says.

Here it comes. Here it comes.

'No.' Minoo shakes her head firmly and takes a few extra sips for good measure.

'I've only just opened it,' he says thoughtfully. Then he shrugs his shoulders. 'I hope I'm not coming down with the flu. Everything tastes strange when I'm getting sick.' And with that he knocks back the whole glass.

Holy shit! Minoo almost blurts. It's as if she's paralyzed, expecting Gustaf to fall off his chair, clawing at his throat. 'I feel a bit dizzy,' he says.

Minoo swallows. 'Maybe we should go to your room,' she suggests.

Gustaf looks confused. 'So you can lie down for a bit,' she says.

'Maybe you're right.'

His voice is toneless, but he gets up.

My God, Minoo thinks. Ida didn't react like that. What if we've given him too much?

She hears footsteps coming up the basement steps, heavy and quick. Minoo's thoughts run wild. Where does Gustaf keep his doppelganger hidden all day – and what better place to put a doppelganger than in your basement? Maybe his dad is in on it, or maybe he's even masterminded the whole thing – or else it's just a big mistake and both Gustaf and his father are innocent but Minoo has given Gustaf a fatal dose of a magic potion.

Minoo flies out of her chair and puts her arm around Gustaf, who looks as if he's about to faint.

The basement door opens and Gustaf's father steps out.

'I was going to ask if you'd made enough food for me . . .' Lage starts, but then he catches sight of Gustaf. 'Are you all right, Gurra? You look pale.'

'I felt dizzy but now I'm fine.'

Lage walks over and lays a hand on Gustaf's forehead. 'You're not warm anyway.'

'Minoo thinks I should lie down for a bit,' Gustaf says.

'Maybe he overdid it at practice.' Minoo turns to Gustaf. 'Come on, let's go up to your room.'

Lage looks at Gustaf with concern. 'Come and fetch me if he gets any worse. I'll be down here.'

'Yes, you will,' Gustaf says.

'My mother's a doctor,' Minoo jabbers. 'The flu going around is pretty nasty. It hits you out of nowhere and you're as sick as dog.' Minoo takes Gustaf's arm and lets him show her the way to his room on the second floor.

'Can you turn on the light?' she asks, as they enter the darkened room.

'Yes,' he answers, and collapses onto his bed with a heavy thud.

It takes Minoo a second to pick up on it – it's like when

little kids are trying to be funny and answer exactly what you ask them, no more.

'Where's the switch?' Minoo asks.

'To the right of the door.'

She turns on the ceiling light. The bed that Gustaf is lying on is unmade. Otherwise the room is tidy.

On the wall beside the bed there's a photo of Rebecka and Gustaf. Their faces fill the frame so it's impossible to determine where it was taken. You can only tell from the light that it was shot outside. They look happy. At that particular hundredth of a second that the camera captured, they had no idea of what was in store for them.

Gustaf may have known, she reminds herself. Far from depicting a happy couple, it may be of a murderer and his victim.

She feels a gentle shove. It's not hard to interpret. Vanessa thinks Minoo should get a move on – and she's right. Who knows how long the serum will last. A drop lasted about a minute with Ida. Minoo has figured out that they should have at least ten minutes but they've already lost some time. And Gustaf is bigger than Ida.

Minoo sits on the edge of the bed. The list of questions she's prepared is in her jeans pocket. She leaves it there. 'Did you love Rebecka?'

'Yes,' Gustaf answers, without hesitation. 'More than anything else in the world.'

'When you were at her grave, you asked for her forgiveness.'

Gustaf nods and a tear trickles from the corner of his eye,

continues along his temple and disappears into his blond hair. He's lying completely still, looking at Minoo with a frightened expression.

'Did you have anything to do with her death?'

'Yes,' he answers.

Minoo's blood runs cold. 'Tell me about it,' she forces herself to say.

'It was my fault. Everyone said Rebecka had an eating disorder, but I was too much of a coward to ask her straight out. I didn't want to upset her, and I didn't want her to think I was hassling her. I never realized how serious it was. I should have spoken to her about it.'

He continues looking at Minoo with big, frightened eyes.

'You think Rebecka killed herself, don't you?' she says.

The question seems to confuse him. 'Yes,' he says. 'She jumped from the roof of the school. It was my fault. If I had been a better boyfriend, it would never have happened.'

Minoo glances at the photo and wonders if Rebecka can see them. She hopes not because she feels so ashamed of what she's doing.

'Were you up on the roof with her?' she asks.

'I was waiting for her downstairs. She was having her meeting with the principal.'

He lays a hand on Minoo's arm. His fingers are cold. 'I hoped the principal would talk to her about her eating disorder. Maybe get her to open up about it, so I wouldn't have to. I was such a coward.'

'Have you done anything special this autumn? Have you contacted anyone?'

'What do you mean?'

Minoo feels another impatient shove, a reminder that time is running out. 'Have you been in contact with any demons?'

He looks confused. Like a child who's been asked a far too grown-up question.

'Have you engaged in any supernatural activities?' Minoo continues.

'No.'

It's clear he has no idea what she's talking about.

'You may not even know about it. Think for a second. Has anything strange happened?'

He shakes his head.

'Do you ever hear a voice inside your head telling you to do things?'

He shakes his head again.

'What's the first thing that comes into your mind when I say "blood-red moon"?'

'Blood orange.'

'Do you have a doppelganger?'

'No,' he says weakly. 'I don't think so.'

'I can't handle this,' Vanessa says.

Minoo understands how she feels. To see Gustaf so afraid and vulnerable is almost more than she can bear. It's like something out of the Spanish inquisition. But she has another question, and she can only hope Gustaf won't say anything about the kiss because, unlike him, Vanessa won't forget everything afterward.

'Did you follow me into town one day and then meet me by the overpass?'

'No.'

'I met you there, and we . . . spoke. Do you remember that?'

'No.'

'And yet you were at the cemetery. That was when you visited Rebecka's grave for the first time. You were in two places at once. How was that possible?'

Gustaf shakes his head. 'I don't understand,' he says. 'Your questions are so strange.'

Minoo can't take it any more. She tries to coax his fingers from her arm, but he's holding it in an iron grip. She strokes them gently, hoping that will calm him.

It works. His grip loosens and she gets up.

'I'm sorry,' she says.

'What are you saying sorry about?'

'All of this.'

'I like you, Minoo,' he says.

'I like you, too,' she says, and discovers she means it. 'I wish I could tell you how Rebecka died, but it wasn't your fault.'

'Minoo, what are you doing?' Vanessa whispers.

But Minoo ignores her. It's very easy to ignore someone who's invisible. 'I want to ask you to try to remember one thing.' Minoo says. 'Try to remember it somewhere deep inside you. Can you promise you'll try?'

'I promise I'll try,' Gustaf says.

'It wasn't your fault. Rebecka loved you.'

Fresh tears well in Gustaf's eyes and Minoo nods, trying to ingrain it into his subconscious. 'She would never have left you by choice,' she says.

Gustaf smiles cautiously. 'I'm tired,' he says.

'You should sleep for a while.'

Gustaf shuts his eyes and Minoo and Vanessa stay in the room until he's dropped off. Then they sneak out, careful not to wake him.

CHAPTER 51

Vanessa has had a long shower, and she still doesn't feel clean. When she and Minoo had separated, they had agreed that they would never reveal what Gustaf had said to anyone. They texted the others that they were sure Gustaf wasn't the killer, and that he didn't know about his doppelganger. Nothing more. The rest is nobody else's business. Not even theirs. That's why she feels so dirty. She never wants to rummage around in someone's innermost thoughts again.

Now she's almost inhaling the sausage stew Sirpa has made for dinner. Vanessa is on her second helping, but her hunger shows no signs of abating. As always when she's been invisible, her body craves nourishment. And lots of it.

'Slow down, Nessa,' Wille says, and has a hard time not laughing.

'Mind your own business,' she says, her mouth full of rice drenched in tomato sauce.

'You'll end up weighing a ton if you go on like that.'

'And I'll still be better-looking than you.' She pours more milk and downs it in three gulps.

Sirpa watches them nervously.

'Sorry I'm gobbling it,' Vanessa says. 'It's just so delicious. As usual.'

'Good,' Sirpa replies.

She looks as if she means it, but Vanessa knows it must be difficult for her to have another mouth to feed. Especially such an unusually voracious one. Of course Vanessa gives Sirpa half of her allowance each month, but it won't cover much. 'Thanks so much for dinner,' she says, and swallows a last piece of sausage.

She starts clearing the table. She's too restless to sit still. When Sirpa stands up, Vanessa tells her to go and watch TV. Sirpa smiles gratefully and disappears into the living room. Wille stays where he is, rocking back on his chair as he sticks a bag of tobacco under his lip.

Vanessa piles the dirty dishes on the counter and fills the sink with water. Then she starts to scrub the plates with the brush. The water is so hot that beads of sweat pop out on her forehead. It's good to concentrate on something mundane.

Suddenly she feels a pair of hands slide around her waist.

'You know,' Wille says, kissing her neck. 'I saw an ad for a cheap trip to Thailand in a few weeks.'

'I'll still be at school.'

Thailand, Thailand, Thailand. He's been harping on about Thailand for months.

'Fuck school,' Wille mumbles. 'Let's go. I think I can get some money from Jonte.'

She sidesteps to escape his hands. But they're on her again and she shakes them off, more firmly this time.

'What's the matter?' he asks.

'Can't you leave me alone for one second?'

'Why are you so grumpy?'

'And why are you stuck to me like a frigging Band-Aid all the time?'

He remains behind her. She feels his irritation radiating out from him.

'I just want a cuddle,' he says.

'And I want to be left alone. Is that so difficult to understand?'

'Why are you so pissed off all the time?' He walks back to the kitchen table.

Vanessa dries the dishes while she waits for him to speak again. She knows he can never stay silent for very long.

'I took a look at those links you sent me,' he says finally.

She turns with a glass in one hand and the towel in the other.

'They're not for me,' he continues.

Vanessa squeezes the glass so hard it should have cracked. 'You didn't see anything you liked, or what?'

'I don't want to be a fucking telemarketer, Nessa.'

'Then what the hell *do* you want, Wille?'

He laughs feebly, not seeming to realize how angry she is.

'I don't know . . . I guess I think things are pretty good the way they are for me. For us.'

'And then what?'

'What does that mean?'

So, Vanessa knows that the end of the world is

approaching, yet it's Wille who has trouble thinking about the future.

'If you want a decent job, then you'll just have to go back to school,' she says.

'Fuck that. I was never any good at school.'

'There are vocational schools.'

'Yeah, but . . . I don't know.'

'So you're happy with the way things are? Is that what you're saying?'

'Well, it would be cool if we had our own place, of course. Maybe you can hook us up with one once you've got a job?' Wille says jokingly.

She can tell he thinks he's being cute. She'd like nothing better than to hurl her glass at the wall. She probably would have, too, if it hadn't belonged to Sirpa, just like everything else around them. And Vanessa doesn't want to explode: she can't take responsibility for what might happen.

She sets the glass on the counter and lays the towel on the table in front of Wille. 'You can do this,' she says.

'Nessa, I was only kidding! I understand we can't live like this forever, but I don't have a clue what to do.'

'I know you were kidding. But I have to go out for a bit – and if you want us to keep being together, then I'd advise you to shut up.'

Vanessa walks through the town without knowing where she's going. Thoughts are spinning in her head like a nausea-inducing merry-go-round. There are way too many Vanessas now, and she no longer knows which is the real one. The Vanessa she is when she's with Michelle and Evelina is different, for example, from the Vanessa who's trying to save the world. And then there's the Vanessa she has to be when she's with Wille, and the Vanessa who's trying not to be too much of a burden on Sirpa, plus the Vanessa who wants to leave school with at least a passing grade in her final exams . . . She's lost her way among all her different personas.

Vanessa looks at the tall high-rises that surround her. She's ended up near Linnéa's place. She hears music coming from a few of the apartments around her. It's Saturday night and she's only just realized it. When did her life become so dull that she no longer has plans for a Saturday night? Getting drunk might help. Evelina and Michelle were talking about a party, she remembers.

Vanessa hesitates. She doesn't want to be alone, but she doesn't want to see them either. Michelle will obsess about Mehmet, whom she's just started dating, and Evelina will whine that she's never going to meet anybody, even though they all know she's the best-looking of the three of them.

When was the last time she felt like seeing Evelina and Michelle? So much has happened in Vanessa's life since last summer. There's so much she can't talk to them about.

It would have been easier to go back to being the old Vanessa. Christ, she wishes she could.

Vanessa looks up at the high-rises again. Maybe it isn't pure chance that she's ended up here.

She heads for the entrance to Linnéa's building, takes the

elevator up to her floor and rings the bell. Nobody comes to open the door and she feels disappointed. It makes her realize how much she wants to see Linnéa.

Vanessa rings again, and hears a toilet flush. When Linnéa opens the door she's wearing the same Dir En Grey shirt as she was that night with Jonte.

'Hi,' Vanessa says.

'Hey,' Linnéa answers.

'What are you doing?'

'Nothing.'

'It's Saturday night,' Vanessa says. 'Shouldn't you be having fun?'

'Who says I'm not?' Linnéa says. She looks so grimfaced when she says it that Vanessa starts laughing.

Linnéa stares at her for half a second. Then she laughs, too. It turns into one of those hysterical, can't-breathe-can't-stop-laughing fits and Vanessa can't even remember the last time she had one. They laugh till they almost choke, then make the mistake of catching the other's eye, which sets them off again.

They sit opposite each other on the sofa and talk. A stream of morose-sounding boys and girls with guitars plays on Linnéa's computer, but strangely it doesn't depress Vanessa. Instead the music, with the dim red lighting, envelops her in a soft, warm sensation.

Their conversation flows naturally. Linnéa tells her what the *Book of Patterns* has revealed about protective magic. Vanessa tells Linnéa how she poured the serum into Gustaf's cola, but leaves out the details of what he said. 'You know I dated Gustaf once?' she says instead.

When she registers the shock on Linnéa's face she giggles. 'For a whole afternoon in first grade. I used to do this thing back then . . . Any boy who managed to swing in sync with me on the swings during recess could be with me for the rest of the day.'

'So you were cheap even then?' Linnéa says, cackling harshly.

'If only it was that easy to decide who to be with now,' Vanessa says, and giggles.

They laugh as they recall when Ida was forced to confess that she was secretly in love with Gustaf. They talk about how five or six girls used to bike around his house, around and around, in the hope that he would look out of a window and see them. Magic or not, he's always had girls under a spell.

Then they talk about Minoo and whether or not she's a lesbian. Vanessa is convinced she is. Linnéa says definitely not.

'I think I like her, but I don't understand her. I can't figure out when she's pissed off and when she's just Minoo,' Vanessa says.

Linnéa laughs and nods. 'I think she may be a little pissed off with me,' she says.

'What for?'

'A misunderstanding.' Linnéa doesn't elaborate.

'We Chosen Ones are a pretty strange bunch,' Vanessa says.

'Aren't we though? Look at the two of us,' Linnéa says, and grins.

509

'Who would've thought you and me would be sitting here like this? I've always like hated you. Or, at least, I've been jealous of you over the whole Wille thing.' What *am* I saying? Vanessa wonders. But it feels okay. She had almost forgotten how it felt to be so relaxed. And she realizes she needs to talk about Wille. Linnéa will understand. 'I don't want to break up with him,' she says, 'but he's driving me crazy.'

'Do you have to live with him?'

'It's complicated,' Vanessa says. She can't bring herself to explain why she isn't living at home. It sounds so pathetic when she imagines the story from Linnéa's perspective. Linnéa, who doesn't even have a mother. Linnéa, whose father dances drunken jigs in Storvall Park.

'I don't understand how I can be in love with someone who pisses me off so fucking much,' Vanessa says. 'Or why I'm always so fucking pissed off with the person I love.'

'Don't ask me.' Linnéa leans back on the sofa.

'Why not?'

'You should never give advice about other people's relationships.'

'But at Monique's you said—'

'That was a mistake.'

Linnéa sits cross-legged and looks straight at her. 'Don't you get it?' she asks. 'You deserve someone better than Wille. But if I say that, and you break up with Wille, I'm the one you'll be angry with if you regret it. And if you decide to stick it out, then you'll know what I think and hate me for it.'

510

'But I won't—' Vanessa protests.

'I just mean I don't want to be the girl you blame everything on later,' Linnéa interrupts.

Vanessa doesn't know what to say. She feels as if she's just been paid a compliment that's really nice and really strange at the same time.

'But he doesn't call me any more,' Linnéa says.

Vanessa sinks a little deeper into the sofa, and gets a flashback of how Jonte and Linnéa looked when they were lying there that night. It feels like a lifetime ago. 'Are you still seeing Jonte?'

'No. I plead temporary insanity for that whole thing.'

Vanessa giggles and wriggles to adjust her position on the sofa so that her feet are resting against Linnéa's legs.

Everything's going to work out. Somehow.

CHAPTER 52

Minoo is standing in the forest near Kärrgruvan. It's spring and the leaves on the trees are a verdant green. It's almost painful to look at them. She hears water burbling and looks down. A stream is flowing at her feet. A thousand little suns glitter on its surface. A pair of black feathers float past. It's strange that she can know it's a dream without waking up.

Minoo?

Rebecka's calling to her.

Minoo?

Minoo is suddenly in a hurry. She starts to run along the water. She has to find Rebecka. But her feet keep sinking into the damp earth. A little deeper with each step.

Minoo!

She's stuck.

And in the water she sees Rebecka. She's lying on her back in her white nightgown. Her long reddish-blonde hair spreads out around her pale face. Her eyes are angled up at the sky, her mouth open as if in ecstasy. In one hand she's holding a garland of flowers. Their colors are unnaturally vivid against the black water.

She is the drowning Ophelia.

'You're not Rebecka,' Minoo says, angry and disappointed.

Rebecka looks at her. It's Rebecka's face, Rebecka's body. Rebecka's voice. And yet it isn't.

The stream eddies and ripples around her, but she's floating, motionless in the middle of the current. She's speaking but her mouth isn't moving.

The woman who posed for this painting was Elizabeth Siddal. She fell gravely ill afterward. The bath she was lying in was fitted with lamps to stop the water from getting cold. But one day they went out. The artist didn't notice. He was absorbed in his painting. And little Lizzie said nothing. She just suffered in silence. All so that he could fulfill his vision. To be reduced to an image comes at a high price.

Somewhere in real life the doorbell rings, but Minoo clings to her dream.

'What are you talking about?'

I thought your mind was your superpower, Minoo. You have to wake up now. You have to find the courage to see yourself as others do. And you have to let go.

The dream dissipates and she's awake. The doorbell rings again.

Minoo's father is unshaven and has dark circles under his eyes. Anna-Karin smells the coffee on his breath when he says he's unsure if Minoo is up yet. Maybe it would have been better if she'd waited a few hours before coming here. But she had to do it before her courage failed her.

He shows her into the front hall and shouts at the ceiling that Minoo has a visitor.

'I'm coming!' Minoo's voice replies.

Anna-Karin takes off her coat and follows him into the living room.

'Would you like something?' he asks. 'Coffee? Tea? Milk? Water?'

'No, thanks,' Anna-Karin mumbles, and looks around the big, bright room.

The furniture is expensive. Four packed bookcases with a built-in TV cabinet stand along one wall. There's real art – not the usual Ikea prints or hangings embroidered with some proverb that Anna-Karin's mother is so fond of. 'A penny saved is a penny earned', 'There's no place like home', 'A merry heart makes a cheerful face.' They're everywhere in her house. As if she were trying to convince herself. Anna-Karin feels pangs of shame as she imagines what Minoo's father would think of those wall hangings.

You can see into the big kitchen with its white cupboard doors and dark wooden floor. The study door is ajar: a brand-new laptop stands on a desk next to a steaming coffee mug. Even more bookshelves.

How many books can you have in a home? Anna-Karin wonders. Where do they find the time to read them all? Do they, even?

She lets her gaze fall on a painting that doesn't depict anything, just colors and shapes. Her mother would scoff at it and say that any five-year-old could've painted that. But Anna-Karin likes it.

'I'm Erik Falk,' Minoo's father says, holding out his hand.

Anna-Karin realizes she's been standing there staring, like a fool. She takes Minoo's father's hand and meets his eyes for a split second.

'Anna-Karin Nieminen,' she mumbles. It's strange to introduce herself with her last name. 'Minoo and I are in the same class. We're working on a project together.'

'Is it the play?'

Anna-Karin has no idea what he's talking about. She opens and closes her mouth like a fish out of water. That's how she feels in this house.

'Minoo said something about how you rehearse on Saturdays.'

'That's right,' Anna-Karin answers. She was within a hair's breadth of ruining Minoo's alibi for their meetings at the fairground. 'But today we're going to do some chemistry,' she says, and hopes that Minoo's father won't ask any more questions.

Finally she hears footsteps on the stairs and Minoo appears in the doorway. Her black hair is in a ponytail and her eyes are still a little puffy from sleep.

'Hi,' she says, without managing to hide her surprise.

'Should we get started on the chemistry?' Anna-Karin asks.

Minoo catches on. 'Of course. Let's go up to my room.'

Anna-Karin notices how easily Minoo moves through the house, as if there's nothing special about being surrounded by nice things.

They walk down a long landing. She glances into a

bathroom with an old map of Engelsfors on the wall. The deep bathtub has lion's feet. That was where Minoo was attacked.

Minoo takes Anna-Karin into her room and shuts the door.

The wallpaper is striped yellow and white and brings out the warm tones of the lacquered wooden floor. A red comforter has been thrown rather sloppily across the bed, and a large art book lies on Minoo's bedside table. The books on the shelf are neatly lined up, no doubt in alphabetical order.

The chaos in Minoo's room is concentrated on the desk in front of the window. It's overflowing with textbooks and notebooks, which threaten to engulf the closed laptop.

'So it wasn't Gustaf,' Anna-Karin says.

'Not the real one,' Minoo says. 'I mean . . . he doesn't know he has an evil doppelganger.'

Anna-Karin goes to the bed and sits down. 'I'm glad it wasn't Gustaf,' she says. 'Even if that means we still don't know who did it.'

Minoo sits down next to her. Waits.

Anna-Karin doesn't know where to begin. Eventually she takes a deep breath and starts with what she feels is most important. 'I'm sorry,' she says. 'I'm sorry I just dis-appeared.' She glances at Minoo, whose dark eyes gaze at her intently.

Anna-Karin has always been a little afraid of Minoo. She often seems so intense, almost angry. When Minoo is impatient, when she thinks you're being stupid or childish or doing something wrong, you can feel it in your whole body. And then that laser stare.

'You know the accident when the barn burned down,' Anna-Karin begins. 'It wasn't an accident.' She doesn't tell her everything, as she did with Nicolaus. She starts with the fire, but leaves out Jari and her mother. It's still difficult to own up, especially to the fact that at first she didn't resist, that she almost welcomed her death.

When she gets to the part about Grandpa she starts to cry. She wipes away the tears with the back of her hand. She doesn't want Minoo to think she's trying to gain sympathy.

'Why didn't you say anything?' Minoo asks.

She's angry. Just as Anna-Karin thought. Her courage falters. 'I was ashamed. I shouldn't have gone into the barn alone.'

'When you resisted . . . did you see anything?' Minoo asks.

Anna-Karin is unsure what she means. 'I didn't see whoever did it,' she says.

'No, but did you see anything else? Something in the air, maybe?'

'No. Why?'

Minoo shakes her head. 'Forget it,' she says. She doesn't look angry any more.

Anna-Karin is so relieved that she starts crying again. Maybe there's hope that they'll forgive her. 'If only I hadn't used my powers at school. Everyone told me not to,' she chokes out.

Minoo furrows her brow. 'What does that have to do with the attack?'

'Whoever attacked me must have noticed I was using magic, like you warned me might happen. It fits with what we know about protective magic, too. Nicolaus told me about it. If you're the one who's visible now, I must still be protected. But maybe the one who attacked me realized I was Chosen anyway—' Anna-Karin breaks off. Catches her breath. 'I've been thinking about something,' she says. 'The one who's trying to kill us is the same element as me. An earth witch. Maybe that's why I could put up such resistance. And maybe that's why he hasn't tried again. Because I was too strong.'

'The voice,' Minoo muses. 'Isn't that how *you* get people to do what you want?'

Anna-Karin flushes. 'More or less. Although I've never taken over someone's body like that.'

Minoo nods slowly. 'Do you think you could make a person think they saw someone who wasn't there?' she asks.

'I don't know,' Anna-Karin answers. 'Maybe. I've never tried.'

'If an earth witch can do that, it might explain why Rebecka saw Gustaf on the roof. If Gustaf was an illusion, and someone else was actually there . . . But that doesn't make sense . . .' She looks straight at Anna-Karin. 'Are you sure the fire was caused by magic?'

'It started so suddenly and came from several different directions at the same time. And then I had this feeling . . .'

'But earth witches shouldn't be able to perform fire magic.'

'No,' Anna-Karin answers.

Minoo's expression is blank, yet intently focused. 'But Rebecka could,' she says, almost to herself. 'And she would have been able to get the barn door to slam shut again.'

'Rebecka?'

Minoo opens the drawer of her bedside table. She pulls out the notepad she always seems to have with her and flips through it. 'When you and Ida experienced Rebecka's death, you said something happened just before she died. As if she was incinerated from within.'

Anna-Karin nods. It's not a memory she enjoys revisiting.

'What if the murderer took her power?' Minoo continues.

'Yes,' Anna-Karin says breathlessly. 'It was as if he took everything that was her.'

'Her soul?'

Anna-Karin nods again. She doesn't know if she believes in souls, but that's the best word to describe it.

Minoo is absorbed in her notes. Anna-Karin doesn't want to disturb her. She looks around the room. Fingers the red bedspread. Notices the big book on the bedside table again. The front cover shows a painting of a couple who are about to kiss. Anna-Karin wipes her hands on her jeans before she dares touch it.

The book is heavy. It falls open automatically to a page in the middle, as if Minoo often looks at it. There are a few books like that in Anna-Karin's house, too. Thick paperback novels about people from the Stone Age that always open where they're having sex with each other on animal skins in caves.

Anna-Karin looks at the image printed on the thick, glossy paper: a portrait of a dark-haired woman in a blue dress. She's holding a pomegranate in one hand and looks sad. She's somehow familiar too.

'I think I get it now,' Minoo says.

Anna-Karin looks up.

Minoo lowers the notepad. 'If the murderer is an earth witch, he may have used his power to force Elias to commit suicide. When Elias died, he took his power, too. The principal said that wood witches can "shape and control different kinds of living material". That might mean that wood witches can change their appearance, like a magic disguise.'

'So after Elias was murdered . . . the killer could make himself look like anyone?'

'We don't know that for sure,' Minoo says, 'but he could at least have looked like Gustaf.'

'And then he got Rebecka's powers . . .'

'Telekinesis and fire. Those were the powers he used in the barn.'

Minoo gets up and starts pacing back and forth. She reminds Anna-Karin of the principal.

'We have to sum up what we know,' Minoo says. She lets down her hair and slides the rubber band onto her wrist. 'The murderer is an earth witch. When he kills us, he can take our souls and our magic. Now he has wood and fire. He didn't manage to kill you or me. Why not?'

'Because I'm an earth witch,' Anna-Karin suggests again, 'and maybe because he's weaker outside the school.'

Minoo stops and gives her an appreciative look. 'Just what I was thinking. The school is an evil place, and all that.'

'But why did he let you live?'

'Because he discovered that I don't have any power?'

'I don't think so,' Anna-Karin says. 'You're still a Chosen One.'

That vacant yet intently focused look has returned to Minoo's face.

She's standing in half-profile toward Anna-Karin and the light from the window illuminates her cascading hair.

Anna-Karin looks at the woman in the blue dress. And then at Minoo. 'Speaking of doppelgangers,' she says, 'the woman in this painting is the spitting image of you.'

She holds up the image to Minoo.

'She is not,' Minoo says.

'Yes, she is,' Anna-Karin says. 'Maybe not if you make an exact comparison of every feature, but taken as a whole, she looks a lot like you.'

Minoo stares at the painting as if it's a Chinese poem Anna-Karin is asking her to recite. 'But she's beautiful,' she says.

Anna-Karin lowers the book. Minoo doesn't say it in the way Julia and Felicia would have, as if she's fishing for a compliment. She means it.

'So are you,' Anna-Karin says.

Minoo snorts. 'You don't have to lie,' she says.

'I'm not.'

Minoo looks annoyed.

'First, I'm a massive pizza-face, in case you hadn't noticed.'

'I have zits too.' Anna-Karin says.

'Not as many as me.'

Now it's Anna-Karin's turn to get annoyed. 'Maybe not exactly as many but some people have a lot more. And you're pretty. You could be her reincarnation.' Anna-Karin points at the image with an index finger.

All the color leaves Minoo's face. She looks as if she's about to faint.

'Are you all right?' Anna-Karin asks. Now she feels stupid. It was a ridiculous thing to argue about – whether or not Minoo is beautiful.

'I don't feel too good,' Minoo mumbles. 'I'm sorry, I have to lie down again. Thanks for telling me.'

Anna-Karin closes the book and gets up. Minoo tries to smile at her. 'I'll head home,' Anna-Karin says. She remains standing there for a moment, but when Minoo doesn't say any more, Anna-Karin pats her shoulder a little awkwardly and tells her to get better soon.

When she comes downstairs, Minoo's father is in the kitchen reading a newspaper. He doesn't look up and Anna-Karin doesn't say anything. She puts on her coat and sneaks out of the front door as quietly as Pepper.

CHAPTER 53

Minoo has a free period. She climbs to the top floor of the school and follows the hallway leading to the attic door. The bathroom up here has just been reopened. The graffiti-covered door was replaced during the Christmas break but is already filling with new messages. Some are dedicated to Elias and Rebecka, but a few are about other people, other lives.

Minoo presses down the handle and enters. For a school bathroom it's almost unnaturally clean. Even if people write things on the door, they rarely go in. Something keeps them away.

The white tiles gleam around Minoo. She's back where it all began.

She walks up to the stall in which Elias died. Of course there are no traces. What had she expected?

Minoo looks at the sinks. The mirrors have been removed. Maybe they were afraid that someone might feel the urge to copy Elias.

But Minoo is happy she can't see her reflection. She's studied it far too often for far too long, and always hated what she saw.

When Anna-Karin said she looked like the beautiful woman in the painting, she couldn't believe it at first. But when Anna-Karin used the word 'reincarnation' all the pieces fell into place.

You have to wake up now.

You have to find the courage to see yourself as others see you.

'Reincarnation'. That was the word Max used.

I love you, Minoo. I've loved you since the first day I set eyes on you.

That hadn't been the first time he'd seen her.

Minoo looks like the woman in the painting. The woman in the painting looks like Alice. His greatest love. That was why he couldn't kill Minoo. It would be like seeing Alice die all over again.

I won't do it. I won't listen to you!

Max is the murderer. He killed Elias. He killed Rebecka. He tried to kill Minoo and Anna-Karin.

It makes sense, yet she still can't believe it.

She takes the little brown bottle from the pocket of her cardigan.

She has to know for sure.

'If you're going to move home there will have to be some rules.'

Vanessa and her mother are the only customers at Monique's. It was Vanessa's suggestion that they meet here, on neutral territory. Now she's regretting it. She wishes they were in a place where she could scream uninhibitedly at her mother. Slam a door or two, maybe.

'Rules?' she repeats, and raises an eyebrow.

Her mother spins her spoon in her hand. She's hardly touched her coffee or the biscotti on her plate.

'Well, we can hardly go back to how it was before.'

'I agree,' Vanessa says, sure they're talking about two different things.

'I haven't been strict enough. You've been allowed to go out partying and meeting boys since you were far too young.'

'Like mother, like daughter?'

The spoon stops spinning. Her mother meets her gaze. 'Yeah,' she says. 'I guess so.'

'But that's all over now? It's time to be a real mother?' Why do I do that? she wonders. Why do I ruin everything from the start?

'If you're going to take that attitude . . .' Her mother starts to stand up.

'I'm sorry,' Vanessa says. The word leaves a bitter aftertaste in her mouth. But her mother sits down again. That's the important thing.

'You have to see it from my perspective, too,' Vanessa continues.

'Don't you think I'm trying to?'

Vanessa sips her coffee to stop herself from screaming, 'No!' to that question. 'I really don't know,' she says. 'You don't seem to care. You haven't tried to get in touch. Not even at Christmas.' She speaks quickly, so her voice doesn't shake.

'Of course I care!' her mother says.

Vanessa still doesn't trust her voice so she shrugs.

'I've asked Sirpa not to say anything, but we've talked to each other at least once a week,' her mother says. 'I thought it best that you came to me when you were ready.'

She reaches across the table to Vanessa, but Vanessa leans back in her chair.

'Why do you want to come home anyway?' her mother asks. 'Aren't things working out between you and Wille?'

'Everything's great,' Vanessa says, and hears how defiant she sounds, how obvious it is that she's lying. She looks out of the window. 'It isn't fair to Sirpa,' she says.

'Is that the only reason?' her mother asks.

Vanessa looks at her hands. Only now does she become aware that she's also spinning her spoon. She knows what she wants to say. Why is it so difficult? 'I miss you – Melvin and you.'

'And we've missed you. A lot.'

Her mother's voice sounds thick and Vanessa doesn't dare look at her. She's afraid she's going to start crying.

'I want it to work,' her mother says, sighing heavily. 'I want us to be a family.'

'So do I,' Vanessa says. 'But there's one thing I have to know: don't you think on some level – just a tiny bit – that Nicke's behavior might be out of line sometimes, too? That maybe it isn't always my fault that things aren't working.'

'I've never said it was only your fault,' her mother says, in the martyr voice that Vanessa hates.

She clenches her fist, lets her nails dig little red half-moons into her palm. 'You said something about rules.'

'You can be out late only on weekends,' her mother says.

Vanessa doesn't object. She's an expert at slipping out and in without her mother noticing.

'I'm not going to try to stop you from seeing Wille,' her mother says. 'I just have one request. Please, Vanessa, be careful. Don't let yourself be dragged into anything. Promise me that?'

'I don't know what you're talking about, but okay.'

'And maybe it's not such a good idea for Wille to come over to our house.'

Her mother looks away, and Vanessa knows instantly that that's Nicke's condition. 'I don't think he'll want to,' she says. 'Not after how he was treated last time.'

'I can understand that.'

It may not sound like much, but that's the closest her mother has ever come to admitting that Nicke was wrong.

'We've fixed the pipes in the shower, by the way,' her mother continues, with a hint of a smile, 'so now you won't get scalded every morning.'

'Did Nicke manage to . . . ?'

'No,' her mother says. 'We had to call in a contractor. They tore out everything Nicke had done and started again. It ended up being twice as expensive as it would have been if we'd brought them in from the beginning.'

Now Vanessa sees an unmistakable smile at the corners of her mother's mouth. Maybe there is hope, after all.

The last class is physics and they're working in pairs. Minoo lets her partner Levan build the ramp that they'll let a little car roll down to show . . . something or other. She can't concentrate on the problem. She can't think. She avoids looking at Max. Avoids looking at Anna-Karin. She has to concentrate on not hyperventilating. Levan is building and measuring. Minoo's hand takes notes automatically.

She sticks the other into her pocket and fingers the little glass bottle. Glances at Max's coffee cup that is on his desk. There's five minutes to go before the end of class. Max is at the back of the lab, turned away from her, helping Kevin Månsson.

'I'm just going to blow my nose,' she tells Levan.

She walks to the front of the class. The paper towel dispenser is mounted on the wall behind the teacher's desk.

She glances in Max's direction. He's still bent over Kevin, explaining something. She wishes she could hear what they're saying so that she knows whether they're in the middle of a discussion or about to end it. Ironically, the survival of the Chosen Ones and the future of the world may depend on Kevin – on whether he's dim-witted enough to need Max's help long enough to allow Minoo the time she needs.

She pulls out the truth serum bottle from her cardigan pocket. Her fingers are slippery and it slides in her grasp, but she doesn't drop it.

She unscrews the top. The mug is on the desk, with some black coffee left in the bottom. He always finishes it when class is over.

Minoo casts a nervous glance over her shoulder. Everyone is staring at their ramps. Max is still with Kevin. It's now or never.

Just do it, she thinks.

She holds out her hand, squeezes the little rubber top of the eye dropper and pulls it back, unsure whether anything came out. There are just a few drops left in the bottle. Her heart is pounding.

Max has left Kevin and is now wandering around the room with his hands clasped behind his back.

Did he see her? She has no idea.

His face is expressionless. Normal.

She pretends to blow her nose and returns to her desk. Step one is accomplished.

The bell rings. Levan has already put away their equipment and gives her a sour look. He's had to do all the work. 'Sorry, I'm tired today,' she says apologetically.

'It's okay,' he says curtly, and packs his bag.

She puts her books into her backpack as slowly as she can, while the last of the other students shuffle out. Why are they so slow? She wants to yell at them to hurry up.

Eventually she and Max are the only ones left. He's holding his coffee cup. Has he drunk it? She tries to read his face. 'Everything all right?' he asks.

She forces a smile that causes her mouth to tremble.

'Of course. Why do you ask?'

'I can see something's wrong,' he says.

She walks up to his desk, meets his gaze. His beautiful greenish-brown eyes. A murderer's eyes.

He looks at her as he empties his coffee cup. His Adam's apple bobs as he swallows.

Max clears his throat. Swallows again. 'Isn't it very . . . stuffy in here?' he says.

And she knows it's working.

'Was it you?' she whispers. 'Was it you who killed Elias and Rebecka?'

Waiting for the answer feels like falling through space, faster and faster with each passing millisecond.

'Yes,' Max says.

And there's the answer. The one that changes everything.

The love she's felt for him, which seemed so huge and eternal, evaporates. She never thought you could stop loving someone so suddenly. But the Max she loved doesn't exist. He never did.

'Did you disguise yourself as Gustaf by the overpass?' she asks.

'Yes. I wanted to be close to you.'

'Why Gustaf?'

'You seem to like him. Everyone likes Gustaf. Rebecka trusted him.'

'Do you know who the other Chosen Ones are?'

'Just you and Anna-Karin. There are three more.'

So Vanessa, Linnéa and Ida aren't in immediate danger. That's a relief. Then a terrible thought takes hold of her. Something Anna-Karin had suggested yesterday and that she hasn't really considered. *The killer could make himself look like anyone . . .*

'Have you ever taken on the form of anyone else? Me or Anna-Karin?'

'I've tried,' he says, 'but for some reason I can only look like other men. They told me that some are limited in that way.'

'"They"?'

'The ones who blessed me,' Max answers, without batting an eyelid. 'They told me about you. About what I have to do.'

'Have you seen them? Met them?'

'No. At first they were just voices in my dreams. But now they're there when I'm awake. They're always with me. At this very moment they're telling me to be silent, but I can't.'

'Why?' she asks. 'Why are you killing us?'

'I made a pact with them. But that's changed now.' He looks at Minoo with a glazed expression and smiles. 'You needn't worry, Minoo. They have a new plan for you.'

The hair on the back of her neck stands up. 'A plan?' she asks.

'They haven't told me the details yet. The important thing is that they've agreed to let you live. That's all that matters to me.'

'But you have no problem with killing those you don't care about?'

'I don't like to do it, but it's necessary.'

'Necessary?'

Max shuts his eyes. The serum has stopped working. He refocuses on her as if he has only just become aware that she's standing there. 'What were we talking about?' he asks.

Minoo opens her mouth but is unable to speak. It's as if she's run out of lies.

And Max sees it.

Or are the demons telling him what happened? They aren't affected by the serum. Max's eyes harden.

She tries to head for the door, but he grabs her wrist tightly and pulls her to him. 'Let go!' Her voice is so weak, like in one of those dreams where you can't scream, only whisper.

'What have you done?'

'Nothing.'

'What have you done?' he repeats.

'I don't know what you're talking about,' she whispers. 'I have to go.'

Max lets go of her. 'I won't harm you, Minoo,' he says pleadingly.

She wants to throw up when she remembers how she kissed him.

How could she have kissed him twice without realizing he was the murderer? And how can she tell the others?

'I don't know what you're talking about,' she says again, and runs out of the classroom.

CHAPTER 54

They've crammed themselves around Nicolaus's kitchen table. Nicolaus is standing beside the counter, petting Cat distractedly.

Minoo's tense shoulders are pulled up so high that they're almost earrings. She leans forward with her hands on the tabletop. She's going to be strong now. She's going to tell them. Across the table she meets Anna-Karin's eyes. Anna-Karin has also been forced to reveal her secrets to the others.

Minoo has rehearsed what she's going to say, over and over again, in her head. She tries to gather her courage, to suppress the shame that, on some level, she knows she doesn't have to feel – but what good is that when she feels it so intensely?

Now everyone's looking at her.

'It's Max,' she says. 'Max is the killer.'

That wasn't how she had intended to start.

'Max?' Anna-Karin asks.

'Max who?' Vanessa asks.

'He's our homeroom teacher,' Anna-Karin says. 'The math and physics teacher.'

'The good-looking one?' Ida asks.

'What makes you think it's him?' Anna-Karin asks.

And Minoo explains, without looking at them: about Max and Alice and the woman in the painting, about the evening she was at his house, about the kiss by the overpass, about Gustaf's doppelganger, who was Max, about everything Max had confessed to her in the classroom.

The only thing she doesn't tell them is the plan that Max was talking about, the one that the demons have devised for her. It's too frightening.

'How could you be so fucking stupid?' Vanessa says.

'I didn't know until yesterday,' Minoo stammers.

'That's not what I'm talking about,' Vanessa says. 'I'm talking about the truth serum! Anything could have happened! How could you use it on him while you were alone with him?'

'I had to.'

Linnéa has sat there silently, watching Minoo. But now she leans forward and smiles coldly. 'So what would have happened if Max had killed you? Then we would never have found out he was the murderer.'

'I wanted to be sure it was him,' Minoo says.

'Exactly. So you wouldn't have to tell us your dirty little secret.'

Minoo doesn't know how to answer.

'And you kissed Gustaf when we thought he was the killer,' Linnéa continues. 'That's pretty fucked up.'

'He kissed me, but I pushed him away.'

'But for a second you liked it,' Linnéa says. 'Even though you thought Gustaf was the killer, you liked it.'

'I never said that.'

'You didn't have to.'

Linnéa is dissecting her alive, Minoo thinks, picking her apart bit by bit and showing how disgusting and disturbed she is.

'That's enough,' Vanessa tell Linnéa. 'Jonte was selling drugs to Elias, and look what you were doing with him!'

Minoo doesn't know who they're talking about, but it's clear from Linnéa's face that it hit home. She falls silent and sinks back into her chair.

'I don't think any of you is without fault,' Nicolaus says. 'We have to move on.'

'But what should we do?' Ida asks.

'Whatever it is, we'd better do it soon,' Anna-Karin says. 'Now that Max knows that Minoo knows.'

The significance of Anna-Karin's words slowly sinks in.

They had waited for this moment all autumn and winter. They've practiced and prepared themselves. Now the waiting is over. When Minoo looks at the others, she wonders if any of them is ready to meet Max, who had already killed two of them.

'You know what I think?' Linnéa says. 'People like him shouldn't be allowed to live. He's made his choice.'

'I agree,' Ida says.

'He's a human being,' Nicolaus says.

'Exactly,' Linnéa says. 'He's just a human being. It must be possible to kill him, even if he is blessed by demons.'

'"Thou shalt not kill,"' Nicolaus reminds her.

'"An eye for an eye, a tooth for a tooth,"' Linnéa retorts.

'Can we skip the Bible quotes please? We can't kill him,' Minoo says.

'You have no right to speak on this issue,' Linnéa says. 'You've got feelings for him.'

Minoo is about to protest when Anna-Karin stands up and glares at Linnéa. 'I'll never agree to kill anyone,' she says. 'We can't cross that line.'

'Two for, two against,' Linnéa says. 'It's up to you, Vanessa.'

It's absurd, Minoo thinks. We're sitting here voting on whether or not to kill someone.

'I agree with Anna-Karin,' Vanessa says.

Linnéa stares at the table.

'That's it, then. There's no more to say.'

'Oh, how lovely it is that we're all friends again,' Ida says sarcastically. 'Am I the only one who still hasn't gotten over the fact that Minoo was fooling around with a teacher?'

Suddenly Cat gives a drawn-out meow and bolts into the living room like a bat out of hell.

Ida's head drops forward as if she's caught sight of something interesting on her stomach.

A charged sensation rushes through Minoo. She recognizes it from the night at the fairground. The night when they all learned their destiny.

Ida's chair slides slowly out from the table with a scraping, squeaking sound. Its feet leave long marks in the wooden floor.

It's deathly silent. Everyone looks at Ida.

The chair stops abruptly. Ida's breath is a barely discernible cloud of smoke. And then she starts growing . . . taller?

No, Minoo realizes. The chair is levitating.

'She's back,' Nicolaus mumbles.

Ida's head lifts and she looks at them with wildly dilated pupils. A thin dribble of ectoplasm runs from the corner of her mouth. 'My daughters, I'm happy to see you,' she says, in the warm, gentle voice that isn't hers. 'But you still don't trust each other. If you're going to prevail, you must trust each other implicitly.'

She looks at them one by one, and Minoo sees her gaze linger on Linnéa.

'You must face your enemy together. You must stand united. Only then can you defeat him. The Circle is the answer. The Circle is the weapon.'

'You must give them something more!' Nicolaus says. He goes to Ida. His hand is reaching out as if he wants to touch her but doesn't dare.

Ida meets his gaze. 'That's all I can give,' she answers. 'And that's all you need.'

'Who are you?' Minoo asks. 'Are you the witch from the seventeenth century?'

Ida looks at her. 'Yes. But there's no time for more questions now,' she answers, as her voice continues inside Minoo's head: *Let go.*

Ida looks straight at her with her huge pupils.
That is the key to everything, Minoo. Let go.
A faint smell of smoke wafts through the room.

CHAPTER 55

The other bed in Grandpa's room at the hospital is now empty and tightly made up. They're alone, Anna-Karin, her mother and Grandpa.

My family, Anna-Karin thinks.

Her mother's fingers drum on the metal frame of Grandpa's bed. It's obvious that she needs to go out for another cigarette. She's already complained that there are no smoking rooms in the hospital. Not even a balcony. They expect you to trek all the way to the front entrance before you can light up.

Anna-Karin stares at her short, stubby fingers, which still show signs of scalding. Suddenly the fingers are still.

Briefly Anna-Karin thinks she has inadvertently forced her mother to stop. She glances nervously at her face, which looks normal. Anna-Karin can't take her eyes off her. This may be the last time they see each other. There's a good chance that Anna-Karin won't survive the night.

Her mother shifts impatiently. 'What's with you?' she asks.

'Nothing.'

'Well, I'm going for a cigarette,' her mother says, and stands up.

Once she's disappeared, Grandpa opens his eyes. He smiles at Anna-Karin. 'Gerda? Is that you?' he asks. A tear rolls down her cheek. Grandma Gerda died years ago.

'No, Grandpa. It's me. Anna-Karin. Your granddaughter.'

He seems not to hear her. Instead he gestures feebly for her to come closer. She leans down to him. Grandpa looks at her probingly.

'It's time now, isn't it?' he says. 'The war has come?'

Anna-Karin nods. It has.

It was Minoo who had devised the plan, once the seventeenth-century witch had left Ida's body, a plan in which Anna-Karin will play the most important role. A plan that none of them believes in, she knows, but they have to stop Max now.

Grandpa blinks in the light. He asks for some water and Anna-Karin holds out the blue plastic sippy cup, tipping it gently toward his mouth. It's like helping a child.

'I wish I was young and strong enough to be in uniform,' Grandpa says dreamily, when he's finished. 'I was so small when my papa went off to war.'

'Don't think about that,' Anna-Karin says. 'You just concentrate on getting better so we can take you home.'

'I'm no warmonger, as well you know, Gerda,' he says, 'but I'm no pacifist either. Some wars are necessary. Some things are worth fighting for. You have to be ready to lay down your life to do the right thing.'

'I know,' she says.

'But a bear is at his most dangerous when he's been forced into a corner. Remember that,' Grandpa says.

'I will.'

He seems to have said what he wanted to. His body relaxes and he shuts his eyes again. Anna-Karin takes his hands and holds them until she's sure he's fast asleep. 'Goodbye, Grandpa,' she whispers. 'I love you.'

The frozen expanse of Dammsjön Lake stretches before them through the windshield. Wille has stopped the car at the water's edge. It's a mild day, too warm for any skaters to venture out on the ice.

Vanessa catches sight of her face in the side mirror. She's aged – not with wrinkles or anything like that: she just looks older. More grown-up. There's an expression in her eyes that she hasn't seen before.

She rolls down the window a little and breathes in the damp, soft smell that is a sure sign spring isn't far away. Everything is still. Only the wind sighs in the treetops.

'I miss you already,' Wille says.

'But I'm here.'

'You know what I mean.'

As soon as she had gotten back to Sirpa's apartment last night, she'd told them she was moving home. Sirpa seemed relieved but tried hard to conceal it.

Wille has just helped Vanessa back to Törnrosvägen with all her things. She knows he's afraid that she'll leave him. But he has no idea that this may be the last day of her life.

You've still got nGéadal hanging over you.

541

Vanessa looks out of the window. There's the spot where she and Wille usually make their campfire in the summer. At this time of year, the little copse where she and Wille have their secret nest is just a few low trees with bare branches. So much has happened since they were last here, on the night of the blood-red moon. And tomorrow morning it will all be over. Tonight they are going to seek out Max. No matter how it ends, it will be over.

Wille interrupts her thoughts when he takes her hand and squeezes it hard. 'What are you thinking?' he asks.

'Nothing in particular.'

How could she tell him that she's wondering if she'll ever see this place again?

'I know I'm hopeless,' he says, 'but I'm trying. I just have to figure out what I want to do. Maybe things were easier for people like me when there wasn't as much choice. You know, you had to work in the mines or whatever all your life.'

Vanessa turns to him and gives his hand a hard squeeze. 'I'm sure it would have been great to live in those days,' she says. 'I would probably have died at the stove while I was boiling turnips and giving birth to our seventeenth child.'

She tries to laugh, but Wille just gazes at her. 'I'd never want to live without you,' he says.

She reaches for him and they hug each other. She kisses him gently, blotting out all other thoughts. There's no past, no future.

Then she pulls him closer to her, clings to him with a

desperation that's not at all like her. She wants to get as close to him as she can, and it's not easy when there's a gear shift in the way.

'Come on,' she says, and clambers between the seats. She sinks down in the wide back seat and pulls off her jacket.

Minoo seals the envelope and lays it in the drawer of her bedside table.

'Dearest Mom and Dad,' the letter begins.

Of course she hasn't written about what they're going to do tonight. But she tells them an important truth: that she loves them. That if anything happens to her and they find this letter, they must never think it was their fault.

If they don't manage to neutralize Max tonight, their bodies will probably be found tomorrow morning. Five young girls who have taken their own lives in some magnificent final celebration of the infamous suicide pact.

Minoo gets up, goes out to the landing and down the stairs. Her mother and father are, for once, sitting in the same place. They're in the living room, reading, with classical music playing softly – Ravel.

She feels strangely calm, even though she should be terrified. For the first time since it all began, she has a clear goal. They know who the killer is and they're going to stop him.

Let go. That's the key to everything, Minoo. Let go.

Those words have become part of her. She doesn't know what they mean, yet something inside her understands.

It's like when she came up with the plan. After Ida had

slumped in Nicolaus's kitchen and become herself again, there it was, clear as day.

Anna-Karin has to force Max to break the demons' blessing. Then she'll force him to go to the police and confess to murdering Rebecka and Elias.

In other words, Anna-Karin will lead the attack, but everyone has to be there.

The Circle is the answer.

Minoo thinks back to when they broke into the principal's house, how she and Vanessa couldn't move until they'd joined hands. It was when Ida and Anna-Karin had joined hands on Lucia night that they could share Ida's vision. And Vanessa, Ida and Minoo had joined hands during the ritual when they had created the truth serum.

All the talk about how they belong together and are connected to one another isn't just talk: it's fact. Together they are stronger. When they merge their energies, the combined effect is greater than that of the individual parts.

Tonight they will go to Max's house and ring his doorbell.

Anna-Karin should be able to carry out the first attack with the help of invisible Vanessa.

They will force Max back into the house. Then Linnéa, Ida and Minoo will go in after them to let Anna-Karin feed off their energy while she's fighting Max.

The Circle is the weapon.

Minoo stands there for a moment in the living room doorway, looking at her mother and father, thinking through everything she's written in the letter and hoping it will be enough for them to understand how much she loves them.

Her mother looks up from her book and Minoo walks into the room. She sits on the sofa between her parents.

'Feeling better now?' her mother asks.

'Yes. I don't think it was flu after all,' Minoo says.

She skipped school today for the first time in her life.

'It's been forever since we sat here all three of us,' her mother says, and puts an arm around Minoo, stroking her hair a little distractedly.

'M-hm,' Minoo answers, and leans against her.

'You haven't said whether there's anything special you want for your birthday. It's not far away, you know. Almost too late if I'm going to order something.'

'I'm happy with what I have,' Minoo answers, and means it.

Her father looks up from his book. He's been completely absorbed in it. It feels right, just as it should be. A perfectly normal Tuesday evening. Minoo just wants to sit there and listen to the piano music and the faint rustle as they turn the pages.

CHAPTER 56

Vanessa is late.

It was hard to leave home. She'd had dinner with her mother and Melvin. Her mother was psyched about an appointment she had made with a tattoo artist for a picture of a snake biting its tail. Apparently it's a karma symbol. Frasse lay farting under the kitchen table and sniffing loudly at the pungent outcome. Then he yawned and fell sleep. Melvin played with his penguin and some kitchen utensils on the floor, occasionally banging Vanessa's leg with a whisk to get her attention.

On the way to Nicolaus's house, Vanessa tries to hold on to the warm, calm feeling inside her. The sun is on its way down over the city and the sky is bright pink. She avoids the pools of melted water, and the treacherous patches of ice.

Her phone rings and she pulls it out of her jacket pocket. It's Minoo.

'Where are you?' She sounds stressed.

'I'm almost there.'

'Is Linnéa with you?'

'No.'

'I've tried calling her but she's switched off her phone.'

Vanessa stops to look around the empty parking lot behind the City Mall. A lone homeless man is sitting on a bench, kicking at a pigeon that's ventured too close. At first she thinks it's Linnéa's father, but when she looks again, she sees it isn't. 'I'll go over to her place and take a look,' she says. 'Call me if she shows up.'

The evening sky is reflected in the windows of the dirty-gray concrete high-rises, transforming them into squares of red and gold.

Vanessa walks briskly toward the entrance. She senses that something is wrong. Terribly wrong. She tries to think of possible explanations for what might have happened. Linnéa must have dropped her phone. Or left it at home. She's probably on her way to Nicolaus's place – at any moment Minoo will call to say she's arrived. Because Linnéa wouldn't let them down. She wouldn't, would she, now that they're about to take on Elias's killer?

As the elevator lumbers upward, Vanessa tries to keep at bay any thoughts that something may have happened to Linnéa. That Max may have exposed her. It would be easy to persuade everyone that Linnéa had killed herself. A dead mother, a dead best friend, an alcoholic father . . . Just the fact that she wears strange clothes makes her an obvious suicide candidate in the eyes of Engelsfors.

The elevator stops and Vanessa steps out. She stands there silently, listening. It's so quiet. She wonders if anyone lives on this floor other than Linnéa. The two nearest doors have no names on them.

She tries to repeat what they did when they were practicing at Nicolaus's house and sense whether Linnéa is in her apartment, but it's impossible to tell. There are so many traces of Linnéa – the air is thick with her energy.

Vanessa's gaze drops to the floor. The green concrete floor with spattered droplets of black and white paint.

Wet footprints lead to Linnéa's door.

The tracks are large. Clearly those of a man.

Vanessa hates the stupid girls in movies who always do exactly what she's about to do. The ones who don't call their friends or wait for back-up, but go straight into the unknown house where the serial killer is probably lying in wait for his next victim.

But this is about Linnéa. There's no time to lose. Vanessa concentrates and becomes invisible.

Slowly she presses down the door handle.

It's unlocked. Vanessa enters Linnéa's hall and shuts the door behind her.

Someone is standing in the living room. The figure is outlined against the light from the windows and it takes her a while to see who it is.

Jonte.

He's wearing the dark blue down jacket that Linnéa sometimes wore. He's staring out into the hall, straight at Vanessa.

Vanessa freezes. Can he see her?

He furrows his brow and disappears into Linnéa's bedroom. Vanessa hears him open the wardrobe, rummage among her clothes, then go through her drawers. It's obvious he's looking for something, and that he's in a hurry.

Vanessa hesitates. Jonte shouldn't be here. Or was Linnéa lying when she said she wasn't seeing him any more? Does he know where she is?

Minoo still hasn't called. So Linnéa still hasn't arrived at Nicolaus's place.

Vanessa drops her invisibility and walks into the living room. Jonte hears her footsteps and comes out of the bedroom. 'What the fuck are you doing here?' he asks. His gaze is unusually alert.

'What the fuck are *you* doing here?' she responds. 'And where's Linnéa?'

'I don't know. The door was open when I got here.'

Vanessa is scared now. It isn't like Linnéa to leave the door unlocked. 'I thought you'd stopped seeing each other,' she says.

'So did I. But she turned up at my place today—' He stops himself. Looks at Vanessa cagily. 'Are you two friends all of a sudden or what?'

'Sort of,' Vanessa answers curtly.

Jonte looks at her seriously. 'She's done something really fucking stupid. I have to get hold of her. If you know where she is—'

'What's she done?' Vanessa cuts in.

Jonte ignores the question. 'If you see her, call me,' he says. 'I'm going into town to look for her.'

He makes for the door but Vanessa pushes past him and stands in his way. Jonte looks at her threateningly but he can't scare Vanessa. She's far too scared already.

'Get out of my way,' he says.

'Tell me what she's done!'

She sees that he's hesitating and makes another attempt. 'If you don't tell me I can't help her.'

Jonte sighs. 'You have to promise not to say anything about this to Wille.'

'I promise.'

Jonte nods. 'She was fucking on edge when she came to my place. She only stayed a little while. It was a few hours before I noticed what she'd done.'

'Can't you just spit it out?' Vanessa almost screams.

'I had a gun in the basement,' Jonte says slowly. 'She's taken it.'

Minoo can't sit still. She's pacing back and forth in Nicolaus's living room with her phone in her hand. Anna-Karin and Ida are sitting on a couple of spindle-back chairs. Their faces are tense. No one has said a word for ten minutes.

When Minoo's phone rings, everyone jumps.

'It's Vanessa,' she says to the others.

She listens and tries to take in what Vanessa is telling her. All of Linnéa's talk about revenge wasn't just talk. She'd never had any intention of going with them tonight. She was going to settle this alone in her own way.

She's planning to shoot Max.

'I'm on my way over to his house now,' Vanessa says.

'No!' says Minoo. 'It's too dangerous!'

Nicolaus comes in from the kitchen with Cat behind him.

'I have to stop her,' Vanessa says.

It's obvious that she's not going to let herself be talked out of it. Minoo's brain is working at top speed, searching for arguments to stop Vanessa running straight into Max's clutches. There isn't even room in her mind to be angry with Linnéa – the situation is too critical. Everything has come crashing down. 'Please, Vanessa, wait. You're not going to solve anything by running over there. We don't even know if Linnéa is there.'

'If anything happens to her . . .'

Minoo's gaze falls on the framed map of the town hanging next to the silver cross. 'Give us ten minutes,' she says. 'Let's try to find her first.'

'We can't wait!' Vanessa shouts.

'Five minutes, then. Just five minutes. I've got an idea. Please.'

Vanessa is silent for a second. 'Okay,' she says.

Minoo hangs up.

'What's happened?' Nicolaus asks.

She tells him as fast as she can, continues talking even when Ida and Nicolaus try to interrupt with questions. 'We have to find Linnéa,' she says finally.

'That dear child,' Nicolaus says. 'I never thought she'd . . . I thought all her talk of revenge was just an empty threat.'

'I thought so, too,' Minoo says, and lifts the town map off its hook. 'Ida, you have to find her with the pendulum.'

Minoo places the map on the table while Ida takes off her necklace and moves closer. 'It's such a big area,' she says, peering at the map. 'I don't know if it'll work.'

Anna-Karin gets up and goes over to her. 'Take my hand,' she says.

Ida hesitates. Then she grabs Anna-Karin's right hand. Anna-Karin stretches the other to Minoo, who clutches it.

Ida starts swinging the pendulum over Max's house. The seconds tick past. Everyone's eyes are transfixed by the little silver heart.

'She's not there,' Ida says, and Minoo feels a powerful sense of relief.

Ida continues swinging the pendulum over Engelsfors, the area where Max lives and toward the center of town.

'Try the school,' Anna-Karin says suddenly.

Ida moves the pendulum again. At once it swings in a wide clockwise circle. 'She's there.'

'Is Max with her?' Nicolaus asks.

'I don't know if I can pick up his energy.'

'Try,' Minoo says.

'Maybe it'll help if you think about him. You know him better than anyone,' Ida says, sarcastically.

'I'll think of him, too,' Anna-Karin says.

Minoo shuts her eyes tightly and thinks about Max. She tries to pretend he's standing in front of her. She sees his face, which had meant something entirely different to her just a few days ago. Then he was the light of her life. Now he is darkness.

You know him better than anyone.

No, Minoo thinks. Quite the opposite. I was the one who didn't understand what he was.

'I've found him,' Ida says, and Minoo opens her eyes.

Ida's face is glistening with sweat. She lowers the necklace. 'He's at the school, too.'

CHAPTER 57

Nicolaus pulls up in the parking lot behind the school and turns off the engine. The heater that has been humming at Minoo's feet falls silent, and the windshield wipers are stilled.

It's snowing again. Fluffy flakes float slowly over the outside world.

Minoo looks toward Engelsfors High School, looming in the darkness ahead. Only a few streetlamps cast a yellow glow across the playground. The windows are blackened squares. Impossible to see into. But someone inside would have no difficulty in seeing out.

They have to cross the brightly lit parking lot. It's either that or making their way across the equally well-lit playground outside the main entrance. There's nothing to hide behind on the way into the school.

Someone knocks on the side window beside Minoo, who jumps in shock.

It's Vanessa.

She tears open the door and cold air gushes into the car.

'Linnéa is in the cafeteria,' she says. 'I felt her energy. She's alive.'

As she speaks, she casts nervous glances at the school.

Nicolaus pulls out his bunch of keys and hands it to Vanessa. 'This one leads to the kitchen entrance over by the loading bay. A hallway goes straight from there to the kitchens.'

'Is Max with her?' Minoo asks.

'I don't know. I couldn't feel him.'

'Excuse me, but has anyone considered this may be a trap?' Ida says.

Minoo glances at her in the rearview mirror. She feels like an idiot. That idea hadn't even occurred to her. They've all been so focused on saving Linnéa.

'Like with Anna-Karin's grandfather in the barn,' Ida continues.

'Maybe it is,' Anna-Karin says. 'But what choice do we have? We have to risk it.'

Ida clearly isn't happy with that, but she doesn't object.

'Are we still keeping to the same plan?' Vanessa asks.

'Yes,' Minoo answers.

She turns to Anna-Karin, who nods.

There's so much that Anna-Karin would like to say to Nicolaus and thank him for, but there's no time.

Minoo steps out of the car and folds the passenger seat forward. Ida clambers out, but Anna-Karin pauses and meets Nicolaus's gaze.

'I wish I could go with you,' he says.

'We need someone to wait for us, too,' she says.

'I'll pray for you.'

They run across the parking lot. The school rises up into the night sky. It's as if it's growing before Anna-Karin's eyes. She tries not to think of how exposed they are in this open space.

They climb onto the loading bay where a wide metal door leads into the school.

Vanessa pulls out the bunch of keys.

'Wait a minute,' Ida says. She stands with her hands shoved into her pockets, looking down at her boots.

'If I die and you guys make it . . . there's a horse at the stables. Troja. Could one of you make sure he's taken care of?'

'I will,' Anna-Karin says.

Ida nods.

'Okay,' Vanessa says, and vanishes. 'Let's go in.'

Vanessa opens the door. It's surprisingly easy and swings back without a sound. A ramp leads down into the darkness before them.

Anna-Karin takes out her cell phone and switches on the light.

'Turn it off,' Minoo whispers. 'We don't know what's in there.'

Vanessa takes Anna-Karin's hand and they form a chain with Vanessa first and Ida last.

Ida closes the door. The darkness that envelops them is more complete than Vanessa has ever experienced before.

All four stand stock still, listening.

All they can hear is their own breathing and the faint hum of the heating system.

Cautiously, Vanessa moves forward, clasping Anna-Karin's hand. With her other, she gropes along the rough wall.

She doesn't dare try to sense if Linnéa is still alive. All her power is focused on sustaining her invisibility. And stopping herself rushing ahead in a crazed panic.

It feels like being blind, walking along with wide-open eyes yet seeing nothing. It's impossible to tell how far she's come or what's waiting just ahead of her. Her whole body is in a hyperactive state, ready to react to the slightest sound. After a while Vanessa doesn't know whether it's the silence or the heater that's humming in her ears. Then, she's hearing whispers.

Vanessa . . .

The voice becomes clearer. And she knows, without being able to explain how, that it's Linnéa's.

Vanessa . . .

The voice is afraid, forlorn, but she's alive. Linnéa's alive. Vanessa picks up the pace. She senses that Anna-Karin and the others can't quite keep up – too bad.

The deeper into the school she gets, the more difficult it is for her to sustain her invisibility. There's a strange resistance to it, all the more terrifying as it had become so easy for her.

Vanessa's hand reaches a corner and she stops. Her fingers touch a smooth surface. A door? She finds the handle. Presses it cautiously. Of course it's locked. She whispers to

Anna-Karin, asking her to turn on the light on her phone. They have to take the chance.

Vanessa takes out the keys and tries them one by one in the light from Anna-Karin's phone. They rattle and clatter deafeningly in the cramped claustrophobic space.

Please . . . please . . . help me . . .

The voice is desperate, filled with pain. Vanessa's hand trembles when she finds a key that slides into the lock. It opens with a click. Anna-Karin turns off the light before Vanessa cracks open the door.

Anna-Karin crouches as she moves behind the invisible Vanessa into the kitchen.

On the right side a big rectangular opening faces the cafeteria dining area. It's where the students collect their food from the stainless-steel trays that stand on the kitchen side. A faint light from the dining area falls through the serving hatch, glinting off the counters and the tiled walls. Plastic racks in different colors stand next to the silent dishwasher. It smells like dishwashing liquid, cooked food, steam and metal.

Anna-Karin is crawling along the floor on all fours. To the left of the gaping serving hatch, a set of swing doors leads into the dining area. Linnéa is out there somewhere.

She stops next to the swing doors. They open excruciatingly slowly when Vanessa goes through to scout around.

Anna-Karin turns her head to look at Minoo and Ida, who are huddled on the floor behind her. They nod. It's time for her to start. Anna-Karin shuts her eyes. Focuses her mind.

Slowly she releases her power, afraid it will surge forth like a flood wave and drown her. But instead it seeps slowly into her body. And then it stops.

She's never experienced this before. The power is there, but where once there was an unstoppable torrent, there is now barely a trickle.

Fear takes hold of her.

She might have been able to overpower Max at home on the farm, but now she's on his turf.

The school is a place of evil.

When Vanessa steps into the dining area, she stops and scans the room.

The chairs are upside-down on the tables with their legs in the air. The only light is coming from the side room, where the most popular students eat.

Her heart is pounding, *thump-thump-thump*, with every step she takes.

When she gets closer she hears a voice speaking fast and low. At first she thinks it's Linnéa, but then she realizes it's a man.

He sounds young. Younger than Max.

Something isn't right.

Vanessa presses herself hard against the wall and slowly moves closer. She doesn't want to take any unnecessary risks. She's never felt so unsure of her power before, of whether it'll hold out.

'Come on,' the strange voice says. 'Tell me. Believe me, I don't want to do this.'

Vanessa's heart is beating even faster now. She has almost reached the entrance to the side room. She drops to her knees and crawls the last stretch. The air is charged with magic. As she goes further into the force field, ever closer to its source, it takes almost all of her energy to remain invisible.

She peers around the corner into the room. The tables have been pushed aside, creating an open space in the middle.

Linnéa is sitting on a chair. Her ankles have been secured to its legs with duct tape. Her hands are tied together behind her back. Her makeup has run down her face and she looks exhausted.

'Don't do this to yourself,' says the boy in the black hoodie squatting in front of her. 'Just tell me who they are.'

Vanessa can't see his face, but she's sure it isn't Max.

Linnéa shuts her eyes. Whimpers.

Vanessa.

The voice is in her head again. And, for a terrifying moment, Vanessa glimpses what is going on inside Linnéa.

She's fighting for her life. A foreign presence is trying to force its way into her consciousness, but she's resisting. And she's very strong. Even though the intruding power is pushing hard, she's keeping it at bay. But she's tiring. She won't be able to keep it up for much longer. Vanessa feels that clearly.

Now the boy gets up. And Vanessa sees who it is.

Elias.

The shock is so powerful that she almost lets go of her

invisibility. Because Elias is standing there, large as life.

'Do you remember when we used to hang out down by the docks?' he asks Linnéa, in a voice full of nostalgia. 'We sat there smoking and talking. You said that if I fell in, you'd come after me. Do you remember that?'

'You . . . can't know that,' Linnéa gasps.

'You told my mom and dad when I really did jump in that time. It was your fault I ended up in the psychiatric hospital. At first I hated you, but then I saw that you did it out of love. I know you love me, Linnéa. I'm your brother. You're my sister in all but blood.'

'Stop it . . .' Linnéa groans.

'Look at me,' Elias says gently, and stares at her intently.

There's a tug at Linnéa's eyelids and they open again. 'I know you're not Elias.'

Vanessa spots the gun lying on a table. She'd been against killing Max, but now she wouldn't hesitate to shoot him to save Linnéa.

'It makes no difference who I am,' he says softly. 'Elias is waiting for you, Linnéa. You can be together again. Stop fighting it.'

Linnéa shakes her head. Vanessa begins to crawl toward the table.

'Come on,' Elias pleads. 'I just need two more names. Tell me who they are and it'll all be over.' He bends down till his face is just a few inches away from Linnéa's. He fixes his eyes on her. 'Tell me,' he whispers.

And Vanessa feels how the magic streaming out of him

strengthens. With her eyes glued to the gun, she crawls on toward the table. She barely dares to breathe. Just a few feet to go. Once she convinced Nicke to show her how to use a gun. Now she tries to remember what he'd said. Where's the safety?

Linnéa squirms in her chair. 'Minoo . . .' comes out of her.

'I know that already,' Elias says patiently. 'Anna-Karin . . . One more. Just give me one more and I'll be satisfied.'

'No!'

Linnéa's tortured voice echoes through the cafeteria. It's physically painful for Minoo to hear it.

Vanessa should have come back by now.

'We can't wait any longer,' she whispers to Anna-Karin. 'Can you influence him from here?'

Anna-Karin looks panicked and shakes her head.

'No,' she murmurs. 'Maybe if I can see him . . . but I don't know.'

'Then we have to go out there.' Minoo turns to Ida. 'All three of us.'

Vanessa has almost reached the table. One hand, one knee at a time.

Elias is standing in front of Linnéa, his hands hanging limply at his sides. His face is strangely stiff, as if it were made of plastic.

Plastic that suddenly melts and morphs into another face. The body fills out with muscles, grows taller.

Max.

He raises one hand to his forehead and presses the tips of his fingers to it.

'You said it would get easier!' he says into the air. 'I don't want to do this!'

Vanessa rises to her knees and reaches for the gun. If only she can get hold of it, everything will be over. Not even Max can survive a bullet.

Just as she's about to pick it up, Max grabs the handle. Their hands miss each other by a hair.

'I don't want to hurt you,' he says, and aims the gun at Linnéa. 'But if you don't tell me their names I will kill you.'

'You think I care?' Linnéa says hoarsely, and meets his gaze. 'You think I'd have come to your house if I cared?'

Max sticks the gun into his waistband. Looks at Linnéa. Then he raises his hand and slaps her so hard that the chair falls over backward.

Vanessa stifles a scream.

And Max turns. A surprised smile spreads across his face when he sees her. 'And there you are,' he says softly.

Vanessa doesn't think, just gets up and rushes straight for him.

Max makes a sweeping gesture.

Anna-Karin is halfway across the dining area when Vanessa flies through the air, flung by an invisible force. She crashes into a table. The chairs crash to the floor. Vanessa is lifted four feet into the air, then pinned to the table. She screams in pain.

Minoo grabs Anna-Karin's hand and holds it tightly. Ida takes the other. Anna-Karin can feel their energy streaming into her. And her own power is there. But it's nowhere near as strong as it was when she was using it routinely here at school.

Max comes into the main dining area from the side room. He looks at Vanessa intently as she writhes on the table. Anna-Karin realizes that they have only one chance to do this and it's now: the moment before he's seen them.

Let go of Vanessa, she commands. *Leave her be.*

Max turns.

Minoo had seen the black smoke swirling around Vanessa as she flew through the room. Now it has settled over her body on the table, like a thick, oily fog.

More smoke shoots out of Max. It streaks toward Anna-Karin and, in the next moment, her hand is wrenched from Minoo's.

Anna-Karin is tossed violently upward, smacking hard into the ceiling, where she remains for a few seconds, pinned against the white tiles. Then the smoke drags her along the ceiling until she slams into the far wall. She slides down to the floor and lies there lifeless.

Minoo's other hand is empty now.

Ida has let go. She's running back toward the kitchen.

But she doesn't get far. The smoke moves quickly and quietly toward her.

She falls to the floor. A ring of fire ignites around her. Minoo can see her terrified face behind the high flames that keep her prisoner. A faint smell of scorched linoleum spreads through the room.

Minoo turns toward Max. The black smoke is still coiling around him, dancing, creating patterns in the air, as he moves toward her. It's like a living organism. It's almost beautiful. Alluring.

'Minoo,' he says, and smiles.

That's the worst thing. That he seems so happy to see her. As if what he has just done doesn't matter.

'I know you don't understand now,' he says, 'but all I want . . . the only thing I've ever wanted . . . is for us to be together. We belong together.'

Rage fizzes through her blood. 'But I don't,' she says, and is surprised by how strong and confident her voice is.

Max stops short. He looks hurt. The black smoke writhes around him, sending out long feelers that approach Minoo but pull back at the last moment.

Minoo stands her ground. Her body is filled with unfamiliar signals. Something is swirling in the air around her, flowing in front of her, intoxicating her with its power.

'Minoo,' Max says weakly. 'What are you doing?'

'I'm letting go.'

The black smoke between them thickens.

But it's not just coming from Max. It's streaming out of Minoo, twisting and churning with long black tentacles.

She's powerful. She's a whole army. She's plugged directly into something that is staggeringly more powerful than she is. They are many. They are one. Together they move toward Max.

He looks at her in panic. He can't move. The smoke envelops him, stops him running away as she approaches, engulfs them both in a swirling black maelstrom.

'Please, Minoo,' Max says, dropping to his knees at her feet. 'I love you.'

The words don't move her. She knows what she has to do. Minoo lays her hand on his forehead. She shuts her eyes and sees: the demons' blessing.

Like a shimmering black aura it surrounds Max. The demons' magic. The black smoke streaming out of Minoo chokes it.

The aura fades. Eventually there's nothing left. The blessing is broken.

She feels Max's life force leaving his body, sucked out by her hand, filling her and making her even stronger and more powerful.

Something is stuck inside Max, something that is struggling to make its way to the surface. She helps it pull itself out.

It's like a weight that suddenly releases.

And Minoo's eyes fill with tears, because now she feels it so clearly.

Rebecka. She's been trapped inside Max. But now her soul radiates through Minoo, fills her with light. All that was her is inside Minoo – and then she's gone. Free at last.

Soon afterward comes Elias. Minoo recognizes him as if she'd known him all her life, and long before that. His soul passes through her and disappears.

Minoo's fingers grab Max's forehead, boring themselves

into his hair. His body sags and she sinks to her knees beside him as he drops onto his side.

She is filled with him. Impressions, thoughts and feelings, everything that he's experienced. Everything that is him flows through Minoo, as if picked up by a hitherto unknown sense.

Memories.

Max drags Linnéa from his car across the playground. Her hands and feet are tightly bound, but she tries to resist.

He opens the door to his house to find an unknown girl with long black bangs standing outside. She pulls out a gun and tells him he's going to die for what he did to Elias. But he sees in her hesitation that she won't shoot. She's no killer. And he knows that she's a Chosen One. That she'll help him find the others. What a gift.

He wakes, as if out of a dream, and sees Minoo in front of him in the classroom. They whisper to him that he has exposed himself. They're angry but he's afraid. Afraid she'll misunderstand, that she won't realize he'll never harm her again, that they belong to each other.

The barn is burning and the cows are bellowing in panic. He runs away with *Their* strident voices in his head. *They* threaten to renege on their promise. They won't let Minoo live after all.

Minoo asks if he can wait for her. He can wait forever.

He's in the classroom looking at Anna-Karin: she's changed so much during the year. He knows how such things happen. Why didn't he pick up on it sooner?

Minoo is so beautiful when he sees her by the overpass.

He knows he shouldn't but he kisses her anyway. He's made a new pact with *Them*: they'll let her live.

The awful moment in the bath when he defied *Them* for the first time.

The first kiss.

Suddenly she's outside his house and he wonders if he's dreaming when he sees her.

He discovers that Minoo is the one he must kill.

He rips Rebecka's soul out of her body as he begs her forgiveness.

She falls.

Rebecka turns and sees his face, sees him as Gustaf.

Rebecka at the City Mall.

He tries out Elias's power for the first time. Sees himself transformed into Gustaf in the mirror, the one Rebecka trusts, who can get close to her if need be.

He sees Rebecka jogging along, knows that she's his next victim. They whisper to him that she's stronger than the first. That he has to prepare himself carefully.

The prophecy was wrong, the voices say. The Chosen Ones are seven. Six left.

He stands outside Minoo's window, wishing she hadn't been the one to find Elias. He wonders how she is and wishes he could comfort her.

He watches as the gurney with Elias's body is rolled out of the school and feels relieved. It's over.

Through the closed bathroom door he hears the mirror shatter.

He enters the classroom and sees Minoo for the first time.

Alice is alive again.

Minoo becomes aware of yet another weight deep inside Max. Like an anchor that clears the bottom and is slowly being drawn up to the surface.

His soul.

The memories come faster and faster.

He hangs up the poster of Persephone that is so much like Alice it's painful to look at. A pleasurable self-torture.

So many nights he lies awake and thinks of the awful things he's committed himself to carrying out. He reminds himself that it's worth it. Alice is worth it.

From the first moment he hates Engelsfors. The town is like the one where he grew up.

The years of teaching, women who come and go, friends he secretly detests. Those who think that the world is only what you see with the naked eye.

They have promised he'll have Alice back. A fresh start.

The years of guilt.

And everything slows down again.

The funeral is like a fog. No one had known she was so unhappy.

The call from the police in the morning. They had found her body on the cliffs below the house.

The party's in full swing, the music blaring. He's shaking with adrenaline. The 'friend' he's selected is there. 'If anyone asks, I've been with you all evening,' Max says, because he's suddenly noticed something new about himself. Still, he's surprised when he sees his friend's eyes glaze. Max is giddy with his first taste of magic. Getting others to obey.

He wants her to die. Better that no one has her if he can't. If only she would just kill herself. He wishes it with all his heart. And that is when she gets up and climbs onto the windowsill. He know he's making her do it. They look at each other, shocked. It's just a moment. And she submits to his wish and lets herself fall.

The windows stand wide open to let in the warm summer air and she perches on the sill, her forehead on her knees. She says, 'Please, Max, go away.' He tries to convince her that he loves her, that they belong together. 'Didn't you hear what I said? I never want to see you again,' she says.

Alice, whom he loves so much, who showed him the painting of Persephone. Together they laugh at how alike Alice and Persephone are.

Alice, the very first time he sees her. He knows she's going to make him happy.

Max's soul will soon surface. Minoo becomes aware of a scream growing louder and louder, filling her head. It's Max screaming in pain. She is inflicting that pain.

She can sense the darkness of his childhood and knows that if she doesn't let go now, she'll be doing the same to Max as he did to Rebecka and Elias. She's going to rip out his soul, take everything from him.

Let go.

And Minoo gently lets go, feels how the weight sinks back into the depths. The scream fades out. Everything falls silent.

Minoo opens her eyes.

The black smoke is gone.

She kneels on the floor. Max's forehead is red where her hand lay. His eyes are closed. His chest is moving slowly.

It's over.

Part 5

CHAPTER 58

The June air is refreshing after the rain, as if someone has thrown the windows wide and aired out the world. The ground is still slippery and muddy in places and it's rough going, as Anna-Karin pushes Grandpa's wheelchair across the farmyard toward the main house. Nicolaus offers to take over, but she refuses: she has to do this herself.

Grandpa is staring silently ahead. Anna-Karin is unsure that he recognizes her but doesn't want to ask. His lucid moments come more often now, and she knows he finds it demeaning to be fussed over.

He's recovering. But her mother refuses to acknowledge it. When Anna-Karin suggested they take him to see the farm one last time, she simply said there was no point. 'Don't be ridiculous. It would only upset him, assuming he understands where he is.'

Nicolaus helps her get the wheelchair up the front steps. 'I'll wait out here,' he says. 'Take as much time as you need.'

Anna-Karin looks at him gratefully and unlocks the front door. Luckily it's wide enough for the wheelchair.

They enter the empty hall. Continue into the kitchen. The

living room. The front room, which they stopped using after Grandma died.

Nothing hides the blemishes. Wallpaper has come unstuck, paint flakes along the baseboards, and there are brownish-yellow spots on the ceiling above where her mother used to sit and smoke.

Somehow the rooms look smaller when they're empty. Shouldn't it be the other way around?

They had once been full of life but now they're empty. That's the difference, Anna-Karin thinks. Before it was a home. Now it's just a house.

Grandpa still hasn't said a word, but he reaches back and pats Anna-Karin's hand when they leave the house. Nicolaus helps her down the steps. She's afraid they'll accidentally tip the wheelchair so Grandpa falls out and hurts himself. She doesn't want to imagine what her mother would say if anything happened. She has no idea they're here – doesn't even know that Anna-Karin still has a key.

Anna-Karin aims at Grandpa's cabin and pushes the wheelchair ahead of her. She follows his gaze toward the new building going up where the barn had stood. Jari's father, who bought the farm, has decided to raise pigs.

'It doesn't look the same,' Grandpa says.

'No,' Anna-Karin agrees. 'It doesn't.'

It doesn't smell like coffee in Grandpa's cabin. When Anna-Karin pushes the wheelchair into the empty kitchen, she wonders if she's done the right thing in bringing him here. The kitchen, the little bedroom and the shabby bathroom are so dreary and desolate. Anna-Karin looks at

Grandpa. He seems thoughtful. She pushes him up to the window where he used to sit.

She squats next to him and looks out. They gaze up toward the big house, at the meadows where there are no longer any cows grazing. The early summer twilight glows above the treetops.

It's beautiful here, Anna-Karin thinks. She understands why Grandma and Grandpa chose this particular farm, on this particular spot, when Engelsfors was a town full of promise.

'Anna-Karin,' Grandpa says.

She meets his clear gaze.

'Staffan wasn't a bad man,' he continues. 'Your father. He was afraid, but he wasn't bad.'

Anna-Karin is speechless. It's hard for her to get the words out when she asks, 'Then why did he disappear?'

'I don't know. That was between your mother and him. But he loved you, Anna-Karin. He did. In his way.'

'Not enough,' she mumbles, and warm tears are running down her cheeks.

Grandpa wipes them away. 'He was wrong to go, but I don't think he had a lot of love in him to start with. Mia was drawn to those boys. The ones who didn't have much to give. But whatever love he had, he gave to you. The little he had to give was yours, Anna-Karin. I'm not saying it was enough, but I want you to know that.'

Anna-Karin takes Grandpa's hand. His skin is softer than it's ever been. As if it's thinned.

'I've worked all my life,' Grandpa continues. 'I worked,

ate and slept, then started again from the beginning. But lately I've been thinking. I haven't been fair to you, Anna-Karin.'

She shakes her head. 'Don't say that, Grandpa—'

'I'm old and I can say what I like. And I'm telling you I did wrong. I closed my eyes to how things were for you. When those young thugs at school were picking on you, Mia always told me to stay out of it, that she'd been bullied, too, and she'd survived. She said I'd only make things worse if I got involved. But I should have anyway.'

He squeezes Anna-Karin's hand, and she feels he's gotten some of his strength back. A strength that she can see in his eyes, too, when he looks at her.

'Can you forgive me, Anna-Karin?'

'I'm the one who should be apologizing. The fire was my fault.'

'Answer my question. Otherwise I'll never have any peace.'

Anna-Karin takes a shuddering breath and nods.

'You were just trying to get back some of what others had taken from you throughout your life,' he said. 'You went too far, but that was my fault, too. I should have been honest with you. I should have told you that you must cherish your gift, not abuse it.'

Anna-Karin isn't even surprised. 'You've known all along, haven't you?' she says.

'Only as much as my own mind could grasp, and that's not much,' Grandpa answers. 'Now I want to go out into the fresh air.'

They make for the front garden. Nicolaus is sitting in the car, waving to them, as they walk past.

Anna-Karin pushes Grandpa along the dirt track running between the fields. He slips back into a haze again, but continues talking, alternating between Swedish and Finnish.

Sometimes he calls her Gerda, sometimes Mia, sometimes Anna-Karin. He tells her about the family of foxes that lived in a burrow by the edge of the forest. He warns her against false prophets. He tells her about the Norwegian refugees the farm's previous owner had taken in during World War II. He describes the late nights when he used to play cards with Anna-Karin's parents, while Grandma Gerda baked flatbread and sang along to old records. Anna-Karin wonders if they were the same songs her mother was singing in the autumn.

Eventually he falls silent. Anna-Karin turns the wheelchair and pushes it toward the car. Grandpa is going back to the nursing home at Solbacken. It's only temporary, her mother says, while she and Anna-Karin settle into a rented apartment in the center of town.

But Anna-Karin knows. There's a room in the apartment that Grandpa could have, but her mother hasn't put any of his things in it. She's decided to leave him at Solbacken.

CHAPTER 59

The full moon is like a white shadow in the light morning sky. Minoo is following the little stream. Her feet and bare legs are damp from wading through the tall, rain-drenched grass.

Two black feathers float past in the water. Then she catches a whiff of smoke.

Minoo.

She looks up. Rebecka is standing on the other side of the stream. She looks so much like the real Rebecka that it hurts.

Her face has color again. Her eyes are alive.

'I know you're not Rebecka. Why can't you appear as yourself?' Minoo asks.

Do you know who I am?

'You're the one who speaks through Ida. The one I've dreamed about. The witch from the past.'

Rebecka doesn't answer. Suddenly Minoo is unsure whether she's dreaming or awake. 'What do you want?' she asks.

I'm worried about you, Minoo. You can't bear this alone.

'What do you mean?'

You know what I mean.

Minoo looks at Rebecka, who is shimmering against the dark background of the forest.

You must tell them.

'Is that all you have to say?'

Yes.

'Are you sure? Nothing more than that? Like which element I am? And why my power is to take people's souls? Am I like Max? Is that why the demons have a plan for me? And why haven't they done anything now they know we're the Chosen Ones?'

You need the others' help.

'Go to hell,' Minoo says, and wakes up.

Minoo had forgotten to close the curtains last night, and now sunlight is streaming into the room. Out in the garden the birds are twittering deafeningly. There's something almost desperate about their warbling song: 'Here I am! Here I am!'

It's the first time for at least three months that she can remember a dream. She doesn't usually remember even the nightmares, but she wakes up feeling stiff and sore as if she'd fought a battle in her sleep.

She opens the wardrobe and catches sight of the sky-blue cotton dress she wore when she graduated up from middle school. She glares at it contemptuously. Now it seems pathetic that she drove all the way into Borlänge with her mother to buy a dress she wore only for a few hours. And she had thought those hours were so important.

She pulls the dress over her head and combs her hair with her fingers.

Her mother and father have gone to work. A bouquet of lily-of-the-valley stands in a vase on the kitchen table, with an envelope leaning against it. Minoo opens it and pulls out a card with a picture of a summer meadow. *Have a great summer! Big hugs and kisses, from Mom and Dad* is written on the back. The envelope also contains a gift certificate for an online bookstore.

Minoo holds the card, tracing her mother's elegant handwriting with her index finger.

She's happy that her parents aren't here. It's so hard to pretend everything's normal. She doesn't know how she's going to handle a long summer break.

It's as if a thick pane of glass separates her from the rest of the world. Nothing taking place on the other side affects her. She's mute inside. Sometimes it scares her, the numb feeling, but it's still better than what she was feeling before: desperation, fear, sorrow.

She leaves the envelope on the kitchen table, looks at her watch and realizes she should have left fifteen minutes ago. She picks up her bag and a worn pair of summer shoes. She has no intention of hurrying.

'Where is she?' Adriana Lopez asks.

Vanessa, Linnéa, Ida and Anna-Karin are sitting on the stage of the dance pavilion in their end-of-the-year outfits. In Anna-Karin's case it's not so much an end-of-the-year outfit as an outfit she's wearing for the end-of-the-year – jeans and her old jacket.

Ida, on the other hand, is wearing a white dress and is sitting on her hands so she won't get it dirty.

Linnéa is sitting cross-legged next to Vanessa, biting her nails. Today they're pink. She's wearing a dress she finished making yesterday, covered in black and white checks with lots of black bows and a tulle skirt. She has fastened a huge bow to Vanessa's pink dress, just below the neckline. Yesterday it had seemed a fun idea. Now Vanessa wonders if she looks gift-wrapped.

The principal paces back and forth across the stage. A few of the buttons on her blouse are undone. Vanessa tries to stop herself from staring at the burned skin beneath.

'She's coming,' Ida says. 'I can feel her now.'

A few minutes later Minoo appears. She's wearing a light blue dress that Vanessa recognizes from the last day of middle school. Her hair is standing out like a black cloud around her head. 'Sorry I'm late,' she says, in the toneless voice she always uses these days.

The principal nods. 'Sit down,' she says impatiently.

Minoo climbs onto the stage and sits next to Vanessa.

'I realize you're all eager to get off to the end-of-the-year celebration, but I have to speak to you first. I've got some good news,' the principal says. 'The Council has decided to let you begin training in defensive magic this autumn. We'll start in August.'

If it weren't so pathetic, Vanessa would have burst out laughing. Only now, a year after Elias's death, does the Council think they should learn how to protect themselves.

Since April the principal had 'put the training sessions temporarily on ice'. Even she must have started to lose interest when they never managed to find anything in the *Book of Patterns*. Toward the end, they didn't even have to lie to her any more. Ever since they had defeated Max, the book has been a big wall of silence. No more rituals, exercises or incomprehensible pieces of advice have appeared to them. The grumpy old hag is grumpier than ever.

The Chosen Ones have met up regularly at Nicolaus's place to continue their old magic practice. Minoo has taken part only passively, and the others haven't objected.

They know nothing of her power. Nicolaus's theory is that when she defeated Max she somehow reflected Max's magic back at him. No one knows what's inside Minoo, what she can actually do. And although no one says so, they're afraid of her.

'So, the Council thinks we're ready to learn a little self-defence?' Linnéa says.

'The situation demands it,' the principal answers. 'Things may have been calm since Christmas but whoever attacked Minoo may still be lurking close by, biding his time.'

The only thing the principal knows about Max is what everyone else knows: nothing. They were careful in choosing which clues to leave for the police.

It was Nicke who had found Max lying unconscious in the cafeteria. There was also an unregistered gun with his fingerprints on it. The newspapers speculated whether the incident might have had anything to do with the suicide pact, but their interest soon faded. The story wasn't as exciting when it featured a math teacher in a coma instead of a bloody corpse.

'It may seem that everything's over,' the principal continues, 'but it's only just begun. What you've experienced so far is nothing compared to what's coming.' She pauses. 'I know you have great powers. You've matured over the course of this year and have achieved a great deal.'

If she only knew, Vanessa thinks to herself.

'I look forward to continuing to work with you in the autumn. Now you'd better go if you're going to get there in time for the fun,' the principal says. Then she smiles warmly, surprising Vanessa. 'Have a great summer, girls. You really deserve a break.'

CHAPTER 60

Anna-Karin is sitting at the back looking out across the packed auditorium. Ida, Julia and Felicia are in the choir onstage. They're beaming.

Jari isn't here. He left with the other seniors a few days ago and most have stayed at home today. Anna-Karin still feels ashamed when she sees him, and she probably will for the rest of her life.

Erik, Kevin and Robin are sitting in a row in the middle. They've spread themselves out and talk loudly to each other, ignoring Ove Post's attempts to silence them. Erik waves to Ida, tries to make her lose her concentration. Anna-Karin has heard rumors that they've started dating. She shudders when she thinks of what their children would be like.

She remembers Grandpa's words: *When those young thugs at school were picking on you, Mia always told me to stay out of it, that she'd been bullied, too, and she'd survived.*

Her mother has almost never talked about her childhood. Had she been bullied at school, too? Is that why she is how she is? Had she been an Anna-Karin once upon a time?

Had they tortured her until something broke that couldn't be fixed?

Mia was drawn to those boys. The ones who didn't have much to give.

Maybe she'd thought she didn't deserve better.

Anna-Karin wonders how broken she is. If she'll ever be free of her hatred. And if she doesn't succeed, will she end up like her mother?

Because the hatred is still inside her. It bubbles up sometimes, threatening to overwhelm her. Then it's hard to stop herself using magic. But she's resisted. Not for the Council's sake or the investigation, whatever's happening with that. No, she's resisted for the sake of the others.

She's doing it for Vanessa, who's passing a soda bottle between herself, Michelle and Evelina. Anna-Karin can smell the alcohol all the way over here.

She's doing it for Linnéa, who's sitting with the alternative crowd, leaning against the shoulder of a blue-haired girl and occasionally glancing at Vanessa.

She's doing it for Minoo, who was sitting alone until Gustaf Åhlander sat next to her. Anna-Karin has tried to speak to her. She knows, of course, how it feels to be afraid of your powers, afraid of what you can do, but Minoo refuses to open up to her. She's shut out the whole world.

She's even doing it for Ida. Ida, who's been in love with Gustaf since fourth grade. Ida, who loves the horse Troja. Those are two subtle traces of a more human Ida, and that's what Anna-Karin has to hold on to.

Just as siblings don't choose each other, the Chosen Ones

haven't either. And, like siblings, they have to learn to live with each other.

Evelina and Michelle are yelling drunkenly in Vanessa's ears, one on either side of her, like great big Evelina-and-Michelle-shaped headphones.

'Come with us!' they bray.

'But I don't need to pee.' Vanessa laughs.

'Just come anyway! It's us tonight!' Evelina says, and swigs from the bottle of beer.

Vanessa laughs again. 'I'll wait here,' she says, and shoves them toward the bushes further down Olsson's Hill.

She straddles Wille. Mehmet, Lucky, Jonte and a few others are there, too. Music is playing from a portable speaker. She kisses Wille and he kisses her back, and all she needs to know about them is in that kiss. Everything's going to work out.

'Check out the old hag,' Lucky says.

Vanessa reluctantly pulls away from Wille's lips and looks up.

Mona Moonbeam is standing on the path smoking a cigarette. Today she's wearing a brown suede jacket with tassels. Her feet are stuffed into a pair of boots. They've even got spurs on them.

And Mona Moonbeam is looking straight at Vanessa. A hint of a smile playing on her lips. It feels like a challenge. Vanessa stands up on unsteady heels and adjusts the bow at her neckline.

'What are you doing?' Wille says.

She giggles when her head spins.

'I'll be back in a minute,' she says. She walks up to Mona and stops a little too close to her. Mona takes a step back. 'Can I have a cigarette?' Vanessa asks.

Mona lights one for her and hands it over. They look at each other as they both take a drag. Mona's cigarettes are strong. They taste like old socks.

'Did you want something?' Vanessa asks.

She hears Evelina and Michelle burst into a fit of laughter in the bushes.

'Haven't seen you for a while,' Mona says.

'Maybe we don't need your stuff any more.'

'You will. You haven't even started to understand how powerful your enemies are.'

But she doesn't frighten Vanessa who, on this particular day, has decided not to give a shit about any of that stuff, or about responsibility, the apocalypse, Nicke or any other evil in the world. It's summer vacation now.

'Aren't you going to say anything about how I'm going to die, too?' Vanessa asks. It annoys her to discover that she's slurring her words. It ruins the effect. 'Maybe you should go back to fortune-teller school because, as you can see, I'm pretty fucking alive, aren't I?' she adds.

Mona chuckles. 'I may not have told the *whole* truth about that symbol,' she says.

'Is that so? Why doesn't it surprise me that you reinterpret your fortunes when they don't come true?'

'*nGéadal* really does stand for death,' Mona says. 'But death can also symbolize transformation, change. Leaving oneself behind and starting afresh. Being reborn, so to speak. Your whole life getting turned upside down to the point that you have to re-evaluate *everything*.'

Mona leans close, her lips beside Vanessa's ear. The smell of cigarettes and incense makes her feel vaguely nauseated. 'In your case *nGéadal* lay very close to *muin*. Love.' Mona leans back and blows a cloud of smoke into Vanessa's face.

'Have a nice summer,' she says, and saunters away.

Vanessa is left standing in the cloud of smoke.

'What the fuck was that about?' Wille shouts.

Vanessa watches Mona go. She almost feels sober. She drops Mona's cigarette and stamps on it.

The canal is glittering in the sunlight. The church is on the other side. The cemetery. She knows what she has to do.

'Nessa!' Michelle shouts from the bushes.

But Vanessa is already on her way.

Minoo walks across the cemetery. The envelope with her report is folded twice in her hand. Top marks in everything except PE, as always. But she doesn't feel the usual sense of relief. It's more like the memory of relief.

When everyone had hugged each other and said goodbye for the summer, she had slipped out of the classroom. Then she walked to the stream that she had dreamed about last night. Even though she knew it was impossible, she hoped Rebecka would be waiting there for her.

She wasn't.

Ever since Minoo had felt Rebecka's soul, she's clung to a

childish hope that her friend would return from where she is now . . .

When Rebecka's grave comes into view, Minoo sees that someone is already standing there. No, not at Rebecka's grave. At Elias's.

It's Linnéa.

Minoo deliberates whether to stay or go. But then Linnéa turns around and sees her. 'Hi,' she shouts.

'Hi,' Minoo answers, and goes up to her.

Linnéa is holding a big bouquet of red roses. The plastic wrapping is still on it. 'I stole them,' Linnéa says. 'It's a bit of a tradition. Elias used to steal flowers for me. Once he came with a whole flower box from Monique's.'

Minoo smiles. It feels as though she hasn't done so for a long time. Like she's forgotten how.

Linnéa sits on the ground between Elias and Rebecka.

'The principal knows,' she says. 'She knows it was Max and she knows that we were the ones who put him where he is. She also knows we were practicing at Nicolaus's place.'

It takes Minoo a moment to absorb what Linnéa has just said. It's typical of her to blurt out some earth-shattering revelation without warning.

Minoo is just about to dispute it when she realizes that what Linnéa has said explains everything.

That strange look the principal had given Minoo in the fairground last winter. Now she understands that it was a look of encouragement. The principal had been forced to pass on the Council's orders. That was why she had told them not to go after Gustaf. But all the time she had known what they were doing and had left them to it. She had bought their subterfuges, their lies. She must have realized they were practicing on their own. And when Max had ended up in a coma, it couldn't have been hard to work out the rest.

'When did you realize that?' Minoo asks.

'I've known for a while.' Linnéa pokes at a tuft of grass with her shoe. 'I'm so glad you came here. I've been wanting to talk to you about something, but I haven't known how to say it . . . What happened in the cafeteria. You can't keep it pent up inside you. It'll kill you. You're already dying from it.'

'What do you mean?' Minoo mumbles.

'You loved Max. He was a murderer. But you loved him. That's not something you get over just like that.'

'As soon as I found out it was him—'

'I know. But you had all those feelings for him before. And it must have been devastating to find out what he'd done. I'd have hated myself if I'd discovered I had a crush on Elias's killer.'

'I'm over it,' Minoo says.

'Okay. Fair enough,' Linnéa says. 'But you aren't over the black smoke.'

Minoo stares at her. Linnéa knows things Minoo hasn't told anyone.

'I can understand it scared the shit out of you,' Linnéa says, 'but it won't get any better if you keep quiet about it. Maybe together we can find out why Max's and your magic looked the same and why no one else could see it.'

'How do you know all this?' Minoo asks. She has the

feeling she should know. That she should have put two and two together ages ago.

'Do you remember Vanessa said she could hear my voice in her head that night? That was something new. I didn't even know I was doing it. But . . .' She hesitates. Her hands sort of wrestle with each other. 'It started last summer.'

'Okay,' says Minoo, in as neutral a tone as she can muster.

'At first I didn't understand what it was. I mean, it was so . . . impossible. In the beginning it just happened now and then. I sort of picked up things.'

She can't say it, Minoo realizes. She wants me to expose her.

And at that moment she realizes how it all adds up. All at once, a thousand odd moments are explained.

'You can read minds,' Minoo says. 'That's your power. You've been able to do it all along.'

At first it looks as though Linnéa is going to deny it, take back everything. But then she slumps down and nods. 'The first time we met, it was pretty new,' she says. 'Just before we found Elias. I knew you'd come into the bathroom because you usually hid there during breaks. It just popped into my head.'

Minoo doesn't know what to say. She thinks about all the things she's thought about Linnéa since then, and all the things she's thought when Linnéa's been around. And then she thinks that Linnéa may be reading her thoughts at this very moment. 'Why didn't you tell us?' she asks.

'You're one to talk! I kept quiet because I knew everyone would react the way you are now. I don't need to read your mind to see that you're terrified about what I've heard you think.'

Linnéa seems to be on the verge of tears.

'You don't understand what it was like in the beginning,' she continues. 'Sometimes it was as if everyone I met just started screaming into my head. That was why I wrote in my diary that you gave me a headache. You think so *much*. But Anna-Karin was the worst. Her endless thoughts controlling others were like fucking primal screams right into my ear.' Linnéa looks at her pleadingly. 'But I've learned to control it now. For the most part. It's only occasionally that I hear things. And I'm becoming better and better at switching off.'

'But you were the one who really went for the principal about not telling the truth. And you were sitting there the whole time and—'

'That was the whole point! I was trying to tell you that the principal knew a lot less than she claimed.'

'But we could have used you right from the start! Maybe we could have found Max a lot sooner!'

'I tried,' Linnéa said. 'I tried to listen to everyone who was a suspect. I listened to Gustaf and every time he thought about Rebecka he felt so guilty. I really thought it was him. I never checked up on Max because I barely knew who he was until you told us.'

'Does anyone else know?' Minoo asks.

'Yes. The principal.'

Minoo has no surprise left in her. 'How?' she asks.

'I read her thoughts when she showed us her scars. She thought about the man she loved and what the Council had done to him. I was shocked. And she saw that I reacted. That was when she realized it. Or she already knew. Mind-reading is common among witches. According to the book anyway.'

Minoo is quiet for a long moment. She should be angry with Linnéa. But Linnéa's right. She herself is harboring a big secret. A secret she's not sure whether she's ready to share with the others.

But I'll have to one day, she realizes. Linnéa is right about that.

'Do you hate me?' Linnéa asks.

'No,' Minoo answers. 'But you have to tell the others.'

Linnéa nods and sighs heavily.

'I won't say anything,' Minoo says. 'But you can't wait too long.'

'Neither can you,' Linnéa says, and catches sight of something.

She gets up slowly. Minoo turns.

Vanessa is walking toward them in her tight pink dress. One of her heels gets stuck in the grass and she stumbles. They hear her swear.

Linnéa touches Minoo's arm and points. Anna-Karin is lumbering along with her hands in her jacket pockets, her long hair swinging around her face.

Tears flare in Minoo's eyes. She looks around the cemetery and, sure enough, Ida appears from the opposite direction. She's pushing her bicycle between the gravestones.

Minoo becomes completely calm.

Everyone gathers around Elias and Rebecka's graves. They look at each other but no one says a word. No one needs to explain why they're here.

They are the Circle. They've fought together for their lives. And they'll do it again.

Linnéa takes the bouquet of roses and divides it into two. One she lays on Elias's grave. The other on Rebecka's.

Minoo thinks about Rebecka's and Elias's souls. About how alive they felt in the moment she set them free.

'Do you think they're here now?' Anna-Karin asks.

Minoo shakes her head. She can't explain why, but suddenly she's certain. 'No,' she answers. 'They're where they should be.'

She takes Linnéa's hand and adds, 'And so are we.'

EARTH

FIRE

AIR

WATER

METAL

WOOD

Acknowledgements

Thanks to our wonderful publisher Marie Augustsson, who felt the magic right from the start and never doubted us – or at least did a good job of hiding it. Thanks also to our editor Sofia Hahr who brought in a fresh pair of eyes when we had stared ourselves blind. Cartwheeling pompom girls, balloons and cakes to Eva Ehrnström, Karin Rowland and the whole incredible team at Rabén & Sjögren/Norstedts, who have given our baby the best possible chances of making it out in the big wide world.

Thanks also to Lena, Maria, Lotta and Peter at Grand Agency. You have guided us and always made us feel chosen.

Thanks to Kim W. Andersson who managed to boil down our vague wishes into three cover illustrations that turned out more beautiful than we ever could have imagined.

Thanks to Pär Åhlander who managed to find a format that summed up everything we wanted to convey and didn't give up until he had achieved perfection.

Thanks to Catharina Wrååk, who read the first chapter at a very early stage and gave us good advice that saved us a whole lot of extra work.

Thanks to Tommy and Stefan Runarsson who taught us what Anna-Karin's life was like on the farm, and Anna Bonnier who helped us fill in the gaps in Linnéa's background. Thanks also to Maria Sadeghzadeh and her family, Elisabeth Östnäs and Camille Tuutti.

Mats would like to thank Margareta, who let us hold our sect-like writing camp for two in her beautiful house, and for producing such a splendid daughter of course. Sara would like to thank her mother – for always reading, supporting, challenging and being there to discuss books, writing and life in general. Thanks for all the stories!

Sara would also like to thank Margit and Micko Strandberg – for their warm reception during our research trip to Bergslagen and for producing such a gifted and handsome son, of course. Mats would like to express his gratitude to his parents – for always being allowed to come home, lock myself up in my old room and only show my face downstairs in time for dinner. I love you more than anyone in the world.

Mats would like to thank Micke – when two people work together things can get pretty crazy on occasion, so thanks for letting me mentally kidnap your wife the whole time. Your patience with my existence is boundless . . . 'right?' Sara wishes she could write a ten-page thank you to Micke for his total support, enthusiasm, humor, patience, friendship and love. Sometimes words really aren't enough.

Sara would also like to thank her sister Sofia – for your enthusiasm, good advice and Frasse. And thanks to her dad

Claes for good comments, and LucasArts games for teaching her proper keyboard technique.

A big thank you to those of you who have read the manuscript in various stages and provided valuable input and encouragement. A few of you are: Elin Borowski, Elisabeth Jensen Haverling, Siska Humlesjö, Viktoria Aponte Persson, Mathilda Elfgren Schwartz, Johanna Paues Darlington, Rickard Darlington, Minna Frydén Bonnier, Anton Bonnier, Hans-Jörgen Riis Jensen, Anna Andersson, Emelie Thorén, Johan Ehn, Lina Neidestam, Pär Åhlander and Levan Akin.

Thanks to all our friends and colleagues for their support and for putting up with our disappearing off to Engelsfors – and with the fact that once we finally did return to reality for a visit, that we did so in the form of a strange creature with two heads.

And a special honorary thank you to the literary Typhoid Mary, alias Helena Dahlgren, who brought us together because she sensed that we would like each other. Little did you know how right you were – and what a monster you created.

A preview of
Fire
the next volume in the Engelsfors Trilogy

CHAPTER 1

Sunlight floods in through the tall windows and picks out every dirty old stain on the white textured wallpaper. A fan on the floor is slowly turning from side to side. The room is still unbearably hot.

'How did your summer go?'

Jakob the shrink, who is wearing shorts, sits back in the brown leather armchair.

Linnéa can't resist a little probe into his thoughts. She registers his discomfort at the chair seat's leather sticking to the back of his thighs and then his genuine pleasure at seeing her again. She backs off instantly. Feels a bit ashamed.

'Fine, thank you', she replies, as the thinks: *The summer's been horrible . . .*

She focuses on the framed poster behind Jakob. All pastely geometric shapes. She can't imagine anything blander and wonders what point Jakob wanted to make by hanging it just there.

'Has anything special happened that you would like to talk about?' he asks.

Define 'special', Linnéa thinks and glares at the blue triangle that hovers above his shaved skull.

'Not really.'

Jakob nods and doesn't say anything more. Ever since she realized that she is a mind-reader, Linnéa has now and then asked herself if he might not have a milder variant of her power, if he isn't somehow able to sense what's going on in her head. He always seems to know when to be silent in a way that makes her want to talk. Mostly, she resists, but this time the words bubble up.

'I've had a fight with one of my friends. Several of them, actually.'

Linnéa lets one of her flip-flops dangle. She hates sandals. But when it's this fucking hot you have no choice.

'So, what happened?' Jakob's tone is neutral.

'I was keeping something secret. Something the others should've known, but I kept it to myself. And then, when I finally told them they got furious with me because I hadn't let them in on it earlier. And now they don't trust me.'

'Can you tell me the secret?'

'No.'

Jakob just nods. She wonders what would happen to his professional composure if she told him the truth. He wouldn't believe her at first, obviously. But she could go on to describe how, before she learned to control her ability better, she sometimes, against her will, picked up what he was thinking. Which is how she knows that he was unfaithful to his wife last fall. He was sleeping with a colleague. His darkest secret.

Jakob would become anxious. Always ill at ease whenever she was around. Just like the Chosen Ones.

A few days after the end of semester assembly, they finally revealed their secrets to each other. Minoo told them the whole truth about what happened that night in the school dining hall, about the black smoke that no one else could see and that came pouring out of her and Max, who had been blessed by the Demons. Anna-Karin described how she had cast a spell over her mother that lasted all Fall semester and admitted how far she had gone with Jari. Heavy secrets, but nothing in comparison with what Linnéa had to confess. That she could read their minds. And that she had been doing it for almost a year. Without saying anything.

Since then, nothing has been the same. They've been meeting regularly all summer to practice their magic skills and, each time, Linnéa has been aware of the others avoiding her eyes. Throughout the summer vacation, Vanessa has hardly said a word to her. When Linnéa thinks about that, she feels as if a super-sharp electric whisk has been thrust through her chest, churning her heart to mush.

'How did you react when they turned on you?' Jakob asks.

'I tried to defend myself. But I understood why they did, of course. I mean . . . like, if I had been one of them, I would've been so fucking angry.'

'Why didn't you tell them the truth before?'

'I knew they would freak out.'

Once more, that psychologist-style silence. Linnéa stares hard at her feet. The polish on her toenails is black.

'Anyway, it felt kind of good, too,' she went on.

'What felt good?'

'It felt like having the upper hand.'

'It can be tough to let other people come close, truly close to you. There are times when being alone gives one a sense of security.'

Linnéa can't stop the laughter. It erupts with a snort.

'What's so funny?' Jakob asks.

She looks up and sees his gentle smile. What does he know about being alone? Not alone, as in everyone else is busy tonight, or alone, as in your wife is away at a conference. But utterly, painfully alone, so lonely it's as if the atoms in your body are pulling away from each other and you're about to dissolve into one great Nothing. So lonely you have to scream into the void just to hear that you still exist. Alone, as in nobody would care if you disappeared.

Inside Linnéa's head, the list pops up. It has been there for as long as she can remember. It's the list named *Who Would Care If I Died*? After Elias was murdered, there are no obvious names left.

Jakob clearly realizes that she isn't going to reply, because he changes the subject.

'Before summer vacation, you told me that you had met someone you felt fond of.'

That murderously sharp, fast whisk starts up again.

'Ancient history', she lies. 'It got too complicated.'

Flipping, flopping, her sandal keeps dangling. She avoids looking at Jakob.

He asks more questions and she answers mechanically, feeding him a small truth here, a large lie there.

There's so much she can't tell him. Like: 'The world is not the way you believe. It is full of magic. Engelsfors will be the center of a battle that's going to cross the boundaries between the dimensions. Good pitted against evil. I and a handful of other junior girls are up against the Demons. And another thing: I'm a witch. You see, I am chosen to vanquish Evil and prevent the Apocalypse. Any more questions?'

4

Besides, there are just as many not-magical secrets that Jakob will never hear about. 'After Elias's death, I started sleeping with Jonte. Sure, the same old Jonte, my ex-dealing pal. And, yes, we smoked together, but I've stopped now. I won't ever do it again, promise. I'm responsible enough to have a place of my own. You and Diana the Social Worker believe me, don't you?'

Any of all that stuff would be a one-way ticket to another institution. Or to new foster parents. Foster parents who wouldn't be like Ulf and Tina. Those two never tried molding her into somebody she was not, never tried to play at being the perfect family. They understood that she hadn't been a child for many, many years – perhaps never. If they hadn't gotten into their heads to go to Botswana and start a school, she would've liked to stay on with them.

'How do you feel about starting school again?' Jakob says and Linnéa realizes that she has been silent for a long while.

'No problem.'

'Do you think a lot about Elias?'

It surprises her sometimes how much it still hurts to hear his name mentioned.

'Of course I do,' she snaps, even though she knows that Jakob didn't intend to get at her. 'I think of him every day. Especially today.'

'Why just today?'

Inside Linnéa, the sense of loss beats like a pulse and she has to concentrate on not bursting into tears.

'It's his birthday today.'

Jakob nods and looks compassionately at her. Linnéa hates him. She doesn't want to be one of the pathetic kids everyone feels sorry for. She's damaged goods, she knows that, but detests seeing it reflected in the eyes of others, resents the way they can't wait to try fitting the broken bits together, get out the superglue and start mending until they think she looks whole.

She probes again and notices that Jakob feels hopeful, believes that he has connected with her and that she's about to open up, tell him more about Elias.

She takes revenge by keeping her mouth shut for the last ten minutes of their session.

I miss you so. It doesn't pass. The pain feels less bad sometimes, that's all.

I hate remembering the last time we met, the fight we had. The real reason was simply that I worried about what was happening to you. Now, I understand what you were going through. I think so, anyway. You had begun to discover new, inexplicable changes in yourself, just like I had.

I thought I was losing my mind and you must have feared it, too. You must have been so frightened.

If only we had talked, told each other our secrets. Perhaps everything would have been different then. If only you had been born anywhere except in this fucking hole of a town.

Perhaps you would still have been alive.

I know it's pointless to think these things, but I can't stop myself.

I draw up lists of all the tiny details that were part of you.

Like the way you always picked the pickles out of the veggie burger. I never figured out why you didn't ask them not to add it. And your favorite authors were Poppy Z. Brite and Edgar Allan Poe and Oscar Wilde. I've underlined the passages you read aloud to me when you phoned me at night. You promised to take me on a trip to Japan before our thirtieth birthdays. Once, you said that if you were a girl you would've liked to be called Lucretia. Wherever did you get that from? You never had crushes on real-life celebs, only on fantasy people like Misa Amane, even though she's so bugging, and Edward Scissorhands.

And you asked me not to forget you if you were to die before I did. Such a truly typically fucking stupid thing to say. As if I could ever forget you.

You are my brother in every way except blood. I love you and will love you forever.

Linnéa carefully rips out the diary page and folds it. She digs a small, deep hollow in the light soil by the rose bush next to the stone on Elias's grave. The white shrub roses are faded already and the leaves have ugly, dried-out edges. She pushes the folded paper into the hole. Buries it. Wipes her hands on her black skirt and sits back.

She can glimpse the rectory between the old lime trees on the far side of the churchyard. Linnéa observes the window of the room that used to be Elias's. The panes reflect the bright blue sky. Elias loved the view over the cemetery. Imagine if he had realized that he was looking at the plot of his own grave.

The air is very still. Within the walled cemetery, the baking sun heats the gravestones. The grass is yellowing and the parched ground criss-crossed with cracks. In June, the *Engelsfors Herald* ran euphoric headlines about the record-breaking hot summer. Now, in August, the records are the numbers of old folk dying of dehydration and farmers having their incomes ruined.

Linnéa's cell phone pings, but she can't even be bothered checking. Olivia, the only one in the old gang who's still her friend, has been texting like crazy all morning. The summer vacation has passed without a sign of life from Olivia, but now that it suits her, she expects Linnéa to jump. No such luck.

She unscrews the top of the water bottle in its fabric case. It makes no difference how much she drinks, she's is still thirsty afterwards. All the same, the rosebush gets the last few drops.

She puts the bottle back and pulls out the three red roses from the rose bed in Storvall Park. Their heads are drooping already. She puts one rose on Elias's grave. Then she goes along to place another one on the nearby grave, where the stone bears Rebecka's name.

Linnéa looks back at Elias's grave. In the beginning she had hoped to be able to pick up the thoughts of the dead. To contact them. But she hasn't succeeded in even sensing whether they are there at all, let alone what might be going on in their minds.

Linnéa used to believe that when a person died, that was it. End of story. Now, she knows that at least souls exist.

They're where they should be, Minoo had said when, after the end of semester assembly, they had met up here, by the graves.

Linnéa hopes that it is true, that Elias exists somewhere else, in a better place.

She recalls meeting Max in the dining hall and what he

8

said when he was trying to make her reveal who the other Chosen Ones are.

Elias is waiting for you, Linnéa.

A tiny part of her is tempted to find out if Max, ally of the Demons, is telling the truth.

You can be together again.

Now she can no longer hold back the tears. She lets them run down her cheeks as she walks away. So fucking what? Since when isn't someone allowed to cry in a graveyard?

One red rose is left in her tote bag. It's for her Mom.

Linnéa is just about to take the path leading to the Memorial Wood when she catches sight of a black shadow moving close to the ground between the gravestones.

She stops.

With a plaintive meow, Nicolaus's familiar slips onto the path ahead of her. The Cat, who has no other name, seems to have lost even more fur during the summer. Its single, green eye is fixed on her.

Linnéa has never managed to read the mind of an animal, but it is easy to grasp that the Cat wants something from her. It stretches itself and meows, then pads along a narrow path leading to the oldest part of the cemetery. Now and then, it stops to make sure that Linnéa is following.

The cemetery is surrounded by low stone wall. The Cat stops in its shadow, next to a tall headstone, almost a yard high and covered with mosses and pale gray lichens.

The Cat meows shrilly, noisily, and gently buts its head against the stone.

'Yes yes,' Linnéa says and kneels.

The ground feels surprisingly cool against her bare legs. She leans forward, scrapes some of the moss off the stone and tries to make out the crumbling letters.

NICOLAUS ELINGIUS
MEMENTO MORI

A chill makes Linnéa's whole body shiver, as if the souls of the dead were present here after all and reaching for her through the soil.

CHAPTER 2

Minoo has made one corner of the garden into her own, where she can sit with her books. She has placed a deckchair in the shade of a sycamore at the back of the house and as far away from it as you can get. Too bad that it isn't far enough for her to ignore what's going on inside it.

Minoo glimpses the outline of Dad through the kitchen window. He crosses the floor with long, clumping steps. Out of sight, he roars something. He's so loud he could make the window panes rattle. Mom shrieks something back at him. Minoo pulls her earphones down and tries to lose herself in a Nick Drake song, but music simply makes her still more aware of the sounds she is trying to exclude.

Mom and Dad always used to deny that they fought,

called it 'discussions' when they got into it about all the time Dad spent at work and his health. But this summer, at some point, they'd stopped pretending.

Perhaps it would be kind of grown-up to think of their fights as 'sound'. Whatever had been simmering under the surface for so long has finally found an outlet. But Minoo feels like a scared little kid whenever she thinks of the word 'divorce'. Maybe it wouldn't have felt so bad if she had had brothers or sisters. But what's at risk now is the only family she has ever known. Mom, Dad and herself.

Minoo tries to concentrate on the book in her lap. It's a detective story by Georges Simenon that she found in Dad's bookshelf. Its back has split, and yellowing pages sometimes drop out when she leafs through it. The book is really good. At least, she thinks so. There's no way she can engage with the story. She feels shut out of the world in the book.

Minoo catches a glimpse of brightness in the corner of her eye. She quickly pulls off her earphones and turns round.

Gustaf is wearing a white T-shirt. It enhances his tanned skin and the golden sheen of his sun-bleached hair. Some people seem made for summer. Minoo definitely isn't one of them.

'Hi, Minoo,' he says.

'Hi,' she replies.

She glances nervously toward the house. All quiet in there now. But for how long?

'You look surprised,' Gustaf is saying. 'Did you forget we were meeting up today?'

'Oh, no. I had just lost track of the time.'

Inside the house, a door slams and Dad roars at top

volume. Mom's response has a lot of swearing in it. Gustaf's face is blank, but he must have heard them. Minoo stands up so quickly the book falls onto the lawn. She leaves it there.

'Come on,' she says and walks off quickly.

At the edge of the garden, she turns impatiently. Gustaf has picked up the book and is putting it on the deckchair. He looks at her, smiles, then hurries to catch up.

Side by side, they amble through Engelsfors. It's impossible to move at anything like a normal pace. The heat is pressing you down to the ground, as if the gravitational pull had been magnified by a factor of ten.

Minoo had never seen the point of lying around on a beach. That is, not until just this summer, when she has been thinking seriously of going to Dammsjön Lake, where the rest of Engelsfors goes to cool down. But the mere thought of undressing in front of other people has always made her stay away. She can hardly bear to show her face in public. The heat wave hasn't exactly done wonders for her skin. A particularly hyper pimple is throbbing at her temple and she tries to pull a strand of hair over it so that Gustaf won't notice.

As hard as it is for her to put her finger on exactly when Mom and Dad started fighting openly, it's just as hard for her to pinpoint when she and Gustaf became friends.

When Minoo finally dared to tell the other Chosen Ones about the black smoke, her alienation from the world of other people felt a little less paralyzing. But she was not the same Minoo as before. Her friend Rebecka had died. Killed by Max, the man Minoo had loved more than anyone else.

Max, who claimed that the Demons had a plan for her. She had no idea what the plan might be, just as she knew nothing about the powers held inside her.

But in the middle of her confusion, Gustaf had been there for her. Early on during summer vacation, he tried to persuade her to come along to Dammsjön Lake but, when she kept being evasive, they went for walks instead. Or else, talked, read or played cards in his garden.

Gustaf is the local football star and one of the most popular boys in the school. Through the years, Minoo has heard so much praise of him, usually over-the-top variants on what a perfect guy he is. As for Minoo, the word she feels describes him best is 'easy-going'. He makes everything seem simple. Since her life generally is the total opposite of simple, the time spent with Gustaf has become a rare zone of ease.

But when she's not with him, paranoia lurks. She wonders why he cares enough to be with her. Maybe she's some kind of charitable project.

They stroll across the Canal Bridge, then follow the swirling flow of black water past the lock gates and take a path underneath the canopies of the trees. A wasp is buzzing around Minoo and she flicks it away.

'How are things with you? Honestly?' Gustaf asks.

The wasp disappears among the trees. Minoo understands that he means what he had heard from inside her home. He has probably sensed all summer that something was up.

'Look, I'm sorry, maybe you'd rather not talk about it?'

Minoo hesitates. He's her escape route and she doesn't want to mess up their friendship.

'Do your parents fight like that?'

'They did when I was little. Now they never do.' Gustaf says and doesn't speak for a moment. 'I don't think they care enough anymore.'

Astonished, Minoo glances at him. She always had the impression that Gustaf's family was like one of these sweet'n'cozy ones in cheesy American sit-coms, the kind where people get mad at each other because of some crazy misunderstanding. And when all is sorted out in the end, cue for hugs all round as everyone agrees they've learned a lesson.

'I try not to think too much about it, but I'm pretty sure they'll get a divorce as soon as I'm out of their way,' Gustaf says. 'I'm the last of their kids who's still at home. I leave and that's it. Nothing left to hold them together.'

'Do you really believe that?'

'You notice when two people are in love, I think. It's like . . . a kind of energy between them. Do you know what I mean?'

Minoo mumbles supportively. She knows exactly what he means. She once felt an energy field between herself and Max. That is, before she found out who he actually was. That he was Rebecka's killer.

'There's nothing like that between my parents,' Gustaf continues. 'I realized that once I'd fallen in love.'

Gustaf falls silent. Minoo knows that he is thinking about Rebecka.

Rebecka's death had brought them together. Now they talk less and less about her. It's Minoo who avoids the subject. As she gets closer to Gustaf, it's more and more difficult to play along with the lie that the death of his girlfriend was suicide.

She sees a familiar shadow sweep across his face and wants to ask him how he feels. Does he still have nightmares about when he watched Rebecka die? Does he still blame himself? She wants to be the friend he deserves.

But how can she be a true friend at the same time as she keeps lying about something so important?

If only it were possible to tell him the truth. But she knows that she couldn't, not ever.

The woodland opens up into a meadow where the summer flowers have faded and died. The old abandoned mansion house stands on the far side of the meadow.

'Did you know that building was an inn once?' Minoo asks to change the subject.

'No, I didn't. When?'

'In the '90s. Dad told me about it. A couple of Stockholm restaurant owners bought the whole thing, moved in and refurbished it. They spent serious money, apparently. And then they opened a restaurant. It got brilliant reviews but, all the same, they had to close the place down after about a year. Zero customers. Dad said the talk in town was all about how they'd show these city folk that in Engelsfors there was no easy money to be made. So there. As if everyone wouldn't have gained by something actually happening here.'

Gustaf laughs.

'Engelsfors strikes again. Typical.'

For a while, they stand looking at the house. It is a grand two-story building made of white-painted wood. Definitely the largest and most beautiful building in the town. Not that the competition is so hot. A wide flight of stone steps leads from the overgrown garden to a veranda where two massive pillars support a large balcony on the second floor.

'Let's check it out,' Gustaf says.

'Sure.'

They start crossing the meadow. The brittle, crackling stems of dry grass reach up to Minoo's knees and she thinks nervously about hordes of starving ticks scenting blood.

'Do you want to stay in Engelsfors?' she asks. 'I mean, after leaving school?'

'I don't know. In some ways, I like the town. It's home. But there's no future here. On the other hand, maybe that's precisely why a person ought to come back later in life. To build something new.'

'What, like opening a restaurant?'

'Do you think they'd come if I was the owner?'

Yes, Minoo thinks. They would come all right. Because you are you.

'I guess so. You're no city interloper.'

Close up, it's easy to see how run-down the house is. The paint is flaking off the walls and, here and there patches of bare wood show. The ground-floor windows are shuttered. Minoo thinks of the work done by the previous owners. Now the old place is decaying again.

Gustaf starts climbing the steps to the veranda, but stops half-way. Listens.

'What's the matter?' Minoo asks.

'I think someone's in there.' Gustaf says quietly.

He sets out along one of the wings. Minoo trails after him, nervously eyeing the first floor windows. They swing round the gable end and step out in the front of the house.

A dark green car is parked on the graveled area near the main entrance. The passenger side door is wide open. Minoo makes out a man seated inside.

He notices them and gets out of the car in one agile movement.

The man is young, their own age, and taller than Gustaf. Wavy, ash blond hair frames his face. His features are near-perfect and so is his smooth skin. His looks would be perfect in one of those upmarket ads where everyone is sailing or playing golf non-stop.

'Hi,' Gustaf says. 'Sorry, we thought the house was empty . . .'

'You're mistaken, obviously,' the guy says.

He speaks with exactly the kind of upperclass Stockholm accent that instantly gets under the skin of most Engelsforsers, regardless of how nice the speaker is. In this case, there isn't a trace of niceness in his voice.

Gustaf stares at him in blank amazement.

Of course he is baffled, Minoo thinks. Gustaf must be totally unused to people being rude to him.

'Sure, yes, our mistake,' Gustaf replies. 'Are you moving in?'

'Yeah, that's right,' the stranger drawls, sounding utterly fed up.

Minoo's ears are burning. She wants to leave. Now. No point in trying to chat, not even Gustaf's charm will have any effect on this guy. He slams the car door shut, flattens the creases in his trousers. Then her looks up and stares intently at Minoo.

She feels that he can see straight through her and that he isn't impressed.

'Come on. Let's go,' she mutters and grabs Gustaf's arm to pull him along.

'Hardly the type to improve the reputation of Stockholm folk round here,' Gustaf says as they cross the meadow.

'Too true.'

When they reach the edge of the wood, Minoo turns for a last view of the mansion house. She catches a glimpse of what might have been someone moving upstairs.

'What would you like to do now?' Gustaf asks.

'I don't know.'

Her cell phone pings in the pocket of her skirt. She checks it.

It's a text from Linnéa.

'Has anything happened?' Gustaf asks.

'No,' she lies. 'Nothing at all.'

Excerpted from **Fire,** Book Two of The Engelsfors Trilogy.

For more information visit

www.worldofengelsfors.com.